"Not too many Canucks have ventured to write humorous books. There is Stephen Leacock, of course. And Robertson Davies cranked out a couple . . . Count Terry Fallis among the few to achieve success at the form. . . . Poignant."

– Ottawa Citizen

"One of CanLit's crowned king of chuckles . . . hits stratospheric heights with his latest well-balanced and unpredictable satire. . . . Fallis is a gifted storyteller."

– Telegraph-Journal

"[A] lighthearted plot involving slamming doors, vaudeville turns, plot twists, and a lot of good-natured badinage. . . . Landon Percival [is] a vivid and dazzling character. . . . [Fallis] displays formidable chops when it comes to narrative pacing, wrangling subplots, balancing comedy and pathos."

– Globe and Mail

"Gently satirical and intelligently frothy, *Up and Down* achieves a delightful weightlessness."

– Andrew Pyper, author of *The Demonologist*

"Fallis spins a hilarious story. . . . Funny and delightful. . . . Quite enjoyable from start to finish."

– Montreal *Gazette*

"*Up and Down* . . . kept me smiling, made me laugh out loud and occasionally moved me to tears. . . . Fallis's hilarious running commentary on the minutiae of modern life recalls the comedy of *Seinfeld*. . . . [A] pleasurable satire."

– National Post

"Terry Fallis brings to vivid life a highly entertaining story of NASA intrigue and public relations highjinks that reminds us of what it means to be Canadian."

– Cathy Marie Buchanan, author of *The Painted Girls*

"Terry Fallis has done it again. *Up and Down* is another hilarious page-turner that also packs an emotional punch. Only a very talented writer can balance humour and pathos so skillfully. Beautifully written, these characters rocket off the page and straight into your heart. This is satire at its finest."

— Ali Velshi, CNN anchor and
Chief Business Correspondent

"Comic. . . . [A] fascinating story of the divergence of Canadian and American values, the importance of family, unlikely friendship, second chances, ageism, a love of Sherlock Holmes, insight into the awe-inspiring world of space travel, and the importance of using your head but following your heart."

— *Winnipeg Free Press*

"A hilarious look at the world of PR."

— *Ottawa Magazine*

"A rollicking good ride. Funny one moment, serious the next, always compelling: a reminder that we can all dream."

— Marc Garneau, Member of Parliament and
Canada's first astronaut

"Terry Fallis . . . is always entertaining."

— NOW magazine

"In the span of one subway ride alone, my emotions wavered more than an astronaut in zero gravity. I surprised myself (and the surrounding commuters) by laughing out loud, and then, with one flip of the page, by having my emotions take a 180, eyes welling up and goosebumps ensuing."

— *Canadian Living*

"[Terry Fallis] has done it again. What a great read!"

— *Waterloo Region Record*

"Terry Fallis has found the cure for Canada's political malaise: a stubborn, old, irreverent Scotsman with nothing to lose. Until Angus McLintock walks out of fiction and into public office, where he would surely save the nation, the only place to find him is right here among *The Best Laid Plans*."

– Tom Allen, CBC Radio host and
author of *The Gift of the Game*

PRAISE FOR

THE HIGH ROAD

"*The High Road* will surely make you laugh. There will be snickers, occasional snorting and hooting, and almost certainly rip-roaring belly laughs."

– Halifax *Chronicle-Herald*

"Fallis writes in pictures . . . that the mind's eye can see clearly. . . . An easy-reading page-turner."

– *National Post*

"Terry Fallis scores again with *The High Road*."

– *Guelph Mercury*

"In a perfect world, the federal government would establish a Ministry of Humour and put Terry Fallis in charge of that department. *The High Road* is brilliantly written and hysterically funny. . . . Do yourself a favour and pick up this book, find a quiet place to read it, and enjoy . . . you will laugh out loud on almost every page."

– Ian Ferguson, author of *Village of Small Houses*

"Doing battle with the prigs and prats that rule the halls of power has never been more enjoyable since . . . well, since *The Best Laid Plans*. Thought-provoking and funny."

– Jim Cuddy, singer/songwriter, Blue Rodeo

UP AND DOWN

Also by Terry Fallis

The Best Laid Plans

The High Road

Gail,
Here's to more
Ups than Downs!

UP AND DOWN

A NOVEL

Terry Fallis

TERRY FALLIS

EMBLEM

McClelland & Stewart

First paperback edition published 2012
Emblem edition published 2013

Emblem is an imprint of McClelland & Stewart,
a division of Random House of Canada Limited

Library and Archives Canada Cataloguing in Publication
is available upon request.

ISBN 978-0-7710-4791-6

Quotes appear in the text from the following works: *The Sign of Four* (1890)
by Sir Arthur Conan Doyle; *His Last Bow* (1917) by Sir Arthur Conan Doyle;
and *A Scandal in Bohemia* (1891) by Sir Arthur Conan Doyle.

Published simultaneously in the United States of America by
McClelland & Stewart Ltd., P.O. Box 1030, Plattsburgh, New York 12901

Library of Congress Control Number: 2013931562

Typeset in Electra by M&S, Toronto
Printed and bound in the United States of America

McClelland & Stewart,
a division of Random House of Canada Limited
One Toronto Street,
Suite 300
Toronto, Ontario
M5C 2V6
www.mcclelland.com

1 2 3 4 5   17 16 15 14 13

David Stewart Fallis
(1967–1986)

Hugh Percival Ham
(1905–1984)

PART 1

CHAPTER 1

"Welcome to the dark side."

Diane Martineau smiled as she said it, but still, those were her words. It was my first day in the Toronto office of the international public relations agency Turner King, and I was already tired of hearing my new profession linked with Lucifer, lord of the underworld. The general manager released my hand and waved me into a chair as she climbed up into hers. She was petite, *très* petite. I put her at barely five feet. In her mid-forties, with shortish dark brown hair, she wore a simple, even drab, tailored black pant suit with a white collarless "top." In the clothes context, I was uncomfortable with the word "top." It didn't spill naturally from my mouth or, for that matter, from almost any guy's. And to be clear, I don't really know what "tailored" actually means, but the jacket curved in at the waist. When she was seated, her tiny black shoes dangled an inch off the floor, leaving her marooned a good two feet from where she wanted to be. No matter. She convulsed twice, her feet flipping up and torso snapping forward, to propel her chair across the black marble floor, gliding perfectly into position. "Docking procedure" may be the better way to describe the manoeuvre that rolled her up to the streamlined chrome and glass desk that would not have looked out of place on the bridge of a Federation starship. I half-expected an order to lay in a course for the Vega system. She caught my stare.

"I know. It's ridiculous, isn't it?" she said, running her hand across the gleaming elliptical surface. "The jackass before me was into sci-fi and spent an obscene sum redecorating before New York toasted him last year. Now I'm stuck with it."

"Well, it's a little much, but hardly a firing offence," I replied, my mouth working faster than my brain. She smiled again and I exhaled.

"There were other factors," she said. "Anyway, it's nice to have you at TK, David. We've got something big going on and your background should put you in the middle of it. So you're going to hit the ground running."

"Well, I guess that's better than just hitting the ground. I think. Um, you do know I've never worked at an agency before, right?"

"Ah, but you *have* spent three years working the press gallery for the Science and Tech Minister. That makes you valuable to us on this big pitch, particularly your work with the Canadian Space Agency," she replied. "Don't worry about life in a PR agency, we'll show you the ropes and try not to let you hang yourself in the first few weeks."

"So, is there anything I should know before, you know, hitting the ground . . . running?"

"Oh, there's a ton of stuff you should know, but like most big, unwieldy, hidebound global PR agencies, we have no well-established and effective orientation program to bring you into this foreign land in a logical and orderly fashion. So you'll get the same treatment everyone else gets. I'll introduce you around, then we'll throw you in the deep end and occasionally toss you an anchor to see if you can adapt and evolve. We'll know pretty quickly if you're going to survive. You'll know slightly sooner, if you're as smart as we think you are."

"That's very comforting," I said. "I'm not sure Darwin would be pleased to see his theory exploited in this way."

The GM leaned towards me, her forearms resting on the cool glass next to a clean steel tray of some kind that I thought might be for serving drinks or cheese. Upon closer inspection, I realized it was actually a MacBook Air computer. I'm not sure I'm as smart as they think I am. But I sure wanted one of those.

"Just before our walk-around, let me offer a few words of advice that you may or may not need to hear." She stared me down, so I stared right back. "In the early going, listen more than you talk. Your nice-guy personality and the chemistry you should be able to establish with colleagues, clients, and new business prospects will take you further than almost anything else. It's one of the reasons I hired you. But we also need you to think, write, and speak with clarity and conviction. If necessary, you can fake the conviction part till it comes, but the clarity needs to be there right out of the gate. Clients deserve your best advice, particularly when they learn your billing rate is $225 an hour. Thankfully, the age of spin is over, or at least on the wane. So always tell the truth and do the right thing, but with care and sensitivity. The idea is to keep the clients for as long as we can. You probably already know this, but at TK, the centre of the universe is New York. When our arrogant U.S. colleagues deign to acknowledge our backwater existence up here, they invariably believe they're far ahead of us—a dubious conclusion when most of them have their heads stuck well up their own arses. So beware. Finally, we exist to make money. We must make money. This desk won't pay for itself." She patted it respectfully. "So always, always use PROTTS to track your time daily on client projects."

I made it almost to the end.

"PROTTS?" It sounded like the intestinal strife tourists suffer after a two-star Mexican getaway.

"Public Relations Online Time Tracking System. Use it, or there'll be no invoice to send at the end of the month—and your tenure with TK will be very, very short."

I nodded. She then reached under some papers on her desk, pulled out one of the most outrageous pairs of glasses I'd ever seen, and put them on. Think 1970s Elton John, with a dash of Dr. Seuss. I'm not sure I can even describe them, but words like "fluorescent," "creepy," and perhaps even "exploding" would only tell half the story. Her specs looked like a bizarre little abstract-post-modern sculpture, with corrective lenses. Since it was my first day at a new job, I managed to keep that observation to myself. Unfortunately, the look on my face was still shouting "Just what exactly is resting on your nose instead of glasses?"

"Don't worry, you'll get used to my eyewear," she said with a smile. "It's kind of my thing. I find it adds a few inches to my presence and makes a very personal fashion statement."

Fashion statement? More like a declaration of war. But I suppose there are worse vices than bizarre specs, though very few that are quite so . . . visible. She then slid forward in her chair, made the perilous descent back to the floor, and glided out of the room, dragging me in her wake to circumnavigate the TK offices. Over the next hour, we met the seventy-five PR pros who were now my colleagues.

Diane introduced me to the creative director, several designers, the consumer products team, the health care/pharma team, the issues and crisis team, the government relations unit, the market research department, the digital and social media group, the financial services team, the technology team, and what she referred to under her breath as the "office overhead," including accounting, IT, the mailroom, and human resources.

Almost everyone wore black. I'd missed the agency dress code memo and was attired in one of my standard-issue Parliament Hill grey suits. I looked a little out of place, perhaps even from another planet. I took off the tie halfway through our tour and stuffed it in my pocket. Even though everyone seemed friendly, with some veering dangerously close to bubbly, I forgot each person's name the instant Diane uttered it, probably because I was still searching for adjectives to describe her glasses. Towards the end, she could see that I was reeling just a bit from the tour.

"I know it's a lot to take in on the first pass," Diane offered. "But it's important to accept that the modern PR agency is a universe unto itself. It is a hydra. When the economy is booming, the multiple heads actually work with one another and sometimes even like one another. But in bad times, it's every head for itself, and decapitations are common," she explained.

I'd heard the word "silos" used to describe the various groups inside an agency, but "hydra" works, too, I guess.

"One last stop," Diane added as we walked into a nice office with lots of glass. I could see people bustling along Bloor Street, ten floors below us.

"Amanda Burke, meet David Stewart."

I stepped forward to shake hands with a tall, lean, very attractive blonde woman, dressed in, yes, a black dress. She was tall to begin with and gained more altitude with four-inch heels that tapered nearly to pinpoints. Diane stayed back a ways so that she wasn't speaking directly into Amanda's shiny belt.

"Amanda runs the corporate comms group and is just back from two weeks in France." She turned to Amanda. "Welcome back, Amanda. This is David's first day."

"I wasn't aware we'd hired anyone new," Amanda said without looking at me. "I've been trying to get approval for a new hire for months."

"I would have involved you in this had you been here, but New York and Washington have really been putting the screws to us to deliver on Project Crimson, and David brings some expertise to the table that is really going to help us win."

"I've got Crimson well in hand, Diane, and I told my team about it last week from Provence. We're all pumped about it, whatever it is. We're good to go, and I think adding a new player at this late stage is a bit of a risk to the chemistry."

I can't always tell the difference between *concerned* and *pissed off*, but with Amanda, the distinction was quite clear. I just looked around the office, moving my head casually, trying not to acknowledge that Amanda considered me an unwanted, unnecessary interloper, or perhaps even unfit for continued life.

"Calm yourself, Amanda. You're running the Toronto end of the Crimson show. David will report to you on a trial basis. If we don't win Crimson, you can keep him – or he can report directly to me until we find the right place for him."

The voice inside my head was screaming "Hello, I'm standing right here!" but I kept my yap shut and continued my careful examination of the wheat-coloured carpet.

"Diane, I don't think it's too much to ask that I be involved in hiring new members of my own team." Amanda still hadn't even looked at me. Yes, wheat was the right description.

"Under normal circumstances, you're absolutely right. But we're being squeezed by D.C. and New York and you were away. I had to move. Let's keep our eye on Crimson right now. We can talk more about where David lives afterwards," Diane said, signalling that this part of the conversation was over. "David will participate in the briefing and brainer this afternoon and we'll finally all know what we're dealing with. See you then."

Diane handed Amanda my resumé and then caught my eye and cocked her head towards the door. The meeting was over. Amanda was just standing there looking like the victim of a purse-snatching. Our eyes finally met as I turned to follow Diane back out into the corridor. I offered what I hoped was an apologetic shrug before I was out the door.

"That went well," I ventured when we were down the hall a ways. "She's clearly been waiting her entire career just for me to arrive."

"Don't worry about Amanda," Diane replied. "She'll warm to you. She's a real pro, works very hard, and is very good at her job. But she also has a bit of a control problem. I've heard some of her colleagues refer to her as 'Commanda.'"

"Nice. So is someone going to tell me what Crimson is all about before I'm supposed to hit the ground running?"

"We won't know much until the briefing this afternoon, but I do know the potential client is NASA."

I had just moved back to my hometown of Toronto after three years on Parliament Hill. I'd headed up to Ottawa right after earning my Honours B.A. in the history of science from McMaster University. I'd always been a space nut, so I wrote my thesis on the societal impact of the manned space program, covering the Mercury, Gemini, and Apollo missions. I had no idea what my degree was preparing me for, but nearing the end of my fourth year, the planets seemed to align. My thesis supervisor passed my name along to a contact in Ottawa on the political staff of the Minister of State for Science and Technology. They were looking for a communications assistant to handle liaison between the minister's office and the Canadian Space Agency. Because I could write and was familiar with such space terms as "escape velocity," "perigee and apogee," "orbital decay," and "angle of re-entry," I got the job and moved to the nation's capital.

When I started, I knew next to nothing about dealing with the vipers' den of the Parliamentary Press Gallery. I've always believed that you learn much more from your mistakes than from your victories. Let's just say that I learned a lot in those early months, and I learned fast. I liked my minister but I didn't see very much of her. My role was a little ill-defined at the outset but I found my place eventually. I was one-third intermediary between the media and my minister, and two-thirds the minister's eyes, ears, and sometimes voice, in our dealings with the Canadian Space Agency. The CSA was an arm's-length but publicly funded agency of the federal government responsible for developing and guiding our indigenous space program and our key space partnerships with NASA, the Russians, the Europeans, the Japanese, and the Chinese.

I had a blast. It was right up my alley. I seemed to be able to get along with nearly everyone and managed to navigate the labyrinth of international relationships that fuelled space diplomacy. I'm still amazed just how far you can go relying only on curiosity, writing skills, manners, and the ability to connect with different people. It kept me moving up the ladder for three years, until my mother's cancer returned.

My father died of a heart attack five years ago, shortly after my mother's first brush with breast cancer. She recovered, from the cancer at least. I'd come home on summer vacation and some weekends to try to do my part and stay connected, but my older sister, Lauren, shouldered most of the burden. Then six months ago, what we thought had been defeated returned with reinforcements, and the siege began once more. Siege was an understatement. My mother's lungs were so riddled with the invader that surgery was not even in the play. Despite my sister's protests that she had everything under control, I resigned from the job I loved and moved back to Toronto. I'd been feeling guilty for three years about my rather carefree existence in Ottawa while Lauren looked after our mother. Now there really wasn't much time left.

My job in Ottawa had been all-consuming, so I was still very much single. It was hard to sustain a meaningful relationship while working in the pressure cooker of national politics. I did have a few less-than-meaningful relationships during my time on the Hill, but they were mercifully short. On a more positive note, I'd banked a whack of dough. Within a week of moving back to Toronto, I made a down payment on a condo across the road from the St. Lawrence Market, on Front Street. It was built in the eighties, a few years before developers discovered that people were prepared to live in 575-square-foot condos. So my unit was 1,120 square feet with a spacious living room and bedroom, and a den of sorts that I turned into a library. As something of a bibliophile, I had collected many history books about science and the space program, lots of novels, and dozens of volumes related to Sherlock Holmes, including several editions of the stories and novels themselves. I loved Arthur Conan Doyle's writing and the characters he immortalized in what were arguably the most famous tales in the world. I often tried to think like Sherlock Holmes when faced with complex problems in my own life, but found I could seldom rise above the Hardy Boys.

When unpacked and settled, I was very happy with my first stab at home ownership. It was only a block from one of Toronto's most beautiful bookstores, and it took me just a ten-minute subway ride north to reach the family homestead near Yonge and St. Clair.

Did I mention that my sister is a saint? Like most saints, she was still single at twenty-eight, and worked part-time at the Deer Park branch of the Toronto Public Library. Most of the librarian stereotypes fit, but not all of them. Lauren moved back into the family home when the cancer moved back into our mother.

Taking care of someone in the final stages of cancer is not a great gig. It leaves next to no time for anything else. When I first visited my mother after moving back to Toronto, I was shocked to see the deterioration since I'd last seen her, two months earlier. She was gaunt and weak, seemed resigned to her fate, and hoped it would come sooner rather than later.

My sister kicked off the visit by chewing me out a bit for abandoning my dream job in Ottawa just to assuage my guilty conscience. I tried to argue that I was acting responsibly and that she deserved help with Mom's care. She snorted a saintly snort. She was so good with Mom. While I flailed around cracking jokes and dodging the big malignant elephant in the room, Lauren knew just exactly what to do, what to say, when to stay, and when to leave.

———

There were about eight people in the boardroom and, it sounded like, plenty more on the speaker phone when we gathered at 2:30 p.m. for the conference call "briefing and brainer." After Googling "brainer," I'd learned that it was PR agency slang for "brainstorm." Got it. I sat down in one of the few remaining plush leather chairs and rolled as far away from the centre of the action as possible while still staying in the boardroom. Several of the folks I'd met earlier in the day on my little tour nodded to me. I nodded back. Diane sat at the midpoint of the boardroom table. Amanda was right next to her, staring into the speaker phone as if it were a crystal ball. She looked a little tense, which for all I knew was how she always looked.

A voice boomed through the static on the line at ear-bleeding volume.

"Okay, let's get started!"

I had an inkling Amanda was startled by the voice by the way she jerked her whole body up and off the chair, before placing her hand on her sternum and breathing heavily. Diane calmly leaned over the speaker phone and dialled back the decibels to prevent any further hearing loss among the Toronto team.

"Hi, Crawford. It's Diane. Go ahead. We're all assembled here in Toronto," said Diane.

"New York is all set, too," piped in another disembodied voice.

"Okay. Thanks for coming together on this, everyone. For those of you I haven't yet met, I'm Crawford Blake, GM here in Washington. I've got with me several of my very smart colleagues. We've got New York on the line and Toronto, too. Rather than taking the next twenty minutes for round-table introductions, let's just introduce ourselves when and if we have something to say. This project, when we win it, will be led out of D.C., with Toronto handling the Canadian component. New York will be hovering around the edges to help out, but it's really a D.C.–Toronto play."

I'd never heard of Crawford Blake, so I pulled out my iPad and Googled him as his pronounced southern drawl draped itself over the meeting. According to the bio that appeared on the TK site,

Crawford Blake, forty-one, was a Washington insider who had worked for three Republican congressmen and served a stint at the Republican National Committee. He was born in, yes, rural Mississippi and had earned a law degree from Alabama State next door. I tuned back in.

"Let me walk you through pretty well all the information we have on this opportunity and you can all hang on to your questions till I'm done, if you don't mind. Okay. Because of a contact of mine on the inside, we're one of three multinational agencies invited to pitch for a nice little project . . . with NASA. Yep, *the* NASA. So rule number one is that none of us ever, ever, cracks a joke that includes the line *'Well, it's not rocket science.'* At NASA, everything is rocket science and they take it very seriously. Here's the deal in a nutshell. To try to tackle our mountain of debt, this Republican Congress, bless their hearts, is threatening to turn off the funding tap to NASA, and to many other outdated and unnecessary agencies. And do you know why they feel comfortable telling NASA where they can put their precious space station?"

Nobody said a word, which was just fine with Blake because he seemed to like owning the floor.

"I'll tell you why. The public no longer cares about space exploration. NASA has been polling for more than fifty years. Back in the early sixties, when we were racing the Russians to orbit and then to the moon, the average American was obsessed with space travel. Nobody went to work when there was a launch. We were glued to our radios and TVs. I'm just barely old enough to have hazy memories of the late Apollo lunar missions and I can tell you, this country was moon crazy. Our family would gather around the TV in the rec room and watch for hours on end. With that kind of public support, Congress kept sending bigger and bigger cheques to NASA and felt good doing it."

Blake paused to catch his breath, but only for a moment.

"Well, my friends, times have changed. Citizens no longer care. A *Simpsons* rerun now draws a larger TV audience than a shuttle launch. In fact, one of the key tracking questions NASA has been asking Americans since the start of the shuttle program in the early eighties is whether you'd rather watch the launch of the shuttle on TV or go out for lunch. The lunch option wasn't even on the landscape until the mid-nineties. But it's definitely on the scene now. In the latest tracking study, for the first time in over thirty years, the majority of survey respondents would rather go out for lunch than watch a shuttle launch. I kid you not. That single finding has pushed NASA off the deep end. Hence their call to us."

"Crawford, Diane here again. Can I just ask whether the public opinion trends are the same here in Canada?"

"Good question, Diane. NASA didn't care much about Canada until you all built that funky mechanical arm for the shuttle. So the polling sample has only covered Canada for the last decade or so and your numbers have also been steadily decreasing, but they're not on as steep a decline as here in U.S. of A. That's one of the reasons NASA wants this to be a continental program. So here's the challenge, put as simply as I can. We need a big-ass PR program to rekindle the public's passion for space flight. We've got to arrest the free fall in our citizens' interest in, and support for, NASA and the important work it does on behalf of all Americans . . . and you all freezing up there in Canada, too. And we'll make a pile of dough while we're doing it."

This guy and his ignorant cracks about my fair country were starting to get on my nerves.

"I'm just about done, but we don't know which other two agencies we're up against, nor do we have any sense of budget for the program, but NASA has their ass stuck between a rock and a very hard place. So I say we go big but not too off the wall. This is still a stodgy group. We've got about two weeks to pull this off. We're pitching NASA here in Washington on the twenty-third and they want a joint American–Canadian team. Okay, I'll shut up now and throw it open for initial ideas."

I'd been watching Amanda for much of Blake's briefing. She was not hard to look at, quite the opposite in fact, and I was intrigued by Diane's description of her as a very dedicated employee who was consumed, perhaps even defined, by her job. She looked like she was dying to say something, anything, just to get into the mix. There was a brief lull after the boss had stopped talking. Cue Amanda.

"Um, it's Amanda Burke here in Toronto. Knowing only that NASA was the potential client, my team has gathered and analyzed the last three years of NASA media coverage here in Canada, including mentions of the shuttle program and the International Space Station. The amount, tone, and placement of the coverage are heading very much in the wrong direction. Even in the social media space, ahhh . . . no pun intended, NASA is not a big topic of conversation. I think we need a more creative, more robust, and more sustained media relations effort to reanimate the public's interest."

She actually had quite a lovely voice.

Her comment triggered a full discussion about what might be done to generate more media coverage. Ideas came thick and fast, including astronaut media tours, more IMAX space movies, weekly news releases, allowing reporters to follow rookie astronauts through their training, even building a mock-up of the space station and touring it across the continent. True to Diane's suggestion, I just listened, but I was not particularly impressed with what I was hearing. It all sounded to me like a bunch of tactics in search of a strategy. I turned my mind to what I thought was really being asked of us. But the unexpected sound of my own name brought me back to the discussion.

"It's Diane again here in TO. Sitting very quietly here in our boardroom this afternoon is the newest member of the TK Toronto team, David Stewart. This is David's first day – he has just joined us fresh from the political staff of the Minister of State for Science and Technology, where he handled media liaison and the government's relationship with the Canadian Space Agency. Even though I suggested he just listen today, I'm going to put him on the spot."

Great, just great. There was a sudden drought in my mouth. Here I am, minding my own business, trying to get the lay of the land in this strange new world, and all of a sudden, Diane decides to toss me my first anchor. With nowhere to hide, I shuffled my chair up to the board table as a condemned man might climb the scaffold stairs.

"David, you've been listening to the ideas fly back and forth, but you've kept your own counsel so far," Diane commented. "Given your experience and expertise, are we on track?"

All eyes in the room and all ears on the speaker phone turned to me. What to do, what to do. My heart rate soared. I've often heard that in moments of high stress, everything slows down, the fog clears, and the perfect response comes into sharp focus. Yes, I've often heard this – I've just never actually experienced it. I knew what I had to do. It was obvious. The path of least resistance was simply to leap on board, ingratiate myself with my new colleagues, build a bridge to Amanda, and support the heavy media relations play being proposed. Yep, all aboard the bandwagon.

"Are we on track? Well, we're on *a track*, I just don't really think it's the right track" were the words I heard coming out of my mouth.

Bandwagons were usually easier to board. I had somehow missed the big fat open door and managed instead to throw myself under the back wheels. By the looks I was getting in the room, no one would be helping me back to my feet.

"What do you mean we're not on the right track?" snapped Amanda. "We've just kicked around dozens of great story ideas here. The media will be lapping it up."

Now that I was out on the limb, it was time to reinforce my branch and hook up a safety line.

"I have no doubt that we could generate a giant stack-o-coverage, but NASA is asking us to re-engage the public, not manufacture news clippings," I explained, not yet knowing exactly where I was headed, other than being ostracized, isolated, and perhaps even unemployed. "More articles and news items will not re-animate the average citizen's fascination with space exploration."

"Okay, new guy, what will?" Amanda threw down the gauntlet.

At that point, I had nothing to lose.

"Well, if we want the public to care about space, we've got to put the public in space, literally. So we run a contest to send a citizen up to the space station where they won't just be PR ballast but will actually have a role in the mission," I said, my words only a hair behind my thoughts.

"We promote it heavily through the social media platforms and use some of the good ideas already discussed to drive some media coverage. But the storyline is about the possibility that you or your next-door neighbour might be heading into orbit. Another shuttle mission to the International Space Station is no longer news. But put a plumber from Edmonton or a nurse from Montreal on board and then you've got a big story, real news."

I decided to quit while I was behind and shut up.

"NASA will never go for that," Amanda interjected. "There's no way we can . . ."

"Whoa, whoa, Amanda," Crawford Blake leapt in. "This is a brainer, honey, so our standard rules apply. There is no 'bad idea' in a brainstorm. We want the team to get creative, so go easy on –" I heard someone on the line prompt him with my name. "– David. It's his first day, after all."

Amanda's face flushed.

"Of course, Crawford. I was just mindful of our time and the need to move us forward," she explained. She looked at me as she said it and nodded. I gave her my best "No worries" look while she responded with a very convincing "Thanks, jerk" expression.

The brainer continued with other ideas advanced and dis-cussed, most of them back in the realm of traditional media relations. I eased myself away from the table and returned to quiet mode. After another thirty minutes or so, the flow of ideas had dwindled to a trickle, so Diane took the reins.

"Crawford, I think we've got some good stuff to work with here. I assume we'll handle blowing out a Canadian approach here and your team will do the same for the U.S. market there. Then we'll bring them together."

"My thoughts exactly, Diane," he agreed. "But let's stick to what we do best, driving earned media coverage. In my experience, the NASA guys are very conservative and easily spooked."

Amanda caught my eye again, this time with what looked like "nannannabooboo" plastered all over her face.

"Just one more thought from north of the border," Diane added. "I'd like David Stewart to flesh out his contest idea a little more and throw together a few slides. Then next week at our status meeting he can walk us through it before we decide on what to include in the final deck."

"Up to you, Diane."

———————

Ten minutes later I was back at my desk in my very own cubicle when Amanda Burke arrived like an Exocet missile, only more explosive. In the classic power play, she placed her hands on my desk and leaned down from above before unleashing her tirade. She was no longer using her "lovely voice." Rather, she spoke in a crazed whisper that carried only four cubicles away in every direction.

"Thank you for shitting on my plan from a very great altitude!" she hissed. "Don't you ever do that again in a boardroom packed with people, let alone with Blake and Diane right there, too. You made me look stupid and I'm running this program, not you. You come here with your vaunted political experience and think you're something special. Well, I couldn't care less if you were actually the minister and not just his lowly media lackey. NASA is my ticket so you'll have to earn your way onto the team. And after today, you're beginning the race well behind the starting line."

"Her" was all I said.

"What?" she snapped.

"You said 'his lowly media lackey' but I was 'her lowly media lackey.' Our Minister of State for Science and Tech is a woman."

"Oh."

"And I'm sorry about what I said. Diane threw me under the bus. I wasn't expecting to be called upon and when I was, all I had was my gut reaction. I had no time to shape it or frame it in a way that didn't appear to, as you so elegantly put it, 'shit on your plan from a very great altitude,'" I explained. "But even though I regret what came out of my mouth in the heat of the moment, it is what I believe. I know your approach will net us the coverage, but unless there's a new and bigger story angle in the play, I don't think we're going to move the needle. I'm very sorry my view emerged in the way it did. But it is what it is."

I spoke quietly, trying to lower the temperature in the room, and smiled once or twice for good measure. To my surprise, Amanda collapsed into the tiny guest chair in front of my desk, which meant it was partly outside my partitioned space. She closed her eyes and rocked slowly.

"God, I am such a bitch," she whispered.

This little sliver of vulnerability caught me off guard.

"Umm, no you're not," I cut in. "You were justifiably upset at the new guy who, you know, had just shit on your plan from a very great altitude." I smiled again and she stopped rocking and lifted her head.

"David, Diane likes to test new people by putting them on the spot. It's her way of seeing if you can handle the heat. She did the same thing to me when I started. I didn't fare much better. I might have warned you," she conceded. "But I was a little stressed with Diane second-guessing me and gushing over you."

"Look, Amanda, I'm just trying to survive my first day in a new job. I have no agency experience. I had to Google the word 'brainer' this morning. I don't even know where the washroom is around here."

Now she actually did smile.

"Okay, fine. I was just taking my paranoia out for a little run," she replied. "But NASA is mine. You can work on it, but I'm running it. Clear?"

"It's all yours," I agreed. "By the way, can you show me how to record my time in PROTTS or whatever the hell it's called?"

CHAPTER 2

"How are you feeling?" I was sitting on the edge of my mother's bed, exercising my gift for creative questions.

The twilight angled into the room through the west-facing window. It took her a minute to focus on who had spoken. Her face was still puffy – a remnant of the steroids she'd taken earlier in her treatment. A few wisps of hair still clung to her head. She'd long since abandoned the wig.

"Not quite myself."

My mother has a way with understatement. I barely recognized her. She only faintly resembled my mother. Not only does cancer take so many lives, but it so often makes its victims seem like different people near the end, which is precisely when you want them to be just the same as they've always been.

"How is the new job?" she breathed in a voice I could hardly hear.

"Oh, my first day went very well. I managed to offend the woman I report to and alienate the entire team I'm supposed to work with to make outer space cool again. The big boss, who is actually quite tiny, wears glasses that could be on display in the Museum of Modern Art and likes to toss grenades to the new kids to see how they'll react. Oh, and my office, at least for now, is a tiny cubicle amidst a half-dozen web designers in an area they call 'the pit.' Other than that, I love it."

"Good boy. And what did you do with *your* grenade?"

"Well, instead of playing the game and deftly reinserting the pin, I just kind of held it where it would inflict the most carnage and waited until it detonated," I replied. "But afterwards, Amanda, you know, the woman I report to and offended, paid me an unexpected visit and we at least began to remove the bigger pieces of shrapnel."

I waited for another "Good boy" before realizing she had drifted off to sleep. Lauren bustled in with a tray.

"Mom, I've got a boiled egg for you and . . ."

"She's just fallen asleep," I said, trying to keep my voice down.

"I know, David. But she really needs to eat to keep up her strength. She has to eat."

I had blundered into a deeper topic than what my mother wanted for dinner. She surfaced again.

"Thank you, but I don't think I can handle food right now."

"Mom, I know. But you need your strength if we're going to beat this thing," Lauren persisted, handing me the tray to hold.

"Honey, please . . ." Mom began, but faltered.

Lauren leaned over her and began to rearrange the pillows to prop her up a bit. Mom allowed her to do this, but she didn't seem eager to venture much off the horizontal.

"Umm, Mom, why don't you just sit there and I'll help you devour this egg." I slid closer and picked up the spoon. Mom crossed her arms in slow motion as a final defence, but allowed me to feed her the egg.

"I promise not to make choo-choo train noises."

Mom fell asleep almost immediately after swallowing the last mouthful. I took the tray and dishes downstairs. Lauren was sitting at the kitchen table, staring at the wall, nursing a coffee.

"Was this a good day or a bad day?" I asked as I loaded the dishwasher and returned the tray to its spot on top of the fridge.

"They're all pretty much the same now," Lauren replied. "She hasn't been downstairs in two weeks and I don't think she'll ever be back down here. She'll never sit in this chair, or turn on that stove, or curse the toaster . . ." She stopped in mid-sentence and I saw that she was about to lose it.

"I know. But at least she doesn't seem in any pain," I offered. What a weak-assed response.

"Yeah, some consolation. What a bastard of a disease that the best we can say about it is that she wasn't in much pain as it took her."

Lauren lifted herself to her feet, dumped her coffee in the sink, and went upstairs to her room.

I don't think I'd ever heard my sister use a word like "bastard." I tidied up the kitchen, looked in once more on Mom, deep in sleep, and left.

I spent the next two days at the office thinking through my Citizen Astronaut contest idea and pulling together a few PowerPoint slides to bring it to life. Despite how much derision it attracts, I actually like PowerPoint, if it's done well. I'd learned the hard way from a senior civil servant in Ottawa how to make the most of the ubiquitous presentation software after he'd pulled me aside following a briefing I'd given early in my tenure in Ottawa. I'd just learned how to animate PowerPoint slides, and I was smitten. When I'd learned that I could liberate, choreograph, and even provide a soundtrack for my bullet points, I seemed to lose any sense of judgment and restraint. In short, I suddenly felt like George Lucas and went hog-wild. Fortunately, the minister didn't attend that particular briefing or my humiliation would have been complete.

It was a presentation on the Canadarm, the mechanical appendage that the Canadian Space Agency built for use on the space shuttle. I considered it an extraordinary achievement and wanted an appropriate measure of drama and gravitas in the presentation. So I developed a background template for the slides that featured a space shuttle along the side, its cargo bay doors open and the Canadarm extended, poised for duty. This left the central zone of each slide free and clear for titles and bullet points. I thought it was masterfully balanced. Then, newly initiated into the glories of custom slide animation, I did my thing. It only took me about six hours to transform what had been five flat slides into a full-on cinematic assault on the senses. Throughout the process, the famous white Hollywood sign kept popping into my head.

When the lights had dimmed and my colleagues had settled around the boardroom table in the minister's office, I stood with the remote control in my hand. I casually explained that I had just "thrown together a few slides" and hit the button to summon the first to the screen. The shuttle first slid into orbit on the edge of the slide. Then as the theme music from *2001: A Space Odyssey*, blared from my tiny and tinny laptop speakers, the Canadarm extended, reached into the shuttle's cargo bay, pulled out the logo for the Canadian Space Agency, and slowly positioned it below the footer line in the bottom right-hand corner of the slide, before the arm retracted to its original position. It was awesome. It was brilliant.

In terms of informing my audience, it was a disaster of epic proportions. It wouldn't have been so bad had I not programmed all five slides to do the same thing. After that opening, I doubt the audience even noticed that each bullet point "launched" from the bottom left-hand side like a text rocket, complete with blast-off sound effects, before settling into its rightful position in the middle of the slide.

Those enduring that first presentation so long ago were polite and said nothing about my special effects, except for that one senior civil servant who took pity on me. His first words after our colleagues had rushed from the boardroom were "Houston, we have a problem." He proceeded to teach me a little about the principles of graphic design and slide composition. He concluded with advice on the restrained and strategic use of animation so that it actually enhanced the delivery of information, rather than distracted, confused, or even frightened the audience. After we'd gotten to know each other a little better, he thoughtfully suggested I donate my original Canadarm PowerPoint presentation to the CIA to assist with the interrogation of reticent prisoners. I saw the light and never again abused the power in PowerPoint.

I kept my contest slides simple, with few words, but solid visuals. I used shots of a shuttle launch, the interior of the International Space Station, a demographic cross-section of Canadians, a few mock headlines that I hoped we might see (e.g., "Citizen Astronaut Contest launched, Canadians get on board!"), as well as a photo of a recent news conference held in the same venue in which I was proposing we announce the contest, the Ontario Science Centre. Steadfastly static bullet points filled in the blanks so that all of the major elements of the program were duly explained. I liked it. Then again, at one time I'd liked my Canadarm presentation, too.

We all reconvened in the boardroom Thursday morning. I hadn't had a chance to share my presentation with either Diane or Amanda beforehand, but they didn't seem too perturbed. I figured they considered my idea a long shot, likely to be cut early on anyway. A laptop was set up and plugged into the projector. Then we waited the compulsory ten minutes it took to fiddle with the laptop settings so the entire slide was visible on the screen. After several bad experiences with computers and projectors, I had revised the tech industry's soothing promise from "plug and play" to "plug and plague." It never seemed to work the first time.

Amanda walked us through a more traditional-looking slide deck with the standard communications program headings, including Background, Goals, Strategic Considerations, Strategy, Target Audiences, Key Messages, Tactics, Measurement, Timelines, Team, and Budget. My mind was drifting after the third slide. Sometimes a bit of "custom animation" would be welcome to keep you awake. As expected from the last meeting, this was strictly a media relations play with lots of solid and creative thinking to drive coverage. Beyond the ideas advanced in the earlier session, the creation of a travelling Canada in Space Museum exhibit that could tour the country was proposed. I liked the idea but still believed that at best, there was really only one media hit per outlet in each city. It seemed like a big investment for a few clippings.

Amanda went on to describe setting up a news bureau of sorts to develop and pitch story ideas on a sustained basis. This would be staffed, nearly full-time, by a team of four in our office, with others contributing potential stories as well. The social media team proposed setting up a "NASA in Canada" blog, Facebook presence, YouTube channel, and Twitter feed. I tried to make up the ground I'd lost in the last meeting by adding a few thoughts and tweaks to some of the stories and commending my colleagues on the others. But I mostly kept my head down in the meeting. Finally, a junior account coordinator blurted out that we should create a NASA mascot, kind of like the San Diego Chicken, so we could tour him/her/it around the country visiting schools, hospitals, and malls. We hemmed and hawed, then killed the mascot idea after what I thought was a surprisingly long discussion.

Finally, at some unspoken signal, two hours in, the meeting just seemed to end. I still wasn't that impressed with what we'd pulled together but I was keeping quiet. I was also still digesting the proposed budget for the Canadian program – just over one million dollars.

"Okay, folks, I think we've got our plan and I think it's solid," Amanda declared. "It may not push the leading edge of creativity, but it will get the job done for a very conservative client. I think it's what they're looking for. I'm going to revamp the deck to include the new ideas we've just discussed, and put it to bed. We owe it to the D.C. office by close of business today so it can be blended with theirs. Nice work, everyone."

I was still fingering my keychain flash drive where I'd stored my contest slides. I wasn't inclined to say anything given how I'd messed up my first meeting, so I didn't. But Diane did.

"Just before we break up, David, will you present your contest idea now that you've fleshed it out a bit?"

I watched people sag back into their chairs.

"Um, sure, Diane."

I really didn't want to get into this, as the plan seemed to have been finalized already, and everyone was keen to get out of there. But I slid my flash drive into the laptop, dragged the file onto Amanda's desktop, and a moment later had my first slide on the screen. I was more nervous presenting in front of my new colleagues than I thought I'd be. My start was shaky, but after zipping up my fly, things seemed to run more smoothly. I confess, I really liked this idea, even though I had just blurted it out at the previous meeting without the benefit of actually thinking it through. But even after a few days of kicking it around inside my head, I was more committed to it than before. Since Yuri Gagarin first left our atmosphere and found himself floating in the great black void, there has always been a mystique about astronauts. They aren't like other humans, but exist on a higher plane. They went into space, while we stayed on Earth to cut the lawn and mind the kids. But the Citizen Astronaut contest finally broke down that barrier and allowed at least one mere mortal Canadian to fly with the elite astronauts. It stood historical convention on its head. And it was this unique shift that I hoped might mobilize a nation, if I could only mobilize a boardroom first.

I spoke for about ten minutes as I walked through my slides.

There was a beginning, a middle, and an end to the presentation, and I seldom found myself reaching for words after the first slide or so. Out of the corner of my eye, I'd seen both Diane and even Amanda nodding with approval, or perhaps with early-onset Parkinson's. When I actually lifted my eyes to look at Amanda, she immediately stopped nodding and gave me a look that seemed to say "Wrap it up, pal, time's a-wasting."

"So coupled with the comprehensive earned media and social media campaign to get the word out, I think there are literally millions of average Canadians who would love to fly on the shuttle and spend a few days floating around the International Space Station, even throwing up in zero gravity, a near certainty for a considerable number of astronauts. And I don't think we'd have any trouble generating entries. It's big and bold, and I believe nothing short of this will meet the challenge NASA has given us. Here endeth the sermon," I said as sat back down.

There was a long pause, and I waited for Diane to announce that she wanted my idea added to the deck before it was sent to D.C. Nope. She was waiting for Amanda.

"Interesting idea but I don't think so," Amanda began. "It's soundly conceived, but we have to be realistic and not push them too far. These are very risk-averse people, according to Crawford. We can't afford to scare them off. If we presented this, we'd blow way over on the crazy-o-meter. Think of the liability issues of sending Joe Public into space. It's a non-starter. Nice effort, but a non-starter."

That hurt. But I wasn't done yet. I looked towards Diane in the hope that she'd overrule Amanda. But she was just looking serenely across the table into space. Okay, now I was done. Diane finally broke the silence.

"Okay, so that's it then. Nice job on developing the idea, David. With a different client in the chair, I think it could have worked," she said as she stood. "Thanks, everyone. Amanda, you can tie it up with a bow and send it off to Crawford."

A minute or two later I was licking my wounds in my cubicle when Diane stuck her head in.

"Don't be bummed at what just happened. That was an impressive performance for an agency tenderfoot. I liked what I saw, so don't stop doing that," she said. "Also, I think you should try to get to know Amanda a bit better. It'll help both of you."

With that, she was gone, and I could turn to Google for a definition of "tenderfoot." I found it in less than three seconds. "A newcomer not yet hardened to rough outdoor life." I could live with that. The NASA deck was still in front of me and with not much on my plate, I idly flipped through it. Something caught my eye and gave me a second reason to leave the pit and head over to Amanda's office on the nicer side of the floor.

"Hi," I said after I'd stood in her doorway for a few seconds without catching her eye. I startled her and she jerked just a bit, then tried to cover it up. Jumpy.

"Oh, David. You know you really shouldn't sneak up on people like that."

She sounded annoyed.

"Sneak up? I just walked down the middle of the corridor in broad daylight and stopped right here in your doorway. You were clearly focused on your work. Next time I'm going to start calling your name gently when I'm getting close." I smiled as I said it.

She'd returned her attention to her laptop by this time.

"I just didn't hear you, that's all," she snapped.

"Well, I guess I walk softly. Diane says I have tender feet."

Amanda didn't get it. Now she looked annoyed, too.

"So, David, what's up? I've got a lot going on right now."

"Has the NASA deck gone to Washington yet?"

"I was just about to push the button. Why?"

"Check out page six, in the capabilities section. There's a mention of GM when I'm pretty sure you mean NASA."

A deep furrow immediately appeared in her forehead as her eyebrows came together in the shape of a capital M. For most, it would have been a lowercase m, but she had very athletic eyebrows. Quite striking, in fact. She abused the wheel on her mouse trying to find the offending slide, and then leaned in closer to read. I heard her sharp intake of breath.

"Shit! I was just about to send this. I would have looked like an idiot in front of Blake," Amanda said as she corrected the line.

"No harm done. How did you manage to type GM instead of NASA?" I asked, genuinely curious.

She flushed a bit.

"I started with an old credentials deck from a pitch last year to GM, just for the capabilities section. I thought I'd caught all the references, but one slipped through. You can't even trust PowerPoint's 'search and replace' function. This would have made me look so sloppy and unprofessional."

"Whoa. Someone else would have caught it before the actual presentation. No harm done. No big deal," I said.

"No big deal?" she asked, giving me her best "Are you on crack?" look. "David, we don't get the chance to strut our stuff with the Washington office very often. Crawford Blake could well be the next TK president, and he's tough. Impressing him can have a real impact on your career. So screwing up in front of him is not on my agenda. Having him discover a stray GM in the deck is almost worse than NASA finding it!"

I just barely stopped myself from backing out of her office. She was so seriously intense. I found my hands in the air as if she were holding me at gunpoint.

"Okay, I got it. I'm glad we found the mistake so that no careers were ruined by an evil Detroit-based multinational."

Fortunately, I had stumbled across her well-hidden sense of humour. She softened and even smiled.

"Sorry, David. I'm mad at myself, not at you. I can't abide carelessness in myself or in others. I read this deck a hundred times and never caught it." She paused, then looked at me again as I lowered my hands, no longer under the gun. "Thanks, David. You saved my bacon."

I thought I might as well strike while the bacon pan was hot.

"So, umm, speaking of bacon, does anyone eat lunch around here?"

She thought about it for a moment, weighing the question.

"Lunch, lunch. That's the midday meal, right?" she asked.

"So you don't eat lunch very often?"

"I hardly ever have time. But I didn't think we'd have this deck done by now. So as soon as I've yanked GM out of it, I think it's ready to go. Give me ten minutes to draft the email to Crawford and I'll meet you in the lobby. I think I've got half an hour before my next meeting."

———

I stopped in to see my mother on the way home from the office, but she was asleep. I offered to stay the night and let Lauren have a night off and sleep at my place. In her mind, it wasn't even an idea worthy of consideration. Lauren seemed locked into her role. I truly wanted to do more, but almost felt like I was trespassing on her turf. We talked for an hour or so, and she let me make spaghetti for us. Then she sent me home so she could get some sleep herself. Mom usually needed her help a few times in the night and Lauren was paranoid about sleeping right through.

I loved my condo. I still got a little thrill from stepping through the door. I'd become a little fanatical about keeping it neat. I lay down on the couch and didn't even turn on the TV. I realized I wanted to show off my new place to somebody, perhaps to anybody. I wondered about knocking on my neighbours' doors and introducing myself but thought that might seem a little odd. While I've always been quite happy in my own company, it occurred to me that perhaps I might be a bit lonely. With all that was swirling in my life, I didn't think I'd freed up enough time in my schedule to be lonely.

My twenty-minute lunch with Amanda had gone well, for the most part. When she'd finally hit Send on the NASA deck, she seemed to lighten up and loosen up. At lunch, I'd learned that she was a couple of years older than I. While I'd been working on Parliament Hill, she'd already been in the trenches at TK for a few years, working insane hours and never saying no to work that came her way. As she explained between forkfuls of a limp salad in the little restaurant in our building, an agency is like a marketplace. Work flows down to those who do it well, do it on time, and do it without complaint. If you look around almost any large PR agency, the junior staffers who are swamped tend to be the good ones, the "keepers." But those who can always be found with time on their hands usually have that extra time for a reason. They've already been tried by the senior consultants or account directors above them, and somehow fallen short. Missed a deadline, missed a meeting, or missed the point. So, repeat business dries up. It's not good news if most others at your level in the organization are crazy busy, and you are not.

Amanda had climbed up the ladder she'd mentioned earlier faster than most. And why not? Why wouldn't Diane promote

Amanda quickly for good performance if it meant TK could get a higher billing rate for her? But from my agency rookie perspective, it seemed to put a lot of pressure on Amanda to keep up the pace of her progress. I made some dumb throwaway comment about shooting stars burning out. Not a good idea, but we got past it. Despite several attempts, I was unable to discover whether Amanda had anything else that occupied her life beyond Turner King. With half a salad still left to eat, Amanda had dashed back upstairs for her 1:30.

I dragged myself off the couch and into the library and pulled down from the shelf the Sherlock Holmes story collection entitled *His Last Bow*. It included one of my favourite stories, "The Adventure of the Bruce-Partington Plans." I'm not sure why I was drawn so often to this story. Perhaps because it's one of only four Holmes stories that featured Sherlock's older brother, Mycroft. Or it might also have been because the missing plans in the mystery are for a submarine. This probably appealed to my interest in the history of science. Whatever the reason, I often reread Sherlock Holmes stories before heading to bed, and this tale more than some of the others. The writing was so good and it was just very cool to be reading the very same words that were first published back in 1912, as the Holmes canon was winding down.

I finished the story and flipped through a few other Conan Doyle books on my shelf, including the second Holmes novel, *The Sign of Four*. I always seemed to gravitate to a line Holmes utters in this story: "How often have I said to you that when you have eliminated the impossible, whatever remains, *however improbable,* must be the truth?"

I fell asleep in the library shortly thereafter.

––––––––––

D.C. in early March was mercifully less humid than in the dead of summer. I'd been to Washington a few times while working for the minister. On our last trip, a year earlier, we'd toured the Smithsonian Institution's National Air and Space Museum. What an amazing place. I remember just staring up at the *Wright Flyer* hanging in the lobby. The sight of it above so transfixed me that I walked straight into the wheelchair of a senior citizen from Baltimore and nearly tipped her into a rack of museum maps. It wasn't quite an international incident, but my minister did speed away from the scene, leaving me there alone to make my apologies. There were no broken bones, and after we eventually staunched the bleeding, the poor woman was actually quite nice about it all. I'm sure the museum staff would have been relieved to know that I'd have no time for a return visit this trip.

There were three of us from TK Toronto heading south for the NASA presentation. I figured my Ottawa stint on the Canadian Space Agency file would punch my ticket to D.C. and I was right. Diane called me a couple of days earlier to let me know I'd be on the pitch team. Diane, Amanda, and I would be the Canadian contingent joining six D.C. TK folks and one from New York. Ten people seemed like a big team, but this was a big opportunity. I sat between Amanda on the aisle and Diane in the window seat, which left me feeling mildly trapped. I think Amanda could probably have kept the Air Canada 767 aloft with tension alone. I wondered if she was a nervous flier, yet she was still rigid and morose back on land at the Dulles baggage carousel.

Diane went in search of a washroom, while we waited for the bags.

"Are you all right, Amanda?" I asked. "You seem a little preoccupied."

"Of course I'm all right. I'm just getting myself psychologically ready to present with Crawford," she explained. "They say you only get one shot with him, so I want to make it count."

"With ten of us on the team, I'm worried that he won't even notice us," I replied. "He'll certainly remember Diane's glasses, but after seeing them, I can't imagine he'll have any sensory capacity left to remember us."

A slight smile threatened the corners of her mouth.

"I know what you mean," Amanda said. "I thought that security guy was going to confiscate them as an unidentified and suspicious object."

"Yep. He seemed quite shocked, perhaps even repulsed, when she actually put them on her face."

After we checked in to the Washington Plaza on Thomas Circle NW, we cabbed it over to the TK office on 14th Street NW for the rehearsal at 2:30 p.m. The vast lobby was all marble and glass, with an Amazonian receptionist in a futuristic booth in the centre. There was actually more glass than I thought.

"Are you all right?" Amanda asked as I bounced my face off the very clean and clear plate glass door.

"I did that on purpose, just to break the tension," I explained. "And perhaps my nose."

I recovered and nonchalantly opened the door while enduring the most unspeakable pain I'd ever experienced. The three of us approached the receptionist with my eyes still streaming.

"Sorry about the door," the receptionist said in greeting. "I usually prop it open to avoid such collisions. You must be the team from the great white north. Welcome to TK D.C., I'm Cheryl."

"Hello, Cheryl. I'm Diane, the TO GM. This is Amanda Burke, account director, and finally, with the red nose and teary eyes, David Stewart, senior consultant."

I waved and wiped my eyes. I've never understood why your eyes water when you hit your nose. Why doesn't your nose run?

"Just have a seat and I'll alert the corner office that you've arrived."

We all sat down and I turned to Amanda.

"Okay. When you're feeling nervous before the presentation tomorrow and you need something to lighten the mood, just think of my nose and that glass door over there, and you'll be fine."

By the time we all heard footsteps coming down a very long corridor behind Cheryl's command post, I could finally see straight again and my eyes were no longer swimming.

"All hail Canada and welcome to Washington!"

We all heard the southern drawl before we laid eyes on the D.C. GM.

"Diane with the fancy glasses, how are you, darlin'?"

"Always great to see you, Crawford. You're looking as tanned and relaxed as ever," replied Diane. "Don't you do any work around here?"

"Not if I can help it," Blake answered. "You know that."

"Crawford, this is the designated account director on the NASA pitch . . ."

"I know who this is. Amanda Burke. It's so great to make your acquaintance at last. I've been so impressed with your leadership on this so far and you look just as I pictured you in my mind's eye."

In the charm department, Crawford Blake was very well-endowed. He kind of made me queasy. Amanda wasn't expecting this southern gentility assault and seemed to succumb to an anxiety aneurysm of some kind. She searched first his face, and then the floor for the words she needed.

"Well, umm, thank you and it's great to meet you too . . . umm . . ."

I was standing right next to her and without moving my lips I whispered his name and hoped he hadn't heard.

". . . yes, Crawford. It's great to meet you Crawford."

Diane jumped back in.

"And Crawford, this is our new guy, David Stewart, who knows the Canadian Space Agency inside and out."

"Well, well, now that's the kind of insight we need on this pitch. I figure the NASA boys will be mighty impressed with the depth of our team."

I just nodded and shook his extended hand, which was big and surprisingly sweaty.

We were escorted to the boardroom, where the rest of the NASA pitch team was gathering. Introductions were made and the bonding began. Amanda had regained her poise and personality and even managed to direct several complete sentences in a row to Crawford, who claimed the big chair at the head of the gigantic polished boardroom table. Lovely, shiny table. I was dying to launch myself headfirst down the length of it in a great slide for life but thought it might not leave the best first impression. Oh yes, and Amanda would probably have had a coronary. Diane was occupied explaining the artistic antecedents of her pair of glasses to two younger TK D.C. fashionistas. Eventually the kibitzing died away and Crawford took control.

"Okay, team, let's get this done," he began. "Let me start by saying that it is wonderful and rare to have the opportunity to work with our colleagues in the land of snow, slush, and ice hockey up there in the province of Toronto. I really must get myself up there for a visit sometime. I welcome the three of you to our warmer climes and hope that we'll have many more chances to work together after we win this thing tomorrow."

We nodded and smiled. Something about this guy was rubbing me the wrong way, but it was hard to cut through the bonhomie to get to what was really bugging me. It was probably just the standard American ignorance of Canada – a very old story. I bet I could name all fifty state capitals, yet I doubted Blake could identify even a handful of Canadian provinces. I decided not to test my theory right then, as Crawford still had the floor.

"We have a truly great opportunity tomorrow to land one of the biggest and most prestigious clients we've ever had at Turner King. NASA is a household name in both our countries and around the world. Their achievements in the last half century have shaped our nation. Regrettably, their influence appears to be waning. Our job is to restore the lustre to NASA and bring the people back to marvel at its miracles. I guarantee you that NASA is as straitlaced an organization as you're ever likely to encounter, and they can be easily spooked. So let's keep it real tomorrow and not scare them with ideas that are too far out there. I've seen the deck and it's a winning presentation. So let's divvy it up and make sure everyone has a piece. If you're in the room tomorrow, you're going to be saying something."

We spent the next few hours mapping out the presentation and then running through it once as if we were in NASA's boardroom.

It was my very first rehearsal for my very first TK presentation. So this was how things worked in the agency world. I admit, I was impressed. But I was also a little concerned about the budget. All elements of the proposed program had been painstakingly budgeted according to the various hourly rates of the professionals involved and the anticipated time required. The North America–wide program came in at just under five million dollars in fees, before expenses. Then in the meeting, Crawford arbitrarily upped the number to six million to ensure we weren't shortchanging the agency. Six million bucks in fees for a year-long continental program still seemed like a lot of dough to me. Then again, we were pitching NASA, famous for purchasing a nineteen–million-dollar toilet for the International Space Station, so perhaps we weren't out of line.

Here's how the show was set up for the following morning:

11:00   Crawford Blake would open and introduce the team before waxing eloquent on the challenges NASA was facing.

11:10   Diane Martineau would add the Canadian perspective on NASA's challenge and outline the goals of the North American program.

11:20   A TK D.C. research consultant named Bridget and I would be up next to outline the public opinion landscape in the U.S. and Canada and identify the strategic opportunities it revealed.

11:30　Amanda and her D.C. counterpart, Michael Crane, would then summarize the program and what results were expected.

11:45　A couple of TK D.C.'s top social media gurus would then explain how tablet and cellphone apps, Facebook, Twitter, and blogger outreach would support the media relations play.

11:55　Finally, two TK measurement experts (one from D.C. and the other from New York) would describe exactly how we were going to evaluate whether we'd been successful in achieving the program's goals.

12:00　Crawford would zip through the estimated budget before opening the floor for questions. Then we would all try desperately to perform as well during the Q&A as we had in the actual presentation.

We ran through our parts once and tweaked the slides a bit. Crawford and Diane left after their parts to have dinner together. After that, Amanda finally seemed to be back in her element and jumped right in the middle of it all. She was still uptight, bossy, and domineering. But without her, the Canadian angle on the plan might well have disappeared. By early evening, we were just going through the motions. Amanda said it was time to quit rehearsing before we became too practised. We needed to leave some adrenalin in the tank for tomorrow. Interesting. I was learning a lot.

When we left, Amanda rushed ahead to open the glass door for me in the lobby. I played my part and stepped very gingerly through the opening with my hands held up in front of my face. For the first time, I heard her laugh. It was nice to see little pieces of the unguarded Amanda surfacing. It seemed she felt good about the NASA presentation.

That night in my hotel room, Google and I dug a little deeper into Crawford Blake. Beyond what I'd learned about him earlier, I discovered that he'd been a baseball star at his rural Mississippi high school. He played third base, the hot corner, and swung a heavy bat. Blake helped lead the team to a state championship in his senior year. The stuff of American dreams.

Just before shutting down, I put my time into the tyrannical time tracking system, PROTTS. Too bad the time wasn't billable, but we were still in pitch mode.

CHAPTER 3

"Oh, that's just great. We're up against the Tupper Group," Amanda sighed as we entered NASA headquarters on E Street sw around 11:00 the next morning. "They are good."

A dozen or so of the most uniformly beautiful people I'd ever seen were milling about in the lobby, all smiles, returning security badges to a harried guard.

"Wow, looks like a *Vanity Fair* photo shoot waiting to happen," I observed. "How do you know who they are?"

"The tall blond woman flirting with that younger suit on the left runs Tupper in Toronto," Amanda explained. "I interviewed with her last year when I was at the end of my TK rope. I'm better now."

We moved over to the other side of the lobby to join the rest of the TK crew assembling there. A few of our folks exchanged casual nods with the Tupperites but there was no overt fraternizing with the enemy.

"Just keep smiling, folks, and act as if we're walking on sunshine," Crawford said under his breath. "Diane, put those funky glasses back on. That'll intimidate them."

When Diane complied, I realized that he'd been serious. Diane turned to face the Tupper Group as they moved en masse towards the door.

"See, they're retreating." Crawford paused until they were out the door before continuing, "Okay, everyone, huddle up."

Again, I thought he'd been kidding but was immediately enveloped in a minor swarm of TK staff as we gathered around our leader. He actually put his arms around Diane and Amanda, who happened to have ended up on either side of him. On cue, we all leaned into the scrum.

"Okay, guys, the nasty people have gone and the field is ours. This is our day. This is our hour. This is our moment. Seize it. We have the team. We have the program. And we have the opportunity. Just do your thing in there and we will win this. Americans will once again be captivated by space travel, and our world and any others they might find out there will be put right."

Unaccustomed to the half-time Vince Lombardi speech, I only just managed to stifle an eye-rolling smile. I half expected him to shout *"Break"* at the end and have us all clap our hands. I glanced at Amanda and was struck by the intensity contorting her game face. She looked like a barefoot Tony Robbins disciple about to sashay across red-hot coals. I confess it was kind of freaky. But then I looked at Diane in her haute couture glasses and realized Amanda wasn't really that freaky at all. It also registered with me that Crawford Blake had failed to acknowledge that Canadians were part of this play too. Typical.

When the coast was clear, we descended on the security guard. He obviously wasn't used to competitive pitches by aggressive, ambitious PR agencies. I watched as Amanda took a little longer than most to enter her name on the sign-in sheet. While the guard was occupied untangling a lanyard, she scanned the paper quickly and even flipped back a page in what I assume was an attempt to identify any of the other agencies pitching. She looked at Crawford and shook her head.

By the time we'd all been issued our visitors security passes, a youngish man was awaiting us wearing a nondescript grey suit with a very "descript" tie of a colour that seemed to swirl at least five different shades of phlegm. Diane was eyeing the tie with undisguised admiration, while nausea seemed the general reaction from the rest of us.

"Turner King, I presume," phlegm tie said.

"We're all here," Crawford replied. "Lead on."

We piled into two different elevators and headed for the executive boardroom on the top floor. We were still ten minutes early. The room was empty of people but clearly had been occupied shortly before. It looked as if the fire alarm had sounded in mid-meeting. Papers, file folders, half-filled coffee cups, pens, and the odd BlackBerry were scattered around the far end of the board table, suggesting an audience of six NASA execs. When phlegm tie left us and we began to hook up Amanda's laptop to the ceiling mounted projector, Crawford actually slipped around to NASA's end of the table and cast his eye on some of the paperwork visible.

"Anything?" Diane asked, keeping a weather eye on the boardroom door.

"Standard scoring sheet. Blank. No sign of the Tupper tally or any other firm's," Crawford whispered, moving safely back to our end of the table before the NASA jury returned.

After a few minutes of increasingly agitated fiddling and cursing, Amanda got our presentation up on the screen and ready to go. We'd been just about to break out our own projector, which of course we had brought with us as a hedge against incompatible technology. But because we had lugged it to the pitch, we did not require it. Murphy's Law.

As agreed in our planning session, we placed the business cards of each pitch team member in six neat stacks where the NASA folks would soon be sitting. We thought this preferable to attempting a round of one-on-one introductions that would have consumed the entire time allotted. Shortly thereafter, we were milling about our end of the table when the double doors to the boardroom swung open and the NASA squad entered – five older men in suits led by a very fit-looking younger woman with shortish dark hair. She was in her late thirties, or perhaps her early forties, or maybe even her late forties. I've never really been very good at guessing a woman's age, dicey practice that it is. I immediately assumed that she was a communications exec because she was wearing what I'd come to accept as the "women in PR" uniform – black pants, a white shirt of some description, and a black jacket. A NASA pin in her lapel completed the ensemble. She had a commanding presence that kept the focus on her.

"Turner King, welcome to NASA," she said as she stood behind her chair. Her colleagues had all dropped into theirs. "Sorry for the brief delay. We were just finishing up our discussion next door about one of your competitors that I'm sure you passed in the lobby. We had built in a half-hour break between pitches so that the firms wouldn't be tripping over each other coming and going but these folks gave us such a creative presentation that we let them slip into overtime."

If she thought she was going to intimidate me at my first PR new business pitch by singing the praises of the agency that had just left . . . she was dead on the mark. I felt a little queasy.

Crawford offered a saccharine smile and was about to speak, but the NASA woman clearly wasn't quite ready to yield the floor.

"I'm Kelly Bradstreet, chief information officer and head of NASA's Office of Communications. I'm in charge of this selection process and the relationship that will follow with the winning firm. I've only been with NASA a short time but my mission is the same one the successful PR firm will be living and breathing, day in and day out. In short, our job is to get the public excited again about space. It's as simple to say as it will be challenging to accomplish. But I have no doubt it can be done, and that's why I came to NASA in the first place."

Kelly Bradstreet, Kelly Bradstreet. I knew that name. It took me a minute to place it but eventually I remembered. I was blessed with the gift of forgetting instantly where I'd put my wallet five minutes earlier while being able to recall nearly everything I'd read in the preceding six weeks or so. Eventually, I remembered a profile piece about Bradstreet in *Time* magazine. Snippets of the article came back to me. She was a marketing hotshot who had been hired a few years ago to rebrand the U.S. Army, which at the time was still saddled with the image of an aging and arthritic Uncle Sam. So she had rebranded one of the oldest institutions in America and triggered lineups at recruiting offices that hadn't been seen since Pearl Harbor. It made her a marketing superstar. How did we not know she'd moved to NASA?

"Now let me introduce the panel before turning the floor over to you."

Kelly's presence had been so dominating that I hadn't even yet looked at the grey-haired contingent of NASA execs seated next to her. It turned out to be the entire senior management team, including the administrator, deputy administrator, CFO, chief scientist, and chief of astronaut training.

I hadn't recognized him until she introduced him, but then it was obvious. The chief of astronaut training was Scott Chandler, the youngest of the twelve Apollo astronauts to walk on the moon. This meant that he was now quite old. I had their faces locked in my head from reading all I could find about the Apollo program when I was just a kid. But they were ageless in my mind, never growing a day older than they were when they walked on another world. I looked at him closely and thought I could just discern faint traces of the astronaut cockiness swagger, not so much in his face, but in his eyes and in the way he held his head. It was very cool to be in the same room as one of the six humans who had actually driven that most expensive of dune buggies, the lunar rover, on that most exotic of beaches.

While seated, Crawford then introduced the Turner King team, having to glance down at his notebook just once when he'd worked his way around the table to where I sat. I was the new guy.

"Thank you, Mr. Blake. Now that we have met one another, the floor is yours. You know how much time you have, so please don't overshoot the clock."

Kelly sat down, looking comfortable and confident but a little out of place alongside her geriatric colleagues. Crawford Blake stood, paused, then began to walk slowly behind the chairs of his team. His southern drawl was wistful, his cadence measured, as he spoke. He wasn't looking at the NASA panel but rather somewhere in the distance. This wasn't what we'd rehearsed.

"My older brother tells a powerful story that has stayed with me all my life. I only regret I was too young to have been there with him. In July of 1969, he was just seven years old, away from home for the first time at a Christian summer camp on Twin

Lakes. It was as remote as you can get in central Mississippi. On the evening of July 21, about ninety campers congregated in the main lodge. The younger boys, like him, wore pyjamas and spread their sleeping bags on the floor. After singing some favourite camp songs and finishing with a handful of spirituals, an old black and white TV set that belonged to the elderly couple who ran the kitchen at the camp was brought out, plugged in, and turned on. The reception was very fuzzy until tinfoil was applied to the rabbit ears. Then, as my older brother puts it, the snow on the screen miraculously parted and the picture took shape."

Crawford paused for effect but kept pacing behind the TK delegation. I had the feeling that if he'd thought he could get away with it, he would have been delivering his soliloquy against the dramatic backdrop of orchestral strings and theatrical lighting. I'd been watching Kelly the whole time and she was beginning to fidget. It started with drumming her fingertips on her yellow pad. Then when I figured her fingers were tired and tender, she escalated to drumming her pen. Crawford didn't notice and almost seemed to be lost in some kind of nostalgic reverie. Or perhaps he was just lost.

"Eventually he could see the nine-rung ladder running down the insect-like leg of the lunar module to the circular landing pad resting on the moon's surface. And he watched, spellbound, as Neil Armstrong stepped down onto the dusty surface and uttered those now-famous words, 'That's one small step . . .'"

"Thank you, Mr. Blake, but I can assure you, the people at this

56

end of the table are very familiar with what Astronaut Armstrong said all those years ago. I wonder if we might move on to hear about the program you are proposing we adopt to fulfil our goals."

Kelly Bradstreet said it calmly but with an edge to her tone that suggested resistance was futile.

I saw anger flash before Crawford could recover and re-plaster the obsequious smile onto his face.

"I can assure you, Miss Bradstreet, we were just about to start into the program. I was just doing a little scene-setting," Crawford replied, remarkably clearly for a man with a clenched jaw and gritted teeth.

"Well, please consider the scene set. Thank you." She smiled back at him as he returned to his seat.

Diane rose, and we were off and running through the PowerPoint slides as we'd rehearsed them the day before. We had not yet distributed the coil-bound copies of the presentation for fear the NASA folks would promptly flip ahead of us in the deck and stop listening. We had decided to hand out the decks at the end.

Diane was a very good presenter and, among other things, managed to put Canada on the map, as it were. I worried that her glasses would be such a distraction that the panel would not be able to focus but they seemed to be with her. Perhaps it was just as a contrast to Crawford's thespian overtones, but Diane spoke well but simply while standing in her place at the table. Bridget and I did the same and made it through our piece on the state of public opinion in both countries. I was nervous. When I'd initially opened my mouth, I thought I sounded like I'd inhaled a shot of helium. But after a few phrases, my voice loosened and seemed to return to its normal register. Bridget was also good and our hand-offs to one another were natural without any of the contrived ". . . and now David will walk you through . . ." transitions. I was pleased just to have gotten through it without a face-plant onto the board table.

After we finished our part, Amanda, who was wearing a "Put me in, coach" look on her face, stood to present the bulk of the program with Michael. She was keyed up and spoke slightly more loudly than anyone else had thus far. But she spoke clearly and not too fast, as did Michael. They worked well together. Amanda even mustered what looked like a smile at one point, unless it was anxiety-induced acid reflux. Now that I was done, I was able to relax and watch the faces of our judges as Amanda and Michael worked their way through the deck. Four of the five NASA men seemed to be either just waking up from or just falling into a deep sleep. The fifth man, Scott Chandler himself, was actually in a deep sleep, his face deformed by the fist jammed under his jaw. But Kelly Bradstreet was very much awake and kept increasing the pace of her pen percussion. I figured if we waited a few more minutes she'd be very close to playing *Wipe Out*. She seemed to be willing Amanda and Michael to get to the point. It was all too much for Kelly when they moved from program activities to program measurement.

"Excuse me," Kelly interrupted. "I'm sorry to cut in but you seem to have finished outlining the tactics and have moved on to evaluation. I don't mean to be rude but if you're simply suggesting we step up our media relations efforts to drive more of the same old coverage we've been generating for fifty years, there's really no point in continuing your presentation."

Amanda was paralyzed with a look that suggested she was standing with a family of deer in the middle of a highway, all of them blinded by high beams. I glanced at Michael and his expression was very much like Amanda's.

"Now just a minute here," Crawford snapped as he leapt to his feet, loaded with invective and with the safety off. "We have worked very hard to develop a program that will achieve your objectives and remain true to the spirit, character, and traditions of NASA. I know you just said that you don't mean to be rude, but I have to say that you really . . ."

Suddenly Amanda regained consciousness and saw the ground racing up to meet us. Just before we hit, she fired our retrorockets and changed course.

"Ahhh, thank you, Crawford. I've got this one. Thanks, thanks," Amanda soothed as she motioned for him to sit down, palming the air in front of her with both hands.

"Well, I was just about to say . . ." Crawford persisted.

"I know, but we're all good here," Amanda pushed back, holding her hand up like a stop sign. "I've got this one, Crawford, if I could just continue. Thanks. Thanks so much."

Unaccustomed to being interrupted, Crawford slowly settled into his chair with a perplexed look on his face – and on the rest of his body, for that matter. Diane had her hand to her mouth with her eyes opened so wide, it made me forget about her glasses. Yes, that wide. Scott Chandler lifted one lid to see what he'd missed. Amanda closed her eyes for just a second, sighed deeply, and then turned back to all of us. For some reason, she looked once at me and then focused on Kelly.

"Ms. Bradstreet, I can understand why you would think we were finished with the major program elements. I should have explained our somewhat unorthodox approach before we started. I apologize, but bear with me please. What we've just finished presenting is merely what we have come to call the PR infra-structure of our NASA plan. We need to sustain and increase the earned media coverage opportunities so that NASA's profile doesn't dip. But we certainly agree that more is needed to reig-nite the public's passion for space exploration. We need a big idea to complement the more traditional media relations approach we've *already* presented."

She leaned over her laptop, but kept talking.

"So thanks for your patience. Now let's skip ahead and unveil the creative centrepiece of our NASA plan. David, over to you," she concluded before sitting back down.

For an instant, I thought she'd said "David, over to you." Surely I was wrong. I looked at Amanda. She gently tilted her head towards the screen while her eyes gripped me in a chokehold.

I broke free from her stare long enough to glance at the screen. It seemed I had heard her correctly. The room was looking at the first background slide in my Citizen Astronaut presentation, minus the title. After an awkward fifteen-second silence, I instantly understood what she intended. And in that moment, something clicked. It might have been Kelly's pen, but I don't think so. Suddenly, I felt calm. This was my idea. I started to get to my feet. I could do this.

I was so focused I barely noticed the pain of smashing my kneecap on the leg of the boardroom table as I stood up, although the noise it made was fearsome. I looked again at Amanda. She nodded encouragement with her acid-reflux smile. Crawford was still sulking, looking at nothing in particular. Diane gave off a serene look with a "Don't blow it" overlay. I turned to the NASA panel and noticed that the one eye moonwalker Scott Chandler had opened earlier had closed again. So I concentrated on Kelly, who seemed to be the decision-maker anyway. She put down her pen and I picked up the remote slide advancer. Breathe.

"A very special breed of men and women has been travelling into space for over half a century. In the early years of the space program, indeed into the late eighties, average Canadians and Americans were transfixed by the human drama of the launch and safe return of Mercury, Gemini, Apollo, Skylab, and space shuttle missions. It was so far removed from the experience of our daily lives that we could only watch in wonder.

"But after more than a hundred space shuttle missions over the last thirty years, slowly but inexorably, the extraordinary has become ordinary. It's still the same highly skilled, heavily trained group of overachievers who get to fly, but the public has lost interest. We've seen too many launches and too many landings. The average citizen has almost nothing in common with the brave test pilots, aerospace engineers, scientists, doctors, and other very special men and women who ride the shuttle into orbit and stay for weeks, sometimes months, on the International Space Station. We can't relate to them or to what they do. The thrill wanes. It's become routine."

I paused for a moment, plotting my next move.

"We agree with you, Kelly, that landing more articles in newspapers and more stories on TV are unlikely to convince the public to leap back on NASA's bandwag . . . er . . . bandrocket. We need something more to re-animate average Canadians and Americans."

I paused again.

"We actually need to give average citizens the chance to ride the shuttle into space, sitting next to the test pilot and nuclear physicist."

I punched the remote and the *Citizen Astronaut* title morphed to life on the slide in a very modest and restrained animation, free of sound effects.

"We want to launch the Citizen Astronaut contest here in the United States and in Canada. It's kind of like Willy Wonka's golden ticket but the prize is not touring a chocolate factory on foot, but orbiting the Earth in the International Space Station."

Kelly was still listening and even nodded a few times as I walked the group through the still hazy details.

- There would be one American winner and one Canadian winner.
- Citizens over the age of eighteen would be eligible to submit one entry each online.
- The contest would be supported by a fully integrated media relations and social media campaign to spread the word across the continent.
- The two winners would be chosen in random draws overseen by a major accounting firm. Just like the Oscars.
- The winners would have to complete successfully a basic citizen astronaut training program before having their flight status confirmed.
- Both winners would have assigned mission duties to complete while in orbit.
- Of course, both winners would be required to sign the mother of all liability waivers.

Kelly sat perfectly still with her hands clasped on the table in front her. I was nearly finished. I'd described the idea and how we would make it happen in as much detail as I knew at that moment. It was time to wrap up.

"In the end, we seek to rekindle the public's support for NASA and excitement about space exploration by actually giving the public a chance to leave this Earth and experience space travel. And we're not talking about some eccentric billionaire business-man who bought his way onto a Soyuz flight after training for six months in Russia. We're talking about opening the possibil-ity of space travel for a farmer in Saskatchewan, a secretary in Halifax, a convenience store owner in Wichita, or a crossing guard in Savannah. It gives every American and Canadian citi-zen a stake in the space program, and a stake in NASA. It's their chance to do what they've only ever watched and dreamed about. That is how you return space exploration to the top of the public's agenda and keep it there."

I sat down slowly, keeping my eyes on Kelly. I felt my knees knocking together under the table. I didn't look at anyone else. Kelly was nodding very slowly while keeping her eyes on me. I took it as a good sign. But for all I knew, she was deciding which expletive to employ when blowing our plan out of the water.

"So let me see if I understand your idea," Kelly began, speak-ing very deliberately. "You want to invite any American or Canadian citizen to enter a contest where two winners would actually fly on a shuttle to the International Space Station, con-duct experiments or complete other mission-related tasks, and then fly back to Earth before returning to their regularly sched-uled lives? Is that really your idea?"

"Um . . . yes, that's it in a nutshell," I replied.

She just looked at me as she thought it through. She raised her right hand, palm facing forward.

"Gentlemen, questions?"

A ripple of energy passed through the panel – a very small ripple.

"Do you know how much it would cost to train complete neo-phytes to fly safely in space?" asked the CFO, who must have finally tuned in while I was presenting.

None of my colleagues was rushing to respond so I felt com-pelled to say something that in the most optimistic light might approach an answer. But I really don't think light comes in such an optimistic variety.

"No, I confess I have no idea. None whatsoever. But wouldn't it be considered a good investment if the contest reinvigorated public support for NASA, and then Congress felt compelled to open up the funding tap again? That's the outcome we're aiming for."

The CFO said nothing. Kelly nodded again. Then Scott Chandler roused himself.

"Son, do you know what a 20G Centrifuge is?"

I was actually being asked a question by an astronaut who had set foot on the moon. Had I known I was to be in the presence of a lunar explorer, I would have worn my "Apollo astronauts do it in one-sixth gravity!" T-shirt. My heart was pounding.

"Yes, sir. I've visited the one you have at the Ames Research Center in California," I replied. I snatched a look at Amanda and

I could tell she was impressed. "It's used to train astronauts and fighter pilots to withstand the g-forces experienced when flying in high-performance fighter jets and spacecraft."

"Very good." He nodded and smiled. "Well, that centrifuge at Ames is always well-stocked with barf bags for those with weaker constitutions who can't hold their lunch past five Gs. I think your idea belongs in one of those barf bags."

"I see," I said, still not quite clear. "I don't suppose you mean that in a good way."

"Putting housewives and shopkeepers in space alongside astronauts who have trained their entire careers for a single shuttle mission diminishes all of us and the legacy of the original seven astronauts, who, by the way, were all friends of mine."

Crash and burn. I was dead.

Well, it was clear we'd lost the astronaut vote on the panel. The role of astronauts has been a topic of much debate right from the earliest stages of the space program. During the Mercury program, the original seven astronauts mentioned by Chandler had felt that they were just human ballast being shot into space in a tin can and that their considerable aeronautical skills were being ignored. They wanted more of a role in the mission. They wanted to "fly" the rocket, not just strap in for the ride. So suggesting that inexperienced civilians should "tag along" for a mission made space flight seem just too pedestrian for the likes of the former Apollo commander. Even in the shuttle era, this remained an issue. On-board computers had the power to guide the shuttle through re-entry and land the shuttle safely without an astronaut ever touching the stick. Yet *every single mission* has ended with the commander actually "flying" the shuttle to a dead stick landing. Screw the computers.

"Thank you, Mr. Chandler." Kelly intervened to put me out of my misery. "Further questions?"

The NASA Administrator piped up next.

"I understand how my colleague feels, but the unfortunate reality is that Congress is squeezing us so goddamned tightly now that I'm looking for spare change in my office couch. Right now, it is not a good scene. It is downright ugly. To make matters worse, Congress has access to all the polling we've ever done, so they know the public has drifted away. So the slashing and burning continues. Do you really think we can bring citizens back to us simply by holding out to them the slim prospect of a trip to the space station?"

"Yes, sir, I truly believe we can." I hoped I sounded more convinced than I felt.

Kelly asked many more questions about how it would all work and I skated my way through them with a little help from Amanda, Diane, and Michael. Crawford Blake was no help. He was still fuming, with arms folded, and wanted out of there. He had gathered up what little he'd brought and seemed to be leaning towards the door.

"Well, thank you for your presentation," Kelly said as she stood up. "Do you have hard copies for the panel?"

Diane jumped in fast as Amanda reached for the copies in her bag.

"Um, no, unfortunately we don't have them with us. Our printer blew a gasket just as we were printing your hard copies this morning. But I received a text during the presentation that they have fixed the problem and the copies have been couriered to you to arrive by the end of the day," improvised Diane.

Very smooth. I realized that the printed decks in Amanda's bag did not include the big idea – my big idea.

"Thank you," Kelly said. "I know you'll be wondering about next steps. Yours was the final pitch, so we now have some thinking to do, and we'll be back to you one way or another soon. Likely within the week."

She paused before continuing.

"And I'm sorry I prematurely cut off the presentation earlier. NASA can only succeed in this if we try bold and creative approaches. The run-of-the-mill media relations program that I thought was the extent of your proposal is something we can do internally, in our sleep. So let me close the meeting with some friendly advice. Don't bury the lead next time. Start with your big idea."

———

"What an unholy bitch she was!" shouted Crawford Blake after the team had reconvened in the TK boardroom an hour later. "I very nearly pulled the plug and took us out of the running.

What a bitch! And where did she come from anyway? Didn't we do a recce on who's running the show over there?"

Diane, Amanda, and I stole a glance at one another. Crawford was the one with the contact inside NASA. Why didn't he know? I decided not to ask. He stomped around the boardroom spitting Mississippi vitriol. Diane, Amanda, and I were getting ready to head for the airport to return to Toronto. With Crawford hovering on the border between livid and apoplectic, the sooner we bolted the better. Amanda had already integrated my slides into the presentation and the printers were spitting out copies ready for binding and rush delivery. So I figured we were free and clear to evacuate. Not yet. Crawford stopped, turned, and faced us, with his hands flat on the table.

"And Amanda, I'm not a big fan of freelancing such a big presentation the way you and David did back there. I really didn't appreciate being shut down like that in front of the potential client."

"Come on, Crawford." Diane leapt in to defend her team. "Amanda did exactly what you would have done. If we still have any chance of winning this account, it's because of Amanda and David."

"I'm so sorry, Crawford, I panicked. I didn't mean to cut you off. I was just trying to save the business and I suddenly remembered I had David's slides on my computer," Amanda explained, looking as if her career were flashing before her eyes.

Crawford paused and dropped into a chair at the table. When he spoke, it was no longer tinged with anger.

"You didn't look panicked to me. You took charge. You reminded me of me, even though it was at my expense. I'll get over it, eventually," he joked. "And if we score the account, I'll get over it even faster."

Diane and Crawford then launched into a separate conversation, speaking in code about TK operational matters. So I turned to Amanda, who still seemed wired from the pitch. It was the first time I'd been able to speak to her since we'd walked out of the NASA meeting.

"Great save when Kelly was about to gas us," I said. "We were cooked, and you saved us. And your hand-off was so smooth, I didn't even know that I had the ball for the first minute or two."

"I know. You had this look on your face that did not inspire confidence, initially," she replied. "But then I could see the penny dropped and you were off. David, I have to admit, you did a great job presenting your idea. You nearly convinced even me this time. I still think it's a long shot but you did really, really well for your first pitch."

She smiled at me. A real smile.

"Thanks. I'm just glad you remembered you had the slides. We'd have been sunk without them."

The boardroom door swung open and Xena the Warrior Princess, aka the TK receptionist from the lobby, stepped in.

"Crawford, there's a Kelly Bradstreet on line two for you."

We all raised our eyebrows in unison. Crawford Blake reached for the phone as my stomach tightened. It was frustrating only hearing Crawford's side of the conversation.

"Hello, Kelly, it's Crawford Blake. Long time, no see. . . .

"Thank you. And I apologize for my abbreviated outburst. We've all been so excited about the NASA pitch so it was tough to hear your initial reaction before we took you through our big idea. . . .

"Yes. Yes. And yes, Diane does have amazing taste in glasses." Diane beamed.

"Uh-huh. Yes. You did? You are? Well that's just fantastic news. We didn't think we'd hear until at least next week. . . .

"Yes, you're right, time is tight. Of course we can start right away."

The phone still to his ear, Crawford gave us the thumbs-up and I experienced my first new business high. It was a surprising feeling of pure elation. Amanda made me do the fist bump. I missed her fist the first time but came around a second time and made contact. Crawford waved his hand to silence us.

"I thought it was all over when the ex-astronaut was so, um, colourfully critical of the idea. . . .

"I see. Well that's good to hear. . . .

"Yes. I understand. It's completely your call, and that will be fine with us," Crawford said, looking at me. "Yes, he's based in Toronto. . . .

"Okay, that's just great. We'll watch for the paperwork and get together next week to kick it off. We'll also hammer out a more detailed plan. Thank you for this news, Kelly. We're all in orbit around here – pun intended. And we'll do everything we can to justify your faith in us. . . .

"We are, too. Oh, and again, sorry about my reaction in the room today. I was a little hot because I knew what was still to come and that you would just love it. Turns out I was right. . . .

"No problem. You were well within your rights. Okay, well, we'll get started. Bye for now and thanks again."

He calmly replaced the phone in the cradle and held his hand there for just a second or two before leaping to his feet and pumping his fist so hard I feared he might dislocate his shoulder. Then he whooped a few times and did a brief but disturbing victory dance that was a little bit bump and grind and far too much Curly from The Three Stooges. It was actually quite frightening, but it really didn't matter.

"Okay, folks, we can ditch the Project Crimson code name and tell the world that we're NASA's agency. We won," he said, still catching his breath.

"Here's the deal. Despite grandpa astronaut's reservations, we won it on the Citizen Astronaut contest idea. The only catch is that there'll be a condition in the NASA contract that young David here plays a senior role on the account team," he said turning to me. "You impressed them. Congratulations."

Amanda looked befuddled for just an instant, but then recovered.

"Okay, but I'm still running the Canadian program, right?"

PART 2

CHAPTER 4

"You're looking fried and frazzled, Lauren."

Oops. I was sitting across the kitchen table from my sister. She supported her forehead with the palm of her right hand and twirled a spoon in her tea with her left. She was not pleased.

"Thanks, jackass. That makes me feel so much better," she said. "You'd look like crap too if you were up every half-hour through the night dealing with whatever Mom's got going on at that precise moment. It could be pain, hallucinations, a congested chest, missing meds, or my favourite, a bedpan malfunction. Sometimes she calls and then doesn't know why when I get there."

Shit. I am such a tool sometimes. Okay, often.

"Lauren, I'm so sorry, I meant it, you know, sympathetically. Honest, I did. I can't imagine what you're going through, but now that I'm here, I can find out. Let me stay here for a few days and you take a break at my place," I offered again. "I'm here to share this. That's why I came back."

Lauren paused and then made eye contact for the first time since I'd arrived a few minutes earlier.

"David, you've been working 24-7 ever since NASA landed. We've barely seen you," she replied. "Look. I know you're serious and you mean well, but it just makes more sense for me to do this. You've got a big-time job now and I'm only part-time in a sleepy library branch. Besides, I don't really think Mom would be that comfortable with you positioning her bedpan or changing her Depends. Her dignity is already in short supply these days."

Ouch. That hurt. There was silence but for the clink of stirring spoon against teacup. I waited, knowing it was coming. There it was, the sound of guilt screeching to a halt and parking on my chest with a jaunty "Okay, I'm here. What did I miss?"

"I'm sorry I've been a bit out of touch the last month. This NASA project is huge and demanding. I've never worked so hard in my life, and it's weighing pretty heavily on my rounded shoulders. We're all working from the crack of dawn till 10 at night, every day. When we launch the contest next week things should slow down . . . somewhat."

Lauren didn't even look up, but kept stirring.

"So, is she feeling any better at all?" I asked.

She almost gave herself whiplash snapping her head up to stare at me, incredulous.

"David, wake up! You know what she's got, and how far down the road she is. Right now she's only ever feeling pain and how slowly time passes. There is no 'feeling better' any more. And there won't be."

And there it was. It hit me so fast, so hard. I'd always managed to keep it at bay, but not any more. It was right there on top of me. I suddenly felt twice my own weight, as if I'd landed on Jupiter, and the lump lodged in my throat felt positively planetary. I squeezed my eyes shut as hard as I could to keep my face dry, and breathed deeply through my mouth. I felt Lauren's hand slide into mine. Even though I'd moved back to Toronto weeks ago, she could see that I'd finally arrived.

Before I left, I tried again to visit with Mom but she was oscillating between light sleep and medicated stupor. Neither state lent itself to conversation. So I just sat on the bed for an hour and tried to remember what she used to look like.

Of course, Lauren was right. I'd been AWOL on the home front since returning from Washington four weeks ago. I'd only managed a couple of visits and even then I'd been preoccupied. I'd tried to explain the inner workings of the contest to my mother, if only to make sure I had it straight, but she nodded off in the middle. And it may not have had anything to do with her disease or treatment. I pledged to carve out more time for my mother and sister. I just didn't know where it was going to come from.

———————

It had been an exhausting month or so since winning the account. Amanda and I, along with a great team of young and dedicated PR pros from whom I was learning a great deal, worked nearly around the clock to get ready for the launch news conference. I was more focused on bringing the contest to life, while Amanda and Diane worked on finalizing the actual plan, budget, and contract. The Canadian plan document was beautiful when finally printed and bound. It was quite different from the U.S. plan, largely because our country is quite different from the U.S. Beyond the disparity in populations, there was a raft of state jurisdictional anomalies that dictated a more complex approach south of the 49th parallel. While the Canadian plan covered more ground geographically, it was simpler to implement, and I was relieved about that.

What had taken the most time was hammering out the contest rules and regs. With NASA's blessing, we signed a non-disclosure agreement and then a partnership contract with National Lottery Corporation (NLC) to help us develop and run the contest in Canada. NLC was satisfied with the global accounting firm TK had contracted to oversee the contest mechanics in both countries. In fact, they had already worked on several national contests with Emily Hatch, a big wheel from the Toronto office of Borden-Bennett. Emily would ensure that the Canadian rules and regs were honoured to the very edge of every serif on every letter of the law. The word "stickler" seemed to have been created in honour of Emily.

After I had briefed the Canadian Space Agency (CSA) very, very unofficially, NASA had approached them officially with the contest idea. NASA was thrilled that the CSA jumped on board so quickly. I was not surprised in the least. Why wouldn't CSA be there? The contest would give the agency national, continental, and even global exposure which could lead to more funding from the feds in the same way that NASA was gunning for more dollars from Congress. It was a win-win, and I knew CSA would see it that way. They signed on fast. In the negotiations, NASA hemmed and hawed and finally agreed to assign a Canadian astronaut to the mission as a kind of escort for the Canadian contest winner. We'd pushed for this and it made sense for us, strategically. The CSA's polling showed that public interest in space peaked when a Canadian astronaut was flying. I learned later that putting a Canadian astronaut on the mission was hardly a major concession. As it turned out, Martine Juneau, a very impressive Canadian mission specialist, had already been scheduled for the flight anyway. How magnanimous of NASA.

The phone in my cubicle emitted its funny sound and I saw "NASA" pop up on the little screen on my phone.

"David Stewart."

"David, it's Kelly Bradstreet."

Uh-oh. What had I done? I was still a little nervous dealing directly with the client. Amanda and Diane had handled most of the NASA liaison, so I was a little concerned to hear from Kelly directly.

"Um, hi Kelly," I stammered. "Um, it looks like we're right on track here. All systems are go for the launch next week . . . to, er, coin a phrase."

"Relax, David, I'm not calling with a problem. You guys are doing a great job. Smooth sailing so far. I wish your D.C. office was doing as well. They're still a few steps behind trying to pull it all together," she said, taking me off the hook. "I've learned through several discussions with Diane that this whole contest idea really came from your brain. Based on your presentation during the pitch, I'd suspected but wasn't sure."

"Well, it's a team effort."

"Yeah, yeah. I know you cooked this up and I just wanted to say thanks for such a great creative idea. NASA has never been known for their out-of-the-box PR savvy and I really wanted to change that. Your idea may just start to turn the ship around. So, well done."

"Thanks, Kelly. Here's hoping it all goes according to plan."

"Well, if it doesn't, at least I know who to ream out," she said. Silence ensued.

"David, that was a joke."

We'd just put the rules to bed, finally securing agreement from all parties, including the heads of the CSA and NASA and Emily Hatch. When Emily's legal hotshots at Borden-Bennett had finished drafting the full set of regulations governing the contest, it might as well have been written in Lithuanian. Emily was kind enough to provide simultaneous translation as I waded through the hefty document. I doubted the North American

Free Trade Agreement was any longer or more indecipherable. While we would certainly use the lengthy legal document as our regulatory bible, I had to draft something for public consumption that outlined the contest rules. The only real change Emily insisted upon from the basic rules we'd come up with ourselves had to do with the way people could enter the contest. We'd just assumed that Canadians would have to enter online. Emily's view was that if the contest was truly to be open to all Canadians, we had to allow entries from those who did not have access to a computer and a high-speed Internet connection. So we permitted mail-in entries as well.

My phone sounded again. I recognized the number immediately.

"Minister, what a surprise," I said.

"Hello, David. I figured I'd never be able to reach you now that you've left the cushy Ottawa life and gotten a real job. But here you are picking up on the first ring."

"Old habits die hard, Minister," I replied. "How's my successor doing?"

"Well, we didn't really think the job warranted a full-time position so my driver is filling in on a trial basis."

I laughed, and so did she.

"Actually, we snagged an ex-journalist from the *Halifax Chronicle-Herald* to fill your shoes and she started last week," the minister explained. "She used to have the science beat, but print is still hurting, so her position was about to be phased out. We're glad to have her."

I'd already heard this news and thought it was a good move.

"I remember her. I think you've made a great hire."

"I think she'll do well. I mean, the job's not that hard anyway, right?"

The minister and I had always had this kind of back-and-forth bantering relationship, and I'd considered it a good sign that she was comfortable joking around with me. I was glad she still felt that way.

Enough kibitzing.

"David, I've just been briefed on this citizen astronaut idea that NASA is pursuing. I'm not surprised that you had a hand in it. So run it by me again without all the big words the CSA egghead was using, will you?"

"Sure, Minister," I started. "Simply put, we want to rekindle the public's enthusiasm for the space program by giving average citizens an opportunity to fly on the shuttle and do a few turns about the Earth on the International Space Station. There'll be one American citizen and one Canadian on the scheduled flight this fall. They'll be trained over the next few months in Florida so that the lucky winners can perform some modest mission-related tasks while in orbit. We don't want them feeling like human cargo. Then they'll return safely to Earth and become instant celebrities. Our lucky Canadian will probably end up on a cereal box and perhaps even snag a reality TV show. Ultimately, NASA's goal is to re-engage the citizenry and turn that public support into dollars from Congress. The folks at the

Canadian Space Agency have similar goals and are hoping the Minister of Finance will send them big bucks in the next federal budget. That's it in a nutshell."

"Okay, got it. Now take me through the mechanics," she continued.

"Okay, here we go. Any Canadian over eighteen can enter online or via snail mail. It's free to enter but you can only enter once. If entrants are caught submitting two entries, both are eliminated. Each valid entry is then assigned a number. The winner is not chosen by some celebrity thrusting her hand into a big drum filled with slips of paper. Too much could go wrong. Rather, a computer uses a random number generator to yield the winning number, which is then matched with an online or paper entry. If everything looks legit, we have ourselves a citizen astronaut, provided of course that a honking big liability waiver is signed. Of course, we vet them before the name is made public just to make sure we haven't randomly selected a sadistic serial killer to represent all Canadians on the space station. That might make for a great horror flick, but I doubt the prime minister would approve. If the candidate isn't found to be keeping human limbs in his freezer, he'll be approved for the program, but not necessarily for the mission yet. Then we announce the American and Canadian citizen winners, before sending them to Florida for some intense civilian astronaut training. After that, if they're up to the rigours of the training program, both citizens will be cleared for the mission. Finally, overseeing it all is a very by-the-book accountant from Borden-Bennett who is rumoured to suffer some kind of a seizure whenever she sees someone jaywalk or jump the queue at the movies. You don't want to mess with Emily Hatch. So that's it, from liftoff to splashdown."

"Well, it sounds fantastic. What a great idea," she said warmly. "So we're up for it, but before we all have a group hug, I do need you to hear me out. If anything goes south, I mean anything at all, I do not want, repeat, *do not want* our government to wear it. Am I coming in loud and clear?" This was the real reason the Minister of Science and Technology had called.

"Crystal clear, Minister," I responded. "You want to bask in the reflected glow of a great Canadian moment, but disappear without a trace if something goes terribly wrong, leaving NASA to pick up the pieces."

I wondered if I'd pushed our relationship too far by characterizing it in that way. I need not have worried.

"You were always a quick study, David," she said. "That is exactly what I want."

"And that's exactly why we're not inviting you or any other elected official to participate in the launch news conference next week," I explained.

"Right. Makes sense," agreed the minister. "I'll chat with the prime minister about it, but we're on board."

My ex-boss and I chatted for a few more minutes before she had to bail for her next briefing.

With the launch news conference a week away, we had secured final approval on all of the materials we'd prepared, including the media advisory, news release, contest backgrounder, plain language rules and regs, bios for the head of the Canadian Space Agency and the overachieving Canadian astronaut, Martine Juneau, and the website where Canadians could find all the information they needed about the Citizen Astronaut contest and, yes, enter the contest.

I'd written some of the materials myself and edited the rest. I was pretty pleased with the work we'd done. But there was some tension in the air as we struggled to get it all done. Amanda was really cracking the whip to keep us just a hair ahead of our strict work-back schedule. For the juniors doing the heavy lifting on the account, fear of Amanda appeared to be a great motivator, although it often led to loathing. Had any of them heard Amanda utter the words "God, I am such a bitch," as I had, they would probably have agreed.

On the Monday before the Wednesday launch news conference, we media-trained Martine Juneau and her boss, Armand Gelinas, the head of the Canadian Space Agency. I was to be an observer in the session and had provided our lead media trainer, Robert, with insight and tough questions to use in the simulated interviews. I'd seen Martine in dozens of interviews and had no concerns about her media skills. Armand, on the other hand, had always struck me as a bit jumpy. I'd been in countless briefings with him while I'd been on the minister's staff, and I still couldn't quite figure him out.

The idea was to rehearse the launch news conference with the two of them, as well as practise the one-on-one interviews and media scrums that would follow the newser. We wanted the best media coverage we could get, so preparing well made sense. I'd often helped my minister prepare for media interviews but I'd never seen how a PR agency goes about training their clients. I was about to find out.

"David, let's go," urged Amanda as she snaked her head into my cubicle. "They'll be here any minute and you don't want to miss this."

Amanda and I had been getting along reasonably well since the pitch in Washington. I was still a little scared of her, but I thought I was beginning to understand her and feel more comfortable around her. When she began to accept that I wasn't after her job, she lightened up and on several occasions actually displayed a sense of humour and a few other traits normally associated with human behaviour. I stood up and turned towards the back door of the boardroom. She grabbed my arm and spun me the other direction.

"Nope. We're going to loiter out in the lobby to see them arrive."

She walked me down the hall, still holding my arm as if I were being escorted out of a courtroom. We reached the lobby and sat down in the guest chairs as if we were waiting to be seen by someone important in the firm.

"Okay, we're just going to hang here for a while and look as if we're supposed to be here," explained Amanda.

"You lost me, Amanda. Why don't we just wait for them in the boardroom? That's where the media training is taking place, isn't it?" I asked. I noticed Eli from the mailroom off to the side of the elevators, a video camera resting on his shoulder, while Robert, from the office next to mine, a former investigative TV reporter, stood further in the shadows.

"Yes, of course the training happens mostly in the boardroom, but it actually starts right here, any second now," Amanda said.

On cue, the elevator dinged, the door opened and out walked Martine Juneau and Armand Gelinas, right on schedule. Robert lunged in front of them as Eli ignited the sun gun on the top of the camera and thrust the lens well into their personal space.

"Mr. Gelinas, Ms. Juneau, can you confirm that we're about to raffle off a seat on the next shuttle so an average Joe can visit the space station?"

Armand Gelinas opened his eyes wider than I thought physiologically possible. He may also have been on the verge of losing bowel control, as he turned to dash down the hall towards the men's room. But he passed right by, swung open the Exit door, and by the sound of his footfalls, sprinted down the stairs. It was the kind of reaction you might expect if he'd been trying to evade gunfire. I finally allowed my eyes to wander back to the elevators where Martine was calmly engaged in what I know to be called an ambush interview.

"I'm afraid I can only confirm that we will be making an announcement next Wednesday about a future space shuttle mission," explained Martine, while smiling sweetly into the camera. "I'm just not in a position to offer any more than that. But I can tell you that the Canadian Space Agency is very proud to be long-time partners with NASA in the exploration of space."

"But come on, a raffle? Are you really going to ask someone a skill-testing question and then let them strap into the shuttle and hit the launch button? What if something goes wrong?" Robert persisted.

"To reiterate, I'm simply not permitted to comment on rumours and speculation. I can confirm that there will be a news conference next Wednesday and I invite you to attend. At that time all will be made clear," she concluded with a smile.

"Come on, Martine. We've got a copy of the briefing note. Your secret is out. We know the Citizen Astronaut contest is just about ready for prime time. What can you tell us about it?"

"I can certainly confirm that next Wednesday we'll be holding a news conference to discuss an important initiative, and you're invited to attend. But right now, I'm already a little late for an important meeting, so if you'll excuse me," Martine said as she sidestepped the camera and walked into the lobby.

To Robert's credit, he did not pursue her further but disappeared with Eli through another door on the far side of the elevators. Martine glanced our way as she approached the receptionist and her eyes held mine as she probed her memory banks for my face.

"Hello, Martine. I'm David Stewart. I used to handle communications for the Minister of Science and Technology. You

and I have met at CSA a few times," I explained, taking her off
the hook.

"Of course, David. I knew I recognized you. How are you – and
what are you doing here?" Martine replied.

"Family matters brought me back to Toronto so I traded in
life on Parliament Hill for life in a multinational PR agency.
This is my colleague, Amanda Burke. She's running the NASA
account here in Toronto."

Amanda beamed as she shook Martine's hand.

"It's an honour to meet you, Martine," said Amanda. "And you
rocked that ambush back there. This could be a short media
training session if you're already that good."

"Well, I've done a fair bit of media over the years but I'm afraid
my boss, Armand, may need some coaching, that is if we can
find him. I have no idea where he bolted to. But from the look
in his eyes, he might be halfway back to Ottawa by now," she
said with a chuckle.

"Fear not, we'll send out a search party," I responded. "Why
don't we head into the boardroom?"

I wasn't kidding about the search party. Armand Gelinas
wasn't answering his cell phone. So after studying his photo on
the Internet, a team of about half a dozen or so Turner-King
staffers fanned out from our office in search of the spooked head
of the CSA. It took about an hour and a half but they did in fact
find him. He was cooling off in a Starbucks down the street trying to figure out his next move. He was not very happy when

he learned that the ambush interview had been staged by our media trainer. He had thought it was an actual reporter lurking in our lobby.

Armand calmed down in the end and only raised the elevator confrontation thirteen more times over the course of the afternoon. I'd had many more dealings with Armand over the years than I had with Martine. Even after what had transpired in the lobby, he may have appreciated seeing a familiar face at the boardroom table. By 6:00 p.m., Martine was still very skilled in the way she handled the simulated interviews we threw her way. Armand? Not so much. But he did improve. His first few simulations were not unlike the shower scene in *Psycho*. But by the end of the day, he could quite ably complete an entire interview and deliver at least a couple of key messages without fainting. I have no idea how he came to be head of the Canadian Space Agency, unless it was someone's idea of putting him out to pasture. We agreed that Martine would try to take the lead when it was time to field questions from the floor at the newser. Armand Gelinas seemed relieved.

We used the Great Hall of the Ontario Science Centre for the NASA/CSA news conference. With Hoberman spheres hanging from the ceiling, slowly expanding and collapsing like living planets, it seemed a fitting venue for our announcement. Amanda was beside herself with anxiety. I'd organized a dozen or so news conferences for my minister in the previous few years, and they'd all gone without a hitch. Then again, whenever a minister of the Crown was holding a newser, reporters always showed up. Apparently, not all news conferences attracted journalists, even though that was the sole purpose of holding them.

"What if no reporters show?" Amanda said to no one in particular. "I'd never live that down. And please don't let me trip on the riser steps and eat the floor."

"Amanda, calm yourself. You'll do just fine. And trust me, reporters will show. It's a joint NASA/CSA announcement. There's never been one on Canadian soil before, so by definition, this is news and they will come," I replied.

The set-up looked great to me. A skirted table on risers sat at the front, with a deep blue backdrop featuring both NASA and CSA logos, along with the words "Citizen Astronaut." There was theatre-style seating for about twenty reporters, and then another set of risers at the back for cameras. Eli, our mailroom camera guy, was already set up to record the announcement so we could post it on YouTube and our Citizen Astronaut website.

Amanda was back on her cellphone again to the office to check on the status of media calls to confirm attendance.

"I don't care that they're not picking up, call again! We have got to have this place filled with reporters, and that means you have to keep calling!" Amanda snapped closed her cell with a look that said keep all sharp objects out of her reach.

"David!"

I turned and saw a beaming Kelly Bradstreet striding my way. Amanda saw her too and moved to intercept.

"Welcome to Toronto, Kelly," said Amanda, as her hand shot forward for the shake.

"Hello, Amanda. Hi, David. This place is perfect. Very appropriate. Nice choice," Kelly said. "It's a bit of a distance from downtown. Do you think we'll have any trouble getting journos here?"

"While it's not downtown, the Science Centre is very easy and fast to get to," Amanda explained. "We'll get them here. It's a NASA/CSA announcement. There's never been one on Canadian soil before. That's news around here."

She didn't even look at me when she said it.

We did a last-minute run-through with Kelly. I explained the proper pronunciation of Armand Gelinas (*Armon Gelina*) and Martine Juneau (*Marteen Juno*) and made sure she spent a few minutes with them in the green room before zero hour. Amanda was now in the zone. With plenty of media showing up, she had calmed down from completely freaked out to excessively agitated.

It all went well, despite the power failure. We were a victim of our own success. We had so many cameras plugging into the central audio feedbox that we blew the breaker about five minutes before show time. In the dimness, I could see that Amanda was close to blowing her own breaker. But the Science Centre

AV guy, bless him, had us up and running again in about forty-five seconds, with a mad dash to the electrical panel down the hall. No problem.

At 10:30, our scheduled start, I counted nineteen reporters, eight bloggers, and six vidcams set up on the risers at the rear. For a Toronto news conference, this was as close to full attendance as you could get. If the announcement went well, the news would travel clear across the country in the coming hours. If Armand Gelinas threw up on his microphone and it all turned ugly, the news would travel clear across the country in the coming hours. The mixed blessing of a well-attended newser.

At the appointed time, Amanda took the steps very carefully, one at a time, as if she were about 104 years old and needed a double hip replacement. Some minutes later, she made it to the fourth and final step and approached the microphone. She was alone on stage. Deep breath.

"Good morning, ladies and gentlemen, I'm Amanda Burke from Turner King and I'm pleased to welcome you to this very special announcement. My role is simply to introduce our guests and get off the stage." She smiled a little self-consciously as she said it, but it went over well.

"Here's how it's going to unfold this morning. You all have the media kits. There'll be three spokespersons available during and following the news conference. We'll also have raw video b-roll of the NASA news conference happening right now in Washington to round out what will be a continental story. So let's get started.

I'd like to welcome Ms. Kelly Bradstreet, chief information officer and head of NASA's Office of Communications, Mr. Armand Gelinas, CEO of the Canadian Space Agency, and of course, Dr. Martine Juneau, Canadian astronaut and NASA mission specialist. Each will make a brief statement, and then Kelly will open the floor for questions. Thank you."

Our three spokespersons were already seated at the skirted table ready to go by the time Amanda had finally made it back down the steps. I toyed with suggesting that we use an inflatable slide to get her back down the next time she chaired a news conference, but decided just to keep that one to myself.

"Thank you, Amanda. Good morning everyone and thank you for coming. I'm Kelly Bradstreet from NASA. At this very moment, the head of NASA is making this same announcement in Washington. Ladies and gentlemen, for more than fifty years, space has been the exclusive domain of a very special breed of human beings. Only astronauts, test pilots, rocket scientists, chemists, physicists, astronomers, physicians, and other extraordinary and highly trained individuals at the absolute top of their respective fields have had the singular opportunity to venture beyond our atmosphere and view the Earth from the depths of space. Yes, we've seen one or two billionaires buy their way onto a mission, but in general, those who have felt the miracle of weightlessness have belonged to a very exclusive club."

Kelly paused and made eye contact with the key reporters we'd pointed out, before getting to the heart of the matter.

"Ladies and gentlemen, we are about to change the face of the space program forever. We are about to open space up to average Americans and Canadians, whoever they are, whatever they do, wherever they live. Welcome to the era of the Citizen Astronaut."

Kelly then proceeded to brief the reporters on the details of the Citizen Astronaut contest, including the eligibility rules and NASA's final say on who would fly. And she was good. She knew what she was doing, and she knew how to command a room. I'd seen her remarks in advance and thought they were fine. But they were so much better when she delivered them than when I'd read them on the page. At the designated point in the program, Kelly invited Armand Gelinas to offer his thoughts on the program from the CSA's perspective. He was a little nervous. I could tell, and perhaps others could too, because he insisted on holding his notes in his hands. The paper was vibrating in his trembling fingers with enough amplitude to fan the front row of reporters. Okay, I exaggerate. But his hands were shaking. He got through his remarks in French and English and threw to Martine Juneau, who would fly with the winning Canadian citizen. Gracious, self-deprecating, bilingual, funny, and above all, authoritative, Martine was a star. How could she be anything but, with a PhD in aeronautical engineering and a Master's in philosophy? The media ate it up.

Much to my surprise, there actually weren't that many questions when Kelly opened the floor. Perhaps I shouldn't have been surprised. After all, the concept and rules of the contest were not hard to grasp. They'd been explained very well. And the media kits provided complete details. As well, the vidcam shooters in particular went rushing out the door as soon as the Q&A wound down. They were clearly trying to get back to their stations to cut and produce their stories in time for their noon newscasts. It had been a slam dunk. Diane had watched quietly from the back and gave me a thumbs-up when it was all over.

———————

"Well, we're out of the gate, and I don't see how it could have gone any better," I said as I raised my glass to Amanda.

She'd stuck her head over top of my cubicle divider on her way out at about 8:30 that night and asked if I wanted to join her for a drink to celebrate. I figured yes was the right call. We walked to a bar down the street from the office. She drank three big glasses of Chardonnay in about forty minutes while I nursed a beer. I wasn't really much of a drinker, but I didn't want to piss her off by ordering a ginger ale when she was clearly in the mood to celebrate.

"I'm just so relieved that we made it through today without any disasters," she said before dissolving into giggles. "And I didn't fall off the stage! Yay!"

"Here's to not falling off the stage!" I said, offering up yet another toast.

Clink went our glasses. Some of her wine sloshed over the edge of her glass onto the floor – probably not a bad place for it at that stage. I'd never really seen this side of Amanda. She was actually smiling quite consistently and had not looked at her BlackBerry for several minutes. Finally, she could restrain herself no longer and she stole a glance at her BB.

"Oh my god," she started. "It's from Crawford Blake. It says 'Amanda, congratulations on what I'm told was a fantastic news conference today up north in Toronto. I knew with you in charge, we were in good hands.' Oh my god!"

She was practically trembling in ecstasy and guzzled another huge mouthful of wine. As she stood up too quickly, hoisting her wine glass high above her, both her knees became better acquainted with the small table between us. It was tipping towards my crotch when I caught it and returned it to its normal upright position. I hadn't caught the beer, but my lap had. She didn't even notice.

"A toast to David Stewart for coming up with this insane idea in the first place, for working so hard to make today a success, and for not trying to take over my job in the process," she intoned.

Then she wobbled a bit and took a few steps to keep her balance.

"Uh-oh. All of a good I don't feel so sudden . . ." she said, swaying a bit.

With that, she promptly sat back down. Too bad her chair wasn't beneath her.

I was happy to help her up and escort her out the door. She leaned most of her weight on me. With right my arm around her, I did my best to keep her upright.

CHAPTER 5

The media coverage over the coming week or so was quite simply off the charts. In the three days following the launch news conference, we had over five hundred stories in print, on radio and TV, online, and in community papers. On the fourth day, as the earned media started to recede, the paid media broke from our sister ad agency, Campbell Creative, including TV, radio, print, online, transit, and outdoor. If you were alive in Canada that week, you knew about the Citizen Astronaut contest.

Our media relations effort also yielded 158 editorials and opinion pieces. Predictably, about a third of them were negative, linked most often to the cost of putting civilians in space. There was also plenty of criticism that the contest was simply a "PR exercise" with no real purpose beyond hype. As I read this, I realized that we needed to do a PR job on the term "PR." Those two little letters attached to my chosen profession were usually delivered with a dismissive head shake, a pejorative tone, and a look that straddled disdain and disgust. In the modern vernacular, "It was just a PR exercise" really meant, whatever "it" was, that it was completely devoid of substance. Or that smoke, mirrors, or both were somehow involved. Or that someone like me was spinning one lonely little positive attribute into a towering all-powerful juggernaut of virtue, while downplaying or even ignoring a boat-load of horrific side effects that threatened (please select one or more of the following options) children, animals, trees, water, air, earth, the ozone layer, the Idaho striped blister beetle, and the entire human race. In my mind, that was the old PR, an out-dated stereotype in decline. I was a practitioner of the *new* PR. As far as I was concerned, my job was to tell the truth, and tell it well. And, no, that's not spin. I believed it.

But I didn't have time right then to rehabilitate the public's view of my profession. I was too busy persuading Joe and Joanne Public to enter a contest that could land them in orbit aboard the International Space Station.

My phone chirped. Phones today don't really ring any more. Chirped is as close as I can come to describing the sound. "TK D.C." flashed into the liquid crystal screen. I love caller ID. I had no idea who would be calling me from the D.C. office.

"David Stewart." I opened with my usual greeting.

"David, it's Crawford Blake."

Uh-oh.

"Oh, hi, Crawford," I said. "Congrats on all the great U.S. coverage. You must be pleased."

"Yep, it was a triumph. I've never seen so much coverage on an announcement in my entire career. I reckon it shows just how many Americans actually want to go into space, the dumb fuckers," Crawford said.

The profanity caught me a little off guard, but I had heard the term before.

"I'm callin' for two reasons. First of all, you folks up there did a fine job driving coverage of the Canadian announcement. Kelly spoke very well of the TK Toronto team and of you in particular."

"Thanks so much. We have a great group of PR pros in this office and they worked very hard under very tight timelines." I was skating. "We were thrilled with the coverage. On a per capita basis, we ended up with more coverage than in the U.S."

Idiot. I knew it as the words were passing over my palate. But I couldn't seem to stop them. Why would I say that?

"Well, we've got so much more going on here stateside than you folks do up there in the wilds. The competition for column inches down here is fierce. So I'm not surprised you got the front page up there. I mean, what else is going on in Canada right now anyway other than ice hockey?"

"Right . . ." I had nothing else.

"Anyway, the second reason for my call is to make sure you understand how important it is that we end up with the right Canadian winner. The goal is to help NASA so we need a classic Canadian winner. You know, young and strapping, hale and hearty, maybe even a hockey player in a lumberjack shirt. We want something quintessentially Canadian. Right, David?"

"Um, I'm a little confused. The winner is chosen through a random draw. We have no role in choosing the citizen astronaut," I replied. "We're not talking about 'fixing' the draw, are we? That would be a huge scandal."

"Did I say 'fix'? No, I did not. You said 'fix' and you should be ashamed of yourself," Crawford scolded. "I'm just telling you to make sure your winner fits with our notion of the ideal citizen astronaut. Are you hearing me, David?"

"But I've got Borden-Bennett all over the mechanics of the draw. If anything is amiss, they're going to blow the whistle and we'll be royally . . . in trouble," I said. "I think you should probably talk to Amanda or Diane about this."

"I'm talking to you, David. And I'm telling you to get me a great Canadian astronaut," he demanded. "Canada will not bring down this program by offering up a lame citizen astronaut."

I was speechless. So, in keeping with the condition, I said nothing.

"Okay, then. Message delivered. Congrats again on the coverage. I'm looking forward to seeing who wins the big prize up in the land of snow and ice." Crawford hung up with a bang.

I held the phone to my ear for a moment or so, stuck in neutral. Eventually, I hung up. Had I heard him right? Did that conversation actually happen? I sat at my desk for ten minutes trying to decide how to handle Crawford's pointed message. After very careful thought, weighing the pros and cons, assessing my options, I carefully conceived an elaborate and brilliant stratagem. I decided simply to forget that I'd ever had the conversation with Crawford Blake. That's right, it had never happened. "Yes," I said aloud. "I'm sure that will work."

———

Lauren called late in the afternoon to let me know that Mom was having a good day and was reasonably lucid. I left immediately and headed over. Mom hadn't had many good days in the last month, so I didn't want to miss her. A nine-minute cab ride and I was there. I let myself in and headed upstairs. Lauren was sitting in the chair placed next to the bed while our mother was propped up on pillows with a magazine opened on her lap. A glass of what was either white wine or apple juice with a straw rested on the bedside table.

"Mom, you're not dressed yet," I teased. "We have to hustle if we're going to make the ski-jumping class on time."

Lauren rolled her eyes but said nothing.

"Sorry, dear, but my skis are still in Innsbruck," Mom replied. "Besides, I'm really not feeling particularly aerodynamic today anyway."

"No worries. Then how about monster truck racing? I've got Grave Digger parked just outside," I offered. As usual, without thinking.

"Nice, David," sighed Lauren. "Very sensitive."

Why couldn't I have chosen Bigfoot instead of Grave Digger.

It's one thing to put your foot in your mouth. But I seemed to have swallowed my whole leg.

"Lauren, I'm kidding. Grave Digger is a black and green monster truck. It's probably the most famous and recognizable monster truck in history. Mom knows that," I backpedalled and looked at Mom.

"Well, I do now," she said.

Just keep talking, I reminded myself.

"Anyway, you look good, Mom. How are you feeling?"

"Sit here, David." Mom patted the bed. "I still feel like I'm in someone else's body, but the fog in my head seems to have receded. I'm drained but more awake than usual."

"I'm just going to head downstairs to put the kettle on," said Lauren as she moved to the door.

I sat down and took Mom's right hand in mine.

"David, while we have a minute and I have the energy," Mom started. "No funeral, no memorial service, no family gathering of any kind with endless plates of inedible squares and egg salad sandwiches. I just don't want any of it. The simplest cremation you can get. Donations to the Cancer Society, if people insist. But that's it. Have you got it?"

I was just looking at her, trying to figure it all out. It was the most animated I'd seen her for weeks.

"Hello, David, hello," she prodded, squeezing my hand.

"Mom, why all the morbid talk? You're going to outlive us all. I mean . . ."

"David. Stop. Stop," she interrupted. "Just tell me that you heard me and understood my wishes. Have I been clear?"

I thought about turning it into a joke, again. That's always my instinct in moments of high drama. I resisted.

"Yes, Mom. I understand what you want. We'll make it happen."

"Good. Thank you. Lauren refuses even to talk to me about it. She's usually so practical about such things, but she just puts her hands up, shakes her head, and walks out."

"Well, I'm not sure I blame her. It's not a conversation we're used to having," I explained.

"Well, it's done now."

Mom lay back and closed her eyes as if a load had been taken off her mind. Then she opened them halfway and looked at me. She was almost back under.

"Use your head . . ." she managed in a whisper.

". . . but follow your heart," I finished, and squeezed her hand. "I will."

She smiled ever so slightly, closed her eyes, and was soon back down deep. That was a line we'd shared since I was just a kid. It was ours. I know it's cliché but my mother believed wholeheartedly and headlong in its truth. I guess I believed it too. The proprietary phrase my Mom and sister shared was shorter, but no less profound. It was, simply, "Be kind."

I gave Lauren a hug in the kitchen as she waited for the tea to steep. Then I headed home.

I didn't know what I had been expecting on the numbers front. There had never been a contest quite like this one, so we had few, if any, benchmarks to help us forecast how many entries might come in. In the weeks following the launch news conference and all that media coverage, the number of entries submitted grew day by day. Online entries were more plentiful than those received through the mail. This was not surprising, given just how much of Canadians' lives are spent online. By the end of the first week, we had over 9,500 online entries and about 300 via snail mail. By the following Friday, the end of week two, we were up to 106,000 entries in total.

Over the next several weeks, we continued to pitch media stories whenever we thought we had a hook that came within a few light-years of hard news. We were constantly issuing news releases as newly created thresholds were crossed, including when we hit 200,000 entries, when we hit the halfway point in the window for entering, when we hit 500,000 entries, when we hit the fortieth anniversary of the first space spew – you know, the first time an astronaut threw up in the space station. Okay, I was just making up that last one. But you get the idea. This "pimping" of the program helped us sustain media coverage, which in turn kept those entries flying in.

"Emily, it's David," I said into the phone. "Just checking in on the count."

I was staying in very close contact with Emily Hatch at Borden-Bennett to keep abreast of the mounting numbers. She was responsible for vetting and approving all entries before they were considered official. I seemed to get along fine with Emily, but she wasn't exactly warm and fuzzy.

"Yes, David. Let me pull the latest numbers," she replied, expressionless. "Here we are. At the end of week seven with one week to go, we're up to a total of 1,235,672 entries, with 34,214 of them submitted by mail."

"We're now at more than 1.2 million entries?" I replied, incredulous. "You're joking!"

"David, I'm a chartered accountant. I never joke about numbers."

"Fair point."

It had been at just over 900,000 less than a week ago. The final rush to the finish line was driving our numbers higher than I ever imagined. Amanda would be thrilled. There were about 24 million citizens over the age of eighteen in Canada. So more than 5 per cent of the eligible population wanted to leave the comfort, safety, and gravity of Earth and visit outer space. Interesting. I desperately wanted to go up, but my role with Turner King took me out of the running.

———

With five days to go until entries closed, I was scanning the top stories on Google News when I saw it. It wasn't a big story, but it scared me first onto the phone with Emily, and then right into Diane's office with Amanda on my heels. She was on a call when we arrived but saw that something was urgent.

"Contest?" she whispered, covering the receiver with her left hand.

I nodded slowly with a "my hamster just died" look of angst etched on my face. Diane promptly pushed a button on the phone and set down the receiver.

"Hang on, Crawford, David and Amanda have just arrived. Okay, guys what's up?"

Great. Just great. Clearly I needed to work on my facial expressions. Diane seemed to have completely misconstrued my look, apparently believing that my hamster was alive and well and running happily on its exercise wheel. At least Diane was not wearing any of her thirteen pairs of glasses, so I was able to make eye contact while constructing and delivering several complete sentences in a row.

"Um, I'm happy to come back later after you're finished with Crawford," I said, nodding my head towards the speaker phone and elevating my eyebrows so they were almost breaking free from their forehead moorings.

"Nonsense," Diane replied. "This will save me briefing Crawford separately on our great progress. Do tell . . ."

"Okay. Well, to get straight to it, we could be in for a nation-wide postal strike in as little as forty-eight hours, leaving us without mail delivery for the final three days of the contest period," I said with all the gravitas I could muster. I couldn't seem to muster much.

In Diane's face, I watched as my hamster suffered a myocardial infarction and fell off the wheel.

"Um, I'll call you back, Crawford, after we've sorted this out if you don't mi–" Diane started as she reached to hang up.

"Fuckin' socialists up there," Crawford shouted. "Why the fuck do you even allow your post office to strike? Just to be clear, we are not delaying the program because you nice Canadians have to spend your tax dollars on a deal with the mailman. Are you hearing me?"

"Crawford, don't worry, we're on it and it won't slow us down. I promise you. I'll call you right back."

"You'd better fix this and fas–"

Diane hung up before his acidic drawl burned any more insulation off the copper wires.

"Yeah, so who cares about a postal strike?" Amanda said. "Who uses the mail service in this day and age anyway?"

"Well, thirty-five thousand Canadians have entered the contest by mail," I explained. "I know that's not a big number next to the online entries but that's not the point. Emily and her integrity SWAT team will not allow us to make the draw if there's even a scintilla of a chance that a single legitimately submitted entry is not included. If Canada Post has a strike in two days, we'll still have three days of mail-in entries stuck in the postal system until they settle with their workers and are back up and running. We're cooked if that happens."

"So we go ahead with the draw without them," Amanda

replied. "It's their own fault for trusting the mail with their entry."

"You haven't spent much time with Emily Hatch, have you?" I inquired. "She has already formally ruled that she'll shut down the draw unless or until *all* eligible entries are duly registered and included. End of story. End of my new job."

"But it's not our fault some Canadians chose a less than reliable delivery vehicle for their entries," Diane observed. "If we don't receive the entries by midnight on June 30, they won't be included in the draw. That's what the rules dictate, right?"

"You haven't spent much time with Emily Hatch, have you?" I repeated. "Well, I'm sorry to let the air out of your very reasonable-sounding position, but Emily is setting the rules. We've given her that power. She's in the news release. And she will not permit a draw until *all* entries postmarked by midnight, June 30, are included. So we'd better pray the union and management come to their senses soon or Crawford Blake is going to come up here and hurt me."

"Shit. Don't they know they're threatening the contest? Maybe we should call the union and ask them to hold off for a few more days till we're done," Amanda suggested, apparently in earnest.

Diane and I looked at one another. I let her take that one.

"Amanda, I think they know what they're disrupting," Diane said. "It's why they're scrambling to get their act together this week. The union is looking for more leverage. Screwing us up and delaying the draw gives them another bargaining chip."

In that final crazed week, the media, bless them, picked up on the link between the postal strike and the contest. Several reporters tried to get someone, anyone, from the Canadian Space Agency to lash out at the union knowing that controversy and confrontation always amp up the news value and help to sell papers. So we rehearsed hard with Martine Juneau late one night so she could walk a very delicate line. We wanted the additional media coverage to drive last-minute entries. But we did not want to engender any ill will among the postal workers when we knew at that stage there were still undelivered mail entries somewhere in the system. She did a fine job with lots of "Well, we're hopeful that differences between Canada Post and their union can be resolved without any interruption in mail service, but you'll really need to speak to them about that. In the meantime, we encourage Canadians who still wish to enter the Citizen Astronaut contest to register online rather than risk mailing it in during this uncertain time" etc., etc. She was very, very good. And the camera liked her, too. And, oh yeah, she's a rock star astronaut. Even hard-bitten jaded reporters think it's kind of cool to interview someone who has actually been in space.

Some reporters saw through the ploy and wanted to speak to the jumpy head of the CSA. But we kept Armand Gelinas sequestered in his office and told the journos in various ways that he was unavailable for comment. A rumour that he was dealing with a nasty and difficult root canal somehow surfaced, festered, and spread. I admit we did nothing to clarify it. He was relieved. So were we.

As it turned out, getting their act together to accelerate a full membership vote was tougher for the union than they'd hoped. By the time they'd given notice of the vote and set up their own polling stations across the country, the Canadian Postal Union was just too late to get in our way. But it was very close and caused me a couple of sleepless nights and the need to stay close to a bathroom.

At midnight on June 30, entries for the Citizen Astronaut contest officially closed. Two days later, 92 per cent of the Canadian Postal Union members voted to strike. The day after that, the workers were walking the picket line and mail service ground to a halt. In my mind's eye, I pictured streams of mail flitting along metal tracks, then slowing down, and finally stopping altogether. Even in my imagination I didn't look too closely at the mail stalled in their tracks for fear of seeing a contest entry.

When the postal workers walked off the job, I picked up the phone.

"Emily, it's David."

"Good morning, David," she replied sounding as formal, professional, even cold, as ever.

I'd already spent some time wondering whether Emily might be taking her role as protector of the integrity of the contest a little too seriously, or was just built that way. I liked her, but she conducted herself as if she were a public defender at the International Court of Justice in The Hague, not an accountant administering what amounted to a big raffle. I decided it was just her personality.

"Okay, Emily, I'm really looking for some good news here. Today is July 3. Entries closed three very long days ago on June 30. I'm assuming, given the outstanding efficiency of Canada Post, that all contest entries postmarked June 30 have been received and duly registered as eligible for the draw. And, further, that the strike has therefore had absolutely no impact on the contest. Right? Help me out here, Emily. Please?"

I held my breath. The stakes were high. If she didn't buy what I was selling, we'd have to wait until the strike ended, whenever that was, to ensure that no straggler entries were stuck somewhere in the post as hostages in a labour dispute. It would delay the Canadian side of the contest for who knows how long, and perhaps kill it altogether. I'd seen her flex her regulatory muscles before, and I was worried, okay terrified. Emily seemed to be a strong adherent to the "no contest entry left behind" philosophy.

"We've been giving this a lot of thought over here. In the Canada Post annual report last year, the average time from postmark to delivery of a letter is four days. Using this as a guidepost, we can't be sure that there aren't some legitimate contest entries still stalled in transit somewhere in the postal system," she began.

"Come on, Emily, four days is almost the same as three days. Can't you cut us a break?"

"I haven't finished yet. I've checked Canada Post's own stats for the first quarter of this year and the average delivery time has been 2.9 days. Apparently it's the Christmas rush that pushes their average up to four days. So on that basis, and since December is still five months away, we are comfortable declaring the Citizen Astronaut contest officially closed and that all legitimate entries have been duly received and registered."

"Emily, I could kiss you!"

"That won't be necessary."

"Actually, it was just a figure of speech," I explained, a little concerned that she thought I'd been serious. "So we're free and clear. That's great news. Thanks so much. Oh, what's the final count?"

"The official tally is 1,723,590 entries."

I stopped by to see Lauren and Mom on my way home. I managed to convince Lauren to leave the house, if only for a walk. I sat down in the chair next to Mom's bed where she lay in a deep sleep. How deep? Well, to try to find a comfortable position in the hard chair, I leaned back, balancing on the rear two chair legs. An instant later I was "balancing" on my back on the floor. The noise I made hitting the hardwood floor was fearsome. I lay there for a moment or two listening for the sirens of the fire trucks surely summoned by concerned neighbours. None came. Eventually, I crawled to my feet, righted the chair, and resumed my seat with four chair legs, plus my own two, firmly planted on the floor. Though my ears were still ringing, Mom never stirred. Not once. The power of the painkillers and the toll of the disease itself seldom left her conscious any more.

I pulled out my iPad from my bag, called up *The Case Book of Sherlock Holmes*, and read Mom "The Adventure of the Creeping Man."

───────

Amanda and I sat in the painfully white lobby of Borden-Bennett's head office on the forty-seventh floor of First Canadian Place. Amanda looked good in a different variation of black on black that I didn't think I'd seen before. We were both feeling buoyant about making it through the contest alive and escaping the noose of the postal strike.

A young man in a black suit approached.

"Hello, I'm Grayson, Emily's assistant. Follow me, if you will."

We walked down an open staircase to the forty-sixth floor and along a corridor to two frosted glass doors. The small flat screen display mounted next to the doors said "Turner King Contest Administration." Grayson swiped his security card and pushed open the doors. It looked like a repurposed boardroom, probably because it was. Two computers sat on a long table along with four cardboard banker's boxes. Emily Hatch stood when we entered. Grayson closed the door behind him when he departed, his crucial mission accomplished.

"Good morning, Emily," I said, extending my hand. "You remember Amanda Burke."

"Hello, David, Amanda."

"So this is where the magic happens, eh?" I asked, surveying the room.

"Well, if you mean, is this where we store all the online and mail entries and make the draw, then yes, this is where the magic happens," Emily replied.

"So when does the magic actually start?" prodded Amanda, who was all business.

"It can start right now."

With that, Emily sat down in front of the first computer and keyed in a few log-in strokes.

Grayson suddenly materialized next to us. I hadn't seen him slip back into the room and was startled. Emily noticed.

"Grayson is here because there must be more than one Borden-Bennett employee in the room when we draw a winning number. It's just a security protocol," Emily explained.

Grayson smiled, so I smiled back.

"Are we all ready?" Emily asked.

"Well, I'd kind of like to savour the moment a little longer and reflect on how far we've come since we started this little . . ."

Amanda cut me off.

"We're ready! Let's do it!"

"Of course."

We crowded around Emily as she opened the random number generator program and typed in the lower and upper bound numbers, 1 and 1,723,590. She then clicked a button on the screen helpfully labelled "generate random number," while my two index fingers offered an arrhythmic drum roll on the edge of the table. We waited only an instant before 541,349 appeared.

"And we have a winner," I declared.

"Almost. All we really have now is a winning number," Emily explained. "Stand by for the winner."

With that, she moved to the second computer and keyed in 541,349. A data base contact card appeared immediately on the screen with the name of the 541,349th person to submit an entry. This was our lucky winner.

"L. Percival, 21 years old, Cigar Lake, British Columbia, V0C 1R0" was all it said in red on the screen.

"That's all we've got on the winner? No phone number or address?" Amanda asked.

"Yes, I'm afraid this is all we have," Emily confirmed. "It's in red, so we know it was a mail entry. Let me pull the hard copy to ensure we've accurately captured all the information provided, though I'm certain we have."

She opened the second banker's box and plunged her fingers into the neatly filed mass of paper and cardstock dividers. It took her a moment to find the one she was seeking but eventually pulled out the 541,349th sheet on which was mounted a small square of paper. There, in handwriting that was just a barely legible blue ink scrawl, was what looked to me like "L. Percival, 21 years old, Cigar Lake, British Columbia, V0C 1R0."

"But the entry asked for their email, mailing address, and

phone number," Amanda said. "Shouldn't we consider this an incomplete entry and draw another?"

"No, I'm afraid not," Emily replied in her accountant and official raffle supervisor voice. "Unless we officially designated certain fields on the entry form as 'required information,' you are under the obligation to find this person, based on what we know. We can only draw a second name after we have exhausted what we call 'best efforts' to identify and contact L. Percival of Cigar Lake, B.C."

————

I spent the afternoon with my old friend Google in search of the elusive L. Percival. There were lots of L. Percivals to be found on the Internet, including a Canadian sports pioneer, Lloyd Percival. But he had died in 1974, having lived his entire life in Ontario. There was a Liza "the lovely" Percival who was a very much alive pole dancer of some repute from Drummondville, Quebec. No, I don't think so. I found a Leon Percival doing time in the Kingston Penitentiary for settling an argument by dumping 150 gallons of hot tar through the passenger window of his father's 1977 Plymouth Duster, in Port Perry, Ontario. Nope. Finally, I tracked down a Lorne Percival who had up until 2009 been known as Lori Percival. But even after sex reassignment surgery, Lorne still lived in Montreal, where he had always resided.

Directory assistance was no help either. There was no record of an L. Percival with a phone anywhere in B.C. Great. In the end, I ran down more than twenty-seven L. Percivals across Canada and hit dead ends with each.

I switched tracks and learned what I could about Cigar Lake, B.C. I found it on a map. It was a smallish, yes, cigar-shaped lake in northern B.C. not too far from Fort Nelson. On the ten-point remoteness scale, it registered a twelve. I wasn't able to find much on the web about the community, so I made a few calls to towns that seemed to be located near Cigar Lake. You'd be surprised how unhelpful people can be when you call them up out of the blue and ask if they know anyone named L. Percival. It wasn't a fun afternoon.

"Why don't we just write to the winner? We have an address of sorts and a postal code," Amanda proposed.

"Yes, that would work were it not for the trifling matter of a national postal strike," I replied.

"Shit," was all she said.

After conferring with Crawford Blake and Diane Martineau, and arguing with the stickler queen herself, Emily Hatch, it was decided that the only way to honour our "best efforts" legal obligations in the matter was to send yours truly out to Cigar Lake to track down the elusive L. Percival, whoever he – or she – was. I'd have to vet the winner anyway to make sure we had a viable choice to put forward to NASA, but I was optimistic. Given our tight timelines, I was really hoping to avoid having to spin the drum again, draw a second name, and go through the vetting procedure again. So the plan was for me to inform L. Percival personally of his – or her – win and at the same time qualify him – or her – as our official Canadian citizen astronaut. We wouldn't be announcing and introducing the winner until later on anyway. Mindful of Crawford's rather pointed directive to find the right candidate, I was hopeful I'd be meeting a strong, chiselled, classic lumberjack type, with all of his hair and teeth, and no police record or weird hobbies. A long shot perhaps, but it was possible. I was headed for logging country, after all.

I was a confirmed big city boy being sent on an important mission to the wilds of B.C. It left me a tad uneasy. Amanda Burke's last words to me before I headed out were "Go west, young man – and bring back the great Canadian astronaut."

CHAPTER 6

The world headquarters of Wilderness Charters was not much more than a Quonset hut perched up on the hill overlooking Williston Lake. I arrived fifteen minutes before I was scheduled to take off in the float plane I'd chartered for the final leg of my journey to Cigar Lake. It was only 5:00 in the afternoon but I was already wiped. My packed morning Air Canada flight to Calgary had been uneventful, if you didn't count the flight attendants dumping a glass of orange juice on my chest. As well, my so-called personal video screen nestled in the back of the headrest of the seat in front of me yielded a stunning crystal-clear picture. Unfortunately, the audio jack in my armrest was broken and could not be fixed by any of the five crew members who tried in turn, one by one. I'd already ordered up a movie so I just sat there and watched it as a modern-day silent movie. Halfway into the film I decided, based on the video, that not having the audio may well have been a blessing.

UP AND DOWN

In Calgary, I hopped aboard a Rocky Mountain Airways connecting flight bound for Prince George in northern British Columbia. I'm not even sure what kind of plane it was, but I had thought that open cockpits and canvas-covered wings were long-gone relics from the early days of aviation. Apparently not. Okay, I exaggerate, but not much. In the twenty-first century, one does not expect to look around the interior of a commercial aircraft and see wood. Nine of us braved the flight to Prince George. I sat very still the entire time with my fingers in my ears, wishing I could turn back the clock to earlier in the day when my principal in-flight concern had been the malfunctioning entertainment system. Of course on Rocky Mountain Airways there was no in-flight entertainment, no in-flight magazines, no in-flight snacks, no in-flight beverages. As far as I was concerned, it was a miracle we were in-flight at all. We landed safely in Prince George. When the plane finally came to a stop and the ear-splitting engine died away, I was as relieved as Charles Lindbergh must have been upon touchdown in Paris. But Prince George was not my final destination.

My rental car was smaller than any automobile ought to be. I was trying to save NASA some money by opting for the subcompact. I won't be doing that again. I had to use a bungee-cord to secure the hatchback because my rather small suitcase just wouldn't fit in the back. What kind of car can't accommodate a single small suitcase? As for the driving, well, my rental wasn't exactly a speed merchant. As I headed up the Alaska Highway, the engine sounded like a sewing machine but lacked the power. The speed limit was ninety kilometres an hour but I could really only get it going up to about eighty kilometres an hour before the vibrations threatened to rearrange my internal organs. It took me nearly three hours to drive the 185 kilometres to Mackenzie.

Named for the famous explorer Alexander Mackenzie, the town was a lumber and logging centre built on the shores of Williston Lake. In fact, the world's largest tree crusher (and no, I really don't know what that is) sat on display at the entrance to the town as a symbol of Mackenzie's roots in logging. Seeing it didn't really help me understand its precise purpose. I parked in front of Wilderness Charters and headed inside.

"You have got to be David Stewart," exclaimed the man sitting at a cluttered desk behind the counter. "Welcome to northern B.C. I'm Chatter Haney."

"Um, yes. You're right, I am David Stewart. Hello."

"Well, Mr. Stewart, I've got good news and bad news," he said. "The bad news is we blew an oil pump on our Cessna the day before yesterday and it won't be fixed until next week."

"Hmmm, the oil pump sounds like it plays an important role in the safe operation of the plane," I said.

"That it does. But have no fear, there is good news, too," Chatter assured me. "I mean, beyond the fact that you've chosen to visit one of the most beautiful untouched, unspoiled parts of this vast country of ours. The mountains and glacial lakes have this almost unearthly and spiritual restorative effect on people – especially those who come from the city. And if you happen to hail from Toronto, well then, son, you are in for the experience of a lifetime."

This was a man who wore his name proudly. He stopped talking just long enough to take a breath before continuing to enumerate the wonders of Williston Lake and the surrounding region. When he paused again a few minutes later, I leapt back in, fearing I might never get another chance.

"So," I interjected, "I think you were about to mention the *good news* part of the equation, weren't you?"

"Right! I knew I was going somewhere with that." He turned and looked out the window, down the hill to the dock, and then pointed. "You see that beaver down there?"

I followed his outstretched finger but could only see a red float plane. Ahh, capital B Beaver.

"That's Doc's plane. She owes us a favour and will get you out to Cigar Lake, and back when you want," he explained.

"Um, okay. Is it safe?"

"A whole pile safer than a Cessna with a busted oil pump. You'll be fine. She's been flying these parts for most of her life." He grabbed the mike attached to what looked like an old CB radio and squeezed the button on the side. "Hey Doc, he's here. I'm sending him down."

I watched out the window as the door of the Beaver opened and an arm waved back to us. I didn't really have a choice. Besides, the Beaver looked a lot safer than the rickety bucket of bolts that had flown me to Prince George.

"Is it okay if I leave my finely tuned pocket rocket in your parking lot for a day or two?" I asked, pointing to the rickety bucket of bolts that had driven me to Mackenzie.

"Done."

"I assume it'll be safe enough in the parking lot. Car theft isn't a problem around here, is it?" I inquired.

He looked out the window again at my car.

"Oh, I'm pretty sure it'll be safe enough."

"All right. Thanks for making alternative arrangements for me," I said.

"Sorry for the inconvenience, but you're in good hands with Doc."

I darted out the door before he could renew his regional tourism patter. I walked back to the car, grabbed my wheelie suitcase, and pulled it behind me along the gravel path. On the polished floors of Toronto's Pearson International Airport it had rolled quite smoothly. But it was not what you would describe as an all-terrain suitcase. Halfway down to the dock, I picked it up and carried it.

A wiry and grizzled old woman climbed out of the cockpit of the Beaver wearing grey, grease-stained coveralls and well-worn hiking boots. At least I thought she was a woman. Her hair was also wiry and grizzled. She was all business.

"Hi, I'm David Stewart." I extended my hand.

She offered her hand and we shook. It felt like one gigantic hand-shaped callous.

"Doc Lanny," she replied, sounding older than she looked. And she looked old. Her voice tipped the balance in favour of her being a woman. But it didn't tip it very far.

"Thanks so much for taking me."

"No problem. Are you staying for a while?" she asked, gesturing to my suitcase.

"Um, no. I just wasn't sure what to bring with me," I explained.

"So you brought it all."

She grabbed the bag. On instinct, I reached out to reclaim it, worried about her snapping a wrist or breaking a hip trying to wrestle it into the plane.

"Here, let me. I can put my own bag in," I said, genuinely concerned.

She said nothing, but the look she gave me had me stepping back with my hands up in surrender. She swung the suitcase up as if it were a bag of marshmallows and pushed it through a small side hatch in the plane behind the cabin.

"You can climb in and sit in the front right-hand seat," she directed.

I did as I was told, only bumping my head twice in the process. She followed, after casting off the line securing the pontoon to the dock and latching the door behind her. She slipped into the pilot's seat and strapped in with the smooth and precise movements of someone who'd done it a thousand times before.

"Buckle up, Mr. Stewart," she said, pointing to the seat belt hanging over the armrest. "And put those on. It gets pretty loud in here."

I did as I was told, latching the lap and shoulder belt and pulling on the headset.

I figured that was the end of the safety demonstration. I knew where the exits were.

Doc Lanny seemed a bit preoccupied and sent a few quick glances my way as she went through her pre-flight checklist. She pushed various buttons on the instrument panel and punched the starter. The single engine sputtered to life and the propeller started its circular journey. We taxied out onto Williston Lake against a light breeze and small waves. Then when we were out from the shore a ways, she opened the throttle and the plane picked up speed. I could see one pontoon below me out the window and I watched as the water around it turned white. I'd never been in a float plane and was surprised by how rough the ride was until we lifted from the water. We climbed gently and she turned to the west, aiming the nose toward a pass between two lines of mountains. The scenery was breathtaking. According to the map, we were flying near the Rocky Mountain Trench that separated the Rocky Mountains to the east from the Omineca Mountains to the west. There were snow-capped peaks on either side of our flight path, with the sun slowly dropping in the west. It was stunning.

"So there aren't many more than a dozen folks living on Cigar Lake," she observed. "Where are you headed?"

I jumped when her voice crackled in my ears. I'd forgotten my headset was more than hearing protection. For the first time I noticed the small microphone that swung down from my left headphone. Right.

"I work at a big PR agency in Toronto, and I'm trying to track down the elusive winner of a contest we helped to run. We haven't been able to reach him. He doesn't seem to have a phone, and with the postal strike, well, it was easier and faster just to send me out to find him. The guy lives on Cigar Lake."

When I looked over, she was staring at me. When she just kept her eyes fixed on me for what seemed like an unduly long time, I eventually pointed out the windscreen as a kind of subtle reminder that she was in fact flying a plane. She took the hint.

"What contest?" she asked.

"Well, I can't really say, but the guy has truly won the trip of a lifetime. It'll be out of this world," I said.

She was staring at me again, for too long. This time her mouth was open. I pointed ahead, again.

"What's the name?" she asked softly.

I really wasn't supposed to reveal the winner's name, particularly when the vetting process had not even begun. On the other hand, how was I going to be delivered to his place without giving up the name?

"All we've got is L. Percival."

The plane violently tipped over on its right wing and nose-dived. I grabbed the seat and hung on. As we shot down, my lunch shot up. An instant later, she righted the plane and brought us back onto an even keel a few hundred feet lower than we'd been. I managed to push my lunch back down where it belonged. I'd already been feeling some nausea from the ups and downs of flying in a float plane. So the manoeuvre she'd just pulled certainly didn't help settle my stomach.

"What the hell just happened!" I shouted into the mike. "What was that?!"

I could hear her breathing hard in my headphones.

"Sorry about that. We caught an air pocket. It happens. I've got her now."

"Well, I hope so. I thought we were going down." I was hyper-ventilating, too.

She looked flushed, and shaken, but said nothing more. We flew on and she kept her eyes front. A couple of times I noticed her shaking her head slowly, probably reliving the ride through the air pocket. About half an hour later, I realized we were turning and descending. Below us I saw the familiar long cigar-shaped lake I had seen before, but just as a map on the Internet.

"I can certainly see why it's called Cigar Lake," I noted as we swung down to start our approach.

She seemed to have regained her composure after the stomach-turning barrel roll and nose-dive we'd executed a half hour before.

"Well, it's probably a better name than Test Tube Lake, or Lake Howitzer, or what some folks call it around here, Phallic Lake," she replied.

"Fair point."

As we circled, I quickly realized that it was not just the waves I could see rushing beneath us but the rocks below the surface of the lake as well. Then at the eastern end of the lake, the blue of the water suddenly deepened and the rocky bottom fell away and disappeared.

"That is one shallow lake," I noted as we passed over land again and made one final turn.

"Yep. A glacier dragged itself through here gouging out a shallow trough except for the one end here where it somehow dug down deep."

We turned again and were back over the east end of the lake heading west at an altitude of about a hundred feet or so. She pointed out a rustic cabin right on the eastern shore.

"That's, um, the Percival place."

Then we were down, touching the water in the middle of the lake, our speed taking us almost to the western shore, where we turned around and started the long taxi back to the Percival dock.

"Why not land from the other direction?" I asked. "It would save you taxiing the length of the lake."

"You don't fly much, do you? I have to land her into the wind. That's how planes work. In this part of the mountains, the west wind is not just prevailing, it's permanent. Every take-off and every landing brings me out here to the west end."

"Do you fly here often?" I asked.

She smiled a little bit and nodded.

Ten minutes later, she eased us toward the dock at the "Percival place" and cut the engine. While we were still gliding through the water, she climbed out of her seat, out the door, and down onto the pontoon. She stuck out her foot to stop the float from hitting the dock and then stepped onto the two-by-eight planks, guiding the plane into position. It was a perfect parking job. She grabbed a rope already fixed to a cleat on the dock and snapped the metal carabiner to a steel eye mounted on the front of the pontoon. She did the same with a second rope securing the aft end of the pontoon. She flipped open the side hatch, reached into the compartment, and swung out my suitcase in one smooth, easy motion. By this time, I'd managed to release the safety belt and crawl out of my seat. I was reminded of my headset only when it pulled rather violently off my head as I made my way to the door. I stepped carefully down onto the pontoon and then jumped gracefully onto the dock. I would have preferred to have landed on my feet, but my knees and then back would have to do.

"Are you all right?" she asked, helping me up.

"Oh, I'm fine. That's my standard float plane disembarkation technique."

"I see."

We stood facing each other. She didn't seem eager to move off the dock. I looked up at the cabin expecting one of the Percival clan to emerge wondering about their surprise visitors. Nothing. All quiet. That was not good. I'd come all this way and no one was home. A red canoe rested on a wooden rack just beyond the dock, making me feel like I was stepping into a Tom Thomson painting. Doc Lanny looked out at the lake for a moment and then stepped toward me.

"Why don't you and I start over?" she said, offering her hand to me for the second time in the last hour or so. She was smiling.

"I'm Dr. Landon Percival. This is my home. I'm the 'L. Percival' I think you've come to see."

A raft of frenzied thoughts collided and collapsed in a heap in my head, which I guess is where thoughts traditionally collide and collapse. In no particular order:

He was a she.

She was certainly not twenty-one years old.

She wasn't a young strapping lumberjack type.

My knees and back still hurt from my Beaver dismount.

How was I going to get back to Mackenzie after breaking the bad news to this old lady that she wouldn't be going anywhere near the space shuttle?

Maybe our terrifying aerobatic routine on the flight here had nothing to do with a rogue air pocket.

Landon is a nice name.

Crawford Blake was going to hurt me. Amanda Burke was going to hurt me. It was quite possible Landon Percival was going to hurt me.

Despite "enjoying" the same lunch twice, once in a roadside restaurant and a second time in the plane, I was suddenly very hungry.

And I was dog tired.

"But . . . I thought you were a twenty-one-year-old 'he,'" I mumbled. "I mean, your entry said you were twenty-one."

Landon looked puzzled.

"No, it did not. I wrote seventy-one. And I don't know why you'd assume L. Percival would be a man unless you just believe that only men would enter a contest to win a trip into space," she replied with an edge, lowering the temperature on the dock.

She may have had a point on why I assumed "she" would be a "he." I opened the front pocket of my suitcase and pulled out the file Emily had given me to help authenticate the winner. I flipped through it, extracted a photocopy of Landon's original entry form, and showed it to her.

"See, twenty-one," I said, pointing.

"Look again, eagle eyes. That's not a two! Do you not know your numbers? That's a seven. That's how I make my sevens, with a tiny little tail at the bottom. See, seventy-one," she responded. "I'm a doctor. Bad handwriting comes with the job."

I was forced to admit upon closer inspection that it did sort of look a little like a seven. But it still looked a lot like a two. I guess I'd just assumed it said twenty-one and that no one in their eighth decade – and their right mind – would be looking for a ride to the space station.

"Okay. So let me see if I have this right. You're Landon Percival. You're a seventy-one-year-old doctor. This definitely is your official winning entry in the Citizen Astronaut contest. You live here in a remote corner of northern British Columbia and fly a plane."

"That about sums it up."

Fantastic. A wasted trip. And now I was marooned here, at least until morning. The sun had finally dipped below the mountains, leaving us in fading light.

"Why did you wait until we landed to tell me who you were?"

"Am I going into space?" she asked.

Awkward. I had to let her down gently.

"Well, that's hard to say, and it's certainly not my call. NASA has the final decision, but with the considerable liability issues around the flight, and given the absolute requirement that you pass the rigorous training program, I suspect that your, um, maturity, sorry, may make it a long shot. I'm sorry."

"Now you know why I didn't tell you until we landed. You would have asked me to turn the plane around and head back to Mackenzie," she replied. "We both know that when you report back to NASA, I'll probably be off the list and you'll just draw another name. Well, now I've got you here and . . ."

"Do you really think abducting me will change anything?" I interrupted. "I'm just the PR guy."

"Abducting you? This isn't a movie," she retorted. "We were running out of daylight and landing on water in the dark is an experience I try to avoid. I'll fly you back tomorrow. And if that doesn't suit you, you're perfectly free to make your own travel arrangements."

I looked around at this idyllic remote lake nestled in the embrace of the Omineca Mountains and remembered the trouble I'd had earlier in the afternoon hauling my suitcase from the car down to the plane. Dragging it 150 miles as the crow flies through untouched mountain passes, lakes, and wilderness might pose a slight problem.

Landon Percival was still standing on the dock in front of me with her hands on what I assume were her hips. It was hard to tell beneath her loose coveralls. Her eyes were closed for a time but eventually she opened them and lifted them back to me.

"Mr. Stewart, I've been waiting a long time for a shot at this. I'm just asking you to hear me out. You'll be back in Mackenzie tomorrow."

She grabbed my suitcase and strode off the dock and up the path to the cabin. I stood there for a time cataloguing my options. It didn't take me long. Then I walked up to the cabin, too.

Landon was lighting kerosene sconces in various locations in the room when I stepped in. The growing light revealed what seemed more a library than a cabin. Built-in shelves on three of the four walls of the main room were full of books. For a biblio-phile like me, it was an unexpected and beautiful scene. Wood and books have such warmth. A couch and matching easy chair sat in the middle of the room around a faded Persian-looking area rug. An old pine box served as a coffee table of sorts. A galley kitchen to the left off the front door featured a pass-through to the small dining area with a table and four chairs.

"Tea?" she asked, heading to the kitchen.

"Please."

She'd put my bag just inside one of the two doors that opened off the main room. I figured they were bedrooms. With Landon in the kitchen, I immediately went to the shelves. A quick scan revealed how her library was organized. One wall was fiction, mainly Canadian, American, and British it seemed at first glance. One wall was non-fiction with lots of history and biography. The third wall was dominated by a stone fireplace with a raised hearth and neat stack of wood.

The bookshelves on either side of the stonework were perhaps the most revealing about Landon. Aviation dominated one set of shelves. There was an array of very old books about bush pilots and their experiences opening up the Canadian north. There was an entire shelf dedicated to books about the de Havilland DHC-2. I recognized the plane on the covers of many of the books as the Beaver now floating at her dock. Another shelf featured books on the history of flight, including biographies of the Wright Brothers and Sir George Cayley, and a small volume on Leonardo da Vinci's examination of birds and his flying machine designs.

The set of shelves on the other side of the fireplace was completely dedicated to the exploration of space. That's right, space. Landon Percival was apparently just as much a space nut as was I. In fact, we had many of the same books chronicling the space programs of the United States and the then Soviet Union. Sputnik, Vostok, Mercury, Gemini, Soyuz, Apollo, Skylab,

Salyut, the shuttle, the International Space Station, they were all there. There were also what looked to be more obscure technical and academic papers on rocket propulsion systems, space medicine, and astronaut training. A few of the books were written in what I assumed was Russian.

Finally my eye fell on the wide mantel above the fireplace. Lying flat was an old leather-bound notebook opened to reveal flowing cursive unmistakably written with a fountain pen. I was about to look more closely until I noticed what was sitting next to it. I have no idea why I hadn't seen them as soon as I'd entered the room, but I hadn't. There, in all its glory, was a well-read edition of *The Complete Sherlock Holmes*, the entire collection of Conan Doyle's famous novels and stories gathered in one volume, published by Doubleday and Garden City Books of New York in 1930. It featured the famous introduction by Christopher Morley entitled "In Memoriam Sherlock Holmes." It stood alone between quite wonderful black, onyx perhaps, Holmes and Watson bookends. I'd been on the lookout for the very same edition. It wasn't a particularly rare book but you didn't stumble across it very often, unless you were in the presence of a fellow Sherlockian.

"You have got to be kidding," I said, just as Landon entered and passed me my tea in a large blue mug. "I fly clear across the country and find, in an old cabin on a remote mountain lake in northern B.C., the 1930 Doubleday edition of *The Complete Sherlock Holmes*. I've been hunting for one of these for some time now. What are the odds?"

"You speak like a fan, steeped in Sherlockiana," Landon said.

"A devoted and long-time fan. I've had a subscription to the *Baker Street Journal* since I was sixteen," I replied. Both of us were smiling now, standing on our patch of common ground.

"I can do better than that. I've had a BSJ subscription since 1953, when I turned fourteen. And they're all right here, every single one," Landon said as she lifted the lid on the pine box with a flourish to reveal several neat stacks of the journals.

I had the full set of the BSJ on CD-ROM, but I'd never actually seen any editions of the journal older than the year 2000 when my subscription started. I sat down on the couch and put my mug on the floor.

"May I?" I asked, as I leaned toward the treasure chest of Sherlockian delights.

Landon abruptly closed the lid.

"After."

"After what?"

"After you listen," Landon replied. "If I'm to be rejected as the citizen astronaut because I've got a few too many miles on me, I want you to know who you're rejecting."

"Landon, I'm sorry, I'm sympathetic, but NASA's going to say that you're a nonstarter. The Citizen Astronaut program is intended to ignite a passion for space in a new generation of Canadians and Americans. We need to build support in the eighteen- to fifty-year-old demographic if we hope to secure adequate funding levels from Congress and the Canadian government. I'm supposed

to be finding a youngish, good-looking, strong, charismatic arche-
type with a Canadian flag tattooed above his heart. As much as
I'd like to see you win this, I just don't think it's in the cards."

She slipped past me to the fireplace, moved the screen, struck
a wooden match on the bottom of its cylindrical container, and
bent down to light the fire that she'd already built. The fire crackled and was soon blazing. A one-match fire. She stood up for a
few moments watching the flames before nodding her head and
coming back to her chair.

"I know I may not be the candidate you had in mind when
you cooked up this contest. But my name was drawn. I won."

I sighed.

"Yes, your name was drawn. I know. But you didn't win a
canned ham at bingo night. We're talking about orbiting the
Earth. So the stakes and the costs are high."

I paused for a moment before continuing.

"I'm really sorry, but it clearly states in the fine print that the candidate must be accredited and approved by NASA and the Canadian
Space Agency even before the winner's name can be announced
and the training starts. They hold all the cards. It's their contest."

"But I'm perfect for this," she said, looking into the fire.
"Winning this contest was justice delayed, but it's justice none-
theless, and I want it. Don't change it to justice denied."

"I'm not following the justice angle."

"Then get comfortable and listen," she instructed.

"Hang on," I replied. "Let me get my notebook."

I owed my colleagues and our client a full briefing on Landon Percival. I knew that Emily would insist on due diligence and a corresponding paper trail from here to the space station if we were going to reject our first winner and draw another. I unzipped another pocket on my bag and withdrew my trusty Moleskine notebook and my favourite Cross fountain pen. In my mind, Moleskines required fountain pens. I had this romantic image of Watson recording his friend's exploits in a Moleskine-like notebook with a fountain pen. I was back in my chair a moment later.

"Okay. My pen is poised and the night is young. You have the floor," I said, with a grand sweep of my hand. Landon adroitly caught the lamp my grand sweeping hand knocked off the end table beside me.

"No, actually, right now I have the lamp."

She did not look pleased.

"So sorry about that," I said. "I'm quite clumsy, if that isn't already evident."

"No blood spilt," she replied, restoring the lamp to its rightful place before turning her eyes back to me.

"When you're seventy-one, few stories are short. But I'll try to tighten it up, so stay with me. It all comes together. Are you quite ready, Mr. Stewart?"

"David, please."

She nodded, sat back, inhaled deeply, and began.

"Hugh Percival, my father, was born in Vancouver in 1899. By the time he was nineteen years old, he was a decorated flying ace in the skies over France in World War I. Against the odds, and a testament to his skill as a pilot, he survived when so many others did not. After the armistice, he returned to Vancouver and became a doctor. As was often the case for returning fighter pilots, he grew bored of seeing patients in his office, and pined for his plane. He struck a reasonable compromise and became one of the first bush pilot doctors in Canada. He bought an eight-year-old Fokker Universal float plane and flew all over northern B.C. delivering babies, setting broken bones, operating when he needed to in less than ideal conditions, and of course signing death certificates when there was no hope. He loved what he did with all his heart. He'd been liberated from the drudgery of a traditional urban medical practice. And he could still fly.

"He met my mother, Dorothy, a schoolteacher in Fort Nelson in 1934, and they were married in '35. The newlyweds moved to this very cabin that he'd built with the help of some local carpenters who were also patients. The barter system was, and is still, alive here, as it probably is in most remote parts of the country. On February 20, 1939, my father delivered me right about where you're now sitting. I'm named after my father's best friend, Rupert Landon, who died over France just days before the peace in 1918. I don't think my father ever quite got over Rupert's death. Perhaps to honour his memory, my father taught me to fly when I was thirteen, and I've been aloft ever since.

"I was home schooled by my mother and finished the equivalent of high school when I was seventeen. My father flew me down to Vancouver when I was eighteen and set me up in an apartment near the campus of the University of British Columbia. I earned a Bachelor of Science in physiology and then went on to medical school. This would have been in 1962. I would go home when I could, but I spent most of the year in Vancouver. When I was twenty-four and almost finished med school, my father flew my mother down to Vancouver, where she was diagnosed with brain cancer. She never left the hospital. They knew little about how to treat that wretched disease back then. Dad was with her for the entire seven weeks of her precipitous decline and I was there for most of it, too. After she passed, I wanted to return to Cigar Lake with my father and put off my final year of medical school, but he flatly refused. I stayed and finished. Then one thing led to another and I found myself living in a much nicer apartment with a roommate, Sam, and taking over an established practice from another woman doctor who had been killed in a car accident. A doctor usually has to start small and build a stable of patients over many years. But I walked into what was already a very successful practice and before I knew it, five years had passed."

I was struck by the simple yet compelling storytelling. She covered a lot of ground with clean efficient sentences.

"Are you still awake, Mr. Stewart?" she asked.

"Of course. I'm not making a shopping list here," I replied, pointing to the notes I'd been taking.

"It's getting late and you're still on Toronto time. I'll just finish this leg of the journey and we'll pick it up in the morning."

"I'm in your hands," I said. "As Sherlock Holmes would say, 'Pray continue.'"

Landon took another big breath and resumed her story.

"On October 17, 1970, I got a message at my office to contact the RCMP in Fort St. John. I knew enough to know that it wasn't likely to be good news. When I reached them, I was told that my father and his plane had disappeared on a flight to a friend's cabin an hour northwest of Cigar Lake to deliver supplies as a favour. By then, he was flying an early de Havilland Beaver that he'd bought in 1958. No trace of him or the Beaver could be found. As you might imagine, I was devastated. I may not have been thinking clearly at the time, yet I've never regretted my decision. Not for a moment. In short order, I sold my medical practice, which was easier and faster than you might imagine. A husband-and-wife team of physicians had just arrived from Montreal and were perfectly suited to take over. I took their down payment and bought a twenty-year-old DHC-2 Beaver from a small charter company just up the coast from Vancouver. It was in good shape and had fewer hours on it than many planes two decades old. It all happened in the space of three weeks. I left my patients, I left my roommate, I left my life in Vancouver and flew my own plane back to this cabin. I was thirty-one years old and had no plan other than to find my father.

"The RCMP had suspended the search after two weeks. Officially, he was presumed dead in a plane crash, even though there was still no sign of wreckage anywhere along the route to his friend's lake. It was odd arriving back here and finding the cabin just as my father had left it before his last flight."

Landon got up and walked to the fireplace. I assumed she was going to stir the fire, although it was still burning nicely. Instead, she reached up and brought down the old leather notebook that was opened on the mantel. She sat down beside me and placed it on the pine box so we could both see it.

"This is my father's. It's a combination diary and flight log. He got used to recording his flights in the Great War and never gave up the habit. Here's his final entry, almost certainly the last words he ever wrote." She gestured towards the page.

I leaned down and read the words penned some forty years earlier.

In a rush to deliver tar paper and shingles to cranky Earl Walker on Laurier Lake. He needs it today so he can fix his damn roof and beat the rain. Damn EW today! Not feeling very well. But tanks are full. Gotta fly now. 2:17 p.m. HP

"Earl Walker was clearly in a hurry that day. Earl Walker never saw my father that day, or ever again."

Landon reached in one of the bookshelves, brought out an empty pill bottle, and placed it on the pine box.

"I found this on the kitchen counter when I arrived that day."

I picked up the bottle.

"Nitroglycerin? Isn't that an explosive?" I asked.

"It can be, but in this form, it's a very common heart medicine my father was evidently taking. It's a vasodilator, probably used to treat angina. But the bottle was empty when I found it. Just another piece of the puzzle.

"So I took over my father's remote practice and spent every other waking moment searching for him. I mapped out his course to Earl Walker's place and then drew a circle demarcating the huge swath of territory my father could have reached that day, based on how far the Beaver could have flown with full tanks. With a range of about 450 miles in any direction, the search area is more than 635,000 square miles. I've spent the last 40 years covering every inch of that vast expanse and have found sweet nothing. I even looked beyond the 450-mile range in case of heavy tail winds. But nothing. It's hard to miss a downed plane with a 48-foot wingspan, but I seemed to have managed it."

I shifted my position on the couch.

"You're about dead to this world. I can tell," Landon said. "Let's stop here and pick it up in the morning. You're in that bedroom. The bed is made. We'll talk when you're conscious again."

I had been caught up in her story but realized she was right. I was exhausted.

"Thanks for sharing your story with me. You've had quite a fascinating life. Quintessentially Canadian."

"Well, there's more to come," she replied.

I looked around the cabin and realized I hadn't yet discovered a bathroom. That wasn't a good sign.

"Um, where might I find the bathroom?"

"You can brush your teeth in the kitchen," she said as she reached for a flashlight and handed it to me. "Otherwise, head out the back door and turn left, down the gangway and you'll find what you're looking for."

I did as I was told and stepped out into the night. To the left, the flashlight illuminated a wooden catwalk of sorts, elevated above the ground. I learned the hard way that it was narrow, with no railing. When I climbed back up onto the catwalk and confirmed that I had no broken bones, I stepped carefully along the wooden planks to what I hoped would be a newly renovated brightly lit bathroom with a full shower and Jacuzzi. Nope, just a classic one-holer outhouse. At least there was a door. I did what I'd come to do, aided by the sound of rushing water somewhere nearby.

Ten minutes later I was horizontal in a single bed with a mattress that I figured was manufactured before the Leafs won their last cup back in '67. Not that it mattered. I was so tired I could have slept perched on a fence post. The mattress sagged and squeaked as I searched for a comfortable position. I eventually found one and started to drift. Landon stuck her head in just as I was heading under.

"I aim to be on that shuttle, Mr. Stewart."

"I know."

CHAPTER 7

Despite how exhausted I'd been the night before, I awoke as usual at 7:00 . . . Toronto time. Unfortunately, I wasn't in Toronto but on the shore of Cigar Lake in northern B.C. where it was 4:00 a.m. and still dark. I lay there drifting in and out of sleep until about 6:00 when the sound of Landon's voice floated up from the dock. I extricated myself from the mattress that predated the Industrial Revolution, and planted both feet on the hardwood floor. Standing there in my boxers I stretched for about thirty seconds, doubling the duration of my standard weekly fitness regimen. Then I peeked out the window. Bad idea.

Landon had just hauled herself out of the water and back onto the dock and was talking to someone. I couldn't quite figure out what she was wearing until I figured out she wasn't wearing anything at all. It's fair to say that I was not expecting to see my seventy-one-year-old host starkers on the dock. I snapped my head

146

away from the window with such violence that I feared a cervical collar might be in my future. She was still talking away but I was too far from the dock to make out what she was saying. I waited until I heard her come back into the cabin and start rooting about in the kitchen before I dressed and eased my way out of the room in stealth mode. I peeked through my fingers like a horror film rookie. All was well. She had donned a garish and reddish terry cloth pull-over robe of some kind, which made for a slightly more welcome sight than the one still seared in my memory from a few minutes before.

"Good morning," I said.

"Well, good morning to you," she replied, while cutting a cantaloupe she'd pulled from what I could now see was a propane fridge. I could see the tops of two tanks through the kitchen window. "I wondered if you were ever going to get up."

"It's only 6:10 and barely daylight. I'm normally down for at least another hour."

"This is my favourite part of the day. The lake is glass, and relatively warm at this time of year. You really should take a dip before breakfast."

"Um, thanks, but I think I'll just take a shower instead," I proposed.

She just looked at me for a moment and then very slowly shook her head.

"This isn't the Hilton. I'm happy to tip a watering can over your head but that's as close as you'll come to a shower."

I'm an idiot. A cabin equipped with a propane fridge and a catwalk to a single-seater outhouse is unlikely to offer shower facilities.

"Right, sorry, of course," I stammered. "I'm obviously still waking up."

She nodded and turned back to the melon.

"By the way, while I was waking up, I heard you chatting with someone down on the dock. Did we have company this morning?" I asked.

"Nope. I was probably just talking to myself," Landon said. "Actually, that's not quite true. I talk to my father as if he were still here. I have for years. I think it helps keep me sane."

Sane? In my mind, talking aloud to someone who wasn't really there wasn't exactly compelling evidence of sanity. But I kept that thought to myself. I was standing next to the pine box and could see her father's short and final entry in the logbook, still opened where we'd left it last night.

But in the light of a beautiful morning, I had to admit that Landon's story was growing on me. It was just so Canadian. There was drama, a vast and harsh land, mystery, perseverance, and the resilience of the human spirit. I thought she was quite a viable Citizen Astronaut contest winner – except for the "seventy-one-year-old skinny-dipper who talks to her long-dead father" part.

When Landon was finished in the one-person kitchen and had gone to her room, presumably to change out of her red muumuu, I splashed some water on my face and brushed my teeth. Then

I braved the outhouse again and the resident mosquitoes, who clearly understood that an outhouse is the perfect hunting ground. There tended to be plenty of exposed flesh and the victim's hands were, well, often occupied, having to contend with belt buckles, pant buttons, and the need for a steady and sustained aim, at least for the male species. Believe me, the "steady and sustained aim" part is tough enough in the dim light of the outhouse, and rendered even more challenging when smacking mosquitoes. I heard Landon rattling about nearby. On instinct, I reached for the flush handle. There wasn't one. Then, on instinct, I reached to lower the seat. There wasn't one. Okay, I guess that's it then. I unhooked the door and started back up to the cabin. Then, in the blink of an eye, I was back in the outhouse, breaking several land speed records in the process. I also suffered some temporary hearing loss by shrieking at the top of my lungs in the close confines of the wooden stall.

The bear on the catwalk was halfway between the outhouse and the cabin. Still in my morning stupor, I'd been a third of the way up before I'd noticed him. Yes, he was actually on the wooden decking, standing on his hind legs sniffing the air, just as they did on all the nature shows. Back in the outhouse, I looked through a crack in the latched door and saw that the ferocious grizzly was still standing and someone was still screaming. Me. The outhouse was actually the perfect refuge given my suddenly tenuous control over various bodily functions. I saw Landon burst from the back door of the cabin banging a wooden spoon on a pot. It sounded to me like she was ringing the gong to announce that dinner was ready – and waiting in the outhouse. I expected to hear "Come and get it!" but she went with something else.

"Go home, Hector! Go on!" she shouted. "Git!"

She kept up the pot percussion and I had the presence of mind to stop my crazed shrieking, though my ears were still ringing. I snuck another peek through the crack and watched as Hector lowered himself to all fours, stepped from the catwalk down to the ground, and sauntered off toward the woods. The beast was utterly unperturbed, stopping once to look back at Landon.

"Go on! Skedaddle!"

I smoothed my clothes, patted down my hair, pushed my heart back down from my throat to its traditional location, and opened the door.

"Oh, hello, Landon. I see the bear seems to have departed," I remarked, feigning nonchalance while my knees knocked. "Was that you making that banging noise?"

She looked at me. She was not buying what I was selling.

"Right. I'm amazed you could hear anything over your blood-curdling screams. I thought you were being probed by aliens," she replied. "Mercy, you nearly gave poor Hector a heart attack."

"That fierce, gigantic grizzly was about to attack," I protested. "He was salivating and getting ready to rush me."

Landon laughed. That's right. She held her pot and wooden spoon to her midsection and laughed.

"Mr. Stewart, Hector probably didn't even see you. He's a very small, very old, nearly blind, somewhat senile black bear that you could probably take if you had to. Did you not see the grey on his snout? In bear years, he's older than I am, and far more arthritic," she explained. "I pose more of a threat to you than that ancient bear does."

"Well, I didn't really get a good look at him before retreating to the outhouse," I said, feeling a bit sheepish now.

"Hector's been visiting me for more than twenty years. He's more curious than anything else."

"Yeah, well, *curious* Hector looked an awful lot like *hungry* Hector to me."

––––––––––

Twenty minutes later, after breakfast, I'd managed to bring my heart rate down to almost normal while keeping a weather eye out the window for a flash of fur. We sat down again in the same spots we'd occupied the previous night. Landon began:

"I'll pick it up where we left off. I'm almost done. By 1983, I'd been living here for nearly thirteen years. Still, not a trace of my father or his plane could be found. By then, I was the only one still looking for him. Many assumed he'd gone down into a lake somewhere between here and Earl Walker's place, but the water usually gives up some sign of a crash. A piece of wreckage, a broken paddle ripped from a pontoon, an oil slick, something. But there was nothing. Nothing at all."

"I'm sorry," I said. "That must have weighed on you."

"Still does. Anyway, 1983 offered a distraction from it all. You probably weren't yet born then but the National Research Council – NRC – started accepting applications for the first group of Canadian astronauts."

"Right. I wrote about that in a speech a few years ago for the Science and Tech minister I worked for. As I recall, it was commemorating the twenty-fifth anniversary of Marc Garneau's first shuttle mission back in 1984, I think."

"Yep. October 5 to 13, mission STS-41-G," Landon interjected. "Long before the creation of the Canadian Space Agency, it was the NRC that selected our first corps of astronauts. Well, I was one of the more than four thousand Canadians who applied."

"You're kidding! You applied to be an astronaut twenty-seven years ago?"

"Yep, and I thought I was a perfect fit. I'm a doctor, I'd been flying for all but the first thirteen years of my life, I was in good physical shape, still am, I'd been training on my own, still am, and no civilian could have been more passionate or knowledgeable about space than I was, or still am."

"Sounds like you'd have been an ideal candidate," I said, and meant it. She looked wistful and tired all of a sudden.

"Well, it didn't happen. They chose six and I certainly wasn't one of them. I wasn't even invited for the preselection testing. I just heard nothing. It took me a long time to recover."

"Maybe they never got your application?"

"Nope, they got it. I was able to confirm that. But that was about all."

"Did you ever find out anything about why you didn't make it?"

"Well, nothing official. They have some kind of a policy against revealing much about their decisions. But thanks to the Access to Information Act, and to some unguarded comments someone made in a meeting for which minutes were taken, I think I have a pretty good idea why I never heard from them."

I nodded but said nothing and just waited for her to continue.

"You know, the original seven Mercury astronauts had to be under forty. In 1983, I was nearly forty-five years old. While it was never spelled out, I figure there was some kind of an age threshold beyond which they wouldn't even review your application. I think it was over before it began."

———

I was trying to slot this new revelation from Landon's past into what else I'd learned about her since arriving. Putting on my PR consultant's hat, it was dawning on me that we had the makings of an extraordinary story here, seventy-one years old or not. I instinctively began to consider how best to present it to media. But then I stopped myself. Hello, reality check. Why bother? It's not that it wouldn't get media coverage. I knew it would be a huge story. But I'd never get the chance to pitch it to reporters because Landon's dream would surely soon be crushed again, just as it was in 1983, and for the same reason. Crawford Blake, and NASA for that matter, would never even consider her. Abort launch. End of story.

"So let me see if I understand all of this," I began. "You're a seventy-one-year-old bush pilot doctor living on the shore of a remote lake in northern B.C. You were rejected by the Canadian astronaut program nearly thirty years ago because you were too old. You've been trying to solve the mystery of your father's disappearance some forty years ago. And now, six years after your old age pension kicked in, you win this contest and still want to venture beyond Earth's safe embrace and visit space. Am I close to getting your story straight?"

"Well, almost," she replied. She hesitated for a moment. "Not that it's anyone's business, but my story isn't exactly 'straight.'"

She had a look on her face that suggested there was more to say.

"What exactly do you mean?" I prompted.

"Well, in the spirit of full disclosure, I guess there's something else you should know," she continued. "Back in the sixties, when I lived in Vancouver, my roommate Sam was much more than a roommate."

"Say it isn't so! I'm shocked," I mocked. "Landon, lovers living in sin during the free-love sixties isn't exactly a stop-the-presses moment. I don't think it'll be a problem. So what happened to him?"

154

"Her. You mean, 'What happened to her?'" she replied and paused, looking down before continuing. "Well, Samantha bolted when it became clear she couldn't really compete with a beloved father who was still missing in a presumed plane crash."

"Samantha," I said, catching up.

"Yes, Samantha," she said. "As in 'the love that dare not speak its name.'"

"Okay, so you're a seventy-one-year-old Oscar Wilde-quoting lesbian bush pilot doctor from Cigar Lake, B.C., who'd like to visit the International Space Station," I said.

She just nodded, satisfied that I had the full picture.

"It would help if you also loved maple syrup and *Hockey Night in Canada,* but I think I can work with what I've got."

"What does that mean?" she asked.

"It means you have an incredible story that I think would have resonated with Canadians if we were ever given the chance to tell it."

"But we won't get that chance, will we?" She wasn't really asking. She was resigned.

"Landon, if it were up to me it'd be an easy call. But I'm just a bit player in all of this. Not even the Canadian Space Agency will have any meaningful role in the final decision. It's all in NASA's hands. If we honestly confront the reality of your situation – and I'm sorry about this – I just don't think there's any hope you'll be given the go-ahead."

"So there it is. I'm rejected a second time."

"Look, I'm sorry. I'll push as hard as I can," I said. "I'll tell them your story and do whatever I can to soft-pedal the age thing. But sooner or later it'll come out. It has to."

She suddenly seemed even smaller and older. I felt terrible and tried to explain it again, to soften it.

"I'm really sorry about this, Landon, but this is a very big deal for NASA. They've staked a lot on this contest idea and it's already pushed them far out of their comfort zone. So they are going to be very, very careful when it comes to approving the citizen astronauts. They're looking for *safe*, very *safe*. I'm sorry to say that at seventy-one, you're just not in the *safe* category. We'll never announce the citizen astronaut until the candidate has been vetted up and down and sideways. That's why my mission out here is shrouded in such secrecy. No one knows who you are, why I'm here, or even that I'm here. So when I get back to Toronto and report on all of this, I know my colleagues and my client will be amazed at your story. How could they not be? But I also know what they'll decide in the end. We'll just draw another name and start the qualifying process all over again."

"Well, maybe I won't keep my mouth shut," Landon said, angry. "I'm the winner, fair and square. I should be on the shuttle."

"No, no, no. Don't do that. You can't go public with this or you'll be disqualified immediately. It's all laid out in black and white in the contest rules and regs. You can say nothing publicly without NASA's approval," I explained. "You'd be making it very easy for them to reject you. I'm truly sorry, but it is what it is."

We sat in silence for a few minutes. Eventually, she sighed, nodded, then stood up.

"I want to show you something."

We headed out the back door but turned right, not towards the outhouse. Down the back porch steps we went and onto a path that snaked through the trees. My eyes darted all around in search of Hector. And I didn't really care how arthritic he might be. We reached a clearing about fifty yards from the cabin. Tree stumps littered the circular space and I realized the land must have been cleared by hand. But I forgot about the stumps when my eyes latched onto the spindly metal contraption that sat at the centre of the clearing.

I couldn't even begin to fathom what I was looking at. A steel post about six feet high was stuck in the ground at the centre. A long metal pole was somehow bolted horizontally to the top of the post somewhere near the middle so that there was twelve feet or so feet of the pole on either side of the vertical post. A small engine was bolted to one end of the horizontal pole, driving a three-foot-diameter three-bladed wooden propeller. At the other end of the pole hung what looked like an old cushioned seat, probably taken from a long-grounded aircraft. Five concrete blocks were stacked on the seat. Even after analyzing what I was seeing, I was unable to figure it out. I didn't even have to ask.

"It's a centrifuge," was all she said.

"A centrifuge?"

"Yes, a centrifuge."

"I see," I replied, still hovering on the outskirts of understanding. "Are you trying to hurl concrete blocks to the other side of the forest?"

"Oh, there has definitely been some hurling happening right here, but it's unrelated to the concrete blocks."

She watched as my wheels turned and finally delivered me. In an instant, I saw it and then wondered how I couldn't have seen it from the beginning.

"No way. You're kidding!" I exclaimed. "Okay. Don't tell me. You've built your own centrifuge to practise pulling Gs for the shuttle launch. Right?

"Actually, it's more to simulate how re-entry feels. But you're on the right track."

She seemed pleased by my enthusiasm.

"Amazing. How does it work?"

"Well, let's do a walk-around and I'll try to explain it," she said as we headed to the centre post. "This is where the real work of the centrifuge happens. While you're seeing only about five feet of the steel post, there's another six feet of it anchored in concrete below the surface. There's a hell of a lot of stress on this post, so I check the foundations and the hardware on top before and after every spin."

I grabbed the post with both hands and tried to give it a little shake. Nothing. Rock of Gibraltar solid.

"Where did you get such a long pole for the radial arm?" I inquired.

"Believe it or not, it's the aluminum mast of a long-retired Starcraft Skylark sailboat we used to sail right here on Cigar. I had a machinist work on the mounting hardware so that it's safely and securely fixed to the post but able to rotate freely about it. I bought an old JLO Rockwell 340 cc twin cylinder snowmobile engine off a neighbour and bolted it to the steel plate I had welded to one end of the mast, the crankshaft running perpendicular to the mast. Then I slapped on an old propeller I had lying around to finish this end."

We walked to the other end.

"Would you mind putting a bit of weight on the mast and holding it there?"

When I had leaned on the aluminum pole, Landon promptly lifted each of the five concrete blocks piled in the seat and set them down on the ground a few feet away. I could immediately feel the upward pressure on my arms as I balanced the weight of the engine and prop assembly on the other end.

"This is one of the old seats from my father's first plane," she explained. "It kind of makes me feel like he's still involved in this."

"Well, it seems appropriate, given that you're still flying when you're sitting in it."

Landon pulled herself into the seat and motioned for me to let go. The old sailboat mast mounted horizontally on the centre post bobbed into perfect equilibrium, the engine and propeller at one end balancing Landon strapped in at the other.

"Okay, Mr. Stewart. All I need you to do now is start the engine on your way up to the observation post on that tree." She pointed as she spoke.

There was a modest tree fort of sorts about twelve feet up hanging between two large Douglas firs. Okay, fort is a bit of an overstatement. It was really just an elevated deck with a ladder up one trunk. I stood in front of the engine, grabbed the pull cord, and yanked for all I was worth. One pull and it started. I looked at Landon and she pointed me up the tree to the observation platform. I obeyed and was soon seated above the centrifuge on a low bench. I pulled out my iPhone and shot some video as Landon squeezed the throttle she'd rigged up using an old bicycle brake handle and cable that ran along the former sailboat mast to the engine. The propeller pushed the air and the centrifuge did what centrifuges do. It began to rotate. What an ingeniously simple design.

Landon was spinning quite quickly by then. I could tell because the freely suspended seat was now angled out to the side, pushed by the centrifugal force of the revolving arm. I was worried for her safety. If the seat ever broke free from the spinning arm, she'd fly halfway back to Vancouver if she cleared the trees. I was getting dizzy and queasy just watching from above. She spun for five minutes according to my iPhone, which is actually quite a long time when you're strapped onto the end of what is essentially a whirling helicopter rotor. I heard the tone of the engine fall and eventually die out completely, leaving the mast to coast around and around, before finally stopping as Landon dragged her feet in the pine needles and dirt. I scrambled back down the ladder, skipping the last two rungs by accident. I struggled back to my feet and helped Landon get out of the seat. With her assistance, I returned the five concrete blocks to the seat, restoring the centrifuge's perfect balance.

"How do you feel?" I asked. "You must have been pulling a few Gs there towards the end."

"Actually, I hit just more than two Gs before shutting her down," she replied.

"How do you know?"

She pointed to a cylinder fixed with chains linking it at one end to the mast and the other to the seat.

"This is a heavy pull scale for load testing. It can register up to 800 pounds. It's positioned so that I can see it when I'm strapped in. At rest, the seat and I together weigh about 150 pounds. So I monitor the scale as I crank up the throttle. Just before I killed the engine, I saw that the gauge was reading over 300 pounds, or slightly more than two Gs."

Landon was standing perfectly still without a hint of dizziness or the traditional temporary wobbling that normally accompanies being spun in a blender for five minutes. I could not relate at all. I would often get a mild case of vertigo after turning a corner.

"You're not dizzy at all after that?" I asked.

"Nope. I was the first two hundred times I did it back in '83, but then, over the years, I just got used to it," she explained.

"I've routinely pulled two and a half Gs in this thing. And sometimes I even secure the seat in the vertical position, facing the centre post, to simulate launch. It's easier to take the Gs at launch because of the direction of the force. But still, it's good practice."

"But it's as if you're completely unaffected by being whipped in circles for five minutes."

"It bothers me even less now. Researchers have actually discovered that there's something about the geriatric physiology that makes it easier to accommodate G forces. I guess there are at least a few benefits to growing old."

"Oh yeah, it must be a great comfort to senior citizens everywhere knowing that they're better able to handle rocket launches," I replied. "So you've really been doing this for years? Why?"

"I've been waiting for my shot and I wanted to be ready. I guess you could say I've been waiting for you and your contest." She was staring at the centrifuge seat as she said this, with a faraway look in her eyes. We stood in silence for a moment or two before she took my arm and led me to the seat.

"Okay, now it's your turn. Hop on, and strap in," Landon said, pointing to the seat.

"I don't think so," I replied. "I'm really not great on amusement park rides. Trust me."

She said nothing but just kept pointing to the seat and smiling. It was a nice smile. Plus, she was my host and personal pilot for the trip back to Mackenzie. I didn't really want to offend her.

I leaned on the seat to offset the weight it was losing as Landon removed the concrete blocks. On her signal, I slipped into the seat.

"How much do you weigh?" she asked.

"About 165."

Landon immediately walked over to a flat tree stump near the observation deck and picked up a large iron disk with a hole in the middle. I recognized it as a weight that would normally be added to a barbell for power-lifting in the gym. She slid it onto a shelf below the engine mount, walked back to fetch another, and secured them both with a couple of shock cords. I was heavier than Landon and this additional weight on the engine end of the mast returned the entire contraption to equilibrium. Simple, but effective.

Landon then made sure I'd secured the harness.

"Are you ready?" she asked.

"No."

"Good. You control the throttle, so you don't have to scramble your innards. Just go fast enough to feel the additional weight on your body."

I nodded.

It occurred to me that I'd never make it as an astronaut. Suddenly, wave after wave of nausea rolled over me. It was a horrible feeling. I didn't know which end was up I was so disoriented. It was even worse when Landon started the engine and I actually started moving slowly along my circular flight plan.

And that's all I remember. I must have passed out. When I came to, Landon was standing in front me with a pail of water. It was shockingly cold as she dumped the bucket on me.

Apparently, I'd thrown up and fainted on my second complete revolution, while still travelling so slowly it was hard to tell I was moving at all. Or perhaps I fainted and then threw up. Either way, I eventually understood why I was being unceremoniously doused with cold water. It took a few buckets, but the last vestiges of my breakfast were finally washed from the seat, my clothes, my hair, my nose, etc. Yes, I was born to this.

"I've never been very good at spinning," I conceded. "Despite being a PR professional."

She took my arm and led me farther up the path where the sound of rushing water grew louder. I could see a mountain stream cascading down the slope to the lake. A wooden box had been placed in the water and was full. The water that didn't flow into the box rushed around it and continued down the slope eventually feeding into the lake. I could see a black plastic hose running from the box down through the woods to Landon's cabin. I got it.

"So this is how you get your water?"

"A tried and true technique. This gravity-fed water box system gives me all the clean and cold water I need, with no pumps required," she explained. "Of course, it's helpful to have a mountain spring rushing by your back door."

I wasn't sure why we were standing there.

"Rinse out your pants and shirt in the stream and we'll dry them on the dock," she instructed.

I hesitated. She wanted me to strip down to my boxers.

"Mr. Stewart, I'm a doctor. I've seen plenty of men in their skivvies. Besides, I bat for the other team, remember?"

I stripped down and was about to dunk my pants and shirt when she stopped me.

"Not in the water box, if you please. We drink from that. Take two steps downstream and we're fine."

Half an hour later, we were sitting on the dock in old-fashioned wooden lounge chairs, known in Ontario as Muskoka chairs, enjoying the sun's warmth. I'd changed by then and was feeling much better, as long as I stayed quite still. Landon got up, walked up the path, and lifted the canoe off its rack in one smooth motion. She supported it on her thighs as she sidestepped back down to the dock and slid the cedar-stripped canoe into the water. She tossed in a couple of life jackets, grabbed the paddle that was stuck in a slot and bracket on one of the plane's floats, and slid onto the seat. She looked my way.

"Hop in and we'll go for a paddle up the lake a ways," she suggested. "You don't have to lift a finger. I only have one paddle anyway. Just sit back and enjoy the ride. I'll take care of navigation and locomotion."

I hesitated.

"Come on, Mr. Stewart, you won't get an offer like this very often."

I did what I was told. I actually made it into the canoe without dumping us both in the lake. I felt pretty good about that. Landon had me sit facing her on a soft life jacket in the bottom of the canoe with my back against the seat. This lowered my centre of gravity, which meant that it also lowered the prospects of tipping the canoe from *certain* to just shy of *likely*. She pushed away from the dock gently and took silent strong strokes. Each stroke was precisely the same. She must have paddled this lake a thousand times. Every time she pulled her paddle back through the water, I felt us surge forward. For the first fifty yards or so off the dock, the water retained its deep blue. Then I watched the rocky bottom rise up and level off about twenty feet beneath us, where it stayed for the rest of our journey up the south shore of Cigar Lake.

"If I'm not flying, this is my favourite mode of transportation," she said, keeping us about twenty yards offshore.

"Except perhaps for the space shuttle," I suggested.

"You got that right," she replied. "Okay. Now that you've heard it all, what happens now?"

"Well, I head back to Toronto and report on our contest winner's suitability for space travel. If I had my way, you'd be confirmed as the Canadian citizen astronaut. Your story is perfect and would captivate the country. You're a bush pilot doctor who was rejected nearly thirty years ago for the astronaut corps. You built your own centrifuge, for crying out loud. This would have been such sweet vindication," I said, but with a melancholy tone that was not lost on Landon.

"But you're not the decision-maker."

"Right. Moreover, I doubt I have enough influence even to get your full story on the table before the hatchet falls," I lamented. "NASA and my bosses in Toronto and Washington will make the call, and I don't think it will take them long. I'm sorry."

"All because I'm a little past my best-before date. Just doesn't seem fair."

"Well, it isn't fair, but they hold all the cards," I said. "I'll try to get all of your story in front of the key players before your age even becomes an issue. But in the end . . ." My voice trailed off.

"Right," was all she said.

We paddled farther up the lake, as I marvelled at the scenery. Take the best Canadian beer commercial ever made, with shots of our fresh water, towering mountains, and big sky, and it couldn't come close to what I was seeing from a canoe on Cigar Lake.

"Did the RCMP ever officially close the file on your father's disappearance?"

"About two months later, they declared him lost in an air crash and haven't done a thing about it since."

"Do you ever wonder what Sherlock Holmes would make of this mystery?" I asked.

She smiled.

"I've reread the entire Holmes canon several times over searching for some insight that might help. I rediscovered my love of

Doyle's writing, but I'm no further ahead in finding my father."

We turned and headed back to the dock.

Half an hour later, my clothes were dry and packed, and my bag was loaded on the Beaver. I took a last look around, taking in the idyllic cabin, canoe, dock, trees, lake, and mountains. I'm not sure I've ever been to a more beautiful and untouched sliver of Canada. I climbed in, fastened my seat belt, and pulled on the headphones as if I'd been flying for years. Landon reached in and started the engine, the propeller disappearing from view as it gathered speed. Then she slipped back out onto one float to cast off from the dock. A few seconds later, she too was buckled in. She pointed us west and hit the throttle. It took us a while to get up a head of steam but we eventually lifted from the surface of Cigar Lake, climbed over the trees at the west end of the lake, and turned for Mackenzie.

"By the way," I said over the headset. "How can I reach you? I mean other than flying back out here."

I heard Landon's voice in my ears as she rhymed off a cell-phone number. I grabbed a pen from my jacket pocket and wrote the number down on the back of one of my business cards I'd found in my wallet.

"You have cell service way up here?"

She pointed out the side window back to the west.

"On the next lake over, a wealthy tycoon from Seattle with more money than brains built a cell tower on his land so that he is always reachable. I can pull in quite a strong signal from my place. I just don't like to give the number out. But I'll make an exception for you."

She reached behind her and grabbed a brown paper bag and handed it to me.

"What's this?" I asked.

"Have a look."

I reached in and pulled out a small tin. I opened it and saw and smelled chocolate chip cookies.

"For the trip home. You'll need something," Landon explained.

"Thank you. That's very kind of you. Can I try one now?"

She just waved her hand in assent. The bag was not yet empty. I reached in again and pulled out the 1930 Doubleday edition of *The Complete Sherlock Holmes*. I was taken aback.

"Landon, I can't accept this. It's in pristine condition!" I protested.

"Ah hell, I've got two more in a box in my closet. Take it. I don't meet too many fellow Sherlock fans. I'd like you to have it. You've come a long way to see me, and I probably didn't make it very easy on you."

"I don't know what to say. It's very generous," I said in all sincerity. "I appreciate it very much."

"Now pass me a cookie, would you?" she asked with hand outstretched.

We flew on. At about the halfway point, even though the air was smooth, I was beginning to feel a little queasy. I must have looked a little green around the gills.

"Use this if you need to," she directed, handing me a large Ziploc freezer bag. "I can't wash down these seats with a bucket of water without short circuiting the entire instrument panel."

I just nodded and opened the bag.

PART 3

CHAPTER 8

"Welcome home, David," Diane said as she settled into the chair at the head of the boardroom table, no paper, no pen. "We weren't sure you were ever going to come back."

It was late Monday morning, the day after I'd returned from my memorable visit to Cigar Lake, B.C. My stomach was almost back to normal, although sitting in a swivel boardroom chair was almost more than I could handle right then.

"By the look of your numbers in PROTTS, you've sustained your torrid pace. You're averaging more than fifty hours a week billable on this project. Very impressive."

Amanda slipped into the room and sat down next to me, her smiling face full of anticipation.

"So, how was it? How's our guy?" she asked, rubbing her hands as if they were cold.

I hadn't provided any kind of an update while I was gone or even when I got back over the weekend. I was still trying to figure out how I was going to handle this.

"Are we waiting for anyone else?" I asked, feeling a little tense.

"Nope, it's just the three of us to start. We've got half an hour before our call with the D.C. team so we thought you could brief us first. You know, no surprises," replied Amanda. "So . . ." She moved her hand in a way that made it clear she wanted me to start talking. So I did.

"Right, well, let me bring you up to date," I began, trying to stick to my plan for as long as I could. "Reaching Cigar Lake was a little less challenging than Shackleton's quest for the south pole, but not by much. The Toronto to Calgary leg was fine but my connection through to Prince George was a little unnerving. The plane was so old I expected Orville and Wilbur to welcome us on board from the cockpit. But we somehow made it, and I went on to Mackenzie by car. Then it was the final push to Cigar Lake aboard a Beaver float plane."

"Okay, okay, we know it was a tough trip to B.C., we got it," chided Amanda. "Tell us about our winner."

"I'm getting there. I'm just trying to set the scene. So Cigar Lake is shaped kind of like . . . um . . . a cigar. We landed and I was eventually delivered to the cabin of our winner, and was introduced to Landon Percival."

"I bet he was over the moon," Amanda said excitedly. "What does he look like? Are we happy with him?"

"Well, actually, Landon is a woman's name. I don't know why we assumed L. Percival is a he, but he's a she."

"Really. Well, that's fine. It's better in some respects," Amanda noted. "What does she look like? Can we see a photo?"

I'd totally forgotten to snap any photos while I was there except for shooting those few minutes of video of Landon whirling in her hepped-up carousel-on-crack.

"Um, I haven't been able to transfer the photos from my camera to my computer yet. I have a glitch somewhere. But she's very nice. Not big. A bit wiry and very strong. Very pleasant looking," I started. "But you won't believe her story. I think we've hit the jackpot with Landon Percival."

"Carry on. We're listening," Diane prodded.

"Okay. In a nutshell, she's passionate about space and has been for almost her entire life. She's a physician and a bush pilot who flies in to remote communities to see patients all through Northern B.C."

"Nice!" Amanda said. "I like that!"

"Wait, there's more. In her spare time, she's spent much of her life searching the area for any trace of her bush pilot doctor father who's been missing and presumed lost in a plane crash, um, some years ago. Finally, and get this, she's been training to be an astronaut on her own in case she ever got the chance to go up. She's in peak physical and mental condition and even trains daily in a home-built centrifuge that simulates the G forces of a shuttle launch and re-entry. She's articulate and intelligent. She's just amazing, incredible."

I spent the next fifteen minutes or so thoroughly briefing them on my visit, while studiously avoiding any reference to her age, sexuality, or penchant for morning skinny-dipping. I knew I'd have to come clean sometime but I wanted them on my side before they learned she was born before the start of World War II. I recounted my encounter with the bear, my trip on the centrifuge, our canoe around the lake, our mutual interest in Sherlock Holmes, and the glories of the monohole outhouse. I was starting to get into my story. Amanda and Diane seemed transfixed, perhaps even spellbound.

"I think you're right, David, she sounds like a brilliant candidate," Amanda said.

"Yes, she certainly has crammed a lot into her life for a twenty-one-year-old," Diane observed. "I didn't know you could actually be a doctor at twenty-one." She tilted her head, puzzled, squinting at me.

And there it was. The end had kind of snuck up on me just when I'd been starting to enjoy my own story. Time to fess up.

"Well, you've hit upon an interesting part of this story, Diane," I started. "You see . . ."

The speaker phone pod at the centre of the board table suddenly blasted its nuclear ring tone, either signalling that a foreign air force was about to start carpet bombing Toronto, or that there was another party on the line eager to speak with us. It was the latter. You might say that the piercing sound caught me somewhat off-guard. You might say that, because in my advanced state of surprise, my reflex was to fling my pen straight up in the air where it stuck fast in a ceiling tile. I mouthed "Sorry" to Diane as Amanda hit the big green button.

"Crawford, is that you?" she asked the sleek speaker phone pod.

"Hello, frozen Canadians. Yes, it's Crawford here and I've got the D.C. team with me. I know we're a few minutes early, but are we all ready?"

"We're all set here. David was just giving us a bit of a sneak peek at our lucky Canadian winner and I think you're going to be pleased," Diane said.

Great, just great, I thought to myself. By dragging out the story, and skirting the seventy-one-year-old lesbian elephant in the room, I was setting myself up for a big fall in front of the entire team. Nicely handled.

"Looking forward to it," Crawford responded, taking control of the meeting. "All right, let's get started. Our agenda for this call is quite straightforward. First, we'll introduce you to our American citizen astronaut. And we're quite excited about him. Then we'll turn it over to Toronto to hear about the Canadian winner. Sound good?"

No one replied, so Crawford filled the silence.

"Okay then, let's start. Here in the U.S., the very first name we drew has passed through our qualification procedure with flying colours and we've already briefed NASA on him and they're happy. So if they're happy, we're happy," Crawford declared. "So let me tell you a bit about him. He exactly fits the model we were hoping to find. His name is Eugene Crank. He's a thirty-eight-year-old deputy sheriff for a small county in Texas. Born and raised a couple states over in rural Mississippi, he's a

God-fearing Christian, married with two sons. He's good looking, in great shape, and is no stranger to the microphone, having won several local karaoke competitions. In my mind, he's the archetypal American hero, protecting his fellow citizens, serving his community, and soon, carrying the dreams of a nation into space."

Unfortunately, I was no longer carrying the Ziploc freezer bag Landon had given me that last time I'd felt close to losing a meal.

"We've now spent some time with Eugene and believe that he is the ideal candidate, which is why NASA was so quick to add their stamp of approval. While he's slightly older than expected, he's just the kind of winner we were hoping to find when we presented this idea to NASA several months ago."

"Crawford, it's Diane here. I assume you've done a full background check on this guy. It would not be good to have something from his past bite us in the ass when the eyes of the world are on him."

"Already done, Diane. He's as clean as they come. He's a lawman, for God's sake. I'm telling you, can we pick 'em or can we pick 'em!"

The D.C. contingent clapped for their fearless leader, so we did too, though somewhat anemically. They couldn't see us, after all.

"Thank you. Okay. Now let's hear about our Canadian candidate. Diane?"

"Thanks, Crawford. I'm going to ask David Stewart to introduce Landon Percival, our Canadian citizen astronaut. David?"

Amanda smiled at me as she pushed the phone pod closer to me so that when I went down in flames, everybody on the call would be able to hear the crash in Dolby surround sound.

"Hi, everyone," I started. My voice was higher than usual. Here we go. "I've just returned from Cigar Lake in northern British Columbia where I spent a couple of days off the grid with Landon Percival. This is a distinctly Canadian story, which is just exactly what we were looking for."

I proceeded to spin Landon's extraordinary tale with every bit of drama and emotion I could muster. Her birth on the shore of Cigar Lake, her home schooling, her stint in the big city, her success at medical school, her mother's tragic and early death, her father's last logbook entry and mysterious disappearance, her return to Cigar Lake to search for her father and carry on his work, her lifelong dream of becoming an astronaut, her years studying space, her own personal astronaut training in the centrifuge she built out of parts from a sailboat and a snowmobile, and her sheer delight and excitement at having been granted the chance to live her dream.

I confess I got caught up in my own performance. Modesty aside, I was on a roll. I was *on*. My ten-minute soliloquy left Diane and Amanda wide-eyed, even though they'd already heard a pared-down version of the story. To be clear, everything I said was the unembellished truth. I just didn't quite tell the whole truth.

As planned, I steered well clear of the Landon Percival danger zones, including her 1983 rejection from the Canadian astronaut training program. It would come out soon enough, I knew. I finished with this.

"Landon Percival is a great Canadian with a very Canadian story. We couldn't have selected a more appropriate candidate. She was born to do this. She was meant to do this. The miracle of her random selection from over 1.7 million entries is, quite simply, destiny. There's no other way to describe it. It was a privilege to spend time with her as she begins the journey to fulfil her destiny."

I stopped talking. Silence descended and then abruptly ended in a burst of wild applause and cheering from both sides of the border. Diane and Amanda were beaming as they clapped. I felt sick. I had to play it this way to honour my promise to Landon. I had to draw them in and get them invested in her story. I needed all of my colleagues hugging one another and singing "Kumbaya." It was the only slim hope we had. Because sooner or later, everyone would know that there were seventy-one candles burning on Landon's last birthday cake. And that would generate a lot of heat.

"Outstanding. Glad you managed to find such a perfect candidate," Crawford said. "Can you send us a photo? I'd like to see what this young woman looks like."

"Um, yes, I'm working on getting photos."

"Okay, folks, that about does it. You all know how important this is and what our next steps are, so let's keep moving and stay on track," Crawford said. "Amanda and David, we'll need to present Landon to NASA for approval, so can you pull together a bio package on her and get it down to me?"

Amanda, always looking for an opportunity to interact with Crawford, piped up fast. I didn't even consider responding.

"Absolutely, Crawford, you'll have it shortly."

"David, one more thing," Crawford said over the noise of his team vacating the D.C. boardroom. "How old is this Landon miracle again?"

I clenched. Better for it to come out now than when were farther down the road. I would have been fired later on in the process. Now I would probably just be kicked off the account.

"She's only twenty-one," offered the ever-helpful Amanda, chipper as ever when Crawford was around.

"Actually, there's a funny story about that," I began, in full back-pedal. "Turns out she's a little older than we thought. But her story is so amazing, I don't think it should be an issue. After all, sixty is the new fifty, right?"

"Shit, she's not sixty, is she?" Crawford snapped. "Tell me she's not sixty. Please somebody tell me our Canadian citizen astronaut is not a decade more than half a century old."

"Um, of course not, no, not exactly, um, no, she's certainly not sixty . . ." I stammered, laughing a little, and watching the moment of truth hurtle towards me like a speeding locomotive.

"Well, thank Christ for that!" blasted Crawford over the speaker.

"Landon Percival is seventy-one years old."

I kind of mumbled the number, but I did say it.

"Sorry, what did you say? You cut out a bit," Crawford asked. Everyone else in the room knew enough to stay silent now.

"She's seventy-one," I repeated, clearer this time, but still a little under my breath, to be honest.

Crawford was getting a little exasperated.

"Sorry, David, we're having trouble hearing you," he began. "That time it almost sounded like you said seventy-one. So can you try it again in your big-boy voice?"

"Landon Percival is seventy-one years old. She was born in 1939, has wiry grey hair, and looks kind of like an apple doll, but with more wrinkles, and she sort of smells like engine grease."

There I'd said it. It was finally out in the open. Diane and Amanda were both staring at me, faces frozen, mouths agape, undergoing what looked like the first recorded case of synchronized strokes. The silence held for an eternity. I couldn't stand it.

It was so quiet you could hear a pin drop, just after Crawford pulled it from the grenade. I jumped back in.

"But I still think she's a great candidate with an amazing story. Let me tell you the best part . . ."

"Stop, David," said Crawford.

"You won't believe this but back in '83, she . . ."

"*Stop*, David . . ."

"She applied to be one of Canada's first astronauts, but was rejected because she was too old. So when I said this was destiny, I . . ."

"*Shut the fuck up!*" Crawford shouted, exhausting every cubic centimetre of air in his lungs.

He paused for effect and perhaps to allow the ringing in my ears to abate, then he spoke in a voice that was barely above a whisper. This made him all the more sinister as the three of us in the room leaned in to the speaker phone pod. In his agitated state, his southern drawl kicked into high gear.

"I do not give a flyin' fuck how good her story is. I do not care if she's actually Amelia Earhart, she's a goddamned ancient old biddy who will not be takin' her walker, readin' glasses, and weak bladder on board the space shuttle. It will not happen. And NASA will never know she even existed. Because you are going to pick another goddamned name and it's going to be a fuckin' ice-skatin', dog-sleddin', snow-shovellin', eh-sayin', very polite lumberjack with a face for TV!"

I have no idea where I found my voice after his tirade, but I suddenly had this vision of Landon, and she was smiling and seemed to be urging me into the fray.

"I really think we should carefully consider moving forward with Landon . . ."

"I really think you should carefully consider your future with this firm, because you have just wasted a half-hour of our professional time that we can never get back with one of the most boneheaded and asinine ideas I've ever heard. Pick a new *fuckin'* winner!"

The image of Landon in my head dissolved and was replaced by a vision of the unemployment office. I was sitting on a frayed blanket on the sidewalk out front, selling pencils . . . in the rain.

The speaker phone went dead, and I followed suit.

My two colleagues seemed to have recovered from their strokes. Amanda started sputtering and looked just about ready to detonate when Diane put her hand on Amanda's arm. Fortunately, Diane had left that day's wacky glasses in her office. I'm not sure I could have handled them right then.

"David, I'm surprised at how you handled this," Diane started in a very measured tone. "Why didn't you come to us beforehand? We could have worked through this and avoided all this unpleasantness."

She was very calm. Amanda was not.

"You just screwed us!" she shouted. "We are royally screwed. Crawford thinks we don't know what the hell we're doing. We're screwed. Screwed! Thanks so much!"

Diane touched Amanda's arm again to quell the outburst. They both waited for me.

"I'm so sorry, it wasn't supposed to unfold like that," I explained. "Crawford called in early, just as I was about to tell you. I swear I was just about to tell you."

"David, telling us thirty seconds before the big teleconference is only marginally better than shocking us on the call as you just did," Diane replied. "Why didn't you tell us over the weekend when you got back? Why didn't you fire us both an email from the Vancouver airport so we could have worked on this together?"

"I don't know. I was so conflicted. I knew she was a nonstarter as the winner but her story is so compelling, and she is so compelling that I just couldn't seem to give up the slim chance that I might be able to convince the team to let her go."

"David, she's seventy-fucking-one!" Amanda shouted.

I sat there looking down at the table. Clearly I'd misjudged the situation.

"You weren't there in her cabin for two days or you'd understand. Before you discard the idea once and for all, will you just please consider what we're giving up here. Seriously, think about this," I implored. "This is all about driving media coverage and getting the public swept up again in the space program. So put yourselves in the shoes of the average reporter and the average Canadian. What's going to be more effective? What is going to make it easier for us to achieve our goals? We could find the kind of citizen astronaut Crawford Blake is looking for, young, male, good-looking, carrying a hockey stick in one hand and a hatchet in the other, apparently saying 'about' differently from Americans, and looking like every other astronaut who's blasted into orbit over the last half-century. Quite frankly, when I look out at my own country in the second decade of the new millennium, I don't see too many Canadians like that any more.

"On the other hand, we could send Landon Percival up to the space station. A pilot. A doctor. A woman who lives alone on the shore of the most beautiful mountain lake you've ever seen. A passionate space junkie who was rejected nearly thirty years ago from our first astronaut training program because she was too

old. An amateur engineer who designed and built a friggin'
human centrifuge so she could train herself to withstand the
G-forces of a ride in a rocket. A Canadian who for forty years has
been searching for her father who disappeared on a bush flight
without a trace in the wilds of northern B.C. in 1970. A winner
who represents Canadian seniors – the largest and fastest-growing
demographic in the country. Now you tell me which astronaut
is more likely to captivate a nation."

I could see their wheels turning and hoped they weren't just
spinning. It looked as if Diane was going to say something so I
put my hand up to hold the floor for a minute or two more.

"We are sitting on an extraordinary story here. It's a distinctly
Canadian story about the land, heartbreak, mystery, ingenuity,
quiet perseverance, courage, and redemption. Up against Landon
Percival and her amazing journey in life, Eugene Crank or whatever his name is, will pale to transparency. He will just disappear. Frankly, Captain America would have trouble capturing
the public's attention with Landon on board. Consider what we
have here. It's pure gold. It's a one-in-a-million story, and we're
going to turn our back on it because she's seventy-one, not thirty-
one? It's just not right."

Again, Diane opened her mouth to say something. Amanda
looked deep in thought, which was a step up from deep in rage
where she'd been a few minutes earlier.

Again, I raised my hand for the final push.

"Almost done," I explained. "Diane, on my first day here, you told me to tell the truth and do the right thing. Well, I think our client, NASA – not Crawford Blake, but NASA – deserves the advice they need to hear, not the advice they may wish to hear, or the advice Crawford wants them to hear. Landon Percival won the contest. She's the legitimate winner. And when Canadians hear her story, their eyes will be glued to their televisions and computer screens from liftoff to landing. And through it all, they will be proud to be Canadian. Besides, I don't think Emily Hatch will even let us pick another winner. If she catches even the faintest whiff of impropriety, she'll shut us down, fast."

Okay, I was done. There was nothing more to say. In fact, I'd probably overdone it but I figured if I was going down, I wanted a fire and an explosion when I hit the ground.

Neither Diane nor Amanda spoke. Diane was nodding her head almost imperceptibly. Amanda was looking at some point well beyond the walls of the boardroom.

My BlackBerry sitting on the table buzzed with a text. On instinct, my eyes went to the screen. It was from Lauren.

"you'd better come home now. and i mean right now."

I grabbed my BB.

"I'm really sorry but I've got a bit of a family emergency. I really have to go now. It's my mother. I really have to go. Sorry . . ."

I was out the door before either of them could say a word.

Her room was dim when I arrived. A few candles burned and one small lamp gave the scene a warm, even comforting, feel. Lauren was seated on the bed holding Mom's hand. She'd been crying, and Mom looked far away. This was different. Lauren held out her other hand towards me when I entered. I took it and sat in the chair pulled up tight to the side of the bed.

"Mom, he's here now. David is here," Lauren said quietly, leaning in close to Mom.

With what looked like a titanic struggle, her eyelids vibrated, then fluttered open. Her eyes were alive and she managed a faint and fleeting smile.

"I'm here, Mom. I'm here. I'm sorry, I've been out of town." I felt terrible for not coming over the previous day, but I had still been jet-lagged from my trip to B.C., not to mention overwhelmed by the challenge Landon had dropped in my lap.

Her grip on my hand was light, as if holding a baby bird. She looked at Lauren as tears gathered in her eyes.

"Thank you," Mom managed, but just barely.

"Mom, don't talk," Lauren said, not quite cloaking the alarm in her voice. "We're both here."

Mom kept looking at her and managed two more words.

"Be kind."

Hearing Mom utter those special words that she and Lauren had shared for so many years pushed me over the edge. It actually felt good not to try to hold it in any longer. Then Mom looked at me and I knew what was coming. She opened her mouth but seemed not to have the breath to push out the words, even in a whisper. She let go of my hand, moved her index finger with care to her temple while staring at me, then dropped her hand to her heart, signing our own special phrase. I took her hand again.

"I will, Mom. I promise."

She almost looked relieved. She closed her eyes and lay very still.

Lauren and I sat with her, still holding hands, for the next two hours as her breathing became ever more shallow. At the end, there were long stretches of silence between very short breaths. And then, there were no more breaths at all. They just stopped. I took my sister in my arms and held her, rocking slightly as she cried, but not for too long. We'd both known the path Mom was on, we just were never quite sure how much farther she had to go. Now we knew.

I led Lauren downstairs to the kitchen and poured her a glass of Shiraz – a big glass. I called the funeral home. I felt calm and a little detached, and wondered if the emotion of it all would come crashing down on me in the coming days. Perhaps, but I didn't think so. I knew and accepted what had just happened. It was terribly sad, but there seemed to be no denial in me.

Two young women from the funeral home arrived about forty-five minutes later with an elderly doctor in tow to certify the obvious. They worked quietly, quickly, and with great reverence for the occasion. Lauren and I stayed in the kitchen. I just didn't want to see them carry her to the discreet grey station wagon parked in the driveway. I wanted my final memory of Mom to be of the three of us upstairs. Lauren agreed.

"I'm so sorry for your loss," the more senior woman from the funeral home said in the front hall half an hour later. The doctor had, apparently, already departed. "We're finished now and will leave you. If there's anything we can do to make this easier, please just let us know. Foster Davidson is expecting your call to arrange a planning meeting for your mother's service and the final arrangements. Here is his card, and this is your copy of the death certificate."

She pressed the business card and piece of paper into my hand.

"Thank you," I said. "We very much appreciate how quickly and efficiently you've handled this. I'll call Foster tomorrow."

I found Lauren upstairs changing the sheets on Mom's bed and tidying up. There was still a bookmarked paperback on the bedside table that Mom had been reading earlier in the week in those few remaining intervals of lucidity. The final decline had been swift and mercifully free of pain. With this wretched disease, there's not much to give thanks for, but a quick and painless end counts.

By the time we were alone in the house, it was early evening. We ordered Chinese food and made phone calls to family members while we waited for our order to be delivered. Everyone said the right things on the calls. There would be no funeral. Mom didn't want one. She would be cremated according to her wishes, with her ashes to be scattered at the family cottage on Georgian

Bay. We'd have the visitation at the funeral home Wednesday evening and Lauren and I would head up north on Thursday.

It was so strange opening the door to receive our Chinese food delivery and make small talk with the young driver as if everything were normal. It was an incredibly powerful and significant moment in our lives, but just another delivery for him. I was shocked to discover that I was ravenous. Lauren dug in as if she hadn't eaten in days. Perhaps she hadn't. We finished the calls to family and then wrote and submitted the obituary to the *Globe and Mail* and *Toronto Star*. It occurred to me that all of these logistical demands were in fact very helpful in keeping us going. There were responsibilities to fulfil, jobs to do, people to call, arrangements to make. It's all part of the therapy.

Lauren and I collapsed on the couch at about 10:00 p.m. and ordered up a movie. It was a forgettable buddy cop comedy that wasn't particularly funny. Yet we laughed hysterically at the lame one-liners, over-acted set pieces, and contrived pratfalls. It was just what we seemed to need.

I slept in the guest bedroom, with Lauren in her room next door. Neither she nor I wanted to be on our own that night. Just before I crawled between the sheets, I emailed Diane and Amanda to explain my situation. I told them I expected to be out of commission until the following Monday. I noted that Emily Hatch was on vacation this week anyway, making the drawing of another contest winner difficult. I suggested we hold off until Emily returned to ensure the integrity of the second draw. I wanted to buy some time. I didn't even bother looking at any emails that night. I turned off my BlackBerry, turned off my bedside lamp, and almost immediately fell into a deep and dreamless sleep closely approximating a coma.

CHAPTER 9

At 2:00 the next afternoon, Lauren and I were in the basement of the funeral home seated at a small board table in the middle of what the sign above the door indicated was The Showroom. Until then, I really had no idea funeral homes had showrooms, but they do. Luxurious and very comfortable-looking caskets were angled artfully from the walls with descriptive feature sheets displayed in Plexiglas stands next to each. It was not unlike looking at expensive cars at the Toronto International Auto Show, but "plush interior" had a slightly different connotation in the funeral home setting.

A very helpful and sensitive Foster Davidson, dressed in a dark grey pinstriped suit, met us in the showroom. Take the classic image of a funeral director, tall, angular, sombre, morose, then amp the stereotype to well beyond caricature, and you've got Foster Davidson. All that was missing were black tails and a very tall stovepipe hat. We were there to make the "final arrangements" and tie down the details for the visitation the next day. Despite Foster's informative twenty-minute dissertation on the proud history, spiritual intimacy, and religious legitimacy of the open casket visitation, Mom had always thought it was creepy to have the body present, particularly with the lid propped open. So her wish was to be cremated right away, but to invite friends and family to pay their respects if they wanted to in one of the funeral home's lovely reception rooms. She also did not want her ashes resting peacefully in some over-the-top rococo urn, positioned on an ornate plinth, surrounded by the bereaved in the middle of the visitation room. She thought that would be even stranger than the open casket, or what she used to refer to as the "convertible coffin with the top down."

"Now let me go and get a selection of our most popular urns for you to consider," Mr. Davidson proposed. "You'll want to know about the features of each model, and of course, the cost. If you'll excuse me, I'll be back in a moment."

He was out the door before we could stop him.

There was something so surreal about calmly comparing funeral product accessories and options as if you were choosing pizza toppings or a set of kitchen knives. I just couldn't restrain myself. At least I waited until Foster Davidson had left the showroom before I turned to my puffy-eyed and fragile sister. I unleashed my very best radio voice and made it up as I went along.

UP AND DOWN

"Ladies and gentlemen, I give you the URNSTAR 2000, the very latest in advanced innovative ash receptacle design. Thanks to the power of secure-lock technology, you can say good bye to those embarrassing ash-cloud moments when inferior lids pop off without warning. But wait, there's more! Lower-priced urns are slippery to the touch. But you'll never drop your loved one in the URNSTAR 2000 with our leading-edge super-grip adhesive surface. You won't want to put this urn down. And you may not be able to. It comes in a variety of soothing colours and is so strong, it is rated to withstand baseball bats and selected small arms fire. So you and your loved one can rest easy. That's the URNSTAR 2000. Our operators are standing by . . ."

I started to lose it towards the end. Lauren looked perplexed for the first two sentences of my little improvised routine, but her resolve eventually crumbled and her face collapsed. Hyenas would have been intimidated by our outburst. We laughed hysterically, loud and long. At one point we were both doubled over, our heads near our knees. It just kept coming, wave after wave. I had thought we had no tears left. Wrong. Our eyes were streaming. Foster Davidson came running, probably ready to call for straitjackets and a padded van. He arrived back in the showroom to find Lauren and me with our heads lying flat on the cool surface of the board table, looking at one another with our arms splayed out to the sides. By then, we were in that satisfying transition from frenzied guffaws to unbridled chortles, with quiet giggles soon to come.

My breathing was almost back to normal, but my throat was a little sore from the workout.

It was one of the few times in my life when my habit of resorting to humour to avoid the serious really seemed to work. It felt like a turning point in our grieving process. It was just such a release. What I'd said wasn't nearly funny enough to warrant our crazed reactions. Clearly, more was at play. It was as if all of the tension and heartache of the last six months, particularly for Lauren, had been released in one massive burst of emotion. I know Mom would have howled along with us. Perhaps she did.

We calmed down enough to assure Mr. Davidson of our mental stability, though he looked wary for the remainder of our meeting. Fifteen minutes later, we'd made all the decisions. It wasn't that difficult. Because we were going to scatter Mom's ashes at the family cottage, we decided against choosing an urn at all. That was probably a wise decision. I doubt we could have handled the selection process without reprising our earlier hysterics.

My BlackBerry chirped as we stepped out of the funeral home. I had a look at the screen and saw that it was Amanda calling. I raised my index finger to Lauren and stepped away to take it.

"Hi, Amanda."

"Hi, David. I'm so sorry about your mother. Are you okay?"

"Thank you. We're hanging in there. It wasn't unexpected. We just didn't know when. In the end, it happened quite quickly, which was probably not a bad thing."

"My mother died two years ago and I'm not over it yet," Amanda confessed. "I'm not sure I ever will be. I think it's why I'm such a bitch sometimes."

"I'm sorry. I didn't know. And you are not a bitch," I assured her, adding "very often" inside my head.

"Well, I was a bitch yesterday. Sorry about that. Even though you should have brought us into it earlier, you made a pretty strong case for Grandma Percival. But I still don't think it will fly."

"Neither do I," I sighed.

"Well, I won't keep you. I know you have other more important matters on your mind," she said. "I just wanted to let you know I was thinking of you. We'll hold the fort till you get back. Don't give all this stuff at the office a second thought. What you're doing is the really important part of our lives."

"Thanks, Amanda. I appreciate it. I'll be with my sister up north on Thursday and probably Friday, but I plan to be back in the office on Monday. I know we've got a lot to do."

I hung up a few minutes later, struck by this softer side of Amanda.

We made it through the visitation the next day, though my legs and back were tired from standing in the same place for three hours. Lauren and I had bought some black foam core at a local art supply store and spent the previous night wading through boxes of family photos. We found about a dozen great shots of Mom and mounted them on the black board in vague chronological order. Foster Davidson supplied the easel, and family and friends crowded around the display.

It's odd. You expect family and friends to attend. That's what family and friends do when someone passes away. What had more impact on me were the visitors I had not expected. Silvio Cartucci was there. He ran the little fruit market my mom went to every week for most of her adult life. He was more choked up than almost anyone else. I hugged him and so did Lauren. Towards the end of the visitation, Diane, Amanda, and several other colleagues from TK arrived en masse. Some of them barely knew me, yet still they seemed to want to be there. That meant a lot to me, as did the unexpected hug from Amanda.

———

We drove to the cottage the following morning. It was a gorgeous day with not a cloud in the sky. Lauren is not really a cottage person, so her plan was to return to Toronto that night. I'm certainly not a cottage person either, yet I felt I needed a day or so up there to clear my head a bit. So we drove separately, Lauren in her Honda Civic, and I in Mom's Ford Fusion. We hadn't yet decided what we were going to do with the Ford, but until we did, I would drive it. I could see Lauren two cars ahead on Highway 400 as we headed north to Georgian Bay. Next to me on the passenger seat was a carefully sealed cardboard box from the funeral home. It was not nearly as secure, fancy, or fashionable as the fictitious URNSTAR 2000 might have been, but it would certainly make it safely to the cottage.

My mother had spent almost every summer of her life at this cottage. She loved it here. It was that simple. The cottage had been passed down through her family from one generation to the next. As an only child, our mother had bequeathed it to us. I can't really explain why, but Lauren and I had never really taken to the cottage life, so when we became old enough to choose, we tended not to spend too many weekends there. Many of my friends thought I was crazy. Maybe I was, but I'm just not really the outdoorsy type. My trip to Cigar Lake – specifically, my unscheduled meeting with an aging Hector, and my time in the outhouse – reaffirmed my big-city tendencies.

When we arrived, it took us a little while to select the ideal spot. We didn't want her final resting place to be right next to any of the paths criss-crossing the property, but rather tucked away on its own. When we found the place, it was an easy call. We decided to scatter her ashes at the base of a beautiful, large white pine about twenty yards up from the shore, in a secluded and peaceful corner of our lot. It was perfect. Lauren cried quietly as I gently emptied the box onto a thick carpet of brown pine needles. I held her hand, and we stood there for a few minutes in silence before heading back up to the cottage. We poured ourselves a drink and then sat on the deck overlooking the water. The prevailing west wind rippled the waves as the sun streamed through the pines and dappled the light all around our feet. Because it was only Thursday, there were not many boats on the bay. We shared a sense of finality now that the last official funereal act was behind us. Lauren dozed in the sun. I just sat there feeling warm, sad, emotionally spent, yet at the same time strangely renewed and invigorated. I couldn't quite understand why.

Late in the afternoon, Lauren pulled out of the driveway for the two-hour journey home. She convinced me that she was fine on her own, though I offered to come home then too. It didn't feel quite right, letting her leave on her own. But she insisted I stay if I wanted to. For some reason I did. After she'd pulled away, I followed the path back down to the deck and dropped into my chair. A loon surfaced just off the dock, quite close. I'd forgotten how big mature loons can be. It paddled around for a time, then ducked again. Because of the angle of the sun and how close the loon was to the shore, I could see it racing like a torpedo beneath the water until it faded from view to the east. I waited to see if it would surface nearby, but I never saw it again.

I'd been replaying my mother's last few hours in my mind when I reached my decision. There was no agonizing, no tortured deliberations, no equivocation. I just seemed to arrive there knowing what I needed to do, as if it were utterly self-evident. I've seldom felt such certainty. Although it seemed I'd just made the call in that instant while sitting on the deck watching a lone loon, I realized in hindsight that the process had actually begun on my mother's final night of life when she looked into my eyes while touching her temple, and then her heart.

I said it aloud, just to hear the words amidst the trees, the wind, the water, perhaps to make them real.

"*Use your head, but follow your heart.*" I said it twice more aloud.

That's what she couldn't say that night, yet still managed to convey with crystal clarity.

Sitting there on the shore of Georgian Bay, I knew. I knew exactly what I had to do. It might cost me my job, my career, and my reputation, but following your heart doesn't really make allowances for such paltry concerns. I turned my plan over in my head for the next hour to make sure it all fitted together. Then I walked back up to the main cabin and reached for the phone. She answered on the fifth ring.

"Landon, it's David. David Stewart."

"Hello, Mr. Stewart. Are you missing Hector and me?" she asked.

"I truly am. And I keep forgetting to flush these newfangled toilets we've got here in the big city."

"So what glad tidings do you bring? They better not have dumped me. I'm a handful when I'm cornered and angry!"

"Well, NASA doesn't actually know about you yet, but my ultimate boss, Crawford Blake, the guy who runs the entire program for our firm in Washington, certainly isn't your biggest fan. If it were up to him – and, by the way, he thinks it is up to him – we'd be picking another winner immediately. He doesn't seem to see any value whatsoever in a more, um, mature and experienced candidate, like you."

"I know the type. And what do *you* think, Mr. Stewart?"

"I think Crawford Blake is a jackass. And that's why I'm calling. I want to freelance this on the sly to keep you in the game a little longer."

"I don't really know what you're driving at, but I like the sound of it," she replied. "What's the plan?"

"It's quite simple. Under deep cover, we're going make it very difficult for NASA to reject you."

"But NASA doesn't even know I exist."

"Not yet, they don't. But if we can figure out how to float it, they will soon," I explained. "We have to get this story into the media without any fingerprints, yours or mine, anywhere near it. If we can just start that ball rolling, the rest will happen on its own."

We talked for a few more minutes as we brainstormed ideas. This was my world, so Landon didn't say very much. But it was helpful just having her on the end of the phone as I proposed and then rejected ways to leak the story while still protecting us. It was still possible that Emily "By-the-Book" Hatch would insist that Landon be given her rightful chance. But NASA could still reject her almost immediately. We batted around a few ways to get the story out to the media, but none of them seemed to be quite right. There was always a flaw somewhere that led right back to me. My mind had been focusing on the Ottawa and Toronto media markets. Hearing Landon's voice on the phone suddenly reminded me that we did actually have reporters stationed in other parts of the country. Yes, there it was.

"Okay, we're getting there now," I started. "When I worked on Parliament Hill, I had a great relationship with Sarah Nesbitt, the science reporter at the *Vancouver Sun*. I don't know why I didn't think of her before. I think the geography, her beat, and the fact that I actually know her, makes her the right candidate for us. If we bring her into this, I'm pretty sure she'd protect me. But we still have to find a plausible way for the story to have come to her without implicating either of us."

For the first time since the call started, there was silence on the line. A minute passed as we thought.

"Wait," Landon said. "You actually spoke to Chatter Haney in Mackenzie, didn't you? Just before we met on the dock, right?"

The name rang a bell. I thought back to my arrival on the shores of Williston Lake and remembered the talkative guy at the charter company who was supposed to have flown me to Cigar Lake.

"I'd forgotten his name until you just mentioned it, but yeah, I spoke to that guy."

"Did you introduce yourself to him, or ever give him your name?"

"Of course. I'd booked his plane and chauffeur to fly me to your place. He had my name and Visa card number."

"Hmmmm. Was it your personal credit card or a company Visa?"

"It was a Turner King Visa," I noted. "I try not to use my own card for business if I can avoid it. Why?"

"Well, then there's our ticket," she said, as if we'd solved world hunger.

"I don't follow," I replied, trying to catch up.

"Why do you think they call him *Chatter* Haney?" Landon asked. "You can't keep his mouth shut with a pair of Vise-Grips."

And so it was done. The plan came together easily after the "Chatter" breakthrough. We mapped it all out, refining it as we continued talking. We played out various twists and turns the plan could take and covered off contingencies for them all that still left us safe and beyond implication. It took about forty-five minutes before I was satisfied we had it right. We reviewed our plan and preparations in great detail along with our respective to-do lists, then Landon hung up to make an important call of her own.

You could never anticipate everything, but I felt comfortable we had our bases (and not to put too fine a point on it, our asses) covered. It all hinged on Chatter Haney and whether my relationship with Sarah Nesbitt was actually as strong as I thought it was. If I'd misread it, we might be in trouble. But I considered it a calculated gamble worth taking. Twenty minutes later, the cottage phone rang.

"Hello," I said, figuring it was Landon but not certain. We didn't have caller ID on the cottage phone. In fact, we still had the original rotary dial from the 1950s. We had only upgraded it from a party line a few years before.

"'One might have thought already that God's curse hung heavy over a degenerate world,'" the voice said in a low, almost furtive tone, and a bad English accent. The line was familiar but I couldn't place it.

"Landon?"

"No, it's Maxwell Smart," Landon replied, her words marinated in sarcasm. "Who did you think it would be?"

"Well, the traditional telephone greeting is a little less cryptic than yours was."

"I was just trying to get into the spirit of things. Spies always greet one another with a coded phrase when they're on an operation."

"Yes, but it's helpful if the co-conspirator is in on it, too."

"Well, I just thought you'd know how to complete that particular line," she said, disappointed.

"I know it's from a Holmes story, but I just can't place it."

"Well, I confess, I'm a little surprised. I had thought you were quite the Sherlockian."

"All right, all right, which story?"

"It's the first half of the second sentence from 'His Last Bow.' Among the most important and studied stories in the canon, wouldn't you agree?"

"I'm bigger fan of the earlier stories," I admitted. "So, can you actually recite the whole line?"

"Of course," she said before switching back into her English accent. "'One might have thought already that God's curse hung heavy over a degenerate world, for there was an awesome hush and a feeling of vague expectancy in the sultry and stagnant air.'"

"He could certainly turn a phrase," I said. "How did your big talk go?"

"Just spoke to the man, and he's on board."

"If he's such a big talker, how do you know he won't give us up if this starts to go bad?"

"Don't worry your big-city head about that. Chatter will never squeal on us," Landon said. "I saved his young son's life four years ago. The man likes to talk, I grant you that, but he'd go to jail before he'd turn me in. We have a green light."

"Does he fully understand how critical his role is and exactly what he can and cannot say?"

"Mr. Stewart, give me some credit," she complained. "I spent twenty minutes on the phone with him. We actually did a rehearsal. That was my idea. Don't worry, he gets it. We are Go."

We tied up a few more loose ends and figured out our contact schedule and our next steps. The conversation was winding down when Landon piped up once more.

"So, Mr. Stewart, I'm grateful for your help, but I'm also curious. Why are you sticking your tender foot so close to a bear trap on my account?"

I wasn't expecting that. I glanced out the window and could just see that big white pine down near the water in that secluded and peaceful corner of our lot. Its branches lifted and settled in the gentle breeze.

"Well, I guess it's become clearer to me in the last few days since I've come back, but it's really not that complicated. I truly believe it's in our client's interest. You won the contest. You have a great story. You *are* a great story. And it helps that sending you up is so obviously the right thing to do," I said. "That's the heart of it."

After we hung up, I sat in silence in the cottage rehearsing the next move in my mind. The call would either be a solid first step down the right path or solid first step into the yawning jaws of that leg-snapping steel bear trap, which I'd then have to drag behind me all the way to the unemployment office.

––––––––––––

Over the next hour, I dialled four times, being sent to voice mail on each attempt. Four times I hung up before the beep. I waited another twenty minutes and called a fifth time.

"Sarah Nesbitt."

"Sarah, it's a voice from your past," I said in greeting. "It's David Stewart."

"David Stewart. Great to hear from you, man. And your timing is impeccable," she replied. "You were about to be a voice from my present. So you've just saved me a call."

"Really? What's up?"

"I was just speaking to your former minister's office about a piece we're doing on the Citizen Astronaut contest," she explained. "You were next on my call list."

"So you must know I'm at Turner King now?" I asked.

"David, I'm a reporter. I try to stay abreast of developments on my beat. It's kind of what reporters do. I've done two stories on the contest already. Your name is at the bottom of every release, and my reading skills are passable. So, yes, I knew you'd made the move to TK."

It was nice to know she more than remembered me.

"And your successor in the minister's office isn't exactly making life easy for me the way you always did," she continued. "I'm missing you and you're looking better and better in hindsight."

"Sorry to hear that . . . I think," I replied. "But perhaps I can help in another way."

"My notebook is open," she said.

"Well, can you close it for a moment? There are some ground rules that come along with this call. But I'm hoping you'll think they're reasonable under the circumstances."

"Okay, my notebook is now closed. Let me know when I can open it again."

"Strictly hypothetically, if I were to pass along the makings of a sizable story to you and you alone, along with a perfectly logical explanation for how you got it – and not from me – will you keep me out of it?"

"Well, without knowing exactly what we're talking about, it's hard to guarantee anything. But you know I've always been fair to you and you've always played straight with me. I'd say there's a solid chance we can make this work. Does that cut it?" she asked.

"I think I can live with that," I replied. "Okay, you can open your notebook again."

"Actually, that was just a figure of speech. But my computer is turned on and my fingers are poised over the keyboard. What do you have?"

"Sit back, and I'll start from the beginning."

My heart rate spiked as I launched into the tale and officially barrelled past the point of no return. It took me nearly twenty-five minutes to recount the whole story from the time Landon's name was drawn, all the way to my crash-and-burn conference call with Crawford Blake earlier in the week. Relying on my notes, I took my time presenting Landon's extraordinary biography. It would be won or lost there. I could hear Sarah's fingers flying as I spoke. I could also hear her breathing deepen at the poignancy of Hugh Percival's disappearance and his final diary entry. But she never interrupted me while I was speaking, unless you count twice uttering "Holy shit" – once when I reached the part about Landon's 1983 astronaut application, and then again when I described her homebuilt centrifuge. As I listened to my own voice, the story seemed even better and more captivating aloud than when it was simply rattling around in my head. I left out any reference to Landon's sexuality or to her penchant for talking daily to her long-lost father. I also kept to myself her daily naked constitutional dip in Cigar Lake. I moved to wrap up my little speech.

"So the bottom line is, seventy-one-year-old Landon Percival, a doctor, a bush pilot, an amateur astronaut in training, a seeker of the truth about her father's disappearance in 1970, an honest and caring Canadian who's worked hard all her life, is the legitimate winner of the Citizen Astronaut contest for Canada. But she won't be going anywhere, and no one will ever know about her."

I paused to let that sink in for a moment. Sarah didn't let the silence reign for long.

"*Why?* Why won't she be flying?" Sarah asked, a note of urgency in her voice.

"Simply put, Landon Percival just doesn't fit the demographic Turner King was looking for," I explained. "NASA has the final say on all candidates. That's why we haven't publicly announced the winner yet. But the reality is that even suggesting sending a seventy-one-year-old into orbit will likely put NASA's lawyers into orbit. Right now, NASA doesn't even know Landon Percival exists, and they never will if my big boss in D.C. has his way. I was kind of flying solo on this and I'm lucky I still have a job. And I may not for long. I simply wasn't able to come even close to persuading him to bring Landon forward to NASA to let them decide her fate. In fact, we've been given direct orders from Washington to pick another winner early next week – and to legally enforce the contest's strict confidentiality rules to gag Landon Percival so no one will ever know about her."

I stopped talking. About thirty seconds later, I heard her fingers slow and then stop on her keyboard.

"Wow. That is one amazing story, David, and I want it. But I'm feeling a little handcuffed here when it comes to protecting you. The people who really count will know that you're the only possible source for this. How am I supposed to use all this without directly tying you to it?" she asked.

Bingo. I was ready for this one.

"Okay. I'm glad you're with me. Here's how it's going to play out. You're going to get a phone call from a guy named Chatter Haney who runs a little one-plane charter outfit in Mackenzie, B.C. In fact, you may already have a message waiting from him. Talk to him. He's known around town for being very curious and having very loose lips. He figured all this out on his own. I had chartered his Cessna to take me from Mackenzie to Cigar Lake to meet Landon. He had my name and my company's name and credit card number. They don't get too many visitors to Mackenzie so my city-slicker ways caught his attention. Then I was professionally evasive when he asked me why I needed to get out to Cigar Lake. So as soon as I left, Chatter Haney headed straight to Google. In ten minutes he had my story figured out. He knew I had to be there to vet the contest winner. Our own news release a few days before pretty well laid out the process in black and white. It never occurred to me to use a pseudonym or cover my tracks on the trip and no one at TK told me to. In hindsight, it probably would have been a good idea. So Chatter Haney called up the only resident of Cigar Lake he figured would have entered the contest, one Landon Percival. Of course, Landon refused even to acknowledge that she knew what he was talking about. But her unusual reticence about it all cemented his belief that Landon Percival was in fact the Canadian winner of the Citizen Astronaut contest. So Chatter decided to contact you, Sarah. And the rest you did on your own. Does that sound about right?"

I waited.

"And you've told no one else about this and won't pitch this to any other outlet?" she asked.

"Nope, and I won't, unless you decide you can't go with this. My goal is to make it very, very difficult for NASA to say no to Landon Percival. So if you tell me you can't use this, I'll move to the next name on my list because time is short."

"And who is next on your list?"

"I'd really rather not say."

I had no one else on my list, but I figured I had the hook well-anchored. I waited for a few seconds.

"Okay, I want it. But this is big, so I'm going to have to get it out fast. If I've got it, I want the *Sun* to break it, not just have the deepest coverage. I won't make the weekend edition, which is a shame, but Monday for sure."

Yes. *Yes!*

"Monday works, Sarah, but to be clear, Tuesday is just too late. I don't want us to have to pick another winner, and the plan is to do that on Monday."

"I can't promise anything, David, but Monday is my target."

"Of course, you'll want to call Landon after speaking with Chatter, but I can tell you right now that you'll get nothing from her, which I know you'll dutifully report in the story. She's bound to silence and it would be nice if she were seen to be honouring her obligations. Obviously, I can't say anything on the record. I suggest reporting that calls to me were not returned. I'll email you the copious notes I took while at Cigar Lake, but please save them to a flash drive and then erase my email. Also, you should leave a message for me at Turner King, not just on my own voice mail, but also with the receptionist, including why you were trying to reach me. It would be helpful if you could also send me an email asking about all of this. I won't respond, just as you might expect NASA's PR flak to behave in this situation. Does that work for you?"

A few minutes later, I said goodbye to Sarah and hung up. Then, before I lost my nerve, I emailed all my notes to her along with Landon's cellphone number using my personal Gmail account. Then I spent ten minutes hyperventilating into a paper bag I found in the kitchen. One minute I was congratulating myself on a beautifully conceived plan, executed to perfection. The next, I was deciding between throwing myself off the roof of the cottage onto the rocks below and running myself over with our old 75-horse Mercury outboard. Then I calmed down. The deed was done and I really had no choice now but to strap in for the ride in the hopes that it would eventually allow Landon Percival to strap in for her ultimate ride. I reached for the phone again when my breathing returned to normal.

"'To Sherlock Holmes, she would always be . . .'" I let my voice trail off.

"'*The* woman,'" Landon snapped. "Come on, Mr. Stewart. That was lame. At least pick a more obscure reference than that."

"What, you don't like 'A Scandal in Bohemia'?"

"Of course I do. Who doesn't? But it's just so, so obvious," she sighed.

I'd actually been quite pleased with it. She was clearly better schooled in the Sherlockian arts than I.

"Anyway, more importantly, the battle is joined," I said with some drama. "You'll soon be getting a call from a Sarah Nesbitt from the *Vancouver Sun*. She's the science reporter and she will already have spoken to Chatter Haney. Just make sure you stick to the plan and don't tell Sarah anything other than 'I don't know what you're talking about.' She'll ask you if you entered the contest. Just say it's none of her business whether you entered. Then she'll ask you if I visited you last week. Again, it's none of her business. Clear?"

"I've got it. This is more excitement than I've had since the centrifuge seat broke off the boom in mid-spin a few years back."

I decided not to ask about that incident.

"Does Chatter Haney fully understand what he can and cannot say?"

"I schooled him on your instructions to the letter and he's on board. He owes me big. Don't worry about him," Landon said.

"Then I guess you're right. Our little plan has a green light."

"I guess it does. And Mr. Stewart?"

"Yes, Landon."

"I'm in your debt for this. I know it's still a long shot. And I know you've put yourself at considerable risk. Thank you."

———

Finally, as the sun was dipping below the trees to the west, I sat at the dining table with my laptop and plugged in my "rocket stick" to give me Internet access. I started by creating a new Gmail address using an unrecognizable name. I then used it to open a new Facebook account and began building a new Facebook fan page entitled "Send Landon Percival to Space." I typed in a brief summary of Landon's story, using simple but powerful language. I provided absolutely no inside information that was not already or soon would be in the public domain. I found and uploaded a photo of the space shuttle with the Canadarm prominently featured as the profile picture. The call to action was for all visitors to hit the Like button and leave supportive comments. I saved the new Facebook fan page but without yet making it live. I wanted to be ready when Sarah's story detonated, I hoped, on Monday.

That night, I kept the paper bag an arm's length away on my bedside table. I used it twice before morning.

CHAPTER 10

Sarah's email arrived just after midnight, Sunday. I'd just returned to my condo after spending the evening with Lauren. I, at least, had the Landon distraction to keep my mind occupied, but I was worried that Lauren might be wallowing. She seemed in reasonable spirits, however, considering the loss of our mother six days ago. But I learned that Lauren did have a distraction of her own. One of the larger downtown library branches had just invited her to apply for a relatively senior position. She decided it was time to get out of the house a bit more and return to full-time gainful employment. She applied. Interviews were already scheduled for the coming week. Knowing for the last six months that Mom's time was limited had allowed Lauren to ease into this new reality gradually. In hindsight, I guess we'd both started the grieving process some time ago.

I clicked on Sarah's email. There was a very brief message with a lonely little hyperlink at the end.

"Here's the piece," Sarah wrote. "It will run as the lead on the front page with a very eye-catching *Sun Exclusive!* banner stretched above the masthead. You and Landon are in the clear. Thanks so much for this."

Wow. Front page. With my heart pounding and my stomach knotted, I clicked on the link. The freshly posted story materialized on the home page of the *Vancouver Sun's* website. The headline summed it up, which, after all, is what headlines are supposed to do.

NASA MAY REJECT ELDERLY ASTRONAUT

The print edition with its explosive front-page story was due to hit the streets in a matter of hours. It was happening. It was really happening. And I was skating on very thin ice, naked, and without water wings. When the plan had come to me, I'd of course played it out in my mind to test it. But I never really thought it might unfold as I'd imagined it.

It couldn't have been a better story if I'd written it myself, which of course I'd offered to do for her. Sarah had felt that passing on the information was wonderful, but that ghost writing the piece for her might just be a bit much for her editor to swallow. I reluctantly agreed. But I liked what she'd made of it. TK's role in the Citizen Astronaut contest, my mysterious trip to Cigar Lake, Landon's contest victory and her amazing life story, the unexplained 1970 disappearance of her father, Hugh Percival, her rejection from the astronaut program in '83, even her home-built centrifuge, it was all there in vivid Technicolor. Initially, I wasn't thrilled with seeing my name in print, but the story would have been conspicuously incomplete without it. In fact, I figured including me in the story actually distanced me from the act of planting it. Yes, Sarah Nesbitt had covered it all, including my posterior. She had hermetically sealed Landon and me in an airtight chamber of denial. She even described, in some detail, just how the loquacious Chatter Haney had brought the story to her, confirming more than once that Landon had not been prepared to share any information or cooperate in any way. I thought Sarah made Landon's reticence sound almost noble. The story also reported that several interview requests sent to me had gone unanswered. Nice.

There were two photos in the story, neither one I'd seen before. The first showed a much younger and not unattractive Landon. The frame of the shot cut out the person obviously standing next to her. It looked like it was taken in an urban setting, probably Vancouver, in the 1960s. The second showed a more recent shot of Landon standing on one pontoon of her beloved Beaver, probably at the dock in Mackenzie as the photo credit read *Mackenzie Times*. Towards the end of the piece, Sarah speculated that NASA would almost certainly reject Landon because of her age, "thus shutting down one senior citizen's dream and denying the world a happy ending to one of the most extraordinary, but until now, unknown stories of our time." I made a mental note to shower

Sarah Nesbitt with rose petals or at least take her out for dinner the next time I was in Vancouver. But it was still early days. In fact, this had really only just begun.

I glanced at the clock, decided it was still early enough in B.C., and called Landon to read her the online story.

"Well, that certainly sounds like a good start, doesn't it?" Landon said calmly when I'd finished reading the article.

"Good start? Sarah has hit it out of the park for us. We are now irrevocably in this thing for the duration."

"Did she have to go on so much about my father and tell everyone that I'm still looking for him? It feels a little odd having that out there and kind of makes me sound a little eccentric."

"Landon, first of all, the mystery of your father's disappearance is one of the most poignant and compelling dimensions of your story. I'm not surprised in the least that it earned a prominent place in her piece. Secondly, searching for a lost father does not make you eccentric. It just makes you a daughter," I countered. "On the other hand, building and 'flying' a propeller-driven centrifuge in a remote corner of a B.C. forest, well, I admit that might take us into the eccentric zone. But it's part of your charm, and it certainly strengthens the amateur astronaut angle of your story."

"So what happens now?" she asked.

"Well, if the story is as big as I think it might be, you'll likely have a few visitors in the coming days, and some of them will be toting video cameras."

"So I just stick to my guns and send them packing, right?"

"Right. But before you unleash Hector on them, let's make sure they get some good shots of you on the dock, working on the Beaver, and generally looking intrepid. Shooting you taking off from the lake would make for some great footage, too. And no skinny-dipping until every last reporter has gone," I insisted.

"Do I let them wander around and take any shots of the centrifuge?" Landon asked.

"I don't think so. I don't think I'd even let them off the dock to use the outhouse. Okay – maybe that. But I don't want you to be seen to be cooperating in any way with the reporters," I said. "Don't worry, I have a plan for getting the word out about the centrifuge. The media will have plenty of video to tell that part of your story."

———

I didn't sleep much that night. It was hard to put my mind at rest when it kept conjuring up ever more creative ways Crawford Blake might employ to separate my testicles from their rightful place of residence. So I headed into the office early. But not early enough. A note on my chair in my palatial cubicle told me to come to Amanda's office as soon as I arrived. It was written in big bold capital letters. In case the urgency might be lost on me, there were nine exclamation marks punctuating the point. Message received.

When I arrived in her office at 7:15, Amanda and Diane were waiting for me. Strangely, Amanda sat next to Diane in the two guest chairs parked in front of her own desk. Only Amanda's feet reached to the floor. When I saw the look on her face, I stopped worrying about what Crawford Blake was going to do to me.

"Sit!" they ordered in unison, though in different keys, and pointed me into Amanda's high-backed leather desk chair.

I sat. Diane started.

"David, first of all, we're all very sorry about your mother and we hope you're okay," Diane said as she leaned over and put her hand on my wrist. "Second, and more pressing right now, we are in such deep shit at this very moment that the three of us may never be found."

"What have I missed?" I said, feigning surprise. "What's happened?"

Amanda tossed a scanned printout of the *Vancouver Sun's* front-page story onto the desk. I grabbed it, scanned the headline, and dutifully doubled over in shock. I thought about upending Amanda's prized chair, hurling it through the plate glass window, and then following it out, but that would have been a bit over the top. Restraint and nuance were the keys to selling this. And they were watching my reaction very carefully. I looked again quickly at the headline.

"What . . . the . . . fuck!" I blurted, then looked up at them. "So sorry. What the hell!"

I stood up as I said it, pushing my chair backwards so it bumped the wall behind me. I read just the lead paragraph of the story and moaned as if the bamboo shoots under my toenails had just been set alight. I rubbed my forehead with my free hand, which I thought was a nice touch.

"Where did this come from? How did this happen?" I shouted, staring at them with eyes wide enough to accommodate a monocle in each. As I raged, I waved the story around my head as if trying to achieve flight. Now, for the *pièce de la résistance.* I threw the article back down, without even having finished it, and then stared them both down, my hands planted on the desk as I leaned towards them.

"Okay, now I'm going to need the complete and unvarnished truth from you both," I said through a clenched jaw. "Were either of you freelancing this story to the *Sun?* Cause I'll be very, very angry if you have. This threatens the whole program and makes us all look incompetent. And why wasn't I informed about this earlier?"

I'd never spoken to them in this tone before. But it was necessary.

"David, of course we didn't throw this to the *Sun.* Why would we do that? Read the rest of the piece. It didn't come from us," Diane replied, with Amanda backing her up with such vigorous head nodding, it gave me a sore neck just watching it.

"We're just as shocked as you are. Read the rest," Amanda urged, pointing to the story that still lay where I'd thrown it.

I calmed down, managed to remember to wheel the chair back under me before dropping back into it, and pretended to read the story as they both sat and watched me. I shook my head a few times, groaned once or twice, and did the forehead-rubbing thing a few more times for good measure. When I thought enough time had passed for me to have read the entire story, I sighed, sat back, and looked up at the ceiling for a moment or two before turning my eyes back to them.

"We've got to get on the blower to Blake and NASA before they find out about this in their morning clips," I suggested. "This story is going to be hot for the next few days at least. It's just the *Sun* today, but by mid-morning, everyone is going to pile on. I bet CTV and CBC will send vidcams out west to track down Landon. This could be huge."

"I already have a call in to Crawford. He's our first priority," Diane replied. "That is, if we all still have jobs by the time we hear from him."

"At least Landon doesn't seem to be behind this," I said with relief. "She's so cut off out there. Besides, she wouldn't begin to know how to orchestrate this."

"No, the story seems to have originated with the guy who was going to fly you in," Amanda said. "Chatter . . . something or other."

Oh, right. I nearly forgot about that part.

"That bastard!" I shouted in rekindled rage. I smashed my fist onto the desk, apparently launching Amanda's pen into the air where it traced a graceful arc and bounced off my head on the way down. I hadn't even noticed it was airborne.

"David, calm down!" Amanda said.

"He screwed me! Nobody told me I should have been using an alias! Shit, shit, shit!"

They'd never seen me this way. *I'd* never seen me this way. Probably because I'd never actually been this way. Then Providence shone, and as if planned and rehearsed, the receptionist noticed me in Amanda's office as she walked past. She stopped and poked her head in, waving a pink message slip in my general direction. She handed it over and slipped back to her post. Serendipity, right on cue.

"It looks like one Sarah Nesbitt from the *Vancouver Sun* was trying to reach me while I was up north scattering my mother's ashes." I held up the message, and then to complete the charade, checked my BlackBerry. "I thought that name was familiar. It seems she emailed me on Friday night but I never opened it. Shit, shit, shit!" I shouted, my fists clenched at my sides, and what I hoped was a kind of crazed serial killer look plastered on my normally quite placid face.

"David, relax! Please." Diane joined the fray. "No one is blaming you for this. But we do have to decide how we're going to handle it, and we haven't much time."

So far, so good. Silence reigned for a moment or two so, I filled it with heavy breathing in my best impression of calming down.

"Maybe we should wait and see how Canadians respond to the story, but I think they'll be in Landon's corner almost immediately. Everyone loves an underdog," I began with brow furrowed. "I don't see how we can go ahead and draw another name when the world knows, or will certainly soon know, that Landon Percival is already our lucky winner. NASA and Turner King would be crucified if she weren't at least given a chance."

I hope I hadn't pushed my luck and moved too quickly to my end-game.

"I fear you're right," Amanda agreed. "I think the only way to divert attention from the fact that we couldn't even protect the identity of the winner will be to announce her fast and focus on what a great Canadian story Landon Percival really represents. Then the *Sun's* big explosive exclusive will turn into a Landon Percival love-in."

"Precisely!" was the word that flashed in my head, though I didn't release it audibly. Instead, I went with something else.

"Hmmm, interesting analysis." I cupped my chin in my right hand, creating what I hoped were cavernous deep-thinking lines in my forehead. "Yes, I think you might actually be on to something there, Amanda. It might be our best, perhaps our only, option."

Amanda seemed pleased. Diane stared into space as she pondered what came to be known as "Amanda's idea." Then she nodded affirmation, but looked very scared while doing it. Then the whole desk vibrated as if struck by a very targeted earthquake. Diane snatched her BlackBerry from the desk.

"Incoming!" she said as she scanned the small screen. "Okay, we've got a call with Crawford at 11:00," Diane said. She eased herself forward and off the chair for the short drop to the floor. "We'll do it in my office."

She then swept out of the room. And having witnessed it, I can report that it's difficult to sweep out of anywhere when you're not quite five feet tall. But she made it work.

"Okay, thanks, Amanda. I'll see you in Diane's office at 11:00," I said as I sat back down and waited for Amanda to leave too.

"Um, you're actually sitting at my desk," she said.

"Oh, right," I mumbled, leaping back to my feet and moving towards the door. "Sorry."

"David?"

I stopped and turned to her as she settled back down in her own chair. She narrowed her eyes a tad.

"You're not playing us here, are you?"

"What? Amanda, how could you even think that?" I protested. "As far as I can tell, this story broke for two reasons, and two reasons only. Google, and Chatter what's-his-name's loose lips. End of story. Well, I guess I mean beginning of story. That's all it took," I explained, trying not to sound too defensive.

I paused and then continued, lowering and softening my voice for the home stretch.

"Besides, I've just returned from scattering my own mother's ashes. I haven't eaten in three days or looked at my BlackBerry until just now. I've got 150 thank-you notes to write and there's something I can't identify growing on a pizza slice in my fridge. I'm a mess. I only came in to work to get my mind off of the last week. Which reminds me, it really was very kind of you to come to the visitation. It really meant a lot to me."

She smiled so slightly I almost missed it, and then she nodded. I made good my escape. I felt bad about my subterfuge but I didn't know Diane or Amanda well enough to trust them yet. If they knew what I was doing behind the curtain, I wasn't yet convinced they wouldn't just hand me over to Crawford Blake on a silver . . . operating table, my nether region prepped.

———————

While it was risky to fan the flames further from my own very exposed cubicle, I really didn't have a choice, and time was running very short. In the next three hours or so, I did it all from my BlackBerry, not trusting my networked office computer. I hit the Do Not Disturb button on my office phone, but used my shoulder to hold the silent receiver to my ear to discourage drive-by drop-ins. I opened a phony YouTube account and uploaded five minutes of Landon Percival strapped into her homemade human blender. Then, from my newly created and fingerprint-free Gmail account, I sent an anonymous email, including links to the *Sun* story and the YouTube clip, to the Canadian Association of Retired Persons. The aptly named CARP was the leading advocacy group for senior citizens in the country, and when they were on the offensive, well, they could be very offensive, and very effective too. I also activated Landon's Facebook fan page and went ahead and set up an untraceable Twitter account with the handle *@Landon_in_space*. The first tweet pointed to the newly live Facebook fan page and included

Landon's full name. I wanted those searching Twitter to have no difficulty finding her. I re-tweeted my initial tweet a few times, directing it in each instance to the most influential Canadians in the Twitterverse. I sent a second set of tweets that linked to Landon's whirligig YouTube debut. I knew that would get us some traction and kick-start a following.

After three hours hunched over my BlackBerry with my head acutely tilted to clamp the prop-only phone to my ear, my BB was hot and smoking, I had muscle spasms in both thumbs, and my neck was in dire need of acupuncture or at least a cervical collar. But in those three hours, I was able to put the communications infrastructure in place that I hoped just might launch Landon Percival into orbit. And by 10:30 that morning, it was already getting a workout.

I trolled through the Canadian media online and was reminded just how fast big stories spread in this country. All major news media websites, including CBC, CTV, Global, the *Globe and Mail, Ottawa Citizen, Toronto Star,* the Halifax *Chronicle Herald,* and the *Calgary Sun* all carried stories about Canada's rumoured citizen astronaut. It wouldn't be long before the story was picked up south of the border. The YouTube clip, still only three hours old, had already attracted 256 views and the number was growing rapidly as the major media sites discovered it and embedded it directly in their stories. Canadian Press, our leading wire service, ran a story that would surely be picked up in dailies across the country the next morning. The

Facebook page had already registered 213 Likes, and somehow, the @*Landon_in_space* Twitter stream had attracted 164 follow- ers in about 20 minutes. Finally, at five minutes to eleven, I had a quick scan of CanadaNewswire, the site that disseminates news releases electronically to media outlets across the country and around the world. I found what I was looking for. CARP had issued a news release at 10:42 with the following headline:

CARP URGES NASA TO LAUNCH
SENIOR CITIZEN ASTRONAUT

Like a prison-break fugitive, I looked around me to make sure no one had been observing my extracurricular efforts. Then I rose and sauntered out of my cubicle for the call in Diane's office, the next big play.

Amanda was already seated as I dropped into the second guest chair in front of Diane's desk.

"Let me take the lead on this," Diane instructed. "Crawford talks a good game about making TK a flatter organization, but in the end, he's still very conscious of seniority. I think he can only process opposing views if they're delivered by some- one who at least approaches his own rank. I can push back. You can't."

"No problem," I said, without disguising my relief.

Amanda eventually nodded in assent, but wasn't as pleased with the directive. Diane dialled and put the call on the speaker.

"What in the name of all that is fucking holy have you all done up there?" said the voice, leaving pure malevolence hanging in the air. "You all have fucked it up, but good."

"Good morning, Crawford," interjected Diane. "I gather you've seen the *Sun* story."

"How did this happen? I ask that you pick another winner. You all try to argue to have this fucking ancient old biddy climb aboard the shuttle. So I direct you a second time to pick and qualify a new goddamned winner. But you say you can't do it until this week for some lame-ass reason. And then mysteriously, miraculously, seemingly out of no-fucking-where, this story breaks. Now what the fuck am I supposed to think?"

"Crawford, we've known each other a long time. We've always been honest with one another. And I have to say, I'm not thrilled with your tone and what sounds like an accusation on your part that we're somehow not being team players on this and are going our own way. That is not what is happening here. You've obviously read the piece so you know that we had nothing to do with the story. A small-town gossip who knows his way around a search engine put two and two together, fed it to a very good and very enterprising reporter who assembled disparate leads and circumstantial evidence into a wholly accurate story. The only thing that might have prevented this, I repeat, *might* have prevented it, is if David had used a phony name to charter a float plane in remote B.C."

"Then why the hell didn't he?" he demanded.

"Crawford, reality check, please. We're a PR agency, not the CIA. It never occurred to me and I doubt very much if it would have occurred to you. Did your people pull the cloak and dagger routine when vetting the American winner?"

"I handled the American winner personally so that there was no chance of botching it," he said pointedly.

Diane scowled and flipped him the bird, which would have had more impact had we been video conferencing. Amanda was so steamed she was vibrating in her chair, itching to enter the fray. Diane gave her the stop-sign hand. Diane was very good with her hands.

"Crawford, let's focus on what we're going to do now to resolve this. We can do the autopsy on how it happened later. And we do have a recommendation . . ."

"I know exactly how we're going to resolve this!" Crawford shouted into the phone. "You are going to issue a news release dismissing and denouncing the *Sun* story and reiterating that the Canadian winner will be announced by NASA within the week. Then you are going to pick another goddamn winner!"

Diane picked up the phone so we could no longer hear Crawford's tirade.

"Crawford, calm yourself and please listen to reason, for the sake of the client. The *Sun* story is breaking across the country. Unfortunately, we're in a bit of a slow news cycle up here right now, so this is going to go big. All the major news outlets are leading with it online and CP has already put a story on the wire about it. If you check CNN.com, you'll see it there as well. This will not go away just because we pick another winner. We've got to make lemonade here."

She paused again, presumably so Crawford could tear a few more strips off her. She remained calm, holding the phone away from her ear and rolling her eyes.

"Crawford, read the piece again. This woman actually has an amazing story. It's a very Canadian story. We have no doubt that the public is going to be behind this Landon Percival woman one hundred per cent. She's a perfect Canadian citizen astronaut on paper, other than the age factor. She's a doctor, a bush pilot, and she applied to our astronaut program nearly thirty years ago and was rejected as too old. This has all the makings of a Hollywood blockbuster. You couldn't make this stuff up. It's priceless."

She had to stop again to listen.

"Hold on, Crawford, stay with me. Our strong recommendation is to kill all this speculation and controversy and give Canadians what they surely want. We need to have NASA announce that Landon Percival is in fact the Canadian Citizen Astronaut contest winner and will be flying aboard the shuttle if, and only if, she can complete the training program. That's how we turn today's unexpected story into a win for us and a win for NASA."

Diane stopped talking and looked at us. Then she tilted her head a bit.

"Hello? Crawford?"

Then she held the phone away from her ear again.

"Okay, I'm sorry. I thought we'd lost the connection," Diane said. "No, it's fine. You go right ahead and think. I'll wait."

She gave us a hopeful look and then bided her time, tapping the desk, as Crawford apparently mulled over what I thought was the only way to go. Several minutes passed until Diane suddenly sat a little straighter in her chair.

"Yes, we can pull that off overnight. Just gen pop though, right?"

She paused again. Other than the classic Bob Newhart routines, I really hated hearing only one side of a telephone conversation.

"Yes, we can do an online gen pop panel of a thousand Canadians and have you the results mid-afternoon tomorrow. We can make the final call then. Yes, that seems fair."

More silence.

"Crawford, we wouldn't have won this business otherwise. We need him to make it go. And don't forget, NASA asked for him."

She gave me reassuring looks as she parried what was clearly my execution order.

"Look, Crawford, you run D.C., and I'll run Toronto. Okay? He stays."

After the week I'd had, learning that Crawford Blake wanted me toasted barely even registered. I no longer really cared. Frankly, I probably should have been fired and certainly would be if my morning's behind-the-scenes work were ever discovered.

After a few more pleasantries, Diane hung up and then collapsed on her desk, banging her tiny fists on the glass top. Amanda and I were beside ourselves with curiosity.

"Okay, we're not dead yet," Diane reported, lifting her head and pushing herself back into a sitting position. "Crawford hates to reverse himself, but as I've said before, he's not a complete idiot. Despite his anger, I think he was starting to see the logic in our recommendation. But we have to do a quick and dirty overnight poll to prove to him that Canadians are four square behind our girl Landon and that we'd be in for a rough ride if we rejected her. If the numbers are strong enough, I think we just might avoid having to pick a new winner. So we have a twenty-four-hour stay of execution. Let's not waste it."

"David and I can rustle up a few questions and get our guys in research to pass them through our online panel tomorrow," Amanda proposed.

Diane nodded.

"Can we wait as long as possible in the day before hitting the online panel?" I asked. "We want tomorrow's media coverage to have had its impact before we pop the questions."

"Good idea," Diane replied. "We can get top-line numbers in minutes after the panel closes, so let's wait to start it until early afternoon."

Amanda and I spent the rest of the day together working through the questions we would pose to the online panel of average Canadians across the country. It was the first time I'd really spent an extended period of time with her. It was nice. She was nice. Really. The hard professional edges she kept sharp in more formal business settings seemed to soften when we were working one on one after everyone else had gone home. It was almost as if the real Amanda emerged after dark. I'd noticed it first when we'd gone for a drink a while back. It was a shame that she seemed to feel that only "tough Amanda" could succeed at TK. I actually made her smile several times and caused her to burst out laughing at one point. Unfortunately, the laugh came when I was taking the inaugural bite of my take-out dinner. The greasy barbecue-sauce–covered chicken breast squirted out from between the obviously well-lubricated buns. Luckily, I caught it deftly, with my lap, so it fouled my Hugo Boss suit rather than the ugly green carpet. I learned that spending ten minutes vigorously rubbing your crotch with a damp dishrag while your colleague laughs hysterically is an excellent bonding exercise. I doubt I'll ever be able to wear the suit again, and I reeked of barbecued chicken for the rest of the evening. On a positive note, I was escorted all the way home that night by three stray dogs and a family of hungry raccoons that clearly favoured southern cuisine.

While I'd been working with Amanda, I made sure I "stumbled upon" the growing Landon Percival presence in the social media channels, pointing out the Facebook fan page and Twitter stream.

"This is big," Amanda said, scanning the positive comments overflowing on the Facebook page.

We were up to 2,349 Facebook fans and had attracted 3,124 Twitter followers. I needed some quiet time to keep up the tweeting or we'd start to lose some of them.

Amanda then clicked on the YouTube link that one Facebook commenter had left and watched in wonder as Landon Percival pulled several Gs in her backyard merry-go-round. Just watching it again made me a little queasy. Or perhaps it was the scent of barbecue sauce that clung to me.

"Unbelievable," was all she said.

Before long, we discovered another Facebook fan page somebody else had created entitled "Hugh Percival's Last Flight."

Again, Amanda uttered, "Unbelievable."

"Um, there's something else you should know about Landon that I haven't mentioned to anyone else yet," I started, deciding to take a chance.

"Okay," Amanda replied, her eyes narrowing in trepidation.

"She's a lesbian. There, I said it."

Amanda gave me a funny look.

"That's it? She's a lesbian? Who cares? She's seventy-one years old. We're in a new century."

"Amanda, I'm not worried so much about Canadian reaction, if it ever comes out at all. But if we pull this off, Landon will be in Houston, Texas, for the training, deep in the Bible Belt. After being a communist, being gay is next on the anti-American list."

"Again, I say, she's seventy-one. She's lived alone on a remote lake for the last forty years or so. It's a non-issue," Amanda concluded. Then she smiled at me.

———

To say that by lunchtime the next day Landon Percival was a household name in Canada would be an overstatement, but not by much. The media coverage was intense and almost universally positive. Nearly all the stories accepted Sarah Nesbitt's research as fact and didn't even bother to question that Landon's name had actually been drawn. I thought this was rather slapdash journalism, although a few outlets called her the "still unofficial Canadian citizen astronaut." But it sure helped our cause. This made it even more difficult for NASA or TK to toss her overboard and pick a new winner.

I'd spoken to Landon after I'd finally made it home from the office the night before and she confirmed that the CBC had sent a camera crew to Cigar Lake. They got some great shots of Landon waving them away from her dock. She looked pretty good and had put on a clean pair of coveralls to pump out the water that inevitably seeped into the pontoons of the Beaver. Then Landon taxied out onto the lake and took off. I knew that because Amanda and I had watched the footage on *The National* on the boardroom flat-screen TV. When I'd asked Landon if she'd actually had anywhere to go when she'd taken off for the camera, she reported that she'd been flying her regular search pattern "hunting for clues, just like Sherlock Holmes, flat on his stomach looking for footfalls in a rug."

Only the CBC and its affiliates had the Cigar Lake shots, but all the other outlets pulled down the YouTube clip I'd helpfully already uploaded. If Crawford Blake had any doubts about how the country would respond to Landon's story, the media coverage banished them, even before the poll results.

By 5:00 p.m., Amanda and I were once again sitting in Diane's office for the most important call of all. We'd already sent media coverage summaries to the D.C. office and fully briefed Crawford on the online panel results. None of that really mattered if this call went awry. Crawford had made it clear that he was running the call and that we should speak only in response to direct questions. What a jerk.

Elevator music played over the speaker phone as we waited for the conference call to start. I don't know who makes the on-hold music selections, but a xylophone cover of "Smoke on the Water" should never, ever have been recorded, let alone aired on a teleconference. It mercifully ended a few seconds later as the call officially started.

"Hey, you all. It's Crawford Blake here in Washington. Thanks for making the time. I know Diane Martineau and the Toronto team are on the line. Who have we got at NASA?"

"Hello, Blake and everyone, it's Kelly Bradstreet here and I'm flying solo today. Actually, I wanted it that way. I'll brief the leadership here afterwards, but I'd like to be the filter and not burden them with the deliberations until we've made a decision here."

"Understood," replied Crawford. "Okay, let's get started. I know we have a hard stop at 6:00. From our call yesterday morning, Kelly, you know that we have our American and Canadian citizen astronaut candidates. For reasons that are obvious, particularly if you happen to live up there in Canada, we'd like NASA to announce the winners as quickly as possible so we can start the next phase of the program and head off a sliver of controversy. But let's review each candidate to make sure we're all on the same page. It won't take too long to consider the American winner. He's exactly what we were looking for when we conceived this idea in the first place. Eugene Crank, thirty-eight years old, a deputy sheriff in the town of Wilkers, Texas, just south of Sabine near the Louisiana border. He's youngish, good-looking, in great shape, and a real patriot. He was born singing the 'Star Spangled Banner' and served in the National Guard. He's a model citizen, Republican of course, just had to slip that in, and is admired and respected by the people he serves and protects. End of story. He is the perfect American citizen astronaut."

"Sounds good to me," Kelly replied. "Shame about his name. 'Eugene Crank' is quite a handle to grow up with. I bet he had a rough ride at school."

"I can assure you, no one ever messed with Eugene Crank at school," Crawford interjected. "He was a star athlete and met his wife when they were both fifteen."

"It's like a fairy tale," Kelly said with what might have been just a whiff of sarcasm. "I think we can give Eugene Crank our stamp of approval," she added. "Let's head north."

"Right. Off to the frozen reaches of Canada," Crawford began, his voice appropriately icy. "Well, we have a bit of an issue in Canada, thanks to a very tenacious reporter and a local village idiot up in what they call British Columbia. The name drawn as the Canadian winner somehow belonged to a Landon Percival. For most of her biography, she sounds great. She's a doctor. She's a bush pilot. Her dream has always been to fly, preferably all the way to space. She even applied for the Canadian astronaut program but was rejected, as we understand it, because she was too old. Now just to put this all in perspective, she was considered too old by NASA and the Canadian Space Agency . . . back in 1983. Yes, she's still alive and kicking today. In fact she's a spry seventy-one years old and still flies her old Beaver around B.C."

"I beg your pardon," Kelly snapped.

"Sorry. Let me be clear," Crawford explained. "I've learned from my Canadian colleagues that the Beaver is an iconic bush plane that helped to open up northern Canada back in the day."

"Ah. I see. Thanks for the clarification."

"Now initially, I was totally opposed to letting this woman through, and I'd already instructed our Toronto team to choose a new winner. Well, we know what happened then. This Landon Percival's story is now all over the goddamn news and seems to have warmed the hearts of Canadians. We did a fast overnight poll to probe Canadians' awareness of, and attitudes towards, our dear Landon Percival and the results are, um, compelling enough to cause a rethink in my position. Twenty-four hours after her story broke, more than half of those surveyed had heard of her, and of that group, over 89 per cent wanted to see her ride the shuttle. There's more data but it just gets uglier."

"And judging from the media coverage today, both in Canada and here in the U.S., this story is still on the rise," commented Kelly.

"Right," agreed Crawford. "So that leaves us in a difficult position. We could reject her again just because she's so old she could break her hip more easily than breaking wind. But my Canadian colleagues have persuaded me that the entire Canadian population would ride their snowmobiles to my front door, string me up from the nearest maple tree, and beat me blue with canoe paddles. I'm not keen to bring that kind of negative publicity down on NASA. So, reluctantly, our recommendation is that this Landon Percival woman be announced as the candidate Canadian citizen astronaut, who will ride the shuttle if, and only if, she can successfully complete the training program."

I could contain myself no longer.

"Well, technically, this Eugene Crank guy will also have to ace the training program or he can't go up either. So both candidates are in exactly same boat, er rocket," I blurted.

"Mr. Stewart is correct," Kelly said. "Actually, in the end, it's an easy call for me. I happen to like Landon Percival and her back story. Having said that, I doubt very much that my colleagues will be too enthusiastic, particularly Scott Chandler, not to mention our lawyers. But I happen to think she adds a new and fresh dimension to the program. In fact, I think she is the kind of citizen we're really looking for. She doesn't look like an astronaut. You could swap Eugene Crank in for any other American astronaut of the last fifty years, and no one would even notice."

"Yes, Kelly, but if I can be direct, neither you nor our Canadian team get to make the final call on who flies," Crawford reminded her.

"Mr. Blake, that was perhaps a little too direct," replied a decidedly cool Kelly Bradstreet. "I may not have the final call. Unfortunately, senior communications execs seldom have the final call. But when I present this to the NASA leadership, I think I know how this story will end."

———

Twenty-four hours later, NASA issued a news release announcing Mr. Eugene Crank and Dr. Landon Percival as the first two citizen astronauts, pending their successful completion of a rigorous training program at the Johnson Space Center in Houston. I didn't really know how Crawford Blake took the news, but then again, I didn't really care any more.

UP AND DOWN

I called Landon as soon as I heard the announcement. Cellphone reception is remarkably good these days, even when bridging the vast distance between Toronto and Cigar Lake, B.C. She later denied it, but I was quite sure I heard the faint sound of weeping.

PART 4

CHAPTER 11

The day after NASA's news release, the phone rang in my cubicle.

"David Stewart."

"David, it's Kelly Bradstreet at NASA."

"Oh, um, hi Kelly, it's David Stewart."

"Yes, I know, you already said that."

Damn.

"Yes, um, right. Sorry about that. I guess I just wasn't expecting to hear from you directly," I babbled.

"Well, I like to stay in touch with the people on the ground, who are doing the heavy lifting," she commented. "Besides, without being too blunt, I sometimes find that Crawford Blake spins so much he's at risk of screwing himself into the ground."

"I understand, Kelly. And to make it easier for our clients, I often say my name twice, usually early in the conversation."

"Good. Very helpful. Okay, so here's the deal. You already know that I was able to get Landon Percival over this first hurdle. She's made it into the training program. But there was a condition that we didn't put in the news release."

"Okay. What kind of condition?" I asked.

"Well, Landon does not exactly fit the typical astronaut stereotype."

"Yes, I know being a Canadian does set her apart," I interjected.

Kelly had the grace to chuckle.

"Right. In any event, the powers that be here at NASA have insisted that she be accompanied at all times by a handler of sorts. A minder who can look out for her, and keep her out of trouble from the time she arrives in Houston for the training to when the shuttle brings her back down, provided she passes the training in the first place."

"Does Eugene get a handler, too?" I asked, a little irritated by NASA's demand.

"Well, that's the rub," Kelly replied. "No. My bosses don't think he needs one, and we don't want any more people cluttering up the program than necessary, so he doesn't get one."

"The double-standard positioning may be difficult," I said.

"Well, I'm hopeful that it won't ever become public that Landon has an escort."

"But if it does, perhaps we could just say that it's always been standard procedure for all foreign nationals to be accompanied while participating in a NASA astronaut program," I suggested.

"Hmmm. I like it," Kelly replied. "That'll be our key message if it ever comes up."

"I'll draft a few different versions for you to consider," I offered.

"Well, write them as you would deliver them, because I'm about to call Crawford Blake and tell him I want you to be Landon Percival's shadow for as long as she's in the program. Her handler," Kelly explained.

I said nothing, because I didn't seem to be capable of human speech at that precise moment, which is often the case when one is flabbergasted.

"Well, you're the logical choice. I've got your bio in front of me, and you've already had some contact with NASA when you were with the minister. And you've already established a relationship with the talented Dr. Percival. You're a perfect fit."

I finally found my tongue resting in my lower jaw, which I picked up off the floor.

"Wow, Kelly. Well, that would be very cool and I'd love to do it, but I doubt Crawford will go for it. Just between us, I don't really think I'm his employee of the month right now after that little *Vancouver Sun* fiasco."

"Are you kidding? If I were you, I'd start claiming responsibility for that story. It gave us great publicity and built more tension and anticipation into the announcement than we could ever have dreamed of. I thought it was brilliant."

"Oh. I see."

"Anyway, I have Crawford Blake in training right now, and I expect that pretty soon he'll actually accept that I'm the client."

"Oh. I see."

"So keep all this under your hat. I just wanted to give you a quiet heads up that the client's first choice to carry our geriatric astronaut's luggage is you," she said. "Am I thwarting any big plans you had for the next eight weeks or so?"

"Um, nope. Not that I know of. If my boss here is okay with it, I'm happy to chauffeur Landon on this adventure. If she agrees."

"Oh, I think she'll be fine with it."

She hung up a few minutes later and I sat back in my chair. I didn't know what to think. I refused to contemplate the idea that I might actually get to do this. I Googled the Johnson Space Center in Houston, where astronauts typically train, and started grazing through the pages. About half an hour later, my phone rang again. The caller ID told me it was TK D.C. Not good. I toyed with the idea of just letting it ring through to voice mail, but I was feeling a little more confident after my Kelly call.

"David Stewart."

"I don't really like you, Stewart. I haven't from the start. And I haven't yet figured out how you've managed to worm your way into the affections of our client, not to mention your colleagues in Toronto. I just don't see it. I thought for a while that you might be a very accomplished swordsman and have been very busy. But I don't think so. You don't look the part. So it must be something else. But I'll find out what it is. Don't you worry."

"Hi, Crawford," I mumbled. "I'm not exactly sure how to respond to that. I've really just been trying to do my job."

"Oh, you've been doing a job all right. And the client has bought it hook, line, and sinker."

"I'm really not sure what you're driving at . . ."

"Yeah, right. Well, pack your bags, buddy boy, you're off to Houston with that grandmother girlfriend of yours. NASA wants you to babysit her for the duration. So have a good time. Diane can give you the gory details."

"Okay . . ."

"I am so totally fucking against this, but our spaced-out client is insisting. And what do I care? When it all goes bad – and trust me, it will all go bad – you'll be right there on the scene to wear it."

"Well . . ."

"I'm not finished," Crawford snapped, which was just fine by me. I had no idea how to respond to his tirade, anyway.

"Do you know what I do when I can't talk a dumbass client out of doing something stupid?"

"Um, no. What?"

"I just grin and bill it."

The line went dead before I could respond with some witty and incisive retort. Then again, I might have had to put him on hold for twenty minutes to come up with one. I hung up and noticed Diane's assistant hovering outside my cubicle. He just pointed to me, then stabbed his thumb towards the corner office.

One week later, I was at Toronto's Pearson airport, sitting in an Air Canada departure lounge waiting to board AC #235 to Houston. A steady stream of people flowed down the wide corridor towards my gate. It was about ten minutes before we were to board, when I heard the noise.

"Mr. Stewart! Yoohooo! Mr. Stewart!"

I can't really describe the sound of her voice when she pushed it to full volume. It didn't really sound like her normal talking voice amplified. Rather, when she cranked it up to 11, it was more like a howler monkey at full wail.

I finally saw her. She had eschewed the moving sidewalk as too slow and was burning up the marble floor with long strides and a determined look. The crowd parted in front of her in self-defence, or perhaps it was simple fear of the unknown. I'd have gotten out of her way, too, had she been barrelling down on me.

"Coming through. Sorry, plane to catch. Pardon me. Coming through!"

When I'd last seen her, she'd been dwarfed by a de Havilland Beaver. So standing there on her own, she now seemed physically bigger than I'd remembered her. I understood why when I got a look at her from the side. She was wearing a bright yellow rain poncho that didn't quite cover the old green canvas backpack slung over her shoulders. From the front, the ensemble kind of made her look like a giant yellow pepper or perhaps the peanut M&M character.

When she finally broke free from the crowd, aided by how

quickly the crowd was trying to break free from her, she rushed over to me, sporting a broad smile. She wrapped her arms around me and squeezed all the air out of my lungs with a Hulk Hogan bear hug. It was a submission hold, and the pressure on my spine ricocheted the word "paraplegia" through my mind.

"Mr. Stewart!" she gushed, holding me out at arms' length for just a second, before pulling me back in for a second bear hug. "You have made me happier than I think I've ever been. You did it. Your media manipulation turned the trick and flicked the switch."

"Whoa, Landon! Always with the jokes!" I said in a loud voice for the sake of the hordes watching us. Then I leaned in to whisper in her ear.

"Keep your voice down. And please, 'media manipulation' is a phrase that should never cross your lips again, or the closest you may come to the space shuttle is on a guided tour of the Smithsonian Air and Space Museum."

I glanced around the departure lounge in case she'd been trailed by some photogs or vidcam shooters, which was a distinct possibility, given her newfound fame. But thankfully, everyone else seemed preoccupied with their own travel plans.

I pulled back to look at her. She nodded quickly with very wide eyes, her entire countenance exuding contrition.

"Sorry," she hissed. "I'm still new at this."

We both relaxed.

"It's great to see you," I said, genuinely pleased. "How was your flight?"

"Well, I really just wanted to get there, I'm just so tickled. But the flight was fine. It's always a bit strange flying as a passenger in somebody else's plane," she replied. "But I have to say that the wings of my old baby are a lot more rigid than the ones on that Airbus."

"That's quite the carry-on bag you're lugging around," I observed. "I can't wait to see what you checked."

"I decided not to check my bag," she replied. "This is the only one I've brought."

"You certainly travel very light for an eight-week trip," I said, trying not to think of the two large suitcases I'd already checked.

"Well, as I recall, the NASA folks make you wear their fancy astronaut jumpsuits from dawn to dusk anyway, so I only brought along a few changes of clothes."

I helped her lower the backpack to the ground, nearly dislocating my shoulder in the process.

"Is it an entirely chainmail wardrobe? This thing weighs a ton," I complained. "Why didn't you check this and save the strain on your back?"

"Check it? Not on your life. I'm carrying precious cargo in here. I don't want Air Canada rerouting it to Kuala Lumpur by mistake," she declared, patting the side of the backpack. She unlaced the top, reached in, and pulled out a magazine. "I decided to bring along my first twenty years of the *Baker Street Journal* for you, 1953 to '73. I haven't looked at them for years and thought you might like them."

UP AND DOWN

"No way! Landon! That's amazing!" I shouted, completely forgetting our "keep your voice down" rule. "You lugged eighty issues of the BSJ all the way from Cigar Lake for me?"

"Well, you'll need something to read while I'm studying and being poked and prodded and spun," she commented. "I think you're going to be bored silly."

———

Diane had briefed me fully the week before. I was to be attached to Landon at the hip for the duration of the training and until the mission itself was over – that is, if she passed through the program and was cleared to fly. The only time we'd be apart would be during the shuttle mission itself. My job was simply to make sure Landon did nothing or said nothing to imperil the program or tarnish the NASA brand. This had required an unanticipated increase to the budget that TK shared with NASA. While I'd be with Landon every waking hour in the coming couple of months, we'd bill NASA for only five hours each day, which conveniently coincided with my daily billable target. So I'd spent an hour or so on my computer the night before I headed to the airport, pumping five-hour days into PROTTS so Amanda could invoice NASA even while I was gone.

———

Houston was hot. And I don't mean the famous Texas "dry heat." This was full-on humid hot. Every time I breathed, it was like inhaling the exhaust of one of the shuttle's solid rocket boosters while swimming in a pool of my own perspiration. We'd just walked out of the air-conditioned comfort of the airport into the blast furnace of just another day in Houston. I looked up and I saw, shimmering faintly like a mirage at the head of what seemed an endless line of taxis, a limo parked at the curb. A uniformed chauffeur held a sign that featured what looked like the NASA logo, but I was too far away to make out the name beneath it.

"That's it," said Landon, staring at the sign in the distance. "Percival."

"You can read that from here?" I asked.

"Of course. Can't you?"

I pulled my two wheeled suitcases towards the limo, losing ground with every step to Landon as she race-walked ahead, shouldering her backpack that weighed only slightly less than a standard refrigerator. When I caught up to her, I'd sweated off about five pounds and was delirious with dehydration. Landon seemed unaffected by the trek and the temperature. She grabbed and loaded my suitcases before the chauffeur could even put away his sign.

"Let's go! We're burning daylight."

––––––––––

The Johnson Space Center is a sprawling complex with heavy security. We were granted entry courtesy of our passports and the close scrutiny of a beady-eyed marine at the gate. It felt like

Checkpoint Charlie in the years before the Berlin wall came tumbling down. But we were in. Landon was like a schoolkid on her first field trip. She gawked out the windows of the limo and kept whacking my leg to point things out to me.

They gave us adjoining rooms, which I thought was taking my minder role a little too seriously. The rooms were quite nice, configured not unlike a high-end motel. There was a queen-sized bed, a spacious closet and dresser, a very nice flat-screen TV, a bar fridge, a desk, high-speed Wi-Fi, and a view of the next building. My newly acquired vintage *Baker Street Journal* copies were stacked precariously on my bedside table, ready for reading.

There was a knock on my door. When I opened it, in the corridor stood a teary-eyed Landon wearing NASA orange astronaut-in-training coveralls. Official patches for NASA, the Canadian Space Agency, and the upcoming mission itself were sewn over her heart. A Canadian flag and "Percival" in upper-case letters were embroidered on the left side. Clothes really do make a statement.

"There were five pairs of these in my closet," she whispered, almost overcome with emotion. "It's really happening. I can't believe it's really happening. I'll never wear anything else again."

"You look very much like an astronaut," I said. "I only got this very official-looking lanyard. It won't get me onto the shuttle, but I'm told it'll get me everywhere else around here."

She leaned in to eye the photo on my card.

"Why didn't you at least smile?" she asked. "You look like you just robbed a train."

A door opened farther down the hall, and out stepped Eugene Crank, decked out in his orange coveralls. I recognized him immediately from the photos I'd seen in the media coverage. Landon did too, and pulled herself together.

"Mr. Crank, I presume," said Landon stepping towards him, her hand extended.

He looked our way, gave a little smile that seemed close to a smirk, shook his head, and walked over.

"Well, well, Mrs. Percival. I figured you'd be holding a news conference by now, to keep up with your clippings," he said.

He reached down to her to shake her hand, but his heart wasn't in it.

"I've never been married, actually, and I'd be quite happy never to see another reporter or photographer in my life," Landon replied. "Congratulations on winning. I'm looking forward to sitting next to you for lift-off."

He smirked again. It was definitely a smirk.

"Well, Ma'am, there's a lot of sheep to shear before you're on the launch pad. Good luck. I'll see you at the news conference."

He turned and walked away from us.

"Well, he seems nice enough," Landon said when he was gone.

"You think so? I thought he was a bit of a jerk."

Kelly Bradstreet ended up chairing the official news conference the following morning to introduce the two citizen astronauts. She'd told me in confidence that Scott Chandler, NASA's head of astronaut training, was supposed to run the newser but had refused, calling the whole program a sideshow. It gave me a glimpse into what her life was like trying to drag the reluctant NASA old guard into the new millennium. Eugene Crank and Landon Percival sat alone at the blue-skirted table with the mission crest on the backdrop behind them. The room was filled to capacity with about fifty reporters, including twelve cameras perched on a bank of risers along the back. I stood at the rear, next to a CNN camera, and even got to meet fellow Canadian and famed CNN host Ali Velshi when he came back to chat with his vidcam shooter.

Kelly introduced herself and then walked the reporters through the Citizen Astronaut program and the goals that underpinned it. She reviewed how popular the program had been with Americans and Canadians, noting the impressive number of entries in each country. Then she introduced, first Eugene Crank, running through his bio, and then Landon Percival. Kelly joked that because Landon was somewhat older than Eugene, it would take her a little longer to get through her bio. Everyone chuckled except for Eugene. Finally Kelly made a big deal of reminding us all that the two contest winners would not be flying the shuttle unless and until they successfully passed the training program and were approved for launch. Both Eugene and Landon nodded.

Then it was time for each citizen astronaut to say a few words. My heart rate spiked until it became clear that Eugene Crank would go first. He pulled a piece of paper from his pocket, unfolded it, and then leaned into the mike placed on the table in front of him. The vibrating paper in his hands, along with his stilted delivery, betrayed his anxiety.

"Good morning, everyone. My name is Eugene Crank and I'm from Wilkers, Texas, where, um, as the little lady already said, I'm a deputy sheriff. I truly believe I'm the right man to fly on the shuttle. I live with danger every day. I've been decorated for bravery on the job. I'm an outstanding athlete, and keep myself in tiptop physical condition. I can handle whatever the good folks at NASA can throw at me. This training is going to be very demanding, and I worry some about my elderly colleague beside me here. But even if there's an empty seat next to me on launch day, I will be on that shuttle when it heads up to the space station in eight weeks. And I'm doing it for God and country. Thank you."

He carefully folded his cheat sheet and returned it to his pocket, his hands still trembling a bit. Landon just stared at him for a few seconds before turning to face the horde of reporters. Eugene ignored her and looked straight ahead. She had no notes and appeared calm even after listening to Eugene. My heart started pounding again, and I was clenching every part of my body that could be clenched as Landon began to speak.

"Well, that was some opening, Mr. Crank. I certainly do

appreciate your concern for me, misguided as it is. And I can report that these nice journalists, the rest of the world, and I are very excited to learn that you're an outstanding athlete. Thank you for letting us in on that," she opened with a smile to Eugene.

Some reporters smiled, others snickered, still others laughed out loud. None of them missed the shot across Eugene's bow. His face clouded over but he managed a weak smile for the cameras as Landon continued, still turned towards him.

"I sincerely wish you well in the arduous training ahead and I truly hope we're both on the shuttle when it launches. I should add I certainly hope we're both on it when it lands, too."

She paused like a pro until the laughter in the room subsided. Next to her, Eugene looked liked he'd just started a drug-free colonoscopy.

"My decision to enter this contest and my boundless gratitude to NASA for this opportunity are driven by the very simple fact that I have always been more at home above the Earth than on it. As Ms. Bradstreet kindly outlined already, I've been flying the mountains and lakes of northern B.C. for fifty-seven years. I've been a physician for forty-five years. Looking at me, I know it's hard for all of you to accept that I'm actually seventy-one – I can scarcely believe it myself – but I know it to be the truth. I freely admit I'm not happy about my age, so I just don't dwell on it much. I've wanted to travel to space for, well, for a very, very long time. I remember my father and I would lie on our dock on Cigar Lake, British Columbia, and look up into the night sky. I just wanted

to be up there among the stars, the moon, the planets, and everything else that inhabits the world beyond our own. I applied to
become one of Canada's first astronauts when that door opened
back in 1983. But I didn't make the cut. Now, nearly thirty years
later, fate has given me another shot. So, here I am, for my father,
for anyone in the world who feels that age has cheated them out
of a dream, and I'm here for me. I'm grateful for the chance that
has been given me, and I don't intend to waste it."

Landon sat back from the microphone. I'd like to say that
I coached her through that perfectly balanced and beautifully
delivered statement, that we'd rehearsed it together until it rang
true with the intended power. But alas, I had nothing to do with
it. Nothing. I'd tried to offer her direction on what she ought to
say. I even provided her with draft talking points so that we might
get out of the gate smoothly. I gave her some unsolicited tips on
public speaking and how to deal with tough questions from
reporters. She thanked me, smiling, but rather firmly told me she
had it well in hand and that I was not to worry.

Not to worry? Sure. No problem. I proceeded to worry so much
I'd barely slept that night. But I did learn all I ever wanted to
know about acne on an overnight infomercial marathon. I lay
there analyzing why I was so anxious. I decided I just didn't want
to give Crawford Blake the satisfaction of watching the wheels
fall off on our very first day. I wanted to get through at least a
week or so before we had to wave the white flag. So you can
imagine how surprised I was when Landon spoke with such

simple eloquence, passion, and even a little emotion. To put it kindly, she'd blown Eugene Crank and his self-centred soliloquy right out of the water.

While the reporters were clearly impressed, they didn't let the silence after Landon finished hang for too long. Kelly stayed at the podium to field the questions and maintain some kind of order in the proceedings. Landon looked serene. Eugene towered over her, even when seated. He looked relieved now, as if the doctor had finally pulled out the scope. The reporters' questions were, for the most part, predictable, run-of-the-mill queries, including the vacuous classics "How do you feel?" and "Are you excited?"

Kelly answered the more technical questions about the program itself and the rules governing it, but referred most questions to Eugene and Landon. When the news conference seemed to be winding down, Kelly called for a last question to keep us on schedule. Always beware of the last question.

"Phillip Lundrigan from *The Family Word*," said the middle-aged, balding, average-looking guy towards the back. "Question for Landon Percival."

I'd taken a quick look at the media sign-in sheet but had not remembered a reporter from *The Family Word* listed. This publication had become a popular vehicle for the Christian right in the U.S. I had no idea why they might be interested in the Citizen Astronaut program unless it was to suggest that a woman's place was in the kitchen, provided that kitchen was not orbiting the Earth.

"I was doing some online research in preparation for this news conference, and I stumbled upon a photograph of you, purportedly from 1968. It's a shot of you holding hands with another woman. No big deal, right? But the caption on the photo, which incidentally is posted on a public Facebook page, reads:

> 'My amazing Aunt Samantha and her partner, Auntie Landon, quietly leading the sexual revolution back in 1968.'

"Dr. Percival, my question is a simple one. Are you a lesbian? Is that your sexual choice in life?"

There was much murmuring and sharp inhalations from the other reporters.

"Hey!" somebody shouted from the back. Wait, I recognized that voice. Okay, it seemed that I had just shouted "Hey!" from the back.

Luckily, Kelly leapt in from the podium before I had time to finish the sentence I had started on pure instinct and anger.

"Mr. Lundrigan, I'm going to rule that question out of order . . ."

"Ms. Bradstreet, it's fine," said Landon over the din. "This was bound to emerge. I almost raised it myself, but when Mr. Crank didn't comment on his sexuality, I decided not to comment on my own. But let me respond – I hope only once – to this extraordinarily invasive question so that we don't have to deal with it again."

Kelly paused, unsure of how to proceed. Eventually, she waved her hand to cede the floor to Landon.

"Mr. Lundrigan. First of all, whether or not I am a lesbian is none of your business or anyone else's and certainly has no bearing on my ability to fulfil my obligations as a citizen astronaut. Secondly, yes, I am a lesbian and have been since I was born. And thirdly, please do not ever again refer to it as any kind of a 'choice.' Your words reveal a profound ignorance of human sexuality. Do you have any other questions?"

"My understanding of human sexuality is not on trial here," Lundrigan sputtered. "If, as you say, your own sexuality is no one else's business, why did you just confess to being a lesbian?"

"As Ronald Reagan once said to great effect, 'There you go again,'" started Landon. "'Confess' is your word, not mine. I merely *stated* that I am a lesbian in the same way as you might state that you are balding, for neither of us has control over these two realities. As for why I announced this in a news conference rather than keeping it to myself, which is everyone's right, well, I just didn't want to be spending the next two months dealing with it. I'm a physician. I've always been inclined to lance the boil rather than wait and watch it fester."

"A final supplementary, if I may," Lundigran said, pushing his luck with Kelly. "Are you a Christian?"

"I'm more of a humanist, but some of my best friends are Christians," quipped Landon. "I do think there's plenty to commend in the Good Book, and I even have a look at it now and then. But I've always believed you should be judged on what you do in life, and not what you read."

Another reporter piped up just before the curtain was to fall.

"Connie Cranston, MSNBC. Mr. Crank, how do you feel about the possibility of flying in space with a lesbian?"

Relieved that his colonoscopy was over, Eugene had been looking more relaxed, at least until the Lundrigan question. Now he looked like he'd just been presented with the hospital's bill for the procedure. He seemed to be trying to create as much space as possible between Landon and him while remaining seated in his chair. So he actually appeared to be leaning away from her at the table.

"Well, I'm a good Christian boy with a nineteen-year marriage to my high school sweetheart. As far as I'm concerned, anything other than love between a man and woman is what my preacher calls an abomination of the Bible's teachings. So I guess I'm not thrilled about all this, but I aim to be on that shuttle when it lifts off, with or without her."

"Although, given how much time we'll be spending together, Mr. Crank, I imagine your wife might be quite relieved to hear that I bat for the other team," interjected Landon with a smile.

———

The rest of the day had been spent doing a series of taped interviews from a smaller satellite media studio at the Johnson Space Center. Because of the number of interview requests, Kelly had wisely split up Landon and Eugene so they were not appearing together on talk shows, although that might have

been interesting. I was there for every one of her twelve interviews that afternoon. For a couple of the early ones, she was
joined by the mission commander, Lee Hainsworth, who had
zipped over from the Kennedy Space Center for two days of
briefings before returning to Florida. All of the interviews were
double-enders, meaning that she was usually alone in the studio, staring into a camera and using an earpiece so she could
hear the questions. The talk show hosts were all on their own
sets with Landon appearing on a TV monitor. I was exhausted
just watching the interviews from the control room but Landon
was energized, gracious, articulate, and animated for every one
of them. It was an impressive performance.

I was the only TK person on site, so as we'd agreed, I stayed
in touch with Amanda throughout the day, and she kept Diane
and Crawford in the loop. I was quite sure that Crawford had
gone from apoplectic to homicidal as he watched the news
conference unravel. I was quite happy to be half a country
away from him.

We didn't see Eugene for the rest of the day, and neither of
us was unhappy about that. After a late dinner that Landon and
I ate on our own in the dining room down the hall from our
rooms, I suggested we watch the media coverage together to
see how the story was playing. Landon declined, saying she was
"hitting the sack."

The coverage went pretty well as I expected it would. Most
TV networks led with the Lundrigan question and Landon's

pitch-perfect response. Other than airing Eugene's homophobic reaction, it was really the Landon Percival show. Under the circumstances, the media play wasn't too bad for us, though I decided not to watch any Fox News coverage. I figured I'd soon be hearing from Crawford and was a little surprised he hadn't called already.

I shut down the TV and fired up my laptop. I went straight to Facebook and typed in "Landon Percival" in the search bar. I couldn't understand how I'd missed the photo that jackass Lundrigan had found. I'd scoured the web for any and all references to Landon Percival and come up with precious little. I'd tried Googling "Landon" but had been inundated with images of Michael Landon from *Bonanza* and *Little House on the Prairie*. After scrolling through fifteen pages of images of him, I'd given up. The Facebook search engine had nothing for me. Then I remembered Lundrigan's words from the caption, "Auntie Landon." I pumped that into the search engine and was rewarded. It was the Facebook page of a niece of Samantha Sharpe. The photo was as Lundrigan had described. A much younger Landon Percival was holding hands with another young woman, obviously Samantha Sharpe. The shot seemed very familiar and I suddenly realized why. I immediately emailed Sarah Nesbitt.

UP AND DOWN

To: *Sarah Nesbitt*
From: *David Stewart*
Subject: *Photo of Landon Percival*

Hi Sarah,
I discovered today that you had used a Facebook photo of
Landon in the Sun *story but had cropped out the other*
woman in the shot when you ran it. I assume you knew
from the photo that Landon is a lesbian. I'm just curious
why you chose to crop the photo and make no reference to
what has become big news today. I very much appreciate
what you did, but I'm still left with my curiosity.
Regards,
David

I hit Send and then went back to Google. I wanted to learn
more about Eugene Crank now that it appeared he was a bit of
a troublemaker. I started with a Google Image search, being careful to run his name in quotation marks. I didn't want every photo
of every Eugene on the planet, just those of Eugene Crank.
Because of his rather unusual name, I figured it wouldn't take
me long. I was right. There were a couple of group shots from a
recent Texas law-enforcement conference, and a headshot of him
in full uniform from the Wilkers Sheriff's Office website. There
was a family shot of him and his wife from a few years ago on
what must be his church's website. And then I found a photo of

a baseball team, the players looking ecstatic with a large trophy on the field in front of them. The caption listed the players, including Eugene, under the heading "Mississippi High School State Champions." That rang a bell. I scanned the players' list in the caption again, and then confirmed it by looking at the player standing right next to Eugene Crank. Unbelievable audacity.

On a whim, I snagged a screen capture of the team photo and emailed it to Amanda with the Subject line: *Just between you and me.*

I checked my BlackBerry just before turning out my light and saw that Sarah Nesbitt had responded.

To: David Stewart
From: Sarah Nesbitt
Subject: Re: Photo of Landon Percival

David,
You asked me why? Well, when I found the photo, don't think I wasn't sorely tempted. My journalistic instincts told me to run with it. But I've always believed that going public about one's sexuality should be the singular choice of the person, and no one else. Besides, I bounced it off my significant other of 15 years, and she thought I should crop the shot, too.
Talk to you soon . . .
Sarah

CHAPTER 12

I awoke at 6:00 the following morning, our second full day in Houston. I grabbed my iPad while I was still horizontal and did a Google News search on "Landon Percival" for the previous twenty-four hours. Twelve pages of news hits came back from as far away as Melbourne and Moscow. Every single one of the stories recounted the now infamous lesbian question. About half the stories included quotations from others critical of Phillip Lundrigan for asking in the first place. Spokespersons for gay and lesbian rights organizations in Canada and the U.S. were all over the story. But at least a third of the stories featured vitriol from the anti-gay movement and hard-core right-wing Christian groups. In several stories I was pleased to see quotations supporting Landon from my former minister. Even though the story was less than twenty-four hours old, many newspapers ran editorials favouring or denouncing Landon's status as a citizen astronaut. As one might expect, there was a certain ideological geography to the editorials.

Starting in Canada, they were mostly, though not exclusively, supportive of Landon. Major dailies like the *Globe and Mail*, the *Toronto Star*, the *Vancouver Sun*, and many others were clearly in Landon's corner. But a few of our own right-leaning papers and columnists used Landon as a platform to rail against same-sex marriage. There was still support for us in the U.S., but it declined as you travelled south. This was not the kind of coverage we'd wanted for the public launch of the program.

I picked up the phone and dialled, even though it was only just past 7:00.

"Kelly Bradstreet."

"Good morning, Kelly. It's David Stewart."

"Well, good morning," she replied, sounding unusually chipper. "I assume you've scanned the coverage. It was almost exactly what I expected, after yesterday."

"That's why I'm calling. It looks like it's running about 50–50 so far. But there are regional pockets of strong opposition. Look, I know this isn't what either of us were hoping for coming out of the newser, but I think it will recede or even improve as the training unfolds and people get to know more about Landon and her story."

"David, I love her story. The lesbian thing caught us all off-guard but she handled it beautifully. And she's such a contrast to Captain America Eugene. I like the tension that's being created between them. We need that to sustain interest. Yesterday took us a bit far afield from the NASA story, but it's only day two. I know we'll get our message out there over the next several weeks and definitely during the mission itself. I just hope Landon makes it through the training."

"I'm relieved to hear you say that," I replied. "I was worried you'd want to talk about easing her out."

"Well, Crawford Blake would like that, based on his four voice-mails to me this morning, but I'm not inclined to do anything for the time being. Let's just try to keep the reporters focused on the training in the next few days."

It looked like Landon would survive a few more days at least.

My BlackBerry buzzed ten minutes later. I glanced at the screen. Yep.

"Hi, Crawford."

"Nice job. You've just hijacked the entire news cycle! Have a look at the coverage. Just look at it. NASA is barely mentioned, neither is the space shuttle. It's wall-to-wall Landon fucking Percival. She is not the client! NASA is paying our fees, and you'd better remember that."

"Crawford, I understand that yesterday didn't exactly roll out the way we thought it would. But I've just been on the phone with Kelly, and she's okay with what went down. Landon turned out to be our big media play on day one, but we've got them hooked now. So when this initial flurry dies down, we can then shift the story back to NASA."

"She's our media hook, is she? She's old! She's a pagan, for Christ's sake, and she's a goddamned dyke to boot. Congratulations, you've scored the trifecta. Tell me she's a commie and my day will be complete. And Eugene got nothing out of yesterday. Sweet fuck-all!"

"I thought Eugene did fine. But he wasn't very nice to Landon."

"Nice? We're lucky Gene will even be in the same room with her. He was very tolerant."

By this time, I had nearly bitten a hole through my tongue. But I was about at my limit. I hate when people use the word "tolerant" to describe how enlightened they are about gays and lesbians. It would never be acceptable to say that someone is "tolerant" of women, or blacks, or Roman Catholics. But somehow it's still okay to be "tolerant" of a lesbian. What's to "tolerate"? I could feel my blood pressure rising but managed to reply in a calm, measured tone.

"I thought it was interesting that Eugene's high school baseball exploits in Mississippi were never mentioned in his bio or in Kelly's introduction yesterday. I gather he was quite the star in his day."

Silence. For what must have been about ten seconds, he said nothing. Ten seconds of dead air on the phone is an eternity.

"Don't you fuck with me, Stewart," he hissed. "You don't know what you're getting into."

Then he hung up. He was right. I really didn't know what I was getting into, but I just couldn't listen to him any more.

I opened my door and on the floor was a photocopied media coverage package with NASA Clips emblazoned across the cover page. There were copies in front of almost every door up and down the corridor. Next to me, there was no clipping package in front of Landon's door. I flipped through the clips and saw a few more articles than I'd seen online, but nothing that changed the pattern.

At 7:45 a.m. there was light tap on my door. When I opened it, a smiling Landon greeted me. She must not have received the clipping package.

"Breakfast beckons," she said. "Let's go."

I closed the door behind me and trotted to catch up.

"Um, how did you sleep?" I asked.

"Heavy and deep."

"Did you watch the news last night, or this morning?"

"Nope. I was in my own little world last night," she said.

Good. Perhaps she was oblivious to the media storm she had triggered.

"And this morning, I was too busy reading through the newspaper clippings conveniently left on my doorstep to turn on the tube."

Great.

"Oh, so you've seen all the coverage. Are you all right?" I asked.

"David, calm yourself, I'm fine. After that toad's question yesterday, I knew exactly what would be in the paper this morning. I hope that by tomorrow or the next day, it will have run its course and we can get back to why we're really here."

"You certainly seem relaxed about it all," I said.

"Well, I'd rather it had not happened at all, but it was perhaps inevitable. And better for it to be a distraction now, at the very start, than for it to break two days before launch. Right? It's common sense."

"This is what I do for a living, Landon, and common sense doesn't always prevail when it comes to the media. The beast needs to be fed and I think we might have a difficult week ahead of us. I doubt it'll clear up quite as quickly as we might like."

"As long as they don't throw me out, I can live with what's coming."

———

After breakfast, Landon and Eugene went into a three-hour briefing on the content and schedule of the training program. The rest of the crew, including Commander Hainsworth, Martine Juneau, and the shuttle pilot, Jefferson Rand, were there, too. After I escorted Landon to the classroom in a different building on the JSC campus, I headed back to my room to get ready for our first TK status call. Every second day we had scheduled a teleconference so I could update Diane, Amanda, Crawford, and the rest of the D.C. team. As I walked back outside along a paved path, I could hear faint shouting, even chanting, in the distance. I followed the noise, and then picked up my pace as it grew louder. I started my own chanting in my head: "Please let it not be a well-organized anti-Landon rally. Please let it not be a well-organized anti-Landon rally."

When I reached the main security gate of the Johnson Space Center, my prayers were answered . . . technically. It was not a well-organized anti-Landon rally at all. It was a massive, very badly organized anti-Landon riot. I made a mental note to aim higher when praying.

I stood on the safe side of the fence, hoping not to see five satellite trucks from mainstream media outlets. Right again. There were seven. And it looked as if at least half of them were beaming live reports from the scene, the on-the-spot reporters trying to get close, but not too close, to the two hundred or so very angry and animated demonstrators. Because they were so rally-challenged, three or four different chants were going on at one time, so no one could really make out the message. Although the placards were reasonably clear.

NO DYKES IN SPACE!

SEND HER TO THE PLANET LESBOS!

GROUND LANDON PERCIVAL!

NASA, SAY NO TO LESBIANS IN ORBIT!

I watched a group of demonstrators handing out to media what appeared to be Landon Percival apple voodoo dolls, dressed in miniature orange coveralls. They attached a line of them to the chain-link fence. It was creepy. It was also uncanny just how much the apple doll's face looked like Landon's.

By listening carefully, I could discern at least one chant delivered in that old familiar cadence: "Hey hey, ho, ho, lesbo Landon's got to go!"

How very creative. I'm glad Landon was out of range and sequestered in a classroom. Houston police were out in force but did not intervene. I saw Kelly off to the side of the melee speaking with the senior police officer on the scene. She was smiling and seemed quite relaxed about it all. She saw me and waved, giving me a quick thumbs-up before turning back to the policewoman. I stood there for about three-quarters of an hour. After twenty minutes, five of the seven satellite trucks departed. The remaining two left ten minutes after that. They all had apparently gotten their quota of video. After that, the demonstrators, who were from a particularly extreme local right-wing church, seemed to lose interest. The rally was breaking up as I hustled back to my room in time for my teleconference.

At the appointed hour, I dialled into the conference call line and listened to the repetitive strains of Aerosmith's "Walk This Way" arranged for the pan flute. Mercifully, I had to endure only a few bars of it before the call started.

"Okay. Hi, everyone," Crawford started. "I've got Michael Crane here with me in the room. Who else is on the line?"

"It's Diane, along with Amanda here in Toronto,"

"And it's David here in Houston."

"All right. Let's get going. We've got a lot to cover and an important decision to make," Crawford said. "Well, that was not exactly the launch news conference we were hoping for, now was it? We were lucky to persuade NASA to let Landon Percival even go to Houston. I figure after yesterday and the media coverage this morning, she's on life support right now. We need to decide whether to pull the plug or give her a few more days. I know what I want, but I'd like to hear from the rest of you."

"It's Diane here. I don't think we'd have gotten anywhere near the coverage we did had Landon not been so, um, so newsworthy. I thought she handled herself, under David's guiding hand, very well."

"Diane, we're not looking for media coverage at any cost. We want positive coverage for NASA. They're the client here."

"I hear you, Crawford. But if I were NASA, I wouldn't be too unhappy with yesterday's launch. There was a ton of coverage in both countries, and that should continue as we get closer to the lift-off date. I say leave Landon in the play. She's a media magnet."

Bless you Diane, I thought to myself. I decided I needed to get into the discussion. After all, I was the one in Houston.

"I couldn't agree more with Diane's perspective," I said. "In fact, I spoke to Kelly Bradstreet this morning and she's not unhappy with yesterday's newser. She did note that she'd like more NASA-focused coverage in the coming weeks but I think we can get that by more targeted story pitching. Besides, I don't think we can pull the plug anyway. We're too far down the road already, and NASA will make that call in the end, won't they?"

"Okay, let's get one thing clear," Crawford interjected in a tone that chilled the call. "This is our program. We are their advisers. We have an obligation to provide our very best advice to serve their interests. I've got CNN playing in the background even as we speak here, and there's ugly coverage of an anti-Landon rally at the JSC going on right now. I would have thought that David would have briefed us on that at the top of the call. We've got to stop this and stop it fast."

"I've just come from that so-called rally and it was anemic at best," I spun. "As soon as the cameras left, so did the demonstrators. They're part of the same group that pickets the funerals of those who have died from AIDS saying they deserved it. They are incredibly offensive and they don't represent the views of mainstream society. In fact, I think the protest will strengthen support for Landon and for the client. If NASA backs down because of a bunch of placard-waving wackos who couldn't even chant in unison, then we certainly aren't giving our client good advice. I say we ride it out, have Landon lie a little low for the next week or so, and try to get Eugene Crank up to the plate where he can hit one out of the park, if you know what I mean, Crawford."

"Don't go there, David. I mean it. I think you've been seduced by your wrinkly bush pilot and your judgment is clouded. The coverage we've seen so far, and there has been a ton, has very little to do with NASA. It's all Landon, all the time. And there is absolutely no evidence that this will change going forward. As Diane says, Landon is a media magnet. That's our problem.

That's what we must fix. We need NASA to be our media magnet. I'm going to call my NASA contacts and have Landon cut loose. Toronto, you can start the process to pick a new winner."

"But you can't do that," I protested. "A heap of negative press will rain down on NASA if Landon is kicked off the mission, especially right now when her public profile is so high. It makes no sense. You'll enrage every seniors group and every gay rights organization in both countries. The Canadian media will go ballistic. It's just not right for the client, and it's not fair to Landon."

"Crawford, I have to say I agree with David," Diane cut in.

"What a surprise! I'll alert the media," Crawford cut in, heavy on the acidic sarcasm.

"It just feels premature to jettison Landon right now. David makes some solid points and we ought to listen to what he's saying. I really worry about the backlash here in Canada if you toast Landon. David is closest to all of this and I think his advice is sound."

"David is a little too fucking close to all of this," was Crawford's response. "Look, I don't like to play this card very often. But this account team is not a democracy. I got us in to pitch NASA in the first place. They are a TK client because of my contacts. I'm running this account, and Landon Percival will soon be heading out of the goddamned spotlight and back to whatever godforsaken part of the Canadian wilderness she calls home. End of story. We've already drafted the news release."

"Crawford . . ." Diane began.

"This discussion is over!" Crawford roared, with the finality of a thermonuclear device. "Now I'm going to ask Michael here to brief us on the ongoing media relations program that we'll be undertaking here in the U.S. After that we're going to . . ."

We all heard what sounded like a knock on the door of the D.C. boardroom.

"You can obviously see that I'm running a meeting here," Crawford said angrily to the interloper.

"But she says it's extremely urgent and that you are to be interrupted," said the voice.

"Christ! I'll take it in my office," snapped Crawford. "Michael, take over. I'll be back."

I could actually hear Crawford Blake stomping out of the room. Or perhaps my imagination inserted its own soundtrack. A second or two later, Michael, whom I barely remembered from our Washington pitch so long ago, started his presentation on the media relations play. I was still reeling from Crawford's announcement. I couldn't believe we were about to shoot ourselves in the foot, or in this case, the head, by sending Landon Percival home. On the other hand, I wasn't convinced Kelly Bradstreet would support the recommendation. But her power was not supreme in NASA. Crawford wouldn't even be calling her. He'd go around her to his more senior contacts, and he'd twist the story to his own benefit. I knew that some of the NASA leadership had been dragged kicking and screaming to the citizen astronaut party and would probably welcome the chance to piss in the punch bowl and put the uppity Kelly Bradstreet in her place. Clearly some of them never wanted Landon Percival on board in the first place.

Fifteen minutes later, I realized that Michael was still talking and I'd heard not a word of his presentation. I'd been too busy analyzing our desperate situation and trying to devise a Hail Mary that might save Landon's seat on the shuttle. Maybe Emily Hatch was the answer. I tried to tune back in to the conference call but Michael really wasn't saying anything that interested me any more. As far as I was concerned, Crawford Blake had just set fire to the city and passed Nero's fiddle to Michael Crane.

I was desperate to talk with Amanda and Diane but didn't feel I really could until the call ended. I was just about to email Amanda on my BB when I heard that familiar two-tone chime that announced the arrival of another party to the conference call.

"Hello?" the newcomer said. "Is this the NASA team call?"

"Yes, it is," said Michael. "Who has just joined?"

"It's Margot Spinello here in New York. I'd like to know exactly who is on this call," she asked.

Margot Spinello, Margot Spinello. I knew the name but couldn't place it. A suddenly very deferential Michael ran down the list of participants on the call. I MSNed Amanda on my laptop: *'margot spinello?'*

"So it's just the TK NASA account team on the call?"

"Yes," Michael replied.

"Diane, it's good to know you're on the call. It explains why I kept getting your voicemail in the last hour," Margot said.

"I'm here, Margot. Is everything okay?" Diane asked.

Just then, Amanda's MSN response arrived: "holy shit! TK global ceo in ny!"

"No, everything is most decidedly not okay. What I'm about to tell you is highly confidential and should never be spoken of again. There could be legal implications. About twenty-five minutes ago, I fired Crawford Blake from TK with cause, effective immediately. He has left the D.C. building and is on his way to a meeting with our corporate legal counsel. About fifteen minutes ago I spoke to a Kelly Bradstreet at NASA and informed her that Crawford had been let go from TK, and I briefed her fully on the reason. I also resigned the NASA account. However, by the time I'd finished speaking with Kelly, we were back on the business. Let me explain. Again, all of this is highly confidential."

It was deathly quiet on the line. I thought I knew what was coming. I just didn't know how it had happened.

"Earlier this morning, it was brought to my attention that the American winner of the Citizen Astronaut contest that we conceived and administered, a Mr. Eugene Crank, is a childhood friend of Crawford Blake. More importantly, the selection of Mr. Crank was not the result of a random draw but a purposeful manipulation by Crawford Blake. Five minutes ago, I spoke to the CEO of Borden-Bennett here in New York. He is taking steps to terminate their D.C. office GM and the senior lead on the NASA contest administration. Obviously, their oversight of the draw was inadequate at best and incompetent at worst. They will also make these changes very quickly and very quietly. As you can imagine, they, like us, have every interest in keeping this all below the radar.

"I said earlier that we're still on the account. Let me explain that, too. Kelly believes, and I agree, that going public and invalidating the entire contest would be an enormous public blow to NASA when they are already on their knees. We both agree that the odds of anyone else discovering this, particularly with Crawford no longer with the agency, are slim. The odds are not zero, but they're slim. Crawford's name was neither mentioned in any media materials nor noted in any coverage. So while it's not ideal, the decision has been made to press ahead and deal with any revelations when they arise. I'm not completely convinced this is the wisest or safest approach, but as the client, Kelly Bradstreet should carry more weight in the final decision. And she has decided to ride it out. If we make it through, this approach has the benefit of protecting TK's image and reputation, even though we don't deserve it. We will immediately put in place a crisis contingency plan that will be invoked should this situation ever hit the streets.

"Finally, Crawford told me before I broke my news to him that he was about to recommend that our Canadian winner be sacked and a new one chosen in light of the recent media coverage. I took the liberty of raising this with Kelly Bradstreet and she shut the idea down immediately. Landon Percival is to stay in the program unless she fails the training. Is that understood?"

"We understand, Margot, and we agree," said Diane. No one else dared speak. "That was the advice we'd already given to Crawford, and that he'd rejected."

"Diane, I haven't had a chance to speak to you about this, but as the next most senior TKer on the project, I'd like you to assume overall account leadership on the NASA business."

"I'll clear the deck and take the helm," Diane replied without missing a beat.

"If I could ask the rest of the Toronto team to hang up now, I need to speak to Diane and Michael about the TK D.C. office in the wake of these events."

I hung up, jumped up and down on my bed until I hit my head on the light fixture, and then called Amanda on her BlackBerry.

"Did you send that baseball team photo to Margot Spinoodle?" I nearly shouted.

"It's Spinello," she corrected. "And I might have."

———

That afternoon, Eugene and Landon were in the JSC gym, for fitness testing. The rest of the mission crew were wrapping up their briefings and would return to Florida that evening. I didn't think the testing would pose any problems for Landon, despite her age. After all, she wasn't in training for the Olympic decathlon, just a quick trip into space. Clearly no one had told Eugene about Crawford Blake or that Kelly and perhaps a few other very senior NASA execs knew he was there under circumstances that now looked a bit suspicious. I can't say for sure that he was in on the manipulation that produced his name, but I was quite confident he must have known something about it. Outstanding athlete that he was, Eugene was strutting around in full swagger wearing shorts, a T-shirt, and very expensive-looking Nike cross-trainers.

Landon didn't wear the athletic image quite as easily. When I saw her, I wondered why NASA hadn't provided track suits or some kind of sportswear for the fitness testing. When the NASA officials saw her, I suspect they may have considered cancelling the testing altogether. Without the cosmetic benefits of the aptly named coveralls, Landon's wiry frame was on full display. She was wearing what my mother used to call clam-diggers or pedal-pushers. I can only describe them as green plaid three-quarter-length stovepipe pants that came down to just below the knee, revealing calves that were hairier than Eugene's. On top, she wore a sleeveless button-up collared shirt, probably cotton, with what appeared to be an oil stain on the back. On her feet, grey work socks with red stripes disappeared into what had to be fifty-year-old black and white high-top sneakers. A red canvas belt completed the ensemble. All in all, it was quite difficult to look at her for very long. Eugene practically doubled over in laughter, making no attempt to conceal his reaction.

There were four basic tests employed to measure their overall fitness. The 400-metre run, the standing broad jump, the flexed arm hang, and finally what they called the shuttle run, where you ran back and forth between two lines about 20 feet apart, picking up or putting down a bean bag on each turn. Before the tests began, Landon and Eugene were measured and weighed.

"Good luck," Eugene said, his words dipped in sarcasm. "And be sure you don't hurt yourself. The flexed arm hang can snap an old bone if you're not careful."

Landon smiled and nodded.

"All the best to you, too, Mr. Crank."

She meant it, he didn't.

They ran together for the 400 metres. Or rather, they ran at the same time. She kept up with him for the first 50 metres or so, but then Eugene pulled away, finishing about 75 metres ahead of her. He was gasping for air when he broke the tape. Landon seemed to be breathing almost normally when she finished. The NASA officials checked heart rate and blood pressure for each of them.

Ten minutes later, Eugene crouched at the standing broad jump line, flexing his knees and swinging his arms. Then he exploded up and forward, landing with a great flourish and finishing with a front roll. Landon applauded while the white coats unfurled their measuring tape. After his one jump, Eugene hopped on the spot and shook out his arms as part of his cool-down procedure as if he'd just completed a marathon.

Then Landon took her position, bent her knees, crouched into a tiny ball, and launched herself to a surprising height and distance. At the same time, she unleashed a shriek that could shatter crystal at forty paces. It was like standing next to a train whistle blast, only louder. Startled by the sound, Eugene leapt further than he had in his official jump. Landon seemed satisfied with her distance, even though it fell considerably short of Eugene's jump. Out came the measuring tape again and numbers were dutifully recorded on clipboards.

The flexed arm hang isn't exactly a spectator sport. It entails pulling yourself up on a chin-up bar until your eyes are even with your hands. Then you hold it for as long as you can. Landon went first this time. She pulled herself up to the prescribed position and the hanging began. More than three minutes passed before she started to vibrate and then dropped back to Earth. She rubbed her arms and took some delight in how animated the NASA guys were as they recorded her time.

Then Eugene assumed the position. At 30 seconds his face was red. At 40 seconds, sweat was pouring down his face. At the one-minute mark, I feared he might have an aneurism. Finally, at 82 seconds, he dropped like a sack of turnips to the floor, his flexed arms in full spasm. Landon helped him to his feet and then pulled on his hands to unfold his arms.

"Well, you don't weigh much more than 90 pounds. I'm 210," Eugene complained. It came very close to a whine.

After a twenty-minute break to allow Eugene's arms to return to their normal position, the fitness testing closed with the shuttle run. Based on what I'd seen so far, I thought that Landon might do very well in this event. It required short bursts of speed, and coordination, and agility. I figured a smaller person might be better suited for it. I was right. Back and forth they both flew, stopping, turning, and starting again, while grabbing and dropping beanbags. Landon beat him by a second and a half on the official run, and a full two seconds on the double or nothing round Eugene insisted on.

"This is stupid!" he complained, in the whiny voice that we were getting to know.

———

We all gathered in a small room just off the gymnasium for the results. The lead white coat stood at the front with his master clipboard.

"Congratulations, you're both in very good physical condition. Mr. Crank, you scored in the 89th percentile for your age and build, a very impressive score." Eugene nodded and shrugged his shoulders in the physical equivalent of "Well, duh." "And Dr. Percival, you hit the 96th percentile for your age. We've never actually seen a specimen at your level before. We might write a paper on your performance for the *Journal of Space Science* if you'd agree to some more testing."

"Happy to, boys. Just tell me when and where," Landon replied with a smile.

"So for the record, you're both in great shape, but the numbers tell us that Dr. Percival is actually at a higher fitness level than Mr. Crank."

"Well, I do have an unfair advantage," conceded Landon. "I've had so many more years to get myself in shape."

Eugene walked out.

―――――

With NASA's blessing, a news release was issued late in the day detailing the results of the fitness testing. To try to shift the coverage more towards NASA, neither Landon nor Eugene was made available to the media. Rather, the official NASA fitness examiner spent the late afternoon and early evening fielding media calls.

―――――

Just before I turned out my light, I called my sister.

"Lauren, it's David. How are you?"

"David! Nice to hear your voice. I kind of miss having you around here."

"I miss being there too. Are you okay? How's the new job?"

"I'm fine. I get a bit weepy now and then, but overall, I'm fine. The new job is great for keeping my mind occupied. I'm loving it. This branch is bigger, with more programs, more staff, and more resources. It's been just great so far. It was time, and I've really needed it. Plus, a guy I used to work with at the other library just called to ask me out."

"Hey, that's fantastic! Did you say yes? Do we like him? Does he wear his pants hiked up to his armpits and have a pocket protector?"

"Yes and yes. But I refuse to comment on his pants, and I really don't know what a pocket protector even is," she replied. "I had no idea he was even interested."

"Well, he probably thought it wouldn't be appropriate to ask you out while you were both shacked up at the same branch."

"Anyway, your friend Landon is the toast of the nation. I keep looking for your ugly mug in the background, but I haven't seen you yet."

"Here's hoping it stays that way."

"Are *you* okay, David?"

"Better than I thought I'd be. There's a lot to keep me distracted down here," I said. "You know, like anti-lesbian zealots, dozens of reporters, an unscrupulous deputy sheriff from Texas, and of course our very own geriatric bush pilot. It certainly ain't dull. But I do wish I could be there with you so soon after, um, well, you know. But I'm glad you're okay. I'm happy for you, Lauren, and for your new librarian man. He's one lucky book nerd."

Using the NASA examiner as the only spokesperson on the fitness testing seemed to work. NASA was included in all the stories, even if Landon continued to drive most of the ink. I know it's not a competition. They weren't fighting for a single seat on the shuttle. Both of them would go up. But when you do the fitness testing head to head, you have to expect the coverage to play that way. My favourite story ran in the *Boston Globe*. The headline:

NASA SAYS LANDON FITTER THAN CRANK

CHAPTER 13

The first four weeks of training for the two citizen astronauts flew by. There were daily mission briefings, training sessions for the simple experiments they would conduct while in orbit, frequent visits to the space station mock-up to get a feel for where they would be spending eight days of their lives, and several hours in the shuttle simulator so they could "experience" launches and landings. I was there for it all and found it utterly fascinating. With fifty years of experience behind them, NASA really knew how to train astronauts. Even hovering on the periphery, I felt like I could command the shuttle myself by the end of the program.

Landon was acing everything. She would pop up with answers to questions the instructors hadn't yet asked. Her body of knowledge of the space program, the shuttle, the International Space Station, and life in orbit was vast, simply based on the years of independent research and reading that fuelled her lifelong passion. She impressed the NASA training team and made them forget about her age. In a few instances, she pulled out relevant observations and connections from the Mercury and Gemini space programs of the sixties that the youngish instructors had never even contemplated.

Eugene held his own but could not always disguise his frustration and anger that Landon was unintentionally showing him up in virtually every aspect of the training program. Even though it was not really essential for the citizen astronauts to understand the math and physics underpinning lift-off, launch trajectory, orbit, gravity, and re-entry, Eugene clearly struggled, while Landon knew it all backwards and forwards.

By the end of the first month, it was clear to anyone on the inside who possessed the most primitive powers of observation that Landon was the star of the program. Eugene could see it too.

There were also increasingly invasive medical examinations to ensure that neither Eugene nor Landon was unfit for the mission or would carry anything untoward into space, from malaria and measles to flu and fleas. They both got clean bills of health although Eugene, perhaps as penance for being such a royal pain in the ass, and in a spasm of ironic symmetry, apparently had a very impressive inflamed hemorrhoid. The medication worked quite effectively, but regrettably, Eugene was still a pain in the ass when the doctors were done. Despite TK's penchant for publicizing every morsel of good news even remotely related to the Citizen Astronaut program, there was no "Crank's Hemorrhoid

A-Okay" news release, though I did come up with a draft just to entertain Landon.

In week five, Commander Hainsworth and the rest of the crew of the space shuttle *Aeres* arrived in Houston from the Kennedy Space Center in Florida to commence full crew training with their citizen astronauts. As planned, Martine Juneau became Landon's mission buddy, and they were a match made in . . . orbit. They got along very well and were quite the team during the many training exercises.

One of the highlights that Landon had been eagerly anticipating was the simulation of weightlessness on the famed Vomit Comet. It was a repurposed jet liner with most of the seats removed. Wall-to-wall padding turned the plane into one long cushioned cylinder. All astronauts make several sorties in the Vomit Comet and invariably return to Earth deeply grateful for the soft walls, ceiling, and floor.

The pilot climbs to a lofty altitude and then carves a parabolic arc in the sky. As the nose moves from pointing upwards to pointing downwards, the passengers experience weightlessness for short periods of time. The pilots learned early on to remain strapped into their seats for these particular training flights, flying dozens of these parabolic circuits in one flight. You can find several YouTube videos of astronaut trainees somersaulting in mid-air from one end of the plane to the other, and catching floating Smarties in their mouths during these brief interludes of weightlessness. Why the name Vomit Comet? Well, one hardly needs to ask. Let's just say that human digestion of food works best in the presence of gravity. Human ejection of food works very well in the absence of gravity. After five decades, NASA had learned a thing or two about humans in space. It seems that a predictable portion of astronauts will suffer space sickness during their missions. It feels much like sea sickness, but you just can't lean over the deck rail to throw up. Other than a few rides on the Vomit Comet, there are few pre-flight indicators to help determine who will get sick. Some astronauts will and some won't.

Based on my recent Beaver flights, I realized that I can feel queasy in a swivelling office chair. So I elected to stay on the ground when Landon and Eugene were scheduled for their flight. Thanks to built-in cameras on the plane, I was able to sit in the control room with two NASA instructors and watch the in-flight proceedings live on a large monitor, while my feet remained firmly planted on terra firma. I'd said goodbye and good luck to Landon and Eugene on the tarmac as Martine Juneau led them up the steps and into the plane. They would be the only three astronauts on this flight.

It took about twenty minutes for the plane to take off and reach the required altitude. From the safety of the control room, we could see the padded section of the plane with a couple of rows of seats at the rear, where Martine and the two citizen astronaut trainees were sitting. We also had the plane's audio feed piped through to us. We heard the pilot say that they were ready to start the first parabola. Seconds later, we watched as

Landon, Eugene, and Martine, resplendent in their orange coveralls, unbuckled their seat belts. They held on to grab straps to secure themselves during the plane's climb. Martine was a true professional, offering support and guidance to both rookies. Landon had a giddy look on her face and seemed about ready to burst with excitement. On the other hand, Eugene was already a shade that I don't think I can adequately describe using only the standard colours of the spectrum. And the fun hadn't even started yet. Looking at Eugene, I wondered if facial pallor might be a good indicator of who was predisposed to space sickness. The pilot's voice crackled through the control room speakers indicating the first arc was about to begin. Then Martine was floating freely, pushing herself off the walls and literally flying the length of the cabin. She grabbed on to a strap at the far end and gave Landon the high sign. She needed no encouragement and let herself float, completely weightless. I have never seen a happier person in my life. She just beamed all the way to Martine at the other end, turning over in the air and getting a sense of her own body in this new state. Then it was the gifted athlete Eugene's turn. He pushed off the floor, shooting directly into the ceiling, head-first. The padding enveloped his head so that for a split second he actually looked decapitated. He floated back down and bumped his way along to join the other two. You could tell even before the pilot confirmed it that the first parabola was done. Martine and Landon settled onto a padded bench to await the next period of weightlessness. Eugene missed the bench and hit the floor. He tried to make it seem as if he'd meant to land there, but with one leg folded at a ligament-straining angle beneath him, I don't think anyone was fooled.

Over time, the two rookies seemed to get the hang of it. Martine could tuck and do somersaults, and even performed full layout spins. It was kind of like synchronized swimming, without the water, sequins, and nose clips. Landon was in her element. She eventually seemed nearly as comfortable when weightless as when subject to the force of gravity. She was very coordinated and could easily follow the procedures and exercises that Martine directed. Eugene also completed everything he was supposed to, but looked as if he might die at any moment.

The flight was cut short a few arcs early, thanks to Eugene. There's a procedure commonly used by women when putting on perfume. I can't explain how or why I know this, but I just do. Anyway, they will spritz a cloud of fragrance directly in front of them, and then walk through it to ensure an even application. Well, Eugene put his own unique twist on this manoeuvre. While floating through the cushioned cabin, he honoured the plane's nickname and threw up his hearty breakfast. Then for good measure, he continued floating and passed completely through his own vomit cloud, ensuring an even, full-immersion application. What had been completely *in* him was now completely *on* him. By then, given my tender constitution, I was halfway to throwing up myself. Landon immediately pushed off the back wall and reached Eugene in one quick flight. There wasn't much she could do until the plane levelled off and they once again gained their original weight. So she just held his hand to steady him and seemed to be talking to him. Martine grabbed the microphone off the wall and spoke into it, I assume to curtail the flight. With gravity reasserted, the three strapped into their seats for the landing.

I waited on the tarmac as the metal staircase was rolled up to the plane and the door swung open. Out came Martine, followed by Landon still leading Eugene by the hand and still talking to him. He looked a little out of it. He'd changed into blue coveralls and Landon carried a big clear plastic bag with his contaminated orange ones. His overall look had improved to "gravely ill."

"I was sick as a dog this morning," Eugene mumbled. "In my condition, I should never have been allowed to get into that puke plane."

"I thought your stunt was very impressive, Mr. Crank," Landon soothed. "Not many would have the coordination and spatial ability – while weightless, remember – to capture every last molecule of your airborne breakfast in a single pass. Yet you did it. The plane is still spotless. You saved the crew a massive clean-up job, and I think you should get points for that."

Eugene burped.

Landon winked at me as she escorted Eugene to the van for the drive back to the Johnson Space Center. I was careful not to look too closely in Eugene's hair. But I can report that the smell was absolutely paint-peeling.

Amanda called that night and I could barely hold it together recounting the day's events. It took me ten minutes to tell a four-minute story, because I couldn't stop laughing. We chatted for about an hour and a half. She told me that Diane was really stepping up and doing a great job as the overall account director of the NASA project. Diane had celebrated her promotion by buying yet another new pair of freaky glasses. I can't really remember exactly how Amanda described them, but feathers, two watch batteries, and pressurized neon were mentioned. There was no news about Crawford Blake since his abrupt departure from the company. He'd apparently taken a long trip to Europe and hadn't been heard from since. I told Amanda that Kelly Bradstreet had spent a long time, one on one, with Eugene Crank the day it had all gone down. He claimed Blake had only suggested he enter the contest. He insisted he was completely unaware that his name would be drawn. Kelly wasn't sure she believed him, but at least Eugene seemed marginally more cooperative thereafter. I said nothing to Landon about it all. She was too deeply immersed in her training and there was really no reason to tell her.

"Do you have any regrets about sending the incriminating photo to Margot?" I asked.

"It took me a long time to muster the courage," she replied. "I had worshipped Crawford Blake for years and tried to model my career path after his. But the more we worked together, the more I realized that he's really not that smart. He's just a bully and a blowhard who looks good in a suit. I don't want to get ahead at TK by being a bully. After my last few encounters with him, particularly on the Landon question, it was an easy call to send the photo. And Margot was really supportive. I really think I'm in a stronger career position now than before. So thanks for passing it along."

I realized after I'd hung up that we'd only talked about work for the first twenty minutes or so. After that, we just talked. It was nice.

Turner King continued carpet bombing the media to keep the program front and centre in the minds of Americans and Canadians. And I did my job in Houston, sticking close to Landon as she sailed through it all. At least once each week, I escorted Landon and Eugene to the media studio at the JSC for satellite interviews on talk shows and public affairs programs across the continent. I would work with them both to polish their key messages and hone their delivery. I showed them how to avoid the standard traps journalists would set, from "the long pause" to the "relax, it's over, chat." We covered them all. A NASA videographer accompanied the citizen astronauts throughout their training. I would review and sanitize the footage we released almost daily. I also took the lead on our social media channels, tweeting up a storm about Landon's training exploits. In short, I coordinated with the Toronto TK office so that Amanda and her team could keep the Canadian media on a steady diet of Landon Percival.

At the end of each week in the training program, the TK polling team went into the field with U.S. and Canadian tracking surveys to monitor awareness and probe public opinion. Landon was pulling great numbers in Canada and her ratings were growing steadily. Deeper analysis of the cross-tabs suggested that most Canadians were appalled that there were still sporadic protests at the JSC's main gate about Landon's sexuality. Of course, the survey results were not for public consumption, but the insights certainly informed our ongoing communications plan. As for Eugene, well, the TK D.C. team did a masterful and seemingly impossible job, transforming him from a petty and arrogant jackass in reality into a swaggering Captain America in the eyes of his adoring fellow citizens. The real problem was that Eugene Crank completely swallowed his own PR. He believed the artificially enhanced image of himself that TK manufactured on TV. He conveniently erased from his own mind the daily reality of his mediocre performance in the training.

Best of all, though, the client was happy. In fact, Kelly Bradstreet was thrilled with all the coverage and with the polls that showed public engagement numbers approaching those last seen in the halcyon days of the Apollo program.

Right through to the end of the two-month training program, the gruelling pace of daily briefings, training exercises, and weekly media interviews was sustained. Through it all, Eugene was still sarcastic and petulant whenever he was with Landon, although she never seemed to notice. She was unfailingly supportive in

return. There was one major hurdle they both still had to sur-
mount before they could be cleared for the mission. Landon
had spent decades preparing for it. Eugene had not. Landon was
not worried in the least about the final test. As an "outstanding
athlete," neither was Eugene.

On the Monday of week eight, Landon, Eugene, and I
boarded a NASA flight from Houston to California. We were
headed for the heart of Silicon Valley and the Ames Research
Center at Moffett Field, where Landon and Eugene would
ride in the cramped cabin of the 20G Centrifuge. Technically,
passing the centrifuge test, which really just meant *not passing
out* in the centrifuge test, was no longer an official requirement for standard-issue NASA astronauts. But the chief of astronaut training, Scott Chandler, had insisted that Landon and
Eugene be spun at Ames, just to simulate the Gs they would
pull during the mission.

We landed at Moffett Field and were driven to one of the many
buildings making up NASA's state of the art R&D facility known
as the Ames Research Center. After checking into our quarters
and dumping our overnight bags, we were escorted into the 20G
Centrifuge control room. Eugene and Landon were wearing
their regular orange coveralls. I was wearing khakis and, well, it
really doesn't much matter what I was wearing.

The man himself was waiting for us.

"Scott Chandler, what a nice surprise it is to see you here,"
Landon gushed as she shook his hand.

"Dr. Percival," Chandler mumbled, his face yielding no evidence that in his lifetime he had ever smiled or would ever smile. He didn't just wear his opposition to citizen astronauts on his sleeve. Rather, it was plastered all over his entire body and was thick in the aura around him.

"Good to see you again, Scott," said Eugene. "So you're our spin-master?"

"No, I'd say Mr. Stewart here is our resident spin-master," replied Chandler, pointing an incriminating finger in my direction. "A NASA white-coat will be here shortly to push the buttons. I'm here just as an observer. As chief of astronaut training, I didn't want to miss this."

That was more of a smirk than a smile.

"You may know that I designed the program you've been enjoying these last several weeks. So far, you've both done reasonably well for uninitiated civilians. But we don't send just anyone up into space. Before I flew my Apollo mission, I'd trained for six years, not two months," he said, shaking his head.

"And your program included desert survival training, hours in the zero gravity of the pool, and a few runs on the rocket sled," Landon interjected. "We know we've had it easy."

"Well, it's been easy up to now. Today's little exercise is what will separate the men from the boys," he said as he pointed through the control room glass into the darkness beyond.

He punched a button on the console in front of him and the 20 G Centrifuge appeared through the window in a wash of bright light. The room was all white except for a large blue NASA logo on one wall. An oversized metal arm – as if constructed from a giant Meccano set – spanned the round room and was anchored to the floor and ceiling in the middle. A blue cab was mounted on one end of the arm and a red cab on the other. Just by looking at the centrifuge, it was pretty obvious to even the untrained observer how it worked.

"So how does this thing work?" asked Eugene.

"Well, it's quite simple, Mr. Crank," responded Chandler. "We strap you into a chair in the cab at one end of the radial arm, then we spin you to simulate the G-forces you'll experience. You'll have no trouble with the Gs at launch. They just push you directly back into your seat. No problem. We won't even bother simulating the launch. But re-entering the Earth's atmosphere after the mission is a much tougher proposition. Why?"

"Because the G-force vector is longitudinal, head to toe, not just straight against your chest, as it is at launch," Landon piped up, nodding.

"Exactly right, Dr. Percival," said Chandler. "So, we've oriented the seat in the centrifuge cab to yield the G-axis you'll experience upon re-entry. Coming home, you'll only be pulling about 1.6 Gs, but for some, it's hard to take. And we always build in a factor of safety. So here's the deal. If you can't handle 2.1 Gs here, you won't be cleared for the mission."

"When do we start?" asked Landon, rubbing her hands together as if trying to start a fire between them.

A technician in a lab coat arrived right on cue.

"We start right now," Chandler said.

"I'll go first," Landon offered and headed out the door to enter the big white round room.

We watched through the glass as two more white-coats seated Landon in the red cab and buckled her into the elaborate restraint system. A monitor flickered to life on the main console and Landon materialized before our eyes. The in-cab view showed her face-on to the camera. She looked gleeful and almost giddy. The tech in the control room donned a headset microphone.

"Are you ready, Dr. Percival?" he asked.

"I've been ready for nearly thirty years. Let's fire up this merry-go-round!"

Landon's voice came booming through the speakers in the control room ceiling.

The tech looked at Scott Chandler. The wizened astronaut nodded. Buttons were pushed, switches flipped, and dials turned. The noise of the motor grew louder as the big arm began to turn. A digital reading on the console gave us the G-forces in play in the cab. Suddenly, a very strange sound burst into the control room. It was almost like singing. Well, it was more like a donkey, or perhaps a water buffalo, singing.

Okay, it was singing. Landon was belting out an old show tune in a voice better suited for breaking glass. The readout registered .9 G. The tech immediately dialled back the speaker volume so Landon's singing was no longer painful, just unpleasant.

Scott Chandler was wincing, but he was still watching the monitor. Landon looked like she was having a great time, beaming as she sang. The tech sought and received the signal from Chandler and increased the rotational speed. The readout now said 1.4 G.

"Come on, boys, let's turn this thing. I'm not feeling much more than one G here!" Landon shouted, still smiling.

Then it was back to Broadway as Landon broke in to "June Is Bustin' Out All Over."

Scott Chandler nodded again, and the tech upped the speed once more. The digital readout jumped to 1.8 G. Landon kept singing but her tone changed. When the readout hit 2.2 G, her voice sounded like a cross between Pee-wee Herman and Linda Blair at the height of her big-screen exorcism. This made the next verse particularly excruciating.

2.4 Gs now.

Landon's singing slowed a bit as she spun faster and faster. I didn't dare look out the window to see the whirling arm but kept my eyes focused on Landon's face as she sang through a smile.

"Aren't we well beyond the required G force now?" I asked, getting a little concerned.

"Yes, we are. But I was trying to get her to stop that infernal noise," Scott Chandler replied with a sigh, before nodding to the tech.

The digital readout peaked at 2.6 G just as she growled the song's big finale at the top of her centrifuge-compressed lungs. It occurred to me that the U.S. Department of Defence might be interested in the destructive potential of Landon's vocal cords.

I pulled my fingers from my ears as the cab slowed and the whine of the big motor waned.

"That's it? We're done?" Landon asked, her voice returning to its traditional timbre. "I was just getting started."

Ten minutes later, Landon sauntered back into the control room as if she'd just returned from a nap.

"Congratulations, Dr. Percival," said Scott Chandler with what seemed like resignation. "That was an impressive performance."

"Thank you, sir. It's one of my favourite songs," Landon replied.

"I wasn't referring to your so-called singing."

"Oh. I chose that number especially for this occasion. It's from *Carousel*. Get it?" She chuckled before turning to Eugene. "Well, you're up, my boy. It's time for you to whirl."

Given his Vomit Comet experience, I silently wondered if "It's time for you to hurl" might have been the more fitting declaration.

Eugene said nothing but shuffled out the door following the white-coat, as if being led to the gallows.

"He'll be fine," Landon said.

He was not fine.

At 1.5 Gs, his head lolled over to the right and his eyes turned up into his head. He passed out.

"He pulled a *funky chicken* and he wasn't even at 2 Gs," Landon said, pointing to the monitor.

The tech immediately dropped the speed. Eugene abruptly came to.

"Why are we slowing down?" he asked.

"Well, you passed out at 1.5 Gs," the tech said into his headset microphone.

"What are y'all on about?" Eugene replied. "I was just sitting here minding my own business and enjoying the ride when you cut the engine to this here whirligig."

"Sorry, sir, but we have it all on tape. At 1.5 Gs, you actually lost consciousness, so we stopped the test."

Scott Chandler reached over to turn on the mike mounted on the console.

"I'm sorry, son, but that is what happened. It's surprising but true. Give yourself a few minutes and we'll try it again when you're feeling ready."

I leaned over to Landon's ear.

"Why did you call it a funky chicken?" I whispered.

"Passing out during centrifuge testing has been called a funky chicken for as long as I can remember," she explained. "I have no idea why."

Twenty minutes later, Eugene was ready for his second spin.

"Eugene, it's Landon. Let me give you a couple of tips before you start your second . . ."

"I've got nothing to learn from you. I've got this thing licked now. Just stand back and start her up."

Landon stepped away from the mike, shaking her head.

Eugene's second ride lasted slightly longer than his first, the operative word being "slightly." He made it to 1.8 Gs this time before the funky chicken came home to roost again. He seemed to realize he had passed out this time.

"Damnation! It happened again, didn't it?" he asked.

"I'm afraid so, Mr. Crank," replied Scott Chandler. "I'm afraid so."

We all gathered in a small briefing room down the hall from the centrifuge. Eugene looked like he might soon start crying.

"Mr. Chandler, Eugene made it to 1.8 Gs. Isn't that enough for this mission?" asked Landon. "You said yourself we won't pull more than 1.6 on re-entry, and he'll be safely strapped in the whole time."

"With the lawyers on my ass, I'm afraid we can't take that risk," Chandler said. "You could hit even more than 2.1 Gs on re-entry. Though I hate to say it, you are cleared to fly, Dr. Percival, but I regret we'll have to wash out Mr. Crank."

Eugene said nothing but buried his head in his hands and sustained a low moan that reminded us all of Landon's centrifuge singing.

"Our flight back to Houston doesn't leave for hours yet," noted Landon. "Can we give Eugene one more shot later on?"

"I don't see what trying a third time will accomplish," Chandler replied.

"But it's worth a try, isn't it?" I asked. "He's trained for nearly eight weeks now. Hasn't he earned at least one more shot? It will not go over well to have to announce to the world that the

American citizen astronaut didn't make the grade. It'll over-shadow everything we've tried to do with this program."

"Well, I thought this whole idea was stupid from the get-go. So what do I care?" Chandler grumbled.

"Please, one last try?" implored Landon.

Scott Chandler checked with the tech about the centrifuge's availability later on.

"Okay, Mr. Crank. If you're up for it, you've got one final attempt at 1600 hours. I suggest you relax until then. You've got three hours to turn this around or there'll only be one so-called citizen astronaut riding the *Aeres*."

We walked back to our rooms together. No one said anything. Eugene turned the key in his door and went inside. Before the door could close, Landon followed him in. Wondering why, and not want-ing to stand by myself out in the corridor, I followed Landon in too.

"What's going on?" Eugene turned and asked with an edge. "You want to gloat some more?"

"You sure are testing my capacity for kindness," Landon replied.

She pulled out the wooden chair from the desk and positioned it in the centre of the room.

"Sit in this chair," she commanded.

Strangely enough, he didn't look like he was interested in fol-lowing her orders. What a shock.

"Sit down or you'll blow your one remaining chance to hitch a ride on that shuttle, and all we've gone through in the last two months will be wasted. *Sit!*"

Despite himself, Eugene seemed to sense something in Landon's tone that needed to be heeded. He sat down and folded his arms across his chest looking like a five-year-old on a time-out.

"Look, Eugene. You can do this. You've got one last shot," she started. "I've been spinning myself silly in a centrifuge in my back forty for more years than I care to count. And I've learned the technique that can get you up past 2.1 Gs if you'll just listen to me and practise."

"There is no technique. You just sit and spin and try not to puke and pass out," he whined.

"That is where you're wrong," Landon replied.

"Well, he's been wrong in other places too," I added helpfully.

Landon ignored me.

"We're going to teach you AGSM. And you are going to sail past three Gs this afternoon."

"What the Sam Hill is AGMS?" Eugene barked.

"It's AGSM, and stands for Anti-Gravity Straining Manoeuvre. Here, I'll show you."

She reached out, took both Eugene's arms and wrists, and positioned them close to his body and against the inside edges of the chair arms. Similarly, she then positioned his feet so they were flat on the floor but against the inside edges of the chair legs.

"Okay, when the centrifuge starts up, I want you to push your arms against the frame of the chair as if you're trying to break the arms off it. Do the same with your feet and legs. Push for all you're worth against the inside surface of each chair leg. Strain yourself. Tighten up all your muscles. This will help keep the centrifugal force from pushing the blood from your brain into your extremities. Do you understand?"

Eugene had actually started listening early on and now nodded his understanding.

"Okay. Show me. Give me a red face, Eugene."

He stayed perfectly still, but his arms and legs strained against the confines of the chair. Soon he was vibrating and his facial hue was changing.

"Like this?" he grunted.

"Just like that," Landon agreed. "One more thing. To sustain positive pressure in your lungs, press your lips tightly together, and open them just a bit to breathe in and out. Show me."

Eugene went back to straining against the chair while pursing his lips, turning red, and vibrating. He looked like he was in the throes of the final confrontation with a severe case of acute constipation.

"So how can Eugene sing Broadway show tunes if his lips are pressed together?" I asked.

"David. Eugene is still a rookie. It took me years of practice before I could add Rodgers and Hammerstein to AGSM."

We stayed with Eugene and worked on his "straining training" for the next two hours. We had to stop a few minutes early when he actually did snap both arms off the chair. Landon took that as a good sign. Just before we left him, Landon handed him one the large plastic Ziploc freezer bags she'd handed me during our return flight to Mackenzie so many weeks ago.

"Try to hold it all together until you get out of cabin. Swallow a lot. Then you can use this if you need to, but try to be subtle about it."

———————

At 4:00 p.m., we were all back in the 20 G Centrifuge control room. I can't imagine what happens to the human body at 20 Gs.

"Ready, Mr. Crank?" asked Scott Chandler.

"Ready!" grunted Eugene, already strapped in and in full straining mode.

Landon and I watched the numbers on the digital readout as the arm began to rotate. Eugene wasn't singing, but he was humming something indecipherable.

The red digits on the G scale moved upwards quickly, 1.5, 1.7, 1.9. Eugene was still with us, his face moving through various shades of red as he pushed his arms and legs against the seat frame.

2.0, 2.1.

"Okay, he's there!" shouted Landon. "Shut it down."

Scott Chandler raised his hand to countermand Landon's order.

2.2, 2.3, 2.4. Still, Eugene was with us, his face now shaking with the effort of keeping the blood in his head where it belonged.

"Okay, I think that will suffice," NASA chief of astronaut training said before the tech slowed the big arm. Chandler hit the mike button. "I don't know how you did it, Mr. Crank, but you've passed the G test and are cleared for the mission."

When Eugene made it back into the control room, I noticed the corner of the Ziploc bag peeking out from the now bulging pocket of his coveralls. His face was slowly returning to its natural complexion. He ignored Scott Chandler and walked directly over to Landon. Then he hugged her. He kindly averted his face.

———

We landed back in Houston at 7:30. I was exhausted, even though I'd just sat on my ass all day watching Landon and Eugene scrambling their insides in a giant blender. Watching Eugene strain against the chair in his room for two hours seemed to have taken its toll on me. After dinner, Landon dragged me over to the library and archives at the Johnson Space Center. I had no idea what we were doing there until the friendly librarian set us up on a computer with a large and crystal-clear monitor beneath a sign that read *LandSat Images*.

"You can input a precise latitude and longitude here, and then the database will give you a listing of the dates and times of each satellite shot. Just click on the ones you want to view, and they'll come up on the screen. Hit Escape to return to the listing."

I thought I had an idea what Landon was up to, but watched in silence to be sure.

She punched in a latitude and longitude, obviously from memory, and hit Enter.

The listing of satellite photos spewed onto the screen starting with a date from late last year, and moving back in time. The satellite, one of the earliest to photograph the Earth, shot photos from the time it was launched in 1970 until last year when it had burned up in the atmosphere somewhere over the Pacific Ocean. Landon scrolled down, down, down, through several screens. Yes, I knew what she was doing.

She stopped the cursor at October 16, 1970. She clicked the mouse button. The screen was filled with a black and white satellite photo. I didn't recognize what I was looking at until she zoomed in to the top right corner. A tiny lake, shaped like a cigar, grew larger and larger as she clicked the Magnify arrow on the screen. Soon, only the east end of the lake was visible as it filled the screen. Her hands were trembling.

"Is that your father's Beaver at the dock?" I asked.

She nodded. I could see the same cabin I'd recently visited. But it was a photograph from forty years or so earlier.

"This was taken just one day before my father disappeared."

I knew where she was going. I helped her split the screen so we could open next to it the same aerial shot from the fateful day following. I could see only two differences in the second photo. The surface of the lake looked a little darker in the second photo. And Hugh Percival's Beaver was no longer moored at the dock.

"The satellite takes the shot at 3:46 p.m. each day," Landon said in hushed tones. "This photo we're looking at was literally snapped about an hour and a quarter after my father took off and was never seen again."

I confess it was eerie and moving just to look at it. For the next five hours, we scoured the satellite shots of the surrounding area taken over several days following his disappearance, hoping to see some evidence of her father's fate. In a few hours, we used satellite photos to cover the same ground that had taken Landon the previous forty years to search. But still, we found nothing. Not a single trace. Nothing at all. The satellite photos told a simple story. Hugh Percival and his plane were there on Cigar Lake on October 16, 1970. Then, one day later, on October 17, 1970, they just disappeared from the face of the Earth.

PART 5

CHAPTER 14

Now that Landon had been cleared for the mission, she enjoyed some well-earned downtime. For Landon downtime tended not to involve anything a normal person might consider relaxing. But she was on a mission that did not involve the space shuttle. She spent our last few days in Houston sequestered in the library, immersed in satellite photos at the *LandSat Images* terminal. She could cover so much more ground so much faster than she could flying the Beaver. She was actually mad at herself for never having thought to research this angle before. I reminded her that being an official astronaut granted her privileges not accorded to average citizens, let alone to reclusive doctor bush pilots living on a remote wilderness lake in the wilds of Canada.

I brought her coffee and sandwiches. I used a second terminal to explore the terrain just beyond the potential flight range of Hugh Percival's Beaver, just in case. Several times we found a grouping of trees that were standing one day and lying flat the next. They could have been hit by a plane, but further investigation dashed the theory. In each case when we looked at the same site the day after, more trees were down. It was loggers cutting down trees, not a Beaver knocking down trees. The librarian was sympathetic and let us stay well past closing time. But the hours of searching still yielded nothing, beyond cramped legs and a tender tush.

———————

Eight weeks and three days after arriving in Houston, Landon, Eugene, Kelly Bradstreet, and I boarded a flight for Orlando. We were headed for the Kennedy Space Center, the shuttle's launch and landing site. It was real. This was actually going to happen. In a few days, Landon Percival was going to blast into space and orbit the Earth aboard the International Space Station for more than a week and then land back at Kennedy. When I'd first concocted the idea of putting citizens in space, I was just trying to survive my first day in a new career. I never dreamed it might actually happen. I looked over at Landon in the window seat. She looked every one of her seventy-one years, until she smiled. Then she looked about eighty-three as the smile animated her face, revealing smaller creases nestled into their larger host wrinkles. It was a veritable wrinkle-fest. But she just beamed all the time. I glanced at Eugene, sitting on the aisle. He had come a long way in eight weeks, too. He'd started out as an arrogant, right-wing, conceited jerk who viewed Landon, and everything about her, with undisguised disdain bordering on contempt. Now, as the launch approached, he seemed to have evolved into an arrogant, right-wing, conceited jerk who had come to accept, respect, and even enjoy Landon, largely through her own generosity towards him. I still thought he was an ass, but Landon would hear none of it.

I'd met regularly with Kelly Bradstreet throughout the eight weeks, and we always seemed to be on the same wavelength. I thought very highly of her and had actually grown quite fond of her. She was tough, intelligent, and committed, and had little time for politics and game-playing. The Citizen Astronaut program would never have flown without her dedication and patience. NASA would not have touched this idea with a ten-foot booster rocket without her formidable powers of persuasion. Lately, she'd taken to calling me DS. I'd never had a nickname, other than Dorkpants back in public school, and it kind of made me feel like a big shot (the DS I mean, not Dorkpants).

As I sat on the plane flanked by Landon and Eugene, my thoughts eventually turned to Amanda. She'd been on my mind a lot, recently. Yes, we'd gotten off on the wrong foot on that first day in the boardroom, for which I felt responsible. But we were now well past first impressions. We "liaised" professionally nearly every day, ostensibly to coordinate the ongoing media relations and social media programs. But in the last few weeks, we seemed to have moved beyond "liaising" to actually talking, like normal human beings. Our conversations had grown longer and longer, and further and further away from the Citizen Astronaut program. We were no longer two PR professionals "liaising" about work. We seemed to have become just two friends yakking with one another about whatever was on our minds. It happened so gradually that I barely noticed. I wondered if she had. It had all become so comfortable. I chatted to Landon about it all, and she listened patiently as I tried to work out if something was, you know, going on. She posed a few questions that helped focus my thinking, but I really wasn't very good at picking up on signs and interpreting signals. Given my limited experience in matters of the heart, apart from a few short-lived romances in Ottawa, I missed everything subtler than a two-by-four to the forehead.

We broke below the cloud cover and Orlando bloomed below. Without warning, Landon knocked me out of my romantic reverie with a hard elbow jab to my chest, nearly winding me.

"Wake up!" she said. "We are T-minus three minutes to touchdown."

"And I am T-minus two minutes to normal respiration," I wheezed, rubbing my ribs.

"Come on, I barely touched you."

———

As soon as we reached the Kennedy Space Center, Landon and Eugene joined Commander Hainsworth, Martine Juneau, and the rest of the crew of the Space Shuttle *Aeres*, and my responsibilities as Landon's chaperone effectively ended. It felt weird.

I'd been attached to her for more than two months. Now she was gone, off with her fancy new astronaut friends, and I was all alone, kicked to the sidelines. I felt a little bereft. I know. I'm pathetic. I knew it was going to happen, and intellectually, it all made sense. They grow up so fast. But it did feel strange to be on my own as the launch loomed.

The next afternoon, Kelly Bradstreet stood at the podium and introduced each mission crew member as they filed in and took their places along the table at the front. Their official mission crest served as the backdrop. The news conference was set up like every other pre-launch mission briefing, except this time, two civilians were up on the risers as full members of the *Aeres* crew. The room was packed with reporters and camera crews. Many of the networks had sent their heavyweight reporters and even a few anchors to cover the news conference and subsequent launch. Kelly introduced Scott Chandler, and the aging rocket jockey mounted the steps and stood at the microphone.

"Good afternoon, everyone. Thank you for coming," he began. "As you can see, our crew for this important mission, under Lee Hainsworth's command, has a slightly different composition from our typical lineup. I am very pleased to announce formally what you probably already know. Both of our citizen astronauts, Mr. Eugene Crank from Wilkers, Texas, and Dr. Landon Percival from Cigar Lake, Canada, have successfully completed our training program and have been officially cleared for the mission. They have not had an easy ride. The training program is challenging, demanding, and at times even gruelling. I'm impressed with their tenacity, their energy and enthusiasm, and their dedication to the mission. As one of the original Apollo astronauts, I freely admit that I was skeptical that civilians could be, or even should be, trained to the required level to fly such a mission as this. Mr. Crank and Dr. Percival have altered my view. I wish them well on their once-in-a-lifetime voyage. And it should be noted for history's sake that tomorrow, Dr. Landon Percival will become the oldest woman and the second-oldest human being ever to venture into space. Godspeed."

Landon's eyes were glistening but she was calm and still smiling. On instinct, I started to applaud. Eventually, Kelly, the mission crew, and one reporter joined in. I felt like a bit of an idiot. Journalists don't attend news conferences to clap. It wasn't a pep rally or an awards show.

Kelly bounded back up to the mike as Scott Chandler stepped down and took a seat in the front row.

"We'll hear now from the mission crew," she announced.

In turn, each member of the *Aeres* crew pulled the table mike in front of them closer and said a few words. The real astronauts all spoke beautifully about what the mission meant to them. Martine Juneau delivered part of her remarks in French. I thought the Radio-Canada camera operator at the back was going to have some kind of an excitement-induced seizure. French was rarely spoken at NASA pre-launch briefings. Then Landon spoke.

"I have a few more miles on me than my crew mates, so I am just so grateful for the rare chance to fly this mission and fulfil what has been a lifelong dream. I've been a pilot since I was thriteen years old. I learned how to fly from my father, Dr. Hugh Percival. He often called me 'Sky' because I was seldom looking anywhere else. To this day, whenever I fly my float plane through the remote reaches of British Columbia, I want to fly higher. Tomorrow it looks like I will. And I expect it will be the single greatest moment in what has been so far a wonderful and rewarding life, with few regrets.

"I want to thank Scott Chandler, Kelly Bradstreet, and NASA for putting up with an old broad in orange coveralls, and for having the courage to train and clear me for this mission. They certainly did not take the easy way out. And I like to think I know a thing or two about rejecting the path of least resistance. But I know they chose the right path. I'm sorry if it put several NASA lawyers on stress leave, but they'll be fine when we're back safely on the ground in nine days. I'd also like to thank my friend and shadow, David Stewart, who, for some reason, had faith in me, almost from the very start. I don't think I'd be sitting here this afternoon were it not for him.

"I think I've taxed your time enough. May I just say that I've really enjoyed working so closely with my friend and fellow traveller, Eugene Crank. And I am more grateful than I can ever express to be warming a seat on the *Aeres* alongside such an impressive group of men and women."

On her closing line, she reached over and grabbed Eugene's hand, lifted it up in the air, and gave it a little shake. I withdraw my earlier statement that reporters don't clap at news conferences. It seems they do sometimes.

When the room settled, it was Eugene's turn. He pulled the mike so close to him you'd think he'd mistaken it for an ice cream cone. Then he blew into it to make sure it was on. The screaming feedback from his mouth-to-mike resuscitation answered his question and he pushed it back a bit until the squeal was squelched. Poor guy.

"Um. Hi, y'all. I just wanted to say that other than getting shot at by some punk robbing a gas station in '07, this is the most exciting thing that's ever happened to me. The training wasn't that tough but there were a couple of rough patches. Sometimes you get surprised by who helps you out. Um, I guess I'll see y'all on the other side . . . I mean when we land."

He eagerly pushed the mike away from him. Landon patted his hand. Kelly then opened the floor for questions. No one asked Eugene anything. A few reporters asked the mission commander about the launch and the work they'd be doing on the space station. But most of the questions were for Landon. Even though I'd warned her, I'm not sure she was expecting to be the focus of attention. But she handled it all like a pro. I wondered again how someone who had lived alone for most of her life could seem so at ease and be so articulate. When I asked her later, she wasn't really sure but credited her daily one-sided conversations with her missing father, and her love of reading. She also reminded me that she had briefly practised medicine in Vancouver in the late sixties and so had daily contact with lots of patients. Right. The late sixties, when she was not yet thirty years old. Right. I just figured it was an innate gift.

Kelly called for a final question and pointed to CNN's Ali Velshi. He rose.

"Dr. Percival, in your comments earlier you said you'd lived, and I quote, 'a wonderful and rewarding life, with few regrets.' What are those regrets?"

Landon's near-permanent smile seemed to me to turn wistful, and she nodded her head almost imperceptibly.

"Well, I don't have many," she responded. "It's simple, really. The regrets I carry revolve around people I'm missing. And I'll just leave it at that."

———

Commander Hainsworth and the rest of his crew were whisked out. Landon looked my way but I was on the other side of a very crowded room. She smiled and waved. I waved and mouthed "Good luck" in return. She gave me a thumbs-up and was out the door, dwarfed by Eugene Crank walking in front of her.

I helped Kelly mop up from the newser, providing background info to a few reporters still in the room as they pieced their stories together.

"Nice job, Kelly," I said when the reporters had all left. "Who wrote Chandler's remarks?"

"Who do you *think* wrote them?" she said, grinning.

"They were nice words and he read them well. He almost sounded as if he meant it."

"Thank you. I worked hard on them. They were even better before he toned some of it down," she replied. "You did a nice job on Landon's."

"I take no credit for her words. They were all hers, and extemporaneous too, I think."

Kelly smiled and shook her head. She looked over my shoulder towards the door.

"Gotta go. Have a good time tonight," she said with a wink and a wave, as she hustled to catch up with the crew for a final communications briefing. Good time?

The technicians were almost finished their tear-down, coiling cords and stowing microphones.

"Well, I guess my work here is done," I said to no one in particular. I grabbed my papers and turned for the door.

"Hello, stranger," she said, standing in the doorway. Her smile was one I hadn't seen before. Of course I'd often seen her smile, but this one was somehow different.

"Amanda! What are you doing here? How did you get here? Is anything wrong?" I spewed.

"Whoa. You got to read me my rights before the interrogation." She was still smiling.

"Sorry. I'm just shocked, and, um, and happy, to see you," I sputtered, which was a small step up from spewing.

"I figured after what you've been through for the last couple of months, you deserved some company for the launch," she explained. "Diane suggested I come down to lend a hand. So, I just landed, dumped my stuff in my room, and here I am, a hand ready to lend."

"Well, this is great. It's really nice to see you, and to have you here," I rambled, another step up from sputtering. "And your timing is impeccable. We're off the clock now. With the crew finally all together, the NASA communications team takes over. I'll be in Launch Control in the morning in case Landon has any last-second issues, which she won't. But other than that, we're done. I can see if I can get you into Launch Control, too."

"I already spoke to Kelly. No dice. We're lucky to have one person in there. But she got me a spot in the VIP viewing box outside."

"I'm envious. You'll get a better view from there. In fact, you'll actually be able to feel the launch from there. I'll be watching it on a computer monitor in a windowless room in what kind of looks like a concrete bunker."

"Yeah, but not many people can say they've done that."

"So, how about dinner?" I asked, wondering if I sounded like a work colleague.

Without a rental car, our dining options were limited at the Kennedy Space Center. We rejected the G-Force Grill, Space

Dots, and the Moon Rock Café (I kid you not), and opted for the nicest of the bunch, the Orbit Café. There were lots of tourists and school tours still milling about when we headed in for an early dinner. I briefly worried that the entrées might come in squeeze tubes. They didn't. Actually the menu wasn't bad. But I really don't remember much about the food. Amanda and I just started talking again as we had almost every night for the past month. Except, this time she was sitting directly across from me, not sitting on the phone thirteen hundred miles away. Being able to look at her as we chatted was nice. Very nice. We talked and laughed, then talked and laughed some more. We covered a broad range of topics from Canadian politics to cooking, world travel to favourite comedians, the skin-shedding habits of the albino leopard gecko to Sherlock Holmes. The three and a half hours we spent in the Orbit Café passed in a blur. The next ten hours we spent in my room passed a little more slowly.

———

I barely noticed the first knock. But I heard the second. It was still dark outside. I pulled on a pair of sweat pants and padded to the door.

"'The game is afoot,'" whispered Landon.

"'The Adventure of the Abbey Grange,'" I mumbled, still getting my bearings.

"Good boy," she replied. "Even half asleep you've still got it."

The light from the corridor spilled into my room. She looked past me and saw a head of blonde hair spilled across the pillow. My pillow.

"Is that Amanda?" Landon asked.

"Yes, I guess it is," I answered a little sheepishly.

"Wonderful, David! See, you were right!"

She actually punched me in the arm like a teenage room-mate might.

I looked at the digital clock on the nightstand and it suddenly dawned on me that Landon was not supposed to be standing at my door at 5:45 in the morning.

"You can't be here now, you're supposed to be in pre-launch prep," I hissed.

"Don't fret. I've been there already and I'm heading back there now. Martine is in the getaway car in the parking lot," explained Landon. "I simply could not suit up and climb aboard the *Aeres* without thanking you for all you've done to put me there. None of this would have happened if you hadn't worked your magic at the beginning and held my hand through all of this. Without you, some other Canadian would be on board the shuttle this morning, and I'd be moping around with Hector back at the lake. Whatever else happens, I'll never ever forget what you've done for me."

She hugged me for a long time and I was actually tearing up as she pulled away and trotted back down the corridor. I think she was, too. In the dimness, she looked like a twelve-year-old running off to play, not a seventy-one-year-old bush pilot doctor from Cigar Lake bound for the space station in Earth orbit.

The first faint inkling of morning light glowed in the eastern sky. Amanda slept. I just stood there for a while, too content to move.

———————

Launch Control at the Kennedy Space Center was housed in a low-rise white building. Inside action central, banks of monitors and computers were arrayed on a white tile floor. About thirty or so members of the *Aeres* launch team huddled at their respective stations. The launch director sat nearly at the centre of it all, but he was supported by many others, including the flow director, the tank/booster test conductor, the payload test conductor, the launch processing system coordinator, the shuttle project engineer, and the ground launch sequencer engineer, among many more impressive people, each with their own impressive titles. I was stationed at a very small console at the very back of the room. My job was to stay out of the way and watch the monitor in front of me. If Landon had any problems, I was there to help. I kind of wanted a cool complicated title that no one could decipher, just like everyone else in the room. But it was not forthcoming. Besides, I knew I was very lucky just to have been given a seat in Launch Control. I kept my eyes open and my yap shut.

My monitor had a split screen. One shot showed the inside of the shuttle cabin and the other was the standard NASA outside video feed of the launch pad. The clock said T-minus 36 minutes to launch. On my screen, I could see Landon in her seat. She sat perfectly still. I couldn't see Eugene, as he was not seated on the flight deck, but below. I pulled on the headset plugged into my console and could then hear the standard pre-launch exchanges between *Aeres* and Launch Control. I watched and listened. All seemed well.

I felt a tap on my shoulder. I pulled off the headset and turned to face a man in white coveralls and white hat that made him look a little like a short-order fry cook. I recognized him from the suit-up drills.

"You David Stewart?"

"The one and only," I replied.

"Dr. Percival tried to smuggle this on board in her suit, but we caught it," he said. "You're not supposed to bring anything bigger than a rabbit's foot on the shuttle, and even then, it has to be approved first. We had to take it from her. She was not pleased, but she insisted I give it to you to hold onto until she's back."

He handed me a whitish opaque plastic bag. I took it and nodded. After he'd gone, I opened the bag and pulled out the soft leather notebook that served as Dr. Hugh Percival's diary and flight log. I held it in my hands feeling the years, the flights, and the mystery within. I opened it, turned the well-thumbed pages, and re-read his last entry.

At T-minus 15 minutes to launch, a young woman sat down in the seat next to me and started working the buttons and switches on her console. Her screen flickered to life with what looked like weather maps. I leaned over.

"I'm David Stewart, I'm the pest control coordinator."

She had the grace to chuckle.

"I know who you are," she replied. "Sandra Evans, launch meteorology."

I looked at her monitor and thought I understood what was playing out on the screen.

"So you're in charge of scrubbing the mission if there's lightning in the area?"

"I guess you could say that. But we're good to go today. Skies are clear and the winds are light."

I saw "sww" flashing on her screen with a number beside it.

"What does that mean?" I asked and pointed.

"Southwest winds," she replied.

"Right."

I watched her work a little longer and was just about to turn back to my own screen when the sww changed to sw. It had a familiarity about it. And there it was. It arrived like a speeding freight train. Suddenly, I knew. I was certain. I yanked open the leather notebook and re-read Hugh Percival's final entry again, and then once more. We were five minutes from launch. I grabbed my BlackBerry and scrolled through my contacts. I found the name I was seeking and wrote an email to a guy I knew who worked at Environment Canada. I asked him a very simple question, and then hit Send. I was calm. Somehow, I was sure.

I put my headphones back on for the big show. On my screen, they had started the shower of sparks directly beneath the gaping mouths of the shuttle's main engines. For years I'd thought this was how they fired up the engines. It seemed a rather primitive technique. I did the same thing whenever I hit the starter button on my gas barbecue, and I had the singed eyebrows to prove it. In fact, I learned that the spark shower was merely there to burn off any stray gases beneath the engine nozzles. We were at T-minus one minute, 25 seconds. My thoughts turned to Amanda, then to Landon, then to her father's notebook, and then back to Amanda. Landon now.

The always sedate voice of Launch Control brought me back. It was time.

"Sound suppression water system has been armed," I heard in my headset.

"We have a go for auto-sequence start."

"*Aeres* computers have primary control."

I couldn't sit for this. I stood up, turning my headset into a floorset. By the time I picked it up and pulled it back on, we were in the final seconds. My whole body was rigid with excitement. I hugged myself and bent over, my eyes glued to the monitor. At T minus 15 seconds, I watched the screen as Martine Juneau offered her gloved hand to Landon. She held it briefly in an "all for one, one for all" kind of moment.

"11, 10, 9, we are go for main engine start, 6, 5, 4, 3, 2, 1, booster ignition and lift-off of the Space Shuttle *Aeres* carrying two intrepid citizen astronauts on an unforgettable ride to space."

This was not the slow lumbering lift-off of the old *Apollo Saturn V* rocket. *Aeres* practically leapt into the air. Soon I could hear the roar outside as the sound of the shuttle thundered across the land from the launch pad. On the monitor, I could see Landon and her crew mates shaking in their seats with the massive power of the launch.

"Houston now has control."

Suddenly everybody relaxed in Launch Control. Their job was now done. As soon as the shuttle cleared the tower, Mission Control in Houston took over. I watched as people pulled back just slightly from their consoles, but their eyes remained fixed on their screens. The *Aeres* commander and Mission Control continued their dialogue in unaccountably calm voices.

"Roll program go."

"Good roll program confirmed."

I watched on the screen as the shuttle rolled, orienting itself for the eight-and-a-half-minute flight to orbit. Landon was still vibrating in her seat. Then again, she'd been shaking with excitement for the previous week.

"Engines throttling down now, at 95 per cent."

"Engines now at 65 per cent."

I knew the sequence, what was supposed to happen, and when. I waited to hear the fateful words. They came at about the one-minute mark. I watched Landon as I heard them, but there was no discernable reaction.

"*Aeres*, Houston, go at throttle up."

"Roger, go at throttle up."

No space buff can hear those words without wincing and waiting. It was very shortly after "throttle up" that the *Challenger* exploded over the Atlantic back in '86, losing the crew, including a teacher from New Hampshire. It was the only time an "average citizen" had flown on a shuttle, until today. I winced and waited. All was well. Everyone was calm as *Aeres* streaked across the sky.

Thanks to the camera mounted on the external fuel tank, I watched as the solid rocket boosters were jettisoned, arcing away from *Aeres* on either side.

"SRB separation. You are clear."

"Copy that, Houston. SRB separation and clear."

"*Aeres*, Houston. Negative return."

"Houston, we copy, Negative return."

That meant the shuttle could no longer make the dead-stick glide back to the Kennedy Space Center. They were headed into orbit.

At 8:31 into the flight, the thrill of the launch was all but over.

"*Aeres*, Houston, go for main engine cut-off."

"Copy that, Houston. Main engine cut-off confirmed."

"External tank separation. Clear."

"Confirmed, Houston. External tank separation and clear."

"*Aeres*, Houston, you are confirmed in orbit, right where you're supposed to be. A picture-perfect flight and parking job."

"Copy that, Houston."

After rocketing into outer space and coasting to exactly the right position in Earth orbit, it somehow seemed inadequate to have the feat acknowledged with a simple "Copy that, Houston."

I should have given Commander Hainsworth another few seconds before passing judgment.

"Houston, you've got a grateful crew up here. Thanks for the ride."

A few minutes passed, then the *Aeres* crew started disembarking from their pressurized space suits. It was fun watching this process. It would be hard in zero-G to wriggle out of gym shorts. It was a Herculean challenge to extricate oneself from the clumsy orange space suits. While the flight deck only seated four astronauts, Eugene floated up into view from his seat below. He kept crashing into the walls, ceiling, seats, and other crew members as he jerked and wiggled his way free. I made a note to upload that sequence to YouTube, perhaps accompanied by the theme from *2001: A Space Odyssey*. You could certainly tell the experienced astronauts from the rookies. Martine very quickly, and without even seeming to move, slipped out of her suit and stowed it. Landon, who had watched as Eugene had flown aimlessly and helplessly around the cabin, wisely anchored herself in her seat while she doffed her suit. Underneath, the crew wore light pants and short-sleeved shirts of a tan colour.

So it was done. I'd watched dozens of shuttle launches but none held my attention quite like the *Aeres* launch. I glanced at Landon still strapped in. She wasn't moving much, but neither was anyone else. I knew her mind and heart would be racing. She was in space. The fulfilment of a dream. And it was just starting.

———

I didn't really know what to do with myself. I wouldn't be able to speak to Landon for several hours yet. NASA had granted us two short windows each day where I could talk to her after they docked with, and were safely aboard, the International Space Station. I didn't feel my usual self. I was so pumped up from everything. I felt like punching the air and shouting at the top of my lungs, but I restrained myself. If anyone had paid any attention to my hopping and prancing around, I probably would have been escorted from the building straight into the office of the onsite psychiatrist. My vibrating BlackBerry brought me back. I looked at the screen, then punched the green button.

"Minister, what a surprise."

"David, I just had to call. I expected to get your voicemail, so it's wonderful to catch you. You must be tickled. She made it. She's there. She's really in space," the Minister of Science and Technology said. "We watched the whole thing live here in the office. It was thrilling."

"It's even better witnessing it from here in the crucible. It was astonishing. And Minister, thanks so much for your call to Landon yesterday. It meant a lot to her."

"Well, thank you for suggesting it. I was delighted to wish her bon voyage."

We chatted for a few more minutes, but then she had to go.

I hung up, and then dialled Amanda.

"Hey. How was it from outside?" I asked.

"Hey, David. Hi. I'm still trembling. It was unbelievable. My whole body is still shaking."

"It's kind of you to say, but I'm not really asking about last night," I said. "I meant the launch."

She laughed.

"Oh, you meant the launch. Right," Amanda played along. "Well, the launch was almost as exciting. You can actually feel it when the sound wave finally hits you. And the noise was fearsome. I wish you'd been here to see it."

"Well, I wish I'd been there, too. But it was pretty cool being inside Launch Control for the lift-off," I replied. "So, um, how are you feeling now about everything in the harsh light of day?"

Her voice dropped almost to a whisper. But I heard every word even as I held my breath.

"Are we back to last night, now?" she asked.

"Well, yes, I guess we are," I said, noticing how hard it is to speak when you're holding your breath.

"Just making sure. Well then, David, I'm happy to report that I feel great. I really do. It all feels right to me. No second thoughts. No reservations. Nothing but good feelings."

"What a coincidence. Me too. I'm tired but I feel wonderful,"

I replied, feeling warm and giddy. "And the *Aeres* launch wasn't bad either."

"Yeah, the launch was amazing. And all those people who went to lunch instead are nutbars."

CHAPTER 15

Amanda had to leave later that afternoon. It's amazing how your feelings can intensify in the space of twenty-four hours. It had been quite a day and I wasn't sure I was thinking straight about it all. I couldn't even drive Amanda to the airport. Kelly wanted me available around the clock for any Landon moments that might arise in orbit. I thought they should be more worried about Eugene than Landon, but in the end, I was being paid to be there. I was able to step out of Launch Control for a few minutes to say goodbye to Amanda. It was nice.

We knew, of course, that there was no way I could stay on her team at TK when I returned to Toronto. But we'd cross that bridge then. I figured Diane would be reasonable and put me somewhere else within the organization. As Amanda's taxi grew smaller and faded from sight after the main gates of the Kennedy Space Center, I pulled out my BlackBerry.

"Lauren, it's David."

"Hi, David. Congratulations! I watched it all but I didn't see you," she said.

"You weren't supposed to see me. I'm behind the curtain pulling all the strings," I explained.

"Well, it was amazing to watch the launch knowing that your bush pilot doctor was on board. It made it all so much more meaningful."

"That was the plan. I'm glad it worked," I replied. "How is everything in Toronto?"

"It's getting better. The new job is going well. And I'm still seeing the new guy. So far so good," Lauren said.

"Good. That's all good. But . . ."

"David, I'm fine. The rough moments are fewer and farther between, now. They still come, often when I'm not expecting them. I was flicking through the channels the other night and came across a movie that Mom and I had seen together last year. That set me off for a bit."

"Lauren, that's going to happen. It's supposed to happen," I said. "I think it's been easier for me. I've been consumed with all of this down here. I've thought about Mom a few times, but I've been okay. Distractions are helpful. And I've had more than my fair share of distractions lately."

We spoke for another few minutes. I didn't mention Amanda. I think I was worried I'd jinx it by telling anyone this early. Besides, who knew whether we'd still be on by the time I got back. I hadn't yet figured out whether it was a nice fling or something more. I wondered if Amanda had sorted it out yet. When I'd finished with Lauren, I noticed an email back from my friend at Environment Canada. It said he was swamped but would try to get me an answer and the backup records in the next week or so. I was hoping for a quicker turnaround time, but I'd take what I could get.

When the *Aeres* finally caught up with the International Space Station – ISS – I was back in Launch Control. I watched as the shuttle fired small rockets in short bursts to slow down to the same orbital speed as the ISS. Before moving in to dock, the commander executed what really amounted to a back flip, the shuttle I mean, not him, so that the crew on the ISS could check *Aeres's* heat shield for any damage from the launch. Everything looked fine. All of the special heat-resistant tiles were in place. My monitor still offered the standard inside-*Aeres* view, but the external shot now on my screen was from a camera mounted in the shuttle's docking hatch. I watched as the commander expertly closed the distance to the ISS, deftly firing various positioning rockets to ensure alignment for docking. He was doing this while travelling 17,250 miles per hour, some 213 miles above the Philippine Islands. Unbelievable. He was aiming for the illuminated docking ring on the space station and I watched on my monitor as it came closer and closer before the screen finally went dark. The shuttle had just penetrated what I'd been informed was the "pressurized mating adapter" on the ISS. I know, it sounded like something out of a sci-fi porn flick. I figured I might be able to get a job at NASA cooking up better names for important mission-related components and procedures.

"Houston and station, capture is confirmed," said the shuttle commander.

"*Aeres*, Houston, station free-drift is confirmed."

"Houston, *Aeres*, copy that, free-drift confirmed."

They were docked. I turned my attention to the *Aeres* cabin view and saw Landon and then Martine each punch the air before attempting the traditional high five. Without the familiar tug of gravity, coordinating something as simple as a high five took on new difficulty. It took Landon two swipes before her hand actually connected with Martine's to complete their own small-scale docking procedure.

Thirty minutes later, a third view was automatically added to my monitor. I could now see inside the International Space Station as the four astronauts already there, two Russians and two Americans, got ready to welcome their new guests. The Russian serving as commander of the ISS grabbed a microphone and pulled out the cord from the wall receptacle. He floated pretty much vertically as a crew mate went through the step-by-step procedure of opening the hatch. I could see two of the *Aeres* crew on the other side of my split screen doing much the same thing with their hatch. I saw the station commander move the microphone to his mouth.

"Houston, station, I'm very happy to welcome aboard the commander and crew of the shuttle *Aeres*," he said in a thick Russian accent.

He then rang a bell mounted on the wall as Commander Hainsworth appeared in the hatchway and floated into the space station. He greeted the four tenants of the ISS with hugs before the bell sounded again and the *Aeres* pilot, Jefferson Rand, made his entrance, delivering his round of hugs. After Martine Juneau, the last of the official crew of *Aeres* came aboard the ISS, the bell chimed yet again and the Russian commander read from a small clipboard he'd pulled from its Velcro mount on the wall.

"Finally, I am proud to welcome two citizen astronauts to the International Space Station. We are crossing a new threshold in the history of the exploration of space. Dr. Landon Percival."

I was standing now, unable to sit calmly in my chair as this scene played out a couple of hundred miles above me. I saw a familiar head of grey, wiry hair pop into view as Landon floated into the International Space Station. As she had been since arriving in Florida, she was beaming. She embraced everyone and seemed almost overcome with emotion. She wiped her eyes now and then, but the smile stayed.

"And Mr. Eugene Crank."

Poor Eugene. He was green and sweating when he appeared. He was clutching one of Landon's Ziploc bags, empty, at least for now. He must have smuggled it aboard. In an attempt at nonchalance, he casually pushed off from the main hatchway and took out the Russian commander with an NFL-calibre shoulder block. "Oooofff!" sounds just the same in Russian. Given his proximity to the microphone still clutched in the Russian commander's hand, I could hear Eugene's apology. He didn't sound quite like himself.

I was excited about my first chance to speak with Landon since lift-off. It was set for about an hour or so after their arrival on the ISS. We had two five-minute slots scheduled each day, one in the morning and one in the evening. It was not on the main audio feed, but on a separate channel that gave us one-on-one communication. I'm sure it was being recorded somewhere, but I was told I could speak with Landon with some degree of privacy. As instructed, I reported to the special console on the other side of Launch Control and donned the headset. At the appointed time, I watched on the screen as Landon "flew" over to bob in front of the camera. She pulled on a headset and swung down the mike in front of her mouth. Sometimes her whole face filled the screen, and other times she'd drift up, giving me a very appetizing view up her nostrils. Then she'd correct and hover back into view. I was told she had a small monitor on which she could see me, as long as I stayed in front of what was really just a webcam on my console.

"Landon, can you hear me?" I asked. "Is this thing on?"

I waited and she said nothing, so I assumed the audio connection had not yet been made. But then suddenly she laughed and nodded.

"Yes, I can hear you and now I can see your worried little face, too."

It obviously took a little longer for my words to reach her ears given her current location. I made sure I smiled.

"I don't even know what to say to you other than you did it. You're in space. You're in orbit. I can hardly believe it," I said. In case it was not obvious, I had no plan for these conversations. I was just thrilled to be having them.

"It's all a dream to me too right now. But it's actually not that much different from how I've been imagining it for the last forty years or so."

"What about being weightless?" I asked. "What's it really like?"

"It was odd at the beginning but after a few hours, it's hard to remember what gravity feels like. We're amazingly adaptable creatures, you know," she replied. "It's as close to flying as you can imagine."

"Eugene didn't look particularly adaptable when he made his grand entrance on board the ISS," I observed.

"No. Young Mr. Crank seems be among those who are afflicted with space sickness. It's a crapshoot as to who will be affected. I'm just glad I still feel myself."

"What was the launch like?"

"The shuddering and shaking felt like I was taxiing a float plane through a very heavy chop, but for seven minutes solid. After SRB separation it smoothed out. And then after we jettisoned the external tank, it was smooth as silk. But you can really feel the power you're sitting atop when those engines fire."

"How has it been with the rest of the crew? Is everybody getting along?"

"They're all wonderful. I feel like I've known Martine my entire life. Such a smart and accomplished woman," Landon said. "But I've noticed a change in Commander Hainsworth's demeanour since we docked. He doesn't seem quite right to me."

"Perhaps he's just feeling the weight of his responsibilities," I offered.

"I don't think that's it."

We spoke until the digital timer on my console had ticked off nearly our full five minutes. Then we said goodbye and I moved back to my own station on the opposite side of the room. I watched my monitor for a while and listened in on the main audio feed linking the ISS and Houston. At one point, Lee Hainsworth floated into view as he went about his duties. Landon was on to something. He did not look well. Even the less than crystal-clear reception on my screen showed that his face was flushed and he was perspiring. I also saw him lean over, close his eyes briefly, and wince.

The scheduled live in-orbit crew broadcast started on time that evening. All ten of the ISS occupants gathered at one end of the main section of the space station and arranged themselves in two tiers, not unlike a kindergarten choir on stage for the annual Christmas concert. Except in this case, they were all simply floating at slightly different elevations so they all fitted into the head-on camera shot. The Russian iss commander introduced each crew member and described their respective roles. I watched the *Aeres* commander throughout. He held it together quite well. If you weren't really looking for it, you probably would not have noticed that he was putting on a brave face and wasn't really himself. The only one who looked worse was Eugene.

Each crew member had a turn with the microphone to offer their reactions to being on the space station. Most everyone's comments were predictable and sometimes crossed the line into cliché. Martine Juneau spoke in French for most of her time, which I thought was a nice touch. When Landon had the mike, she spoke briefly and finished with this.

"Since I was a young girl, I've wondered what it must be like to be up here in space and look down upon the blue and white ball that is our home. I've seen hundreds of shots others have taken of Earth from space. We've all seen them. Well, I can report with first-hand authority that the photos just don't cut it. When you stare back at Earth from up here, your ability to take in its full beauty falters. It's just too much. You simply cannot imagine anything more stunning, or more important to protect. I think it will leave its mark on all of us up here."

She then passed the mike to Eugene. I don't exactly remember just what he said, but he sounded like Foster Brooks in the middle of his standard inebriation routine. There was lots of swallowing, silent burping, and vocal changes as he struggled to keep the nausea at bay.

By day four, Eugene had come into his own. He finally seemed to have acclimatized himself to space and no longer looked one shallow breath away from projectile spewing. By this time, he and Landon had completed their mission experiments. Commander Hainsworth got a little better – before getting a lot worse. It was the classic one step forward, two steps back routine. As I watched the daily proceedings on the space station as crew members went about their assigned tasks, I noticed more than one animated conversation between the commander and Landon. I had no audio for these but I could tell Landon was asking him questions and trying to examine him. He seemed to be a reluctant patient. Once, she even pointed to the ceiling and when he looked up Landon quickly put both of her hands around his neck. I learned later she was checking for swollen glands. By the look on his face, he was unimpressed with the subterfuge.

In my twice-daily chats with Landon, she could talk of nothing else. She was worried about him. He thought it was just a severe bout of space sickness, though he'd never been affected before. She thought it was something else.

"He's lost his appetite and has severe pain that radiates across his abdomen," Landon explained. "But he won't tell anyone, thinking it will eventually stop. And he certainly won't tell Houston."

"Well, with us talking about it here, Houston may well know about it now," I commented. "What's your diagnosis?"

"I haven't been able to conduct a full examination, but based on my limited and not always helpful conversations with him, I think it's one of three things: food poisoning, constipation, or acute appendicitis. It doesn't look anything like space sickness, particularly when we've got Eugene as the space sickness poster boy for comparison."

On day six, I saw them again off in a corner in heated discussion. The combination of Landon's finger-pointing and nonstop talking, and the look of acquiescence, or perhaps surrender, on the commander's face made me think she'd had a breakthrough. He let her feel his abdomen and I could see her trying to demarcate what I assume was the pain zone. She shook her head, made a final declaration. He nodded and they both floated out of my view. Ten minutes later, they floated back into the picture and headed for the microphone. He took the mike and turned to face the camera. Most of the other crew members were otherwise occupied but a couple of them had noticed that something was amiss. It was like I was watching a silent movie but I had no difficulty piecing together what was happening. Then the commander spoke through a grimace. His voice sounded strained in my headset.

"Houston, station, I had hoped never to have to say these words, but Houston, we have a problem."

"Station, Houston, copy that. What have we got?"

"What we've got is a sick commander here. Sorry about this. Lots of cramps in my belly, sometimes severe, and bit of a fever. I thought it would pass but it's gotten worse over the last two days, not better."

"Copy that, station. We'll have the flight surgeon on the blower in a minute."

Landon took the mike from Commander Hainsworth.

"Houston, I've done a preliminary examination and I've ruled out food poisoning. We've all had the same food and everyone else is fine. Besides, the commander has eaten very little in the last two days. I don't think it's space sickness either. The commander didn't encounter it in his two earlier missions, and it probably would have passed by now anyway. Even Eugene has finally got his space legs. We can rule out constipation or any kind of bowel obstruction. As of this morning, according to the commander, his bowels are functioning A-okay. So my best guess is an inflamed appendix, which is not the diagnosis I was hoping for."

"Station, Dr. Phillips here. Symptoms please, and don't leave anything out."

Landon kept the mike and responded.

"It's classic appendix. Abdominal pain, loss of appetite, slight fever, nausea . . ."

"Sounds like zero-G Space Adaptation Syndrome to me," interrupted Dr. Phillips.

"I wasn't finished," she snapped. "It's not space sickness. His pain began in the centre of his abdomen, right around the navel. On day two, the pain moved downward and to the right, and hovered right over McBurney's point. And you know what that means, doctor. The nausea stopped on day three. He had a colossal dump this morning but the pain is still intensifying and radiating out from the epicentre at McBurney's point. And the fever is hanging in, too."

"Could be a bowel tear during evacuation," Phillips said.

"Negative. I did a brief internal and there's no sign of blood and the pain isn't quite in the right place anyway. I don't think it's bowel."

"What about food poisoning?" asked the doctor.

"Weren't you listening, doctor? We've all had the same food, and I've confirmed that the commander had nothing in addition to what we all had. He hasn't snuck a tainted cookie when we weren't looking. It's not food."

I could tell Landon was getting angry. In fact, anyone hearing the back-and-forth could tell she was getting angry.

"You're very sure of yourself, aren't you?" said Dr. Phillips, his irritation evident.

"Doctor, I'm with the patient. I've been observing him for the last four days. I've examined him. And, in case you'd forgotten, I've been practising medicine for more than forty years. Diagnosing acute appendicitis is not always easy. But this seems a pretty clear-cut case. We've got to get him down now.

If his appendix blows and we're still in orbit, well, you know the prognosis as well as I do. And looking at him, I think we're closer to rupture than we want to be."

"Station, Houston, meteorology is not good for Florida, hurricane activity in the gulf. We're checking alternative sites now. Stand by."

The commander wasn't looking good. His eyes closed several times during the exchange with Houston and the furrows in his forehead seemed almost permanent. Landon waved Martine and Eugene over and spoke to them off-mike. They took the commander's arms and guided him back towards a quieter area of the space station. Landon was growing impatient. Jefferson Rand, the pilot of the *Aeres*, was now beside her, looking concerned. Who could blame him? He'd have to handle the re-entry and landing of the shuttle himself if Lee Hainsworth was down for the count.

"Station, you can give him some pain meds. You've got morphine on board," said Dr. Phillips.

Landon shook her head and raised the mike.

"Whoa. Hang on. I know he's hurting right now, but dulling his pain will make it tougher for us to know when we're getting close to rupture. I'll give him some codeine but let's hold off on the morphine. As cruel as it sounds, we need the pain to stage the diagnosis."

There was silence for several seconds.

"Understood. But he needs to be on a close watch," replied Dr. Phillips.

"No kidding. As soon as you let me go, I'll be on him the whole time," said Landon. "Look, time is very short. We gotta get him down, now."

There was a pause that seemed long, but wasn't.

"Station, Houston, we've agreed here to shorten the mission and bring you down ASAP. It's blowing too hard at Kennedy, so it's out of the play, but we are clear for touchdown at Edwards. We've just missed the re-entry window for California so we have to go around again. Can you hang on for another hour and a half?"

The pilot took the mike from Landon.

"Houston, station, copy that. We need that time to get ready here anyway."

"Station, Houston. Okay you are go for separation and re-entry. Better get busy."

I watched as Landon headed out of the shot, presumably to check in on the patient. Another split screen appeared, giving me a view of the commander floating horizontally with Martine and Eugene on either side of him holding one arm each. Landon appeared and started unzipping the commander's coveralls. He was conscious, sweating, wincing, and trying to bring his knees up. It was obvious, he was in severe pain. Landon was now looking at his abdomen and asking him questions as she moved her hands to different spots on his midsection. She spent most of her time focused on a spot in the lower right quadrant. I saw her look up and shake her head several times. She spoke some more to the commander and then to Martine and Eugene. They looked very worried. My side started to hurt in sympathy. I just felt helpless, but there really wasn't anything a PR guy could do in this situation.

Forty minutes later, Landon looked increasingly agitated. I saw her check the digital countdown clock on the wall. Most of the *Aeres* crew were already on board the shuttle, getting ready for separation. Only Eugene and Landon were with the commander and would move him aboard the shuttle at the last possible moment. I shuddered at the thought of having to wrestle him into the pressurized space suit for re-entry. Landon hovered over the commander asking a continuous stream of questions to which he could only nod while grimacing, occasionally pointing, and clenching his fists. Landon did more head-shaking. Finally, with about twenty-five minutes to separation, she grabbed the headset mike on a console next to the patient and pulled it on.

"Houston, put the doc back on. We're not going to make it here."

"Phillips, here."

"Doc, based on his symptoms, we're either very close to rupture or it's already happened. Patient is in severe pain. We don't have any more time. If it's about to blow or has already burst, we have no time to get him down. We're too late for that. Peritonitis in space is not how I want to close out my medical career. The toxins rushing through his abdomen could kill him before we touch down. You know that, right?"

"But we don't have any other options. We have to get him down," Dr. Phillips replied.

"Of course there's another option. We open him up here and now and deal with it. If it hasn't ruptured, we're into a routine appendectomy. If it has, we'll do what we can to flush him clean. But we've got to do it now, not in an hour."

"Negative, station," said Dr. Phillips, angrily. "You can't open him in orbit. You're not equipped. There's no general anaesthetic on board. You can't do it. It's never been done. We have to take our chances and bring him down."

"It's too big a risk. I've seen dozens of these and the commander is too close to wait any longer. Do you want that on your record? We've got everything we need. We've got instruments, we've got oxygen. We've got sutures. Eugene is a blood-type match if we need to transfuse. The only thing we don't have is general anaesthetic and suction. We can easily rig up suction using the toilet vacuum hose. I'll just use liberal amounts of local anaesthetic, keep administering it throughout, and Bob's your uncle. It's the right call."

"Are you really proposing to do an emergency appendectomy in zero gravity under local anaesthetic?"

"We don't have time to debate this, Doc. It's a simple enough procedure. It's the best of a set of bad options," Landon pushed. "He's running out of time."

"When is the last time you did an appendectomy?" Dr. Phillips asked.

"My memory's a bit hazy on that. I think bell-bottom pants were on the way out. But it's like riding a bike. And the inflamed appendix hasn't changed much since then, has it? You know this is the right call. We're going to do it. We're out of time."

There was a long pause but Landon was already in motion. Because of her headset, we could all hear what she was saying.

"*Aeres*, we're operating right here and I need help. Get yourselves back in here. Okay, Eugene, your job is to figure out in the next ten minutes how to turn the toilet vacuum into a narrow surgical suction device. Go."

In the next thirty seconds or so, she gave each member of the ISS crew a different job, including getting disinfectant, sterile drapes, basic surgical instruments, and the suture kits from their storage compartments; finding better lighting; and using Velcro tie-down straps to secure the patient to the flat work surface near the toilet. She was running a very tight ship. Eventually, Houston caught up and finally made the only call they were in a position to make.

"Station, Houston here, Dr. Phillips has given the green light but he'll talk you through the procedure. It's critical that no fluids of any kind start floating through the cabin or we could have some problems. Do you copy that, station?"

"Yep," was all Landon said in return.

Eugene floated over with the toilet vacuum hose. He'd already added an extra length of hose using duct tape so it would reach over to the makeshift operating table. He showed Landon the modifications he'd already made.

"It's a start, but the opening is way too big. We don't want to suck out his liver, just the stray blood and toxins in the incision. Can you fit something over the opening to make it smaller? And we need to be able to turn down the power a bit."

Eugene nodded and floated away. Martine moved in with two helmets used in space walks. They were each fitted with strong halogen lamps. Martine used duct tape to secure them to the ceiling above the patient and, with Landon's help, oriented them to illuminate the commander's midsection. Two minutes later, Eugene was back with the back cover of a manual rolled and taped into the end of the vacuum hose so that it telescoped to a much smaller opening.

"I found a rheostat on the electric motor running the vacuum pump and dialled it down. How's this now?" asked Eugene.

"Eugene, you've outdone yourself. This should work well. I knew you had it in you," replied Landon. She beamed at him and held his shoulder while she spoke.

Eugene was chuffed. He said nothing but moved off to hold the plastic tray, where elastic straps secured the basic surgical instruments on board. There were two pairs of scissors, four clamps, two retractors, two sizes of forceps, and two scalpels. Landon disappeared to scrub but was soon back at what passed for the operating table. There was no gown to wear, but she did wear a mask and surgical gloves. Martine held the syringes prefilled with local anaesthetic. Finally, Landon instructed Eugene to duct tape her ankles to the table supports to stabilize her position. She did not want to be the first doctor in history to float away from her patient during surgery.

She pulled off her headset and leaned over to look directly in Commander Hainsworth's eyes, even as he grimaced.

"Here's the drill, Commander," she said. "You've already had a triple dose of codeine. My apologies for what that'll do to your innards when we're back. I see a couple of boxes of All-Bran in your future, but it's a small price to pay. We're going to do this under local. We've got plenty so I'll keep you pumped up with the stuff and you shouldn't feel a thing. But don't be a tough guy. Tell me if you feel it. Okay, lie back and enjoy the ride."

It was hard to see on the monitor with the crowd around the table, but I saw him nod. Landon used her secured ankles to draw herself back down to his now draped abdomen. She put her headset back on.

"Okay. We're going to start. I'll need you to hold him down so he's grounded and stable. He can't be floating. Got it? You monitor his breathing. And you take his pulse every two minutes."

Two crew members pushed down on the commander and held him still. The other two took to their tasks as well. Lee Hainsworth was awake for it all.

"Station, Houston. Okay, Landon, have you swabbed the site with disinfectant?"

"Done."

"Okay, let's inject the local. Go deep with the needle and give about five ccs. Then pull up and give another five ccs closer to the surface."

Landon followed the instructions and then took the scalpel from the tray Eugene was holding. She poked the site with the handle of the scalpel.

"Can you feel that, Commander?"

"Feel what?" he grunted.

"Thank you."

"I can't see the site well enough. Can you move the camera?" asked Dr. Phillips.

A crew member pulled the camera from its Velcro mount and floated up above the patient, directing the camera downwards.

"Better. Okay, time to cut. Let me see where you're going to make the incision."

Landon moved the scalpel along the imaginary incision line.

"Good. But no more than three inches long."

"Eugene, ready on the suction. You've got to catch it all," Landon said.

Eugene gave Martine the tray and lowered the cardboard adapter towards the site. Landon cut into the commander and drew the scalpel along the line. Blood appeared and Eugene did his thing. The incision gaped and Landon made another pass going deeper. More suction. Landon used the sterile gauze to clear away the site and get a look at where she was.

"More local now, Landon," said Dr. Phillips.

"I know, I know," she replied, taking the syringe Martine offered her. She injected the whole area deep within the incision.

"It looks like you're right on it. You'll have to reach in, expose the appendix and draw it up into the incision. You can recognize the appendix by the way . . ."

"I've done appendectomies before, Doc. Just let me do it without all the distracting colour commentary," Landon cut in.

Normally, I'm a bit squeamish, but I found this fascinating and stayed glued to the screen. She had a crew member use the retractors to keep the incision spread. Then she moved her fingers inside. I couldn't see what she was doing but when she pulled back, a very red, swollen, and, at the tip, white little object about the size of my pinkie was front and centre. Behold, the mighty appendix.

"It's ugly and angry near the tip but I don't see any perforations. I think we just caught it in time. It sure looks ready to blow," Landon said.

"Give me some more light, please," asked Dr. Phillips.

The helmet headlamp was retargeted.

"Agreed. It's close but I don't see any perfs," commented Dr. Phillips. "Let's get it out and tie it off. I'll walk you through it."

"No need to navigate, Doc. I've got it. Thanks," said Landon. She then pulled off the headset. It floated away from the action.

"Landon, Landon. I'm the flight surgeon, I'll walk you through it. Landon!"

But she was no longer hearing him. She severed the appendix after holding it inside a clear plastic cup. Thankfully, the liquid oozed rather than gushed. She managed to contain almost all of it in the plastic cup. Eugene used his makeshift suction hose to snag the few droplets of toxins that floated free. None of the foul fluid found its way into the commander's abdomen. She cut the appendix beyond the redness and very close to where it was attached to the large intestine. As she instructed, it was placed in a Ziploc bag and sealed. She quickly sutured the little nub that was left, pushed it inside the large intestine, then added a final suture to keep it there. The commander was awake but kept his eyes fixed on the ceiling. Landon saw him begin to wince so she re-administered the local anaesthetic. It worked remarkably fast, and the patient's face relaxed. Landon pulled the headset back on.

"I think everything is shipshape now," she said.

"Do not remove the headset again. Do not break contact. I'm in charge of this procedure as the flight surgeon. Is that clear?" said Dr. Phillips.

"Calm yourself, Doc. I'm not used to a co-pilot. I needed to concentrate. Are you satisfied with what I did?" asked Landon.

"Well, I probably wouldn't have cut it back quite so far, but it looks okay to me."

"Well, I'm a little closer to it than you are. It was pretty nicely inflamed so I wanted to cut out as much as I could to minimize the potential for infection. I'm going to close now."

Fifteen minutes later it was all over. A couple of rows of sutures, one inside and one on the surface, and the deed was done. Through it all, Eugene, without prompting, kept the incision and the air around it free of blood and any other airborne offering, with his jerry-rigged suction device. Martine took the commander's temperature. It had already fallen, but was still above normal. Then Landon gave him morphine to relieve any post-op pain and help him sleep.

By the next morning, the *Aeres* commander's temperature was normal, and he was feeling much better. The incision was giving him some mild discomfort but it was a completely different brand of pain than he'd experienced for the first several days of the mission. Landon apparently told him that when you cut through all the abdominal muscle right into the gut, root around a bit, slice off an infected appendix, and then sew it all back up again, it's bloody well going to hurt when you wake up.

The cameras were recording the entire time. I, and everyone in Launch Control and Mission Control, could see the commander's rapid recovery. We also watched as he embraced Landon in a mighty hug as soon as he felt up to it. Landon could also be seen speaking individually with each of the crew members, presumably thanking them for their support during the unscheduled in-flight emergency appendectomy. Landon held Eugene's hand when she spoke to him. He smiled and nodded the whole time. It was like watching a reality TV show without the customary bickering and interpersonal histrionics.

"Station, Houston, we've extended your cruise for another day. Kennedy will be clear on weather by tomorrow night, so we'll bring you down early the next morning. Enjoy the down-time. Pilot will land *Aeres*. Commander, you're just on for the ride this time."

"Houston, station, copy that. Re-entry for Kennedy in forty-eight hours."

I wondered if this would ever be made public. I shouldn't have. Kelly Bradstreet met me outside of Launch Control. She was just shaking her head.

"I cannot believe what we've seen in the last twenty-four hours," she gushed. "Who is this woman you found in the backwoods of Canada?"

"I think she found us."

"We're just editing a package of clips from the surgery, includ-ing some of the audio. We're going out with it in the morning in a full court press when we're sure the commander is out of the woods. You better get ready. Landon Percival is already a rock star. But when this breaks, she's going to be an international hero."

CHAPTER 16

To maximize viewership of the *Aeres* landing, Kelly Bradstreet, true to her word, released the emergency in-orbit appendectomy story twenty-four hours before re-entry. Dr. Phillips gave her the green light after witnessing Commander Hainsworth's lightning-fast recovery. It helped that he was in tiptop physical condition. There were no signs of infection. His temperature was back to normal. And Mission Control had returned command of the *Aeres* to him. In fact, at his request, he was even granted permission to land the *Aeres*, even though Jefferson Rand had been assigned the task. I wasn't surprised he recovered quickly. He was an astronaut, after all. I was still shocked he'd gotten sick in the first place.

Landon was oblivious to all the fuss and had no idea Kelly's celebrity-making machine was working overtime. Landon seemed serene. When she wasn't monitoring the commander's recovery, she spent most of the additional time in orbit floating near one

TERRY FALLIS

of the larger windows in the International Space Station watching the Earth passing below. My regularly scheduled ship-to-shore chats with Landon had been suspended during the surgery and immediate aftermath. But I managed to get one more talk approved before re-entry, after life in orbit returned to a semblance of normal. Well, as normal as life in orbit can ever be.

"Landon, can you hear me?"

"Loud and clear, David."

"Again, I don't know what to say," I started. "But if I ever get appendicitis in space, you're my first call."

"I didn't want to operate. I'd much rather have let it wait until we were back on terra firma. Unfortunately, the commander's appendix had other plans. It was pretty straightforward when we were all prepped and set up. Just between us, I was nervous but didn't want the commander or the rest of the crew to know."

"Given my vast experience with in-orbit surgery, I thought you looked in control the whole time."

"It was easier to focus after that know-it-all flight surgeon shut up," Landon noted.

"Well, he never actually shut up," I clarified. "You just couldn't hear him after you pulled off your headset. I can report that he was still talking, actually shouting."

"I acted in self-defence."

"Um, Landon, you should know that as of right now, no one outside of Mission Control, Launch Control, and the White House knows that you made medical history yesterday."

"Good. Let's keep it that way," Landon replied.

"Sorry to disappoint you, but if Hainsworth is still doing well in about an hour, the whole world will know, complete with video, audio, and the full force of the great American hero-making machine."

"Well, the commander fits the bill. He already looks like a hero. He'll wear it well."

"Hello? Earth to Landon – and for once in my life I mean that phrase in its truest sense – *you* are the hero. This is all about you, so get ready."

"Don't I have any say in it?" she asked. "What if I don't want this news to be released?"

"You're kidding, right? You can't be serious," I replied. "Landon, from NASA's perspective, the most creative Hollywood screenwriter could not have come up with a better storyline than the one you've written in the last twenty-four hours. It's *Apollo 13* all over again, but this time, a seventy-one-year-old Canadian bush pilot and doctor has the starring role. It's going to be big, so you'd better prepare yourself. And no, you don't have any say over it. Not this time, it's too big, and it's as good as done."

Mission Control broke in.

"Sorry to interrupt, but Dr. Percival has another call coming in so you'll have to terminate," said the flight director. "It's the president from Camp David."

"Shit."

I don't think I'd ever heard her swear. I hoped it wasn't the first word the president heard. I broke our connection in favour of the leader of the free world.

I assumed it hadn't even occurred to NASA to contact the prime minister, so when Landon got on the line with the president, I called my former minister on her cellphone.

"Minister, it's David," I opened.

"David, I'm just heading into a meeting. What's up?"

"I think you're going to want to hear this."

In under four minutes, I described the drama that had unfolded in Earth orbit the day before, and the media juggernaut that Kelly Bradstreet was about to unleash.

"Amazing. This will get the full American treatment, and the fact that she's Canadian will be lost on the world." The minister sighed. "They'll turn this into a star-spangled extravaganza and the maple leaf will be nowhere in sight."

"That's why I'm calling," I explained. "This is going to be huge. The Prez is on the blower with Landon now. NASA is going public in a big way with this in just under an hour. I think you should book the National Press Building and call a news conference for the same time. You can pipe in the live feed from the NASA newser, then add your praise for Landon's heroic performance, and announce that she'll be coming to Ottawa at the earliest opportunity following her return from space. We can give her the hero's welcome she deserves but make it a distinctly Canadian affair. Why not give her the Order of Canada?"

"I like it. But we'll need help," she replied.

"I'll brief my Turner King colleagues in our Ottawa office and we'll help make this happen."

"Okay, brief my staff at the same time, will you? I'm calling the PM right now."

I hung up, stepped outside, and called Amanda. I went through the same incredible story with her, finishing by briefing her on my call to the minister.

"So I want us to do a three-way with the minister's chief of staff," I said.

"I know our relationship is going well, David, but I think suggesting a three-way with anybody at this stage is a little premature," she deadpanned.

I put her on hold, then conferenced in the minister's chief of staff.

Kelly dropped the big bomb at a Houston news conference with the chief of astronaut training, Scott Chandler, and the flight surgeon, Dr. Phillips, beside her. I watched the whole thing from Launch Control. Despite the NASA firepower at the table, Kelly was firmly in control of this story. She took the lead and welcomed the dozens of reporters in the media briefing room and the hundreds more worldwide tuning in online.

"Welcome and thank you for being available on such short notice for this emergency briefing. Over last twenty-four hours, a dramatic life-or-death story has been playing out on the

International Space Station high above the Earth. I'm very pleased to report that after some very tense moments, the danger has passed, and the crew of the shuttle *Aeres* will soon land safely in Florida. There was a medical emergency on board the ISS affecting the commander of the *Aeres* that could have been extremely serious. Only the skill, experience, and courage of Dr. Landon Percival, one of our citizen astronauts, saved the day, and very likely saved the life of the commander. We have pulled together an edited package of video highlights that really speaks for itself. We'll watch it now and then throw open the floor for questions for Mr. Chandler and Dr. Phillips."

In seven minutes, the skilfully edited video took the assembled reporters through the last twenty-four hours. It started with clips of the initial conversation the commander and Landon had with Mission Control. Then there followed shots of the crew's preparations for the surgery under Landon's leadership as the commander floated in considerable pain. Next, the world watched as Landon performed the first invasive surgical procedure in space. From the look on Eugene's face in the footage, he took his suctioning duties very seriously. Finally, we saw the commander's dramatic recovery over the course of twenty-four hours or so. It closed with video of the commander in conversation with Mission Control when command of the *Aeres* was handed back to him. It was powerful stuff. All that was missing was a moving John Williams symphonic soundtrack, but even Kelly agreed it would have been a bit over the top. But don't think she hadn't considered it.

The questions from the assembled reporters took over an hour to answer. But the timing of the news cycle closed it down as we were heading up to the top of the hour and live remotes and stand-ups had to be organized to break the story. Both Chandler and Dr. Phillips tried to bask in Landon's aura. Phillips claimed to have guided Landon's hands from start to finish. It wasn't long before he was forced to modify his position when it leaked that Landon had in fact performed the surgery unassisted with her headset floating well out of earshot. Scott Chandler having been opposed to the very idea of putting civilians in space, so I was keen to hear how he would respond to reporters' queries. He was very smooth and had suddenly become a staunch supporter of Landon and the Citizen Astronaut program. He beamed throughout and offered very minor variations on the "key messages" Kelly had drafted.

"Landon Percival is exactly the kind of citizen astronaut we were looking to send into orbit. Hell, if she hadn't been on board, there's no telling what might have happened. It's quite possible the commander would not have made it back alive," Chandler responded to one open-ended question. "So I'm very proud that our training program put Dr. Percival in a position to perform so well under such intense pressure."

Yeah, right. It was all about the training. I thought back to the rigorous weeks of preparations and could not recall a single session focused on zero-gravity appendectomies.

———

Commander Lee Hainsworth landed the *Aeres* in Florida, five hours later. Kelly arrived from Houston on a NASA plane about an hour before the shuttle touched down so she could herd the largest contingent of reporters and cameras ever to record a shuttle landing. She brought Dr. Phillips along with her. The *Aeres* circled high above the tarmac bleeding off speed before finally diving to touch down on the runway, its drag chute then deploying to trail behind. I watched from the VIP viewing stand and was feeling quite emotional about it all. I had to keep blinking to deal with my unaccountably watery eyes. No one seemed to notice. The *Aeres* ended up at the far end of the runway, so I turned my attention to the large flat-screen TV monitor nearby.

An ambulance joined the usual convoy of emergency vehicles racing down the runway to greet the returning astronauts. Tendrils of smoke rose from the heat shield on the underside of the *Aeres*. The media hordes were not usually permitted on the tarmac but would pick up the NASA camera feed. But Kelly had arranged for a cordoned area a mere fifty metres or so from the *Aeres*. She was really milking this for all it was worth. After all, that was her job. Kelly herded cameras, tripods, and dozens of reporters into the area, straining the ropes that contained them. After about twenty-five minutes of shut-down procedures, a metal staircase was driven up to the main hatch at the nose. Dr. Phillips and Kelly Bradstreet were first up the steps while the director of the Kennedy Space Center waited on the tarmac below. When the hatch was opened, they disappeared inside. I assumed

Dr. Phillips was examining the commander to make sure this was indeed a happy ending.

A half-hour passed before Kelly and Dr. Phillips descended the staircase again. Kelly stood at the bottom and thrust her hand into the air to signal the media that the big entrance was at hand. She is a pro and had choreographed this moment perfectly. A few moments later, the commander and Landon emerged and waved, no doubt as they'd been instructed to. The crowd of NASA officials on the runway clapped along with a few reporters. The commander towered over Landon and twice reached down to give her a hug. Landon looked a little uncomfortable but seemed to understand this had to be done. I could see Kelly waving at Landon to encourage her to keep waving. With a put-upon look, Landon kept her hand moving through the air in kind of an imitation of a wave. The hero had come home.

The next week seemed more hectic than any before or during the mission. Kelly and the TK team in New York and Washington laid on a media tour that took Landon and the commander to all the major talk shows on NBC, CBS, ABC, Fox, MTV, CNBC, BBC, CNN, and all the rest. Landon was so grateful to have been part of the mission in the first place that she dutifully acquiesced, though she was clearly not comfortable with the adulation heaped on her and the rose petals strewn in her path. I was with her every step of the way. In fact, it was my idea to have Commander Hainsworth display his incision to bring the ordeal alive for the audience. Letterman loved it. The commander? Not so much. Eugene Crank and Martine Juneau handled the second-tier media outlets and they did a great job. Eugene managed to make it seem that the key to successfully completing the emergency appendectomy had been his suctioning skills.

Every show unfolded in pretty much the same way. After a melodramatic introduction usually delivered by unseen vocal talent that sounded like the movie trailer guy (you know the voice: "In a world, caught between good and evil, in a time just after lunch . . ." etc., etc.), Landon and the commander would come out to thunderous applause. The host would welcome them home from orbit. A clip of the surgery would be played to the dramatic ooos and ahhhs of the studio audience. Landon would be modest about her role in kind of an aw-shucks way. Quintessentially Canadian, you might say. The host would then pile on a little too much praise. I would watch as Landon's irritation would start to crack her polite veneer.

"Look, I'm a doctor! I took the Hippocratic oath. He was sick, so I treated him. That's what doctors do. End of story!"

A version of that line would usually find its way into the interview if the host pushed Landon a little too far. The commander would then leap in and guide the conversation to calmer waters. It actually was great TV, even though Landon tired quickly of the spotlight.

My TK colleagues in Toronto toned it down when we finally arrived back in Canada about ten days after touchdown. Landon was itching to get back to Cigar Lake, so Amanda kept the media interviews to a minimum. Landon was approaching overexposed already, courtesy of her American media tour the previous week. On our first day back north of the 49th, there was a major CBC interview that aired in prime time, and a two-page *Globe and Mail* spread. On day two, Landon and I flew up to Ottawa for her – private – meeting with the prime minister and a photo opp. We both sat in the gallery for Question Period that day and the Speaker introduced Landon, sparking a standing ovation from all sides of the House. She stood and gave a little wave, then sat back down in the hopes of abbreviating the applause. It didn't really work. The Prime Minister's Office wanted to do much more to recognize Landon's adventure. She politely but firmly declined. It was time to go home.

———

Because I was accompanying Landon Percival, *the* Landon Percival, I was permitted to go through security with a dummy boarding pass and escort her to Air Canada's Maple Leaf Lounge where business class ticket holders awaited their flights. Many heads turned and a few fingers pointed when we entered, but beyond that, we were left alone. We were in Canada, after all.

"What am I going to do without you looking out for me?" Landon said as she sank into a chair.

"I was going to ask you the same question," I replied. "You don't need anybody. You're the most independent, self-sufficient person I've ever met. You built your own human centrifuge out of a snow-mobile engine, a wooden propeller, and a sailboat mast. I'm still trying to get my toaster to pop up at the right time without setting off the smoke detector. Would you consider moving in with me?"

She found the grace to smile.

"I'll visit sometime, but it's time for me to get back home. Hector will think I've completely given up on him, and he needs me."

We sat for a few moments in silence. I really wasn't sure what I was doing or how I was feeling. This was the end of something that had dominated my life for the previous several months. I barely knew where I was, let alone what was next.

"Is it all settling into perspective yet? Are you feeling yourself?" I asked.

"I don't think I'll ever feel quite the same again," she said, then paused. It was a softer voice that continued. "When you look down on the blue Earth magically hanging in the blackness, your own country moving across your field of view, you are changed. It is inescapable."

I just nodded and held my tongue, not wanting to sully the moment with what would surely be an inadequate response. Fortunately, she carried on.

"You know, I've never credited Eugene Crank with a great deal of emotional depth, but he was very moved by the experience too. I really think it changed him. It was a different person wielding that homemade suction tube."

"Well, for what it's worth, I think you changed him as much as the mission."

"Air Canada flight 156 with service to Calgary and then on to Vancouver is ready for pre-boarding at gate 124," said a woman's voice over the speakers in the ceiling.

"I'll walk you to the gate."

"I'll walk myself to the gate. Let's say goodbye here without the crowds."

She moved in with open arms and held on tight for longer than your garden-variety farewell hug.

"You're back now, so take care of that new woman of yours. You both work too hard, so you need your time together or you're not really living," she said in my ear. Still she hung on to me. "You went out on a very thin limb so I could make it onto that shuttle. It never would have happened otherwise. You put your job on the line for someone you barely knew. Well, that kindness is part of me now, and I'll be passing it on. That's what you do with kindness. I am more grateful than you can ever know. Thank you. And come and visit Hector and me."

She pulled back, grabbed her small carry-on bag, and walked quickly out of the automated sliding doors. There was no time to respond. She was gone. I sat there for a few minutes as people came and went. I shoved a couple of packages of smoked almonds into my pocket and headed for the car. I love smoked almonds.

A few hours later, Amanda and I met Lauren in one of my favourite restaurants in Toronto. I'd wanted Lauren to meet Amanda. They both looked very relaxed and happy. Since I'd returned from Florida, I'd not spent a single night in my own condo. I seemed to have moved into Amanda's. It was nice. The dinner went well. Lauren and Amanda seemed to hit it off well, which was a gigantic relief. I'm not sure how I'd have felt had they not gotten along.

It was quiet in the restaurant, and our booth made it feel like an intimate and safe enclave. Amanda and I were seated on one side of the banquette, Lauren on the other.

"So tell me more about your mother," asked Amanda. "I'm so sorry I never met her."

Lauren smiled and told a couple of funny stories about our mother that made us all laugh. She finished by telling Amanda about the special phrase she and Mom had shared.

"Whenever we said good bye, whether I was going off to summer camp as a kid, or back to my own apartment after Sunday dinner at home, she'd always say 'Be kind.' Short and sweet. 'Be kind.' It was our special line."

Amanda nodded, then looked my way.

"Was there a phrase you had with your mother too?" she asked.

"Oh yeah. We each had one. My mother would always say to me 'Use your head, but follow your heart.'"

The word "heart" sounded like it had been uttered by someone else. It struck me like lightning. All of a sudden, I was weeping.

No, not just weeping, it was more like blubbering. I was a mess in three seconds flat. Lauren reached out and took my hands. Amanda had her arms around me in an instant. It was an awkward position, being embraced by the person next to you while someone else holds your hands from across the table. But I didn't really notice. I was too busy having some kind of a breakdown. The privacy of the booth meant that only the surrounding five tables stopped what they were doing and stared. The other nine parties in the room were oblivious. Our waiter was headed over but pulled a U-turn back to the bar when she saw my meltdown.

About ten minutes later, I started to feel more like myself, and the crying jag faded into that periodic sniffling and spasmodic inhalations that I remembered as a kid.

"What the hell was that?" I mumbled when I eventually found my own voice again.

"It's called grief," replied Amanda, still with one arm around me. "And it's about time you released some of it."

Lauren just smiled and squeezed my hands.

I was weeping again in the car on the way home without even realizing it. I even turned on the windshield wipers, thinking that would improve my impaired vision. Amanda made me pull over. She drove the rest of the way. I cried again in bed that night. Amanda just held me without saying a thing. I had never really known the true meaning of the word catharsis until that night. When the tears stopped, I actually felt amazing.

Amanda whispered in my ear at about 3:00 in the morning after I'd been quiet for a while.

"I like that you can cry."

I hoped not to make a habit of it.

———

"Welcome home, stranger," Diane said as I settled in a chair in front of her shiny sci-fi desk.

"Well, it's nice to be back."

It was Friday morning. I'd spent the first hour after arriving at the office fist-bumping or high-fiving pretty well all of my colleagues. It wasn't my idea. They just kept interrupting me in my cubicle as I tried to hunker down and start writing the Citizen Astronaut program wrap-up report. When the last of them had smacked my pink and swelling hand, I was summoned to the corner office. Diane was wearing a rather sedate pair of glasses, at least by her standards, encrusted with enough sparkly rhinestones to do retinal damage to anyone trying to make eye contact with her. If she'd been in direct sunlight, she might well have been able to set me on fire just by looking my way. Mercifully, she removed them and laid them on her desk when she noticed me averting my eyes.

"Well, you pulled it off," she said. "There were plenty of moments in the last couple of months when I thought it was going south, but each time you somehow pulled it back."

"Kind of you to say, but I was really just hanging on for dear life. Landon made my job easy. She is one amazing woman."

"Don't sell yourself short. We thrust you into a very difficult situation and you delivered time and time again. We've never seen so much media coverage. You kept yourself and TK out of the news. Not only did you keep Dr. Percival out of trouble, she's now a national treasure in two countries. Kelly Bradstreet is singing your praises and that makes the New York bigwigs happy. And the whole emergency surgery thing was pure genius. Kudos on that little gambit."

"Well, um, I admit that Kelly and I were working overtime to keep the story hot for the media, but my influence does not extend to the commander's inflamed appendix, as much as I'd like to claim the credit for it. That little medical situation was pure serendipity. Fortunately, Landon made the most of it."

"Kidding. I was kidding. But by all accounts, you did a great job. And you led the entire firm in the PROTTS race over the last fourteen weeks."

"Hey, that's great news," I replied. "What exactly is the PROTTS race?"

"It just means that you billed more hours in the last three months than anyone else in the entire firm, worldwide."

"So does my picture hang in the lobby of the New York office for a week?"

"No, but your productivity bonus at year-end will probably pay for a lightly used Beemer. That is, if you're still here," she said staring down at me. She was no longer smiling.

"Oh, you don't have to worry, I really like it here. I have no plans to leave," I replied.

"Oh, it wouldn't be up to you. Based on your performance on the Citizen Astronaut program, I'm torn between promoting you and firing your ass."

I chuckled, waiting for the joke. But Diane wasn't close to cracking a smile. So I figured I'd better stop chuckling.

"Um, sorry, I'm missing something here," I stammered. "One minute we're talking a hefty bonus, and the next, I might be out the door?"

Diane picked up a stack of pages stapled in the corner and slid them over to me without saying a word. My heart rate kicked into a higher gear. I picked up the document and started reading. It wasn't good. I was holding a copy of the lengthy email I'd sent to Sarah Nesbitt at the *Vancouver Sun*. I quickly flipped through all of the notes I'd taken during my initial visit to Cigar Lake and painstakingly cut and pasted into the body of the email to Sarah. My email also outlined in excruciating detail the plan I'd laid out for Sarah and that she'd honoured. Without her initial exclusive story, I'm quite convinced Landon Percival would never have been aboard the *Aeres*.

"How did you get this? This was not sent on my TK email. Did you hack into my personal Gmail account?"

For some reason, I was more concerned with how Diane had gotten her hands on my private email than I was with my quickly dimming prospects for continued employment.

"David, you're not thinking clearly. And you obviously weren't when you sent that to Sarah Nesbitt," Diane said. "Yes, you used your own Gmail account, not your TK email. But you had already routed your Gmail through your BlackBerry so that you could receive your personal email as well as your TK email on your handheld, regardless of your location. When you routed your Gmail through your BlackBerry, you actually routed your Gmail directly through the TK servers. So while we don't have your original outbound message to Sarah, her return acknowledgement, which included your earlier email to her, came to my attention earlier this week."

I was in deep. I looked at my still-pink hand, tender from all that high-fiving a few minutes before. How fitting. I was caught red-handed.

"You lied to us and freelanced the story underground. I don't care that it all worked out so well. You didn't trust your team. In most instances, when a TKer goes rogue, they get fired. Case in point, Crawford Blake. You remember him, don't you?"

I had nothing. I was already mentally clearing out my desk and dusting off my resumé.

"Diane, I'm sorry. I did what I thought was in the best interests of the client, the program, and the firm. I tried to convince you and Blake, but I was shut down. If I hadn't reached out to Sarah, we would have picked a new winner and Landon Percival and what she's achieved for NASA would never have happened. You know that. Crawford Blake told us in no uncertain terms to shut her down, and we would have if that *Vancouver Sun* story hadn't broken."

"David, you were a week or so into the job. We didn't know you. We didn't yet fully trust you or your judgment. In hindsight, Landon Percival was a brilliant choice. But back then it wasn't so obvious," she explained. "Knowing you as we do now, if it were to happen all over again, we'd probably have gone to bat for you and Landon with Blake and we might have made it happen. But either way, you just don't cut out the team and backdoor it on your own. That's just wrong. We can't have that in the firm, regardless of how well this has all turned out."

I rose from my chair.

"I'm really sorry that it's all unravelled like this. I understand the firm's position and that what I did was wrong. But I still believe that morally, I made the right call."

"David, this is a PR firm, making the right call, morally, isn't part of the equation."

I nodded and started towards the door.

"I'll clean out my desk."

"Yes, and when you've got your stuff, move it into the vacant office three down from Amanda's. You're now an account director," she said. "Bob the IT guy and I are the only ones who know about your little Gmail escapade with Sarah Nesbitt. Let's keep it that way. It's a good thing I didn't find out about all this until after you distinguished yourself on the account or this might not have been such a happy ending. No more freelancing. Clear?"

"Clear. And thank you, Diane. It's all about the team from now on."

"By the way, I was just kidding when I said making the right call, morally, doesn't matter in a PR firm. You know that, right?"

I nodded again, somewhat relieved.

"And nicely played with Sarah Nesbitt. I couldn't have cooked up a better plan myself," Diane said.

I turned, and was almost out the door when she spoke again.

"Oh, one more thing. You're no longer reporting to Amanda. She told me you two have recently become a little more than office colleagues. So as of right now, you'll report directly to me. I'm very happy for you both, but don't let it get in the way around here," she said.

"Understood. I didn't really want to report to her anyway," I replied. "Too complicated. And she can be mean sometimes."

"Well, I for one am glad she now has more than just her clients and colleagues in her life. She needs you."

———

It took me about five minutes to clear out my desk. I was about to close my laptop for the walk to my new office when an email bonged in my inbox. It was from my contact at Environment Canada. I'd totally forgotten about it. The message simply said, "Hope this is what you were looking for." I clicked open the attachment and read it through, twice. Then I read it carefully yet again just to make sure. I picked up the phone, called Air Canada, turned on the charm, and cashed in nearly all of my frequent flyer miles to book a flight for very early the next morning. Amanda would understand.

PART 6

CHAPTER 17

The early afternoon sun lit up the trees below, their leaves starting to turn in the October chill. Chatter Haney had finally managed to replace the blown oil pump on his Cessna 172. The flight from Mackenzie was uneventful, if you call flying without a passenger door uneventful. You couldn't fly a Cessna without an oil pump. But apparently it was completely acceptable to make the trip with no door. A passenger earlier in the day had snapped a seized hinge clean off while attempting to disembark. Then, while trying to undo the damage, the guy bent the one remaining hinge sufficiently to shear it off too. I don't think Wilderness Charters granted him any frequent flyer miles for that trip. But I was so eager to get to Cigar Lake that I climbed in and buckled the seat belt so tightly that only shallow respiration was possible. Then as the time for take-off approached, I just tried to focus on something other than the open space right next to me. You know, mind over matter. Or in my case, mind over paralytic terror.

Float planes are loud to begin with, but with no door, the noise was almost unbearable. The headphones offered little in the way of protection, so my head was already ringing by the time we taxied out into the lake. As Chatter hit the throttle to get us up to speed, the water hit me. Yes, the pontoons kicked up a fierce spray and I was sitting in the slipstream. I got completely soaked sitting in that doorless Cessna during take-off.

"Don't worry about the water," Chatter barked. "The wind that'll be whipping in here when we're airborne will dry you out in no time."

And he was right. I was dry in about fifteen minutes, and nearly frozen solid. It was a beautiful and warm fall afternoon, but at twelve hundred feet and a hundred miles an hour, it felt like I was entombed in a glacier. Chatter reached behind him and pulled out a moth-eaten Hudson Bay blanket. He dropped it in my lap. When I could work my arms sufficiently, I somehow managed to wrap the blanket around me against the wind.

For most of the flight, Chatter lived up to his name, talking nonstop. After the first five minutes or so, I discreetly turned the volume knob on my headset down to zero, and concentrated on staying warm. Eventually, I recognized Cigar Lake below us. Chatter Haney banked sharply first to the north, and then back to the west to line up our approach. If you're keeping track of the geography, banking sharply to the north really meant banking sharply to the right. For the few seconds of that stomach-churning right hander, the only thing separating me from the forest several hundred feet below was my seat belt and centrifugal force. Chatter told me later that I screamed during the sharp turn. I don't really remember that. As we passed over her cabin, Landon, clad in coveralls, stepped out onto her front veranda and looked up.

When the floats hit the light chop on Cigar Lake, the cold water hit me, again. It was like driving through a car wash in a convertible with the top down, but without the cleansing benefit of soap. As we made the long taxi back to the east end of the lake, Landon made her way down onto her dock. I wrung out the blanket as best I could before wringing out my shirt as best I could. My pants would have to wait. Chatter manoeuvred the Cessna into the parking space at the dock so that he was nose to nose with the larger Beaver. I unlatched the seat belt, grabbed my bag, and in one less-than-smooth motion stepped onto the pontoon below and then onto the dock. I made it without falling this time, even though I was wet, stiff, and half-frozen. Landon was not pleased when she saw the wide open space where the passenger door was traditionally installed.

"Chatter, why did you bother landing at all," she yelled into the plane. "You could have just unlatched his belt, banked, and dropped him in the lake just off the dock. He wouldn't be any wetter!"

He looked away as if thinking and nodded his head.

"That could've worked, I guess. Would've saved some fuel, too."

"You should have flown from the starboard controls so David could at least have had a door on his side."

"Well, the way I figure it, if I'd sat there instead, I'd be the one soaked right now and I don't much like being wet," Chatter replied, apparently seriously.

Landon just shook her head as she pushed on the wing overhanging the dock to angle the Cessna clear of the Beaver and back out onto the lake.

"I'll fly him back. You go and fix that door!" she shouted.

Chatter waved, restarted the engine, and headed back onto the lake. He throttled up and was in the air inside of a minute. When I turned back from watching the take-off, Landon was staring at me with her hands on her hips.

"If I'd known you were coming, I'd have baked a cake."

She stepped forward and gave me a hug, despite my saturated state.

"Come on up and get out of those wet things," she said, taking my bag off my shoulder and slinging it on hers. "I hope you brought a change of clothes."

"Well, I travelled light this time, but I packed enough to be dry and decent."

Despite the hair-raising trip, I was appreciating the beautiful fall day with barely a cloud in the sky. It felt good to be back. I could hear Landon bustling about in the kitchen as I changed into sweat pants and a T-shirt in the same bedroom I'd slept in nearly four months earlier. I hung my wet clothes over the railing of the veranda. When I stepped back into the cabin, Landon handed me a mug of soup.

"Minestrone," she said, nodding towards the soup. "You'll like it. Now come sit. I thought when I saw the Cessna that my guest had arrived a week early."

"You've got company coming?" I asked. "Who?"

"Sam is flying in for a visit. I haven't seen her since she bailed out shortly after my father disappeared."

"*That Sam* is coming? *The* Sam? That's fantastic, Landon!" I said. "I'm happy for you, for you both."

"Well, no cause to celebrate just yet. It'll be nice to see her, but a lot of seasons have come and gone since we were together."

I set the soup down on the pine box and zipped back into the bedroom to grab a file folder from my bag before returning to the main room. I gently lifted Hugh Percival's weathered leather logbook from its traditional resting place on the mantel and laid it on the pine box. Then I snagged the empty bottle of nitroglycerin pills and placed it next to the logbook. Landon watched from her chair but said nothing until I'd settled in mine.

"Are you all set, now?" she asked.

"I am."

"Okay, then, we can start. What on Earth are you doing here? Did you miss seeing my stunning face every day?"

"For the whole trip out here, except perhaps during that last leg, I've been trying to figure out how to tell you something important. But I really haven't come up with anything."

Landon looked troubled all of a sudden.

"Please don't say you can't live without me – I drive on the other side of the road, remember?"

I was pretty sure she was joking but I chuckled anyway to set her mind at ease, just in case she was actually serious. I noticed the second Sherlock Holmes novel, *The Sign of Four*, opened on the arm of her chair, as if she'd been reading it when the Cessna came in. And in an instant, the way in to my news came to me. I put my hand in the air to claim the floor.

"'When you have eliminated the impossible, whatever remains, however improbable . . .'" I paused.

"'. . . must be the truth,'" replied Landon, finishing the sentence in a dismissive tone. "Yes, yes, I know the line. It's from *The Sign of Four*. I read it again only this morning. It's one of the most oft-quoted lines in the Holmes canon. What about it?"

"Well, I don't know quite how to put this, but I think I know where your father's plane is. I think I may have figured it out."

Her eyes widened and she leaned forward, but said nothing. I opened the leather logbook and scanned several pages to check on Hugh Percival's attention to punctuation. It was as I'd expected. Then I turned to his final entry.

> *In a rush to deliver tar paper and shingles to cranky Earl Walker on Laurier Lake. He needs it today so he can fix his damn roof and beat the rain. Damn EW today! Not feeling very well. But tanks are full. Gotta fly now. 2:17 p.m. HP*

"What do you think he meant by 'Damn EW today!'?" I asked.

"Clearly, he was not happy that Earl Walker needed to finish his roof that afternoon," Landon said, as if there could be no debate about its meaning.

"I think it means something else," I began. "Flipping through the logbook, it seems your father wasn't a big fan of the comma. I think he meant that line to read 'Damn, EW today!'"

"You've lost me," she interrupted.

"Hang on, I'm almost there," I said. "I don't think 'EW' means 'Earl Walker.' I'm now convinced 'EW' means 'east wind.'"

She shook her head and sat back.

"David, I've been here nearly all my life and I've never once seen an east wind. The prevailing west wind is as constant as the North Star. You should have just called me."

I opened the file folder and pulled out the printout of the federal government's official meteorology report for northern B.C. for the fateful date and handed it to her.

"October 17, 1970, was one of only three occasions in the last sixty years when there was an east wind in this area. And it was very strong that day," I said.

Landon read through the meteorology report and then set it back down on the pine box.

"Okay, there was an east wind that day. So what?"

I picked up the empty pill bottle.

"What if it happened like this?" I started. "Your father wasn't feeling well that day. He says so in the logbook entry. He'd already

399

run out of his heart pills. He loads up the plane and heads out onto the lake. Because of the rare stiff east wind, he has to take off from the other end of the lake back towards the cabin."

Landon suddenly stood up, looking past me out the window to the lake, but I continued, just to get my theory out in the open.

"What if, just as he was lifting off the surface, he suffered a heart attack and pushed the stick forward? The plane would have nose-dived into this end of the lake, where the water is deeper. So deep that a plane would stay hidden there."

I paused. Landon was still standing up, her eyes on the lake, but she was very slowly nodding her head.

"Landon, you've spent decades scouring the landscape wherever he might have gone down and have found nothing. Not a trace. So the deep end of the lake is not just the only possible crash site you haven't yet searched, but now that you know there was an east wind that day, and that your father wasn't feeling great, it actually makes the scenario plausible."

"I am such an idiot!" Landon snapped and darted out the door.

She grabbed her bathing suit from the railing as she descended the stairs towards the dock. She stopped beneath the veranda and smoothly hoisted the canoe onto her thighs. I offered to help but she waved me off and slid the canoe into the water. She handed me the rope attached to the bow.

"Hold this and look away, young man," she directed.

I took the rope, turned my back, and looked out on the pristine lake nestled amidst the mountains. I could hear the faint sounds of her slipping out of her coveralls and into her bathing suit. Then she hustled back up the path to a wooden door beneath the veranda that opened into what seemed to be a storage area. I could hear her rummaging around.

"Eureka!" she shouted.

When she emerged, she had an ancient brown diving mask perched on her forehead. It was clear where this was going.

"Landon, it's October, the water is freezing. I know, I was soaked in it and thought I felt the first signs of hypothermia," I said.

"David, I swim every day until early November. It's why I look so young and have such beautiful skin," she quipped.

Ten minutes later, I was paddle-less and seated in the stern facing Landon, who paddled from the bow seat. Landon explained that when there's only one paddler in a canoe, you're supposed to sit in the bow seat facing the stern. It makes it easier to control the canoe against the wind. With only a few powerful strokes, she had us a couple of hundred feet off the dock. She coasted for a time and looked first out towards the western end of the lake, and then back towards the cabin. This routine continued for a few minutes, before she paddled the canoe a little closer to the southern shore of the lake.

"Um, what exactly are you doing?" I asked.

"I'm trying to determine the takeoff path my father would have adopted in the event of an east wind. I figure it would be tight to the shoreline so he wouldn't have to fly directly over his cabin. That would mean right about here."

"But I can still see the bottom here," I said as I looked down over the canoe's gunwale into the water.

"You have to be systematic about it. I'm just setting our eastern boundary. The drop-off starts right here, so that's where we'll start."

It's hard for one person to leave a canoe without dumping the other. But somehow Landon managed it. When she'd spat into her mask and cleaned it to keep it from fogging up, she pulled it down onto her face. It was all I could do to keep from laughing when she looked my way. It wasn't a modern and sleek black scuba-diving mask. Rather, it was quite a large brown rubber concoction from the forties with what looked like a big pane of glass on the front. And it looked ridiculous on her. I returned her thumbs-up as she put one leg on each gunwale, then inched her way backwards towards the bow. I could feel the canoe vibrating with her effort as she tried to keep her weight centred. Finally, with her hands gripping the gunwales, she lifted herself up and pushed back, clearing the canoe and landing in the lake. It was quite impressive. I rocked a bit but took on no water. I grabbed the paddle and tried to stay close to Landon as she began a series of exploratory dives in search of a lost plane and a lost father.

There was quite a bit of ground, er, water, to cover. Landon kept lining herself up with a landmark of some kind on shore. Sometimes it was a tree, other times a rock. She obviously meant it when she'd talked about searching systematically. I found that she could hold her breath for quite a long time. She would dive about eight or ten feet beneath the surface so I could still see her hazy form. Then she would seem to hover there scanning as much of the bottom as she could, before surfacing. And she did it over and over again.

I looked at my watch. It was nearly 3:30. Landon had been diving for almost an hour.

"You must be frozen. Why don't we take a break, warm up, and try again later?"

She bobbed next to the canoe with her mask pushed back on her head, revealing a red ring it had left encircling her eyes and nose.

"It's getting deeper now, but I thought I saw something down there that didn't quite match its surroundings. So sit tight for one more look," she said before hauling the mask back down over her face.

She took a few deep breaths before holding the last one and heading back down. She seemed to go deeper this time and stay longer, hanging weightless in the water. Finally, she rose.

"Mark this spot well. Triangulate with something on the shore. We're coming back."

I did what I was told, lining up our position with a tall dead tree and a large outcropping of rock.

"Okay, I need you to lean over the far side of the canoe while I pull myself in over this side."

"You sound like Lucy inviting Charlie Brown to kick the football before she yanks it away and he breaks his back in the ensuing acrobatic fall," I replied.

"Trust me and let's go. We're burning daylight."

I actually did it, and stayed dry. It was close, but she managed to flop back into the canoe while I leaned precariously over the gunwale to maintain our equilibrium. There was lots of rocking, but no tipping, and no water on board. I was quite proud of us.

Landon huddled in the bottom of the canoe wrapped in a towel while I attempted to paddle us back to the dock. While the shortest distance between two points is a straight line, the canoe had a different theory.

"I could see something down there. It was too deep to make it out, but there was a kind of shimmering shape below that didn't seem to fit with the rest of the scene. It's probably a different shade of rock but the edges of the shape were quite straight. It's just too deep to see it clearly."

I nodded, concentrating on keeping the canoe pointed towards the cabin. We made it back, following a somewhat meandering route. As soon as we touched the dock, Landon was up and out of the canoe before I'd even laid my paddle across the gunwales.

"Stay put. I'll be right back," Landon instructed.

I held on to the dock as she disappeared back into the storage room beneath the veranda. There were more sounds of debris being overturned as she searched. Then she was back out the door, labouring under the weight of what looked like a deflated inner-tube with a lawnmower engine in the middle. She made it down to the canoe and, with care, laid down her load.

"What is that?" I asked, getting a closer look at it.

"I gather it's called a Scubuoy. A neighbour gave it to my father I think in the late sixties. We've never used it. It's supposed to be a floating air pump but the inner-tube is shot."

"I don't quite get it," I said, puzzled.

"You will," she said before disappearing up the path and back under the veranda.

Five minutes later she returned with a small gas can, a roll of duct tape, some tools, and a long hose.

She shoved one end of the hose onto a spigot of sorts protruding from the Scubuoy unit and tightened a hose clamp to secure it. Even to me, it was starting to become clear. I noticed that attached to the other end of the hose was a mouthpiece.

"Jacques Cousteau would be proud," I said.

"Well, we got to get it working first," she replied.

"The hose has split down near the motor," I said, pointing to it.

"That's the very reason duct tape was invented."

She carefully wrapped the hose in the sturdy grey tape, starting before the split and ending well beyond it. By this time, I'd managed to get out of the canoe and tie the rope to the dock ring. While Landon smoothed out her tape job, I grabbed the red gas can and filled the small tank on the Scubuoy.

"So let me get this straight," I said. "You don't need to wear a big scuba tank on your back, you can just rev up the old Scubuoy and it'll push air down the hose directly into your mouth?"

"That's it. But you're limited to the thirty feet or so of hose."

"Right."

Landon pointed to the engine.

"Shall we?" she asked

"By all means," I replied, stepping over and grabbing the pull cord.

I pulled and pulled and pulled, generating nothing more than buckets of sweat, an aggravated rotator cuff, and a series of anemic gurgles from the engine.

"Hold your fire!" Landon said before reaching down and connecting the spark plug lead to the spark plug. "Sorry, try it now."

The next pull produced a major backfire, a large puff of very black smoke, and the fleeting but very encouraging sound of the garden variety internal combustion engine. I pulled once more, and it not only started up, it kept running. It sounded a bit rough, but it was working. Landon set the throttle to what we both thought sounded reasonable, then she inserted the mouthpiece where one usually inserts mouthpieces. She pinched her nose and was definitely still breathing. About thirty seconds later she pulled it out.

"Well, it sure doesn't taste great, but I'm pretty sure it's air."

Good enough for me. Landon made one more dash to the storage room and returned with a big flashlight and a tired and faded wetsuit with Scubuoy emblazoned across the back. She pulled it on over her bathing suit, though it was a little big on her. I used duct tape again to seal a tear in the rubber on her left elbow. She had me tape the suit up at her ankles and wrists to prevent water from flowing in. The neck seemed tight enough with the zipper pulled up. Then she held the canoe tight against the dock as I lowered the Scubuoy onto the cedar ribbing on the bottom. She grabbed the hose and mask and settled into the bow seat again. We were both pumped up now. I navigated as Landon paddled us back out to the spot.

"I think you'll have to equalize for the pressure as you go down," I said. "But I'm not certain how you do that. I think you have to pinch your nose and blow, or something like that."

"Yep. I think you're right. Well, start her up."

So I did. Two pulls on the cord and we were in business. Landon used the same technique as before to get back in the water and once again, the canoe stayed upright. She treaded water beside the canoe and pulled her mask into position. I handed her the mouthpiece, which she promptly put in her mouth. Then I loaded the big flashlight into the large Ziploc freezer bag and sealed it. She floated there for a moment, then put her hand out. I passed her the improvised underwater flashlight. She couldn't speak with the mouthpiece in, but she nodded to me before starting down.

I watched her descend slowly, pinching her nose periodically as part of equalizing the water pressure in her ears. I could barely see her at twenty feet, but there was a glow when she fired up the flashlight. As she faded from view into the dim glow, I realized I should have tied a line to her so I could pull her back up if something went wrong. I held the last coil of hose in my hands so she couldn't pull it off the motor trying to get a little deeper. She was down as far as she could go without dragging the canoe under. It was unnerving to have her down so deep, beyond my view. She'd agreed to tug once on the hose every few minutes or so to confirm she was okay and she was pretty good at sticking to the schedule.

She'd been down for about twenty minutes when the periodic signal tugs just stopped. After five minutes of the Scubuoy hose equivalent of radio silence, I was starting to panic. Should I dive in after her? Should I give my own tug on the hose and risk pulling the mouthpiece out of her mouth? Should I bury my head in my hands and moan? As I contemplated these burning questions, I suddenly realized I could see the light below getting stronger. Landon was on her way up. As she got closer, I could see she was looking up. She broke the surface and just held onto the gunwale. She didn't move for quite some time. Eventually she spat out the mouthpiece. I gathered in the hose and shut down the Scubuoy. She lifted the flashlight into the canoe, then used her free hand to pull off the mask. She wouldn't lift her eyes to mine. She just held on and seemed to stare directly into the side of the canoe with a look on her face I'd never seen. She was trembling a bit. Even with the wetsuit, she must have been cold.

"Landon, can you make it into the canoe? Your lips are blue. We should get you back and warmed up," I said in a quiet and even voice. I really wasn't sure what was happening.

That seemed to rouse her and she nodded and started to haul herself in. Fortunately, I was ready and leaned over my side to balance us. It helped having the extra ballast of the heavy Scubuoy resting in the bottom of the canoe. I handed her the towel and she draped it over her shoulders. It was not yet 5:00 p.m. but the sun was beyond the mountains. The light fell and so did the temperature. I paddled us back to the dock as quickly as I could, struggling to keep the canoe pointed at the cabin. Landon seemed to be in some kind of a trance. She was rocking just a bit, pulling the towel around her. I was nearly overcome with curiosity but to speak to her just then seemed like trespassing, so with considerable effort, I held my peace. Just as we glided up to the dock, but before my inept steering crashed the canoe into it, Landon reached down and picked up something from underneath the flashlight, and cradled it in her hands like a newborn bird.

When we finally came to rest, which happened quite suddenly, I grabbed the dock and held on.

"Now go up and get warm, I'll deal with all of this," I said with a little more authority than I usually employed with Landon.

She didn't argue. Her face was very calm, even serene, as she headed up.

"Thank you, David."

I considered my situation and decided to pull the canoe up on the pebbled beach next to the dock before unloading it. Good call. Trying to hoist the heavy Scubuoy up and onto the dock would probably have played out like a scene from *The Keystone*

Kops Go Canoeing, with me ending up in the lake. I stowed everything back in the storage space beneath the veranda and then tried to muscle the canoe back onto its rack. I used the same technique I'd watched Landon use. Unfortunately, I soon discovered that it wasn't precisely the same technique. When I pulled the canoe up onto my thighs, I forgot to compensate for the shift in my own centre of gravity and quickly found myself seated on the ground with the canoe quite literally in my lap. It felt just excellent. I managed to slip out from underneath by rolling the canoe up and over my shins. I'll have to check my files, but I don't think I've ever experienced pain quite like that. It took me another fifteen minutes to position the canoe on the rack. When I finished, dusk had descended. I looked up and saw Landon leaning on the veranda railing watching me.

"I usually position the canoe the other way around on the rack, with the stern at the north end," she observed. "That way I'm already headed in the right direction when I get it in the water."

My heart sank and I briefly considered trying to correct my mistake, the operative word being "briefly." I just shook my head.

"I'm not sure the canoe would survive another attempt," I explained. I looked up at her in the fading light. "Are you all right?"

"I am more than all right. Come up."

Landon had built and lit a fire in the stone fireplace. A mug of hot tea was waiting on the pine box. I collapsed into the chair. Landon sat in her usual place across from me.

"Okay, tell me," I said.

"There's not much to tell. He's down there. He's really there, just as you surmised," she began. "The Beaver is upright with both pontoons pulled away at the front and folded behind, still attached by the rear struts. The prop blades are bent back in accordance with a nose-in impact on the water. The wind-screen is smashed away, but the rest of the plane looks in good shape. It's been sitting just off the dock for more than forty years while I've been flying all over hell's half acre looking for a fiery crash site."

"Um, is he there? Is he in the Beaver?"

"Yes. He's still there, strapped in. Died with his boots on while flying. A perfect way for him to go. He couldn't have planned a more fitting end."

Landon reached for what looked like an oversized wallet sitting on the pine box. A damp water mark was left behind in the wood when she picked it up.

"My father always flew in a leather flying jacket with what was supposed to be a watertight zipper pocket. I was down there for so long because I was wrestling with a zipper that hadn't func-tioned for four decades. It was a tad reluctant to cooperate. But I got it opened and can confirm that the pocket was not water-tight. But I found this, and it's not in bad shape for being down there for so long. I remember this leather wallet."

She was smiling as she spoke, as if a heavy burden had finally been lifted. And I guess it had.

She opened the wallet and passed it to me. There, behind a foggy and yellowing plastic window, was a now stained photo of a young woman and her father standing on the pontoon of the very same Beaver that now rested on the bottom just a ways off the dock.

"I was fourteen in that shot. I'd just soloed for the first time. My father was beyond proud."

I passed it back to her, at a complete loss for words. Landon's eyes were now glistening in the firelight.

"I'm pretty nearly overcome. Reaching space and finding my father have been the two constants in my life. And now, thanks largely to you, I've done both. You can't know what that means. I don't yet know what it means."

She paused and looked into the fire. Then she looked at me.

"Though inadequate the words may be, from the bottom of my heart, from the bottom of my lake, thank you. David, after forty years, you found my father. Thank you."

I swallowed hard.

"Landon, I just pointed. You found him."

———

The day I returned to Toronto, Amanda met me at the airport. I'd been feeling pretty good about my trip to Cigar Lake, but I very nearly forgot about it all when I spied her waiting outside the baggage claim area at Pearson Airport. As I waited for my bag to come down the conveyor, I watched as other passengers with their carry-ons walked through the sliding doors to meet family or friends, or just to catch a cab. Each time the doors opened, I could see Amanda waiting on the other side. She hadn't yet picked me out of the crowd so I could just look at her for the three or four seconds the doors were apart. It was nice.

We went out for dinner that night and I gave her a complete play-by-play of my weekend with Landon. Amanda had been a little skeptical about my east wind theory when I'd told her about it before heading west. Even after I'd shown her the forty-year-old meteorology report, she worried that I was getting my hopes up when the odds still seemed impossibly long. So she was downright pumped and proud when it all panned out.

We ended up closing the place that night. I had no idea where the time had gone. We just started talking and the night evaporated. I barely remember what I ordered or if I ate. Despite being preoccupied with one another, I couldn't help but notice that my BlackBerry sitting on the table was flashing. Amanda, similarly afflicted with the need to check emails as soon as they arrived, saw it too. We both stared at it for a second or two, then I looked at her.

"You can check it," she said. "I'd be forced to check mine if it were flashing, but it's not."

"I'll just take a peek."

I snatched up the BlackBerry and scanned the inbox. There was one new email.

"It's from Kelly Bradstreet," I explained, clicking it open.

I read it and started laughing. Amanda just smiled at me.

"What?" she asked.

"The NASA brass just had a look at the top line numbers from the tracking study that went into the field during Landon's triumphant post-mission media tour."

"Yeah, so dish the news already! I'm dying here," Amanda said.

I scrolled down in Kelly's email to get the numbers for the most important question of all.

"Okay, here you go. It was a North American-wide gen pop survey with a sample size of 3,800. Here's how the all-important 'launch or lunch' question breaks down. The share of those who would rather watch a shuttle launch than go out for lunch jumped from 45 per cent last quarter, to 61 per cent last week," I reported. "Wooo-hooo!"

We had actually moved the "launch or lunch" needle. Amanda thrust her hands in the air and looked on the verge of starting a conga line. No one else still left in the restaurant was prepared to join her, except me, of course.

ACKNOWLEDGEMENTS

In writing this book, I have been blessed with the encouragement and support of so many. As always, I thank Beverley Slopen for her wise counsel and experienced hand. I'm honoured that Doug Gibson is my editor and my friend, and I'm grateful for both. I owe a great deal to superstar publicist, Frances Bedford, who has kept my dance card full of literary festivals and other authorial gigs from coast to coast. I look forward to hitting the road again, for this novel. As well, copy editor extraordinaire, Wendy Thomas, has made this a better book. My thanks also to Doug Pepper, Bhavna Chauhan, and the rest of the McClelland & Stewart team for all of their efforts.

I must also thank CNN's Ali Velshi and everyone on the CBC **Canada Reads** team for all they did for me in 2011. Ali's passion and eloquence in the **Canada Reads** debates yielded a year I'll never forget and a debt I can never repay. I feel the same way about the wonderful people who lead the **Stephen Leacock Association**, and how they changed my life in the spring of 2008. It all started in Orillia.

Canada's first astronaut, Marc Garneau, has been so helpful to me in writing this novel. While the part of this story that unfolds beyond our earthly bounds is clearly fiction, it could be fact, thanks, in no small measure, to Marc. I'm grateful for his time, expertise, and kind words about the book.

Dr. James Fallis and Dr. Martha Bushore-Fallis very kindly helped me capture in words the required technique for removing an inflamed appendix. I am thankful for their medical advice, and for so much more.

Beyond connecting with readers, one aspect of the literary life I've treasured in the last four years has been spending time with some amazing writers. International bestsellers Cathy Marie Buchanan and Andrew Pyper, friends both, are two of them. They were very kind to read this manuscript and offer up such wonderful words about it. They have my gratitude and whatever else I have to give.

Joe Thornley, my friend, and technically my boss in my day job, continues to turn a blind eye as I gallivant from one book event to another. I know I'm very lucky and I very much appreciate his indulgence, and that of my work colleagues.

To my wife, Nancy, and our two sons, Calder and Ben, merely saying thank you is wholly inadequate. Simply put, you have made this little odyssey of mine possible. That thought is never far from my mind.

T.F.
Toronto, 2012

Clarence Johnson

TERRY FALLIS grew up in Toronto and earned an engineering degree from McMaster University. Drawn to politics at an early age, he worked for cabinet ministers at Queen's Park and in Ottawa. His first novel, *The Best Laid Plans*, began as a podcast, then was self-published, won the Stephen Leacock Medal for Humour, was re-published by McClelland & Stewart to great reviews, and was crowned the 2011 winner of CBC's Canada Reads as "the essential Canadian novel of the decade." His follow-up, *The High Road*, was a finalist for the 2011 Leacock Medal. A skilled public speaker, Terry Fallis is also co-founder of the public relations agency Thornley Fallis. He lives in Toronto with his wife and two sons, and blogs at www.terryfallis.com. Follow @TerryFallis on Twitter.